THE
TRADE

SHIRLEY PALMER

THE
TRADE

MIRA®

MIRA

ISBN 1-55166-735-5

THE TRADE

Visit us at www.mirabooks.com

Printed in U.S.A.

First Printing: December 2003
10 9 8 7 6 5 4 3 2 1

This book is dedicated to those who suffer
from this most heinous of crimes.

ACKNOWLEDGMENTS

My thanks go first to editors Dianne Moggy and Amy Moore-Benson for their patience and continued support during the past year. Thanks, too, to Ken Atchity at AEI; to Andrea McKeown for her invaluable input; to L.A. Sheriff's Department homicide detective Sergeant Ray Verdugo, ret.; and to Hae Jung Cho, former director of the Coalition Against Slavery and Trafficking in Los Angeles.

Finally, this book could not have been written without researcher/editor Mignon McCarthy, who not only contributed the facts upon which the entire structure rests, but gave unstintingly of her time, her literary expertise, her enthusiasm and her words. It gives me much pleasure to acknowledge the work she has done.

All errors, of course, are entirely mine.

This is a work of fiction. The events described did not happen. No such club exists in Malibu, nor has there ever been a breath of rumor to indicate otherwise. To serve the story being told, the author has taken some liberty with the topography of this small, treasured Southern California town. For this she begs indulgence.

In the perception of the smallest is the secret
of clear vision;
In the guarding of the weakest is the secret
of all strength.

—Lao Tse

CHAPTER 1

A storm of wind-tossed embers burst through the smoke, crossed the Pacific Coast Highway, caught the dry grasses along the ocean side of the road. A stand of eucalyptus trees exploded into flame. Suddenly visibility was zero.

Matt Lowell forced himself not to jam his foot on the gas. Without the weight of the two horses, the empty trailer was already rocking dangerously. The wind slamming against it had to be gusting at eighty miles an hour.

At Trancas Canyon Road, the traffic lights were out, the Mobil station and the market both dark. On the other side of the intersection, the whirling blue and red light bars across the top of sheriff's black and whites became visible through the murk. A police barricade stretched across the highway, blocking all lanes, north and south.

A deputy sheriff waved Matt down, his sharp arm movements directing him left into the Trancas Market parking lot. Matt recognized Bobby Eckhart. They'd been at preschool together, gone through Webster Elementary and Cub Scouts, surfed the coast from Rincon to Baja. Raised some hell.

Matt pulled over to the median and lowered the window. The acrid stink of disaster caught in his throat—chaparral burning on the hillsides, houses, furniture, lives going up in flames.

"Bobby," he shouted. "I've got to get through."

The deputy looked to see who was shouting, then jogged over to the pickup. "Hey, Matt." Eckhart looked like hell, eyes red-rimmed and bloodshot, his usually immaculate tan uniform charred on one sleeve, and streaked with ash. "The PCH is closed, but we're getting a convoy out over Kanan Dume while it's still open. We can sure use your trailer. Take it over to the creek area, and start loading some of those animals."

Matt shot a glance at the parking lot. Another uniformed deputy was trying to bring some order into the chaos of vehicles loaded with a crazy assortment of household goods; anxious adults riding herd on kids holding onto family pets: dogs, cats, bird and hamster cages. A makeshift corral held a small flock of black sheep, a couple of potbellied pigs, some goats. Horse trailers, rocking under the nervous movements of their occupants, lined the edge of the parched creek. In October when the Santa Ana's roar straight out of the desert, water is a distant memory of spring.

"My horses are down in Ramirez. I've got to get them out."

"Margie Little brought a couple of trailers out of there an hour ago. They're over at the shelter in Agoura."

"Did you see my two?"

Eckhart shook his head. "But you can't get down there, Matt, not now. It's been evacuated, everyone's out." His words ended in a fit of coughing.

Matt put his head out of the window, peered into the blanket of smoke shrouding the highway. "Where the hell are the fire crews?"

"They're spread pretty thin but more are coming. This brute skipped the PCH at noon today, in some places it's burned clear down to the ocean, and now some crazy bastard is setting fires along Mulholland in the backcountry."

Matt's gut clenched. His house was on the beach, and Barney was locked inside. "What about Malibu Road?"

"Blocked at both ends, but it was evacuated earlier today. Escondido, Latigo Shores, everything. Last I heard it was still okay, but the wind's getting worse."

"Bobby, I've got to get through. Barney's locked in the house."

"Oh, Jesus." Eckhart looked stricken, he had known the yellow Lab since he was a pup. "Matt, I'm sorry, but the official word is no traffic on the PCH from here to Topanga, only law enforcement and fire crews. But you slip by, I sure can't follow with lights and sirens." He thumped the top of the cab with a clenched fist, and started back toward the parking lot. Matt let in the clutch.

The emptiness was eerie. No traffic along Zuma Beach. No surfers crossing, their boards balanced overhead. Twice birds literally fell out of the sky—whether from exhaustion or burns it was impossible to know—and hit the road in front of him.

At Ramirez, he pulled into the turn and jumped out of the pickup in front of the tunnel built under the highway to lead back into the canyon. The intricate metal gates barring entry to the tunnel were closed, and he ran to the keypad that would open them, cursing the day they had been installed. A movie star had dazzled the residents when it had come to a vote at the homeowner's association. Then she got married, sold her collection of stuff, donated her property to Nature Conservancy and moved to Point Dume. Only the goddamn gates remained.

Matt entered the code. Nothing happened. Cursing, he banged out the number again. The gates jerked, held. He tried again, jamming a finger at the numbers, slamming a foot against the gate as it jerked. A burst of black smoke billowed from the darkness and he ran back to the pickup.

Matt thought quickly. Maybe Margie got the horses out,

maybe she didn't. If she didn't, she'd open the corral, let them take their chances. A lot of people had had to do that in the 1978 fire, it had moved so fast. Either way, there was nothing he could do about it now. But Barney was at home, locked inside. If he dumped the trailer, he could jam through with the pickup, and be there in ten minutes.

The metal hitch was too hot to touch. Quickly, he reached inside the trailer, grabbed the leather gloves he used for hauling hay. He sent an anxious glance up into the eucalyptus trees. For a long choking moment, he wrestled with the hitch. Then fire swept through the oleanders, jumped to a pair of cedars, ran up the trunks of the eucalyptus. The tossing crowns exploded into flame. A shower of sparks hit the trailer, found the shreds of hay on the floor inside, ignited. Within seconds trailer and pickup were engulfed.

"I'm not going to make it." Matt heard his own voice, maybe in his head, maybe he was yelling. "God, I'm not going to make it."

He raced down the road to the Cove restaurant and the beach. Half a mile seemed suddenly impossible. Melting asphalt grabbed at his feet, fifty-foot eucalyptus trees were going up like oil-soaked torches, burning leaves tossed in the wind like missiles spreading fire wherever they touched. Beyond the trees on his right, the Sunset Pines trailer park was a sea of flames, metal screamed as heat buckled the double-wides, the force of the wind lifting blazing roofs, sending them spinning like giant fiery kites.

At the edge of the water the restaurant was still untouched, the old wooden pier still standing. Not a soul was around. The Cove had been abandoned.

Matt smashed a window in the kitchen door, thrust a hand through to the lock and let himself in. Normally booming with activity at this hour, the interior was utterly still, empty. He grabbed some bottled water from a refrigerator, left by the side door directly onto the beach. The sky was darker, an ominous dirty orange reflecting the fire and the low, late afternoon sun. It had to be close to sunset, but it was hard to tell.

Ash and smoke eddied in the wind, lifting the sand into a murky, eye-stinging soup. The edge of the bluff was in flames, the multimillion-dollar houses fronting the ocean probably already engulfed. Fire ate at the cascading purple ice plant, smoldering clumps dropped into the water lapping at the base of the cliff. The swells on the sea were a dark hammered bronze, the tops of the waves blown apart by the offshore wind.

Without slowing his pace, Matt struggled out of his jacket, stooping to drag it through the water. Debris tumbled in the surf, the bodies of singed birds, fish floating belly up in the unnaturally warmed water. He covered his head with the wet jacket, kept as far as he could from the base of the cliff and the brush falling in great blazing arcs blown by the wind.

The sea dragged at every step. He prayed he wouldn't stumble into a hole—he'd surfed this coast all his life, and with a booming tide like this racing in, he knew the rip could tear a grown man's legs from under him, drag him out to sea.

The beach widened, the bluff on his left was lower now, breaking down into sandstone gullies and he was able to get his bearing. The stairs to what used to be the Edwards place were charred and rocking with every gusts, but still standing. He could hear his breath laboring, and his lungs felt seared. Even this close to the water, the Santa Ana winds drew every scrap of moisture out of the air. In the oven-hot wind howling under a dirty sky, he felt as if he could be the last man left alive on a devastated earth.

He took a swig of the bottled water, warm now from the heat. Ahead, a large seabird, a dead pelican probably, tangled in a fisherman's discarded line—it happened all the time—lay close to the edge of the surf. Matt fixed his eyes on it as a measure of his progress along the beach. As he got closer, he realized it wasn't a pelican. Maybe a doll with a scrap of copper-colored fabric wrapped around it. He glanced down as he passed, took several more strides. Uncertain, he turned back.

An advancing wave broke around his ankles and tugged at the small pale form. It moved, then responding to the pull of the water, started to roll. Matt reached down instinctively to stop its slide to the sea. Suddenly he found the smoke-filled air even more difficult to draw into his lungs and in spite of the heat, the blood pumping through his veins felt icy. He picked up the tiny form, held it against his body, and put his fingers against its throat.

He felt the thready flutter of a pulse.

CHAPTER 2

Matt stripped away the wet silky covering, struggled out of his polo shirt and wrapped the newborn infant, a girl, in the soft cotton. Her eyes were closed, her hands curled into tiny fists. Downy strands of gold hair feathered damply against her head.

He scanned the beach but the blowing sand and smoke and falling ash cut visibility down to a few yards. Rabbits and a couple of raccoons huddled against the low bluff close to a flock of gulls. He could see nothing that could possibly be a human form.

Who would leave a baby like this?

He held the almost weightless bundle against his chest with some idea of warming her with his own body heat, put on his wet jacket to protect them both against falling debris, and started back along the beach toward the stairs up to the Edwards house. If they were still standing, maybe there would be firefighters trying to save it.

He scanned the beach as he ran. Trash thrown up by a polluted ocean was caught in the giant kelp above the high tide mark—nylon fishing line, plastic holders for six packs, bits of Styrofoam coolers. No sign of the mother, no patch of blood, nothing to show that a woman had just given birth. He stumbled across a beam of charred wood and saw the beach was littered with planks.

The stairs. Since he had passed them only minutes ago, the ferocious wind had blown the damaged stairs apart.

He swept his eyes across the low bluff, looking for another way up, handholds, anything, but even if he could find a way, the top of the cliff was blazing. He hesitated—the empty restaurant was closer than his own place, he could go back. But he'd lived in Malibu all his life, seen flames leap two hundred feet in seconds, consume a house in minutes. And the tide was roaring in. He had to get home.

Flooded with relief, Matt jogged across the dry sand, toward his own beach stairs. The small gray clapboard house was intact. The large houses on either side were dark, not surprising. His neighbors used them only on weekends, and that rarely.

For the last hour he'd been running nonstop, across soft sand, in and out of the ocean, holding the baby close as he clambered over the bare rocky reefs that would normally be covered by resting seals as the tide receded. On a night like this, though, they'd stay out at sea.

The sky was a cauldron, the fire dangerously close. He could feel blasts of heat from the thirty-foot flames now whirling south on the ridge above the Pacific Coast Highway as it followed the curve of the coastline toward the enormous expanse of lawn fronting Pepperdine University. That lawn still pissed a lot of people off, they were still arguing about the amount of water used to keep it green, the contaminated runoff draining into the Santa Monica Bay, but in a wildfire it could be a godsend, a break where fire crews could make a stand.

If the wind turned west again as it easily could, a maelstrom like this created its own wind patterns, flames would be across the highway in minutes, take the houses above his on the land side of Malibu Road, jump to the beach side and burn clear down to the water. From what he'd seen, so far the flames had reached oceanside houses in a staggered pattern, driven by the changing wind. His place was vulnerable, clapboard with an old shake roof, it would go in seconds.

He pushed open the door into his smoky kitchen, staggering as eighty pounds of terrified dog hurled himself at his legs.

"It's okay, Barns. It's okay, boy." Matt held off the Lab with one hand and picked up the phone. No dial tone. The line was dead. He shook it in frustration. Of course it was dead—the phone lines were down. This wasn't the first fire he'd been through in his thirty-six years, he should have remembered that. At least he had his mobile.

The baby close against his chest, he searched his jacket. Then again. Patted the pockets in his pants. The phone was gone. He'd dropped it somewhere on the beach.

He laid the child down on the soft couch in the living room, touched her pale cheek. She was cool. Colder than she had been when he picked her up. Matt felt for the pulse in the baby's throat, as he'd done on the beach. He couldn't find it. He flexed his fingers, felt on the other side. No pulse. Maybe he was doing it wrong. He rubbed his fingers on the couch to sensitize them, tried again. Nothing. Heart hammering, he knelt, held the tiny nose, blew gently into the infant's mouth. Once, twice. Again. But he knew it was useless. There was no breath, no heartbeat. The baby was dead. Sometime in the last hour, as they made their way down the beach, she had died in his arms. He had not even known when life left her. Surely, he should have felt something.

He sat back on his heels. She was so delicate, so fragile, she made barely a dent in the cushion. Long lashes fanned her cheeks. He didn't even know what color her eyes were. What sort of woman would abandon her defenseless newborn on an empty beach?

Minutes passed. Barney pushed his nose at Matt's hand, then started to howl as if he knew, a mournful sound that gave a voice to the tangle of feeling swelling in Matt's chest.

Matt put a hand on Barney's head, and took a long, deep painful breath. The smoke inside the house was thicker now, the heat increasing. Barney nudged at him insistently. Matt knew he had to get some water on the roof, and soon. He looked at her one last time, then covered her face with his shirt and got to his feet.

"Come on, boy." He snapped on Barney's leash in case they had to make a run for it, took the Lab with him into his bedroom. Black particles of ash hung in the air and coated every surface; shadows danced madly in the dirty amber glow that was the only light, but it was enough for him to see what he needed to see. He stripped, got into dry jeans and shirt, socks and heavy boots, then retrieved a black carry-on bag from the closet and looked around for the things that were important enough to save.

He picked up the photograph by his bed, an eight-by-ten of Ginn and himself, Barney at their feet, taken last summer, and put it into the bag. The only other things of value were a framed picture of his mother and an album of old photographs of them together when he was a kid. His memory of her had dimmed over the years, only the pictures kept it alive. He took a second to wrap them in a T-shirt before putting them in the bag, threw in a handful of underwear, socks, some jeans on top. He took some of his books from the shelves in the living room, his laptop. He already had Barney ready to run. That was it. Except for the house itself, there was nothing else here he cared about.

He tied a bandanna around his nose and mouth, then grabbed all the towels in the linen cupboard, dropped the bag by the kitchen door where he could get it easily if they had to get down to the water. He slammed the door closed behind him to keep Barney confined in the house, ran along the side of the house toward the little shed of a detached garage facing the road. He could hear the rumble of fire trucks, power horns and sirens on the Coast Highway above Malibu Road. Help was on the way at last and the fire crews would make a stand wherever they could as long as they had water pressure. At least he and Barney could always get down to the ocean, so they wouldn't be trapped. If it came to it, he'd let the house, his mother's house, burn.

Without electricity the garage door was immovable. He climbed behind the wheel of the Range Rover parked inside, shoved the gear into Reverse, hit the gas and rammed the heavy vehicle at the overhead door. The old structure shook but the warped wood splintered at the first attempt and he was through. He got out, grabbed three of Bobby Eckhart's surfboards, shoved them into the back, added a couple of his own. The ladder he kept for repairs had fallen off the wall with the impact. He picked it up, threw it onto the patio, then backed the Range Rover up to the street, away from the structure. Only a block away, a couple of houses were burning.

He unwound the hose on the patio, turned the spigot, let out a grunt of relief when water spurted, then shoved the nozzle into an empty trash barrel and filled it, dumped in the towels. He soaked his bandanna and retied it over his nose and mouth, dragged the hose with him up the ladder to the roof.

If the water pressure stayed strong, if the wind didn't turn, if he could beat out sparks with the towels before they got a hold under the wooden shakes—a hell of a lot of ifs—he had a chance of saving the house. His mother's house.

Matt looked at his watch, saw that it was after midnight. The arc of the night sky from east to west was still red with fire, but something was different. The wind had changed direction and was blowing onshore. He wouldn't call it moisture exactly, but for the first time in hours he felt as if he could take a full breath without cooking his lungs.

He went out to the street again. Everything in the front of the house was gone, the fence, the bushes, a couple of trees, and the bougainvillea that his mother had planted for privacy thirty years ago. At least the house had survived, scorched but still there. Many landside houses above his, and several along his stretch of beach, were smoking ruins. Fire crews hadn't even made it down here until now, when it was all over and the firestorm had moved on.

A sheriff's patrol car cruised by and Matt stepped into the road to wave it down. The black and white slowed. The deputy sheriff looked him over.

"Who are you? This area is evacuated, authorized personnel only."

Matt had been hoping for Bob Eckhart. He didn't recognize the man speaking to him.

Matt said, "I live here. You got a minute? I've got something here you should see."

"You got identification?"

"Sure." Matt reached for the wallet he'd transferred from his wet jeans, flipped it open to his driver's license.

The deputy reached for it. "What happened to your arm?"

Matt held it up, surprised to see a gash and streaks of dried blood. "I don't know, I guess I must've cut it when I broke a window at the Cove to get some water."

"I see." The deputy handed back the license. "Well, I'll have to get back to you, just as soon as I've checked out the end of the road. Things are still pretty hectic." Fire equipment moved along the road, wetting down hotspots, checking roofs. The black and white started to roll.

Matt paced with the car. "No, wait a minute. Listen, you've got to come inside. Sounds crazy I know, but I've got a dead baby here."

The car stopped. The deputy stared at him for a long moment, then pulled off the road. He retrieved a flashlight, played it over Matt's face, along the still-smoking stumps of the bougainvillea, across the newly exposed house and patio. Barney, muzzle pressed against the bedroom window no longer shielded from the street by shrubbery, barked a warning. The deputy picked up his radio transmitter. "This is 103. I've got a report of a 927D at..." He looked at Matt. "What's the address here?"

Matt told him, the deputy repeated the address, then signed off. He stepped out of the car.

"How come you didn't evacuate with everyone else?" His voice was guardedly neutral.

"I wasn't here when the order came. I came home later by way of the beach."

"What's your name again, sir?"

"Matthew Lowell. Yours?"

"Deputy Timms." Ramrod posture, early thirties, dark hair short back and sides, but surprisingly long on top for a deputy sheriff. He followed Matt across the patio, along the deck by the side of the house into the candlelit kitchen.

Matt opened the door of the refrigerator. Except for a small bundle wrapped in a bright-blue polo shirt, the shelves were empty.

"What is this, some kind of joke?" Timms turned a darkening face toward Matt.

"No." Matt gestured to the sink piled with jars and containers, orange juice, mayonnaise, olives, a carton of eggs. "In this heat, I couldn't think of what else to do. And I thought if the house burned, she would be safer, maybe. I don't know. I found her on the beach last night when I was coming home."

"Jesus." Timms reached into the refrigerator.

Matt turned away. Even in the flickering candlelight, he couldn't bear to look again at the little face.

"There's a lot of blood on this shirt," Timms said.

"Must be mine. From when I cut my arm."

"You say you found this baby, you weren't there when it was born?"

"No, I wasn't there when she was born. I found her, I told you.

I took my shirt off and wrapped her in it because there wasn't anything else to use. I didn't realize there was blood on it. It wouldn't have made any difference anyway, that's all I had, my shirt."

"I see. It's a girl," Timms said. "Where did you say you found it?"

"Her. I found her on the beach."

Timms gave him another long, hard stare. "How long have you lived at this address, Mr. Lowell?"

"Most of my life, on and off. It belonged to my parents. We lived on Point Dume but we spent a lot of time here. They planned to tear this old place down and build a decent house, but my mother—" He stopped. Timms would think he was nuts, running on with his life's story. "I've lived here permanently since I got out of college. Fourteen years."

"I see. Well, I can't get the M.E. out here now, they won't get through. PCH is still closed in both directions. I'll have to call this in. You wait here."

The deputy hesitated as if uncertain what to do with a dead child, then put the tiny body back where he'd found her, and started across the kitchen. He stopped at the sound of a voice, and footsteps on the wooden deck.

"Hey, Matt. What's going on? Everything okay?" Deputy sheriff Bobby Eckhart walked in without knocking. Lean and athletic, he was powerful through the shoulders from years of paddling out to meet the surf. Blond hair cropped close, tonight his usually clear gray eyes were swollen and bloodshot.

"Pete, what's going on?" Bobby said to Timms. "I heard the 927D."

"Mr. Lowell here says he found a dead baby on the beach."

"What?" Bobby looked sharply at Matt. "Where?"

"I don't know, exactly. Somewhere this side of the Edwards place. When I was trying to get home."

"Oh, Matt. How old?"

"Maybe only hours. No more than a day."

"That's a rough one, buddy. You okay? You're bleeding."

"It's nothing. Just a cut. I broke a window at Jimmy's place to get some water."

While they spoke, Timms had reopened the refrigerator, and unwrapped Matt's shirt from around the tiny form.

"Oh, jeez, just look at this."

"I've already seen her." Matt went out onto the deck, leaving the two deputies alone. He heard Bobby's calm voice.

"Pete, I think you'd better take it up to the courthouse. They've got the command post set up there."

"You know this guy?" Timms asked.

"All my life. Those are my surfboards in his Range Rover. I keep them in his garage—saves me tracking them down from Las Flores. I catch a few waves after work sometimes."

Timms grunted. "Yeah? Then better if you take the baby to the courthouse and I get his statement."

Matt stared out over the ocean, one of the few remaining places in Los Angeles uncontaminated by city lights, where a star-filled night was visible. But tonight the sky was shrouded, the glow from the fire still coloring the smoke hanging low over the sea.

If he had the juice, he thought, he'd be pissed off at the doubt he could hear in Timms's voice, the guy obviously thought he was lying—but suddenly the events of the last few punishing hours had come up and hit him in the face. He felt wrecked, and knew something in his life had shifted, although he had no idea what that could be.

He turned at the sound of Bobby's voice asking, "Where's Barney? Is he all right?"

"Yes, I've got him locked in the bedroom."

"Timms has gone." Bobby handed Matt a bottle of Evian, and leaned his belly against the railing. "I saw Margie Little. Your horses are over in Agoura. Be good if you could make arrangements for them, the animal shelter is pushed to the limit."

"I'll get them out of there as soon as I can. Your house okay?"

Bobby and his wife Sylvie had a tiny place in Las Flores Canyon.

"Yeah, bit singed is all. Lost the big cedar in front, though. Okay, I've got to go, there's a long night still ahead." He patted Matt's shoulder. "I'll take care of the baby, Matt. Don't worry about it. Maybe you'd better have someone take a look at that arm."

"Sure," Matt said. He did not turn to see Bobby leave with the child in his arms. He listened to retreating footsteps, the sirens racing along the highway. The wind had shifted and was blowing offshore again.

It would be days before this fire was contained.

CHAPTER 3

"Matt, did you hear what I said?" Ned Lowell leaned back from his desk to look out of the window of the office on San Vicente Boulevard in fashionable Brentwood. "What's so interesting down there?"

The small plaza below the window was festive, elegant stores decorated for Halloween with piles of pumpkins and hay bales, kids and adults in costume, witches, dragons, fairies, a lot of Harry Potters. Matt had his eyes on a small pink rabbit with big floppy ears and white tail. Her mother was holding her on a large orange pumpkin while her father took pictures.

"Cute mom," Ned said.

Matt spun his chair around, fitting his feet around Barney, asleep under his half of the partner's desk he shared with his older brother. The office was large, the main decorative feature the display of architectural photographs of Lowell Brothers projects. "I'm listening. What did you say?"

"I said Mike Greffen called about that building downtown on San Julian and Pico. Did you look at it?"

"Not yet. I'd planned to go down on Monday before the fire. Used to be a dress factory. Been empty for years, price should be right."

"What's around there?"

"About what you'd expect in the garment district. Plus some light manufacturing, a few run-down apartment buildings. Pretty grim, but it might be good for studios or workshops."

In fourteen years, they had created elegant offices in abandoned banks for those eccentric souls who found high-rise office buildings sterile, made luxurious pied-à-terre apartments out of crumbling warehouses, built low-cost housing in old railroad yards, for which the city loved them. They had turned deconsecrated churches into concert venues and restaurants, created artisans workshops, art studios and lofts throughout downtown. On the way, Lowell Brothers had received design awards, thanks from a grateful city, and made a lot of money.

Ned rose to his feet, stretched his six foot two plus frame—he had a couple of inches on Matt—rotated his hips, then shrugged into his jacket. Matt noticed how much his brother was looking like their dad as he grew older, the same thick rumpled head of dark hair streaked now with gray, the deepening lines around his eyes and mouth. He'd look like that, too, probably, when he was Ned's age, another ten years. They'd always looked alike.

"I'll call Mike in the morning then. Right now, I've got to get home for trick-or-treating or Julie will kill me. Are you coming?"

"No, I don't think so."

"Why not?" Ned stopped at Matt's desk, and peered into his face. "Matt, you don't look so good. I know it's only been a couple of days, but are you okay? Sleeping, eating, that kind of stuff?"

"What are you, my mother all of a sudden? Get out of here."

Ned lingered. "Listen, this dead baby. You want to talk about it?"

"Nothing to talk about. Get going."

"I know it was a hell of a thing, but it's not your business. You just happened to be at the wrong place at the wrong time. You didn't know that baby. You couldn't have saved it. It happens, shit like this."

"You're right. It does. It just did."

"Oh, come on, you know what I mean."

"No, you're right. It's not my business."

But it felt like his business. Yesterday, Matt had spent a couple of hours with sheriff's deputies walking the beach trying to pinpoint the exact place where he'd found the baby's body. They'd found nothing. No trace.

"So why don't you come over tonight and hand out candy, while we take the boys out to plunder the neighborhood?"

"Not this year." Last year, he and Ginn had still been together. It had been a blast just watching her laughing at the parade of kids, oohing and aahing over the costumes. She was good with kids.

"We've got people coming over later, costumes and some drinks. Julie asked Susan Dean, and I think she only said yes because Julie dangled you as bait. Susan's a good architect, bright, and gorgeous. What she sees in you God only knows." He thumped Matt's shoulder affectionately.

"Now you're my social director, too? I thought you said you were going home."

"If it's still about Ginn, Matt, that was your choice."

"She's the one who left, not me."

"Come on, man. She's thirty-five years old. She wants kids. You don't even want to get married. You think you left her any option?"

"Knock it off, Ned, okay?"

Ned raised both hands. "Sorry I spoke. See you tomorrow."

Matt waited until the door closed behind him. He looked down into the plaza, but the pink rabbit and her family had gone.

He reached for the phone. The deputy who answered said that Eckhart wasn't in the station house. Matt left a message that he'd called.

Traffic was clogged on the Pacific Coast Highway. Fire equipment returning to home bases all over the state rumbled south to the I-10. Going north was a nightmare of backed-up traffic. At Topanga Canyon a young entrepreneur was doing a brisk business, running up and down the line of cars waiting to get through the sheriff's department roadblock, taking money, handing out T-shirts that read "I Survived The Latest Greatest Malibu Topanga Fire."

Matt showed his driver's license to a deputy to prove he was a resident and was waved through. A few restaurants had reopened in time for Halloween but they'd be crowded with people wearing false noses and mustaches, partying and swapping war stories. He stopped at PC Greens to pick up food for dinner.

It was dark when he got home. Instead of the sweet smell of sumac and thyme that grew wild up on the hills, the heavy stink of wet ash pervaded the air, overpowering even the fresh salt spray from the Pacific.

The phone in the kitchen started to ring as he came down the walkway. Barney raced ahead and Matt hurried the last few steps—mad hope, but maybe Ginn was calling to find out whether the house had survived, if the horses were okay, how Barney had come through. She'd found Barns at some rescue outfit, a two-month-old pale yellow scrap with an unusual white star on his forehead, and brought him home, dumped him in Matt's lap on his birthday a couple years ago. Matt let himself into the kitchen, dropped the groceries on the table and picked up the phone.

"Matt Lowell."

"Hey, Matt. What have you been up to?" Jimmy McPhee's voice was loud, jovial.

"Hi, Jim. Heard the restaurant made it okay. I'm glad."

"Yeah, by the grace of the Almighty. Only damage was a broken window in the kitchen, can you beat that?"

"I'm afraid I did that." Matt glanced down at the bandage on his arm. "I took some water from the big fridge, too."

"You were down here? Hell on wheels, Matt, how did you manage that?"

"Dumb luck, I guess. Lost my pickup and trailer at the tunnel, though. They should be cleared out by now. Do you know if the wrecker turned up?"

"Yeah, they're gone. They were a hell of a mess, just a tangle of burned-out metal."

While he listened, Matt filled Barney's dish with kibble, popped a can of Rolling Rock, turned on the television. Reception had been restored, electricity was back on. He hit the mute.

"St. Aidan's is all right, too," McPhee said. "Bit scorched is all. A service of thanksgiving is scheduled for Sunday."

"Okay, I'll try to make it." His only church attendance nowadays was on the Sunday closest to the anniversary of his mother's death twenty-six years earlier when he was ten. She'd gone out to get ice cream one Sunday afternoon, and he'd never seen her again. The drunk who'd killed her was sentenced to two years. So now, around June 20 every year his dad came up from Palm Springs, and the three of them, he and Ned and their father attended morning service at St. Aidan's and had lunch afterward at Jimmy's.

Matt clicked to the local news. The fire was no longer at the top of the hour. Life was returning to normal for the rest of Los Angeles. With hotspots still in the backcountry, it would be weeks for Malibu, months and even longer, if ever, for those who'd lost everything. He turned off the news and waited for Jimmy to get to the point.

"So, James, what's up?" he said when Jimmy let a moment of silence linger.

"Had a couple of sheriff's department detectives asking about you today."

While listening, Matt walked outside to the deck and looked out over the Pacific. A sliver of moon was rising, stars blazed in a clear sky.

"What did they want?"

"Just had I seen you during the fire. I said I hadn't, but they went on awhile, wanted to know if I was sure. You know, bunch of questions like that." Jimmy gave a strained laugh. "What have you been up to? Raiding the old Edwards place while it burned?"

"Thought I might find a Princess Di mug or something."

Blake Edwards, his famous wife Julie Andrews, and their brood of kids had lived in the house for years without raising comment. But after the Edwards's moved, Harrods heir, Dodi Al-Fayed, bought the house and started a major remodel, and Malibu was giddy with the rumor that Princess Di was coming to town.

"They seemed pretty serious, Matt. You in trouble?"

"Not that I know of."

"I've known your dad for thirty years, kiddo, and I loved your mother, God bless her. If you're in trouble, you just have to say the word. I'll help if I can, you know that."

Matt nodded as if McPhee could see him. After his mother was gone, most family celebrations were held at Jimmy's restaurant—birthdays, graduations. He'd had his first legal beer at Jimmy's.

"During the fire after I left the Cove, I found the body of a baby," he said. "Lying on the beach."

"Holy Mother of God! Whose baby?"

"Well, I guess that's what they're trying to find out, Jim."

"Oh, sure. Of course. Poor little soul. How old?"

"Newborn." Matt reached for his beer. He couldn't bring himself to say that the baby had been alive when he'd found her. "Jim, listen, thanks for calling, but I've got to go."

"Yeah, sure. Well, if you need anything, let me know, okay?"

"Sure thing." Matt put a finger on the disconnect, started to replace the phone, then found himself punching out the number he hadn't used for almost a year. After she'd left, he'd ring just to listen to her voice on the machine, always hanging up if she answered in person. But one night, she'd said, "Matt, I know it's you. Please don't keep doing this. Don't force me to get an unlisted number."

It had been like breaking an addiction. Just for today, he'd tell himself, I won't call her. Just for today. Ten months of one day at a time not calling Genevieve Chang.

After four rings, the familiar voice said, "This is Ginn Chang. If you leave your number I'll call you back. If you don't, I won't."

Matt hesitated. He wanted to tell her about the baby, about the cops asking questions about him. He wanted... What? Marriage? A family? He dropped the phone into the cradle, went into the bedroom, Barney at his heels.

The eight-by-ten was back on the table by his bed. Every line was etched in his mind, but he picked it up and studied it. Ginn in hipriding white shorts and a bikini top leaned her narrow back against his chest. He had both arms wrapped around her, his chin resting on top of her head, the half-grown Barney stretched at their feet, grinning as only a happy young Lab could. He remembered the day clearly. Ned and Julie and their boys had come over for the day, Ned with a new digital camera posing everyone until they finally rebelled.

Matt thought about his brother. Ned didn't complicate life. He'd found the right girl when he was twenty-eight, he'd gotten married, settled down, had a couple of kids. No sweat.

Matt replaced the picture on the table. From the moment they met, he'd never doubted that Ginn was the right girl. It was the rest of the story that wouldn't fall into place. The old family album was still on the dresser where he'd put it after the fire. Slowly he turned to a page—any page—as he did sometimes. They were all photographs taken by his dad of their mother and Ned and himself, with their horses at the ranch on Zumirez

Drive on Point Dume; the three of them running on the beach outside this house, throwing sticks for their two Shepherd-type mutts, playing in the surf. His mother always seemed to be smiling. Something he could still remember about her, sometimes the only thing was that wide, sweet smile. He closed the album.

"Come on, Barney. Let's get out of here."

He changed into old jeans and running shoes, and opened the door to the deck. Barney pushed ahead of him, but instead of heading for the gate and the narrow stairs down to the beach, the dog dashed along the walkway toward the street, tail wagging furiously. The automatic patio lights, hanging by a wire from the garage but still working, flashed on as Bobby Eckhart stepped across the beam. He was wearing black jeans, leather jacket, heavy boots.

"Hey, Matthew, you coming or going?"

"Going. I was taking Barney for a run on the beach, but it can wait. Did you come on your bike?" He hadn't heard the sound of the love of Bobby's life, his Harley.

"What else?"

"What brings you here?"

"You called, master?"

Matt laughed. "Come on in. You want a beer?"

"Is the pope Catholic?" Bobby tussled with Barney until they both banged their way through the door into the kitchen. He looked down at his pants. "Look at this. I'm covered in yellow hair. Don't you ever brush this mutt?"

"You know where the brush is kept, buddy. Be our guest."

"Too late. Damage is done." Bobby crossed the kitchen to the refrigerator, opened the door, looked in, stared at the empty interior. "You got something against food?"

"I picked up some stuff on the way home." He didn't explain that no way could he ever open that door without seeing the shirt-wrapped bundle resting on a steel rack. He'd already ordered a new refrigerator, different make, different configuration.

"Sit down. I've got water, warm beer, or scotch. If you want cold, there's a bottle of Stoli in the freezer."

"A glass of your best red will do me fine. Gotta get my sweetie home in one piece."

Matt grinned. "Would that be Sylvie or the Harley?" Bobby's wife was also a deputy sheriff.

"Sylvie's got late duty tonight, that's why I'm here. So I don't have to cook." Bobby peered into the containers of braised beef, roasted vegetables, mashed potatoes.

"I don't know how she puts up with playing second fiddle to that bike."

"She knows she's on to a good thing. She's got us both."

Matt opened a bottle of Merlot while Bobby decanted the food, put it into the microwave.

Matt leaned back in his chair, reached for a couple of glasses, poured the wine.

"So, what's up?" Bobby asked.

"The sheriff's department is asking questions about me," Matt said. "Jimmy McPhee called tonight." He repeated the conversation.

"Routine stuff, nothing to worry about." The microwave beeped. Bobby placed the containers on the table.

"What will happen to her, Bob?"

"The baby? Well, if they can't find the mother, she'll either get a civil burial or transfer her body to a teaching hospital where pediatric surgeons get their training."

The food in Matt's mouth was suddenly a lump impossible to swallow. "You mean—" He wanted to gag. He thought of the delicate body he'd seen, the fragile limbs. "She shouldn't be cut up."

Bobby helped himself to more braised beef. "Yeah, turns your stomach, doesn't it? You know, in one month last year...August, I think, three babies were found on the beach in Santa Monica, about a week apart. Remember that?"

"No."

"Yeah, well. No one notices. Just the flotsam of a big city. Another little Jane Doe, no one to claim her."

"Then I'll claim this one. She should have someone, not end up on a surgical slab, alone."

"You can't just walk in and claim a body. It's not that easy. Why would you want to do that?"

Because she died in his arms. Because maybe he could have saved her if he hadn't been so hellbent on getting home to his house and his dog. Although he still didn't know how.

"Because I found her, I guess. Why not?"

Bobby shook his head. "Matt, just think for a minute how this plays. Single guy finds a baby. She's still alive. No one's around as a witness. Baby dies. Then the guy claims the body, spends a fair amount of change to give this Baby Doe a funeral. What do you think that says?"

"That someone wants to do the right thing? What? You think like a cop, Bobby, you know that?"

"Twelve years on the job, Matt. It'll do it to you every time." After college, Bobby had bummed the world following the waves for a couple of years before he came home, met Sylvie and joined the sheriff's department.

Matt pushed his chair back, got to his feet. He dumped the remains of the food into the trash. "So what's the next step? Do I call the coroner's office?"

"No. You sleep on it for a week, then you call."

"That might be too late."

"Yeah," Bobby said. "You're right."

CHAPTER 4

"See what I mean? It's a prime piece of property." Mike Greffen of Downtown Realty Associates, was resplendent in a well tailored gray suit, white shirt, Hermes tie. He gestured toward the vast empty interior of the almost derelict building. In spite of the brilliant fall day outside, the late afternoon sunlight barely penetrated the second floor windows, multi-paned and washed with a thin film of brown paint. The place reeked of excrement, human and animal, rats, stray cats, the unwholesome stink of the transients who used the place to drink and vomit and crash. "Know what they say about location. Still can't beat it, gentlemen."

Ned stamped a foot tentatively on the splintered wooden planks of the uneven factory floor. A small cloud of dust coated his Nikes. He and Matt wore their usual working clothes, blue jeans, polo shirts, sneakers.

"Wow. Nearly went through there. What do you think anyone can do with this piece of industrial wasteland? Matt, you got any ideas?"

Matt recognized Ned's opening salvo for negotiation on the price. Ned managed their financial affairs, bank loans, mortgages. There wasn't a real estate broker or a banker alive who could best Ned. He could wring the last penny out of any deal.

Matt shrugged. "I'd call in the bulldozers." His cell phone buzzed and he excused himself, walked over to the bank of darkened windows.

"Matt Lowell."

"Matt, it's Bobby. Listen, a heads-up. Better you don't contact the coroner about that matter we talked about last night. Something's come up. Okay?"

"What's happened?"

"I'm at the desk, I can't talk now. Just hang tight, don't make any calls, okay?"

"Too late. I called this morning."

"Shit. Did you leave your name?"

"Of course I left my name."

"Shit," Bobby said again. "Oh well, maybe it won't make any difference. They lose bodies all the time down there, chances are they're no better with telephone messages."

"What bodies? What are you talking about?"

"I can't talk right now. I'll call you tonight. Better yet, I'll come by. Meantime, don't make any more calls to the coroner." He rang off.

Slowly, Matt returned the cell to his pocket. He cleaned a circle in the filthy window with the heel of his hand. Across the street stood a mirror image of the four-story building he was standing in. Someone had enough faith in the neighborhood to try to do something with it, but not enough to trust the neighbors not to make off with anything they could get their hands on. Surrounding the old factory was a new ten-foot chain-link fence topped with a concertina of razor wire.

Matt walked over to rejoin the two men.

"Mike tells me we can turn this dump into luxury apartments," Ned said. "You're the design and structural arm of the firm." For Matt, the thrill of his job was in seeing the aesthetic possibilities in the crumbling buildings they restored. He was good at it, had the imagination to see what could be, probably got it from his father. It also enabled him to see the absence of opportunity, such as this building.

Matt laughed. "Mike, you don't believe that."

"Sure I do. Would I lie to you guys? This is a wicked piece of property. Great potential."

"Yeah, potential to go from bad to worse."

"That building you were looking at, Matt? Across the street there? Sold in less than a week, asking price, and I hear it's going to be gutted and refitted as apartments. It will bring the whole area up."

"In your dreams, Michael," Ned said. "Who'd you sucker into that deal?"

"Unfortunately, I didn't have the listing, but I hear it was bought by some outfit from Canada. I could have offered this one to them, but we've been doing business for a long time. I wanted to give you guys first crack at it."

The three men navigated the dark filth-encrusted stairs and stepped out into the sunshine.

"So don't wait too long, guys," Mike said. "This is a primo piece of downtown real estate, a steal at the price."

He slid into his late model Lexus, tapped his horn at a kid running across the street, and drew away.

"Shall we go for it, Matt?" Ned's tone was doubtful.

Matt eyed the street scene. A couple of guys selling foam-rubber pads and remnants of fabric from the back of a beat-up truck to small round women a long way in time and distance from their Aztec roots. Men with the same flat features leaned against walls, hats tipped over eyes, waiting for God knows what. In the middle of the block, kids converged on an old guy selling ice cream from a handcart that looked as if it had been in use since the fifties.

"Pass. Let someone else take the hassle." Matt looked again at his watch. "See you tomorrow."

* * *

Matt put the Range Rover into the now doorless garage, walked down the side deck past Bobby's Harley, a Softail, parked in the middle of the ruined front garden, and let himself into the kitchen.

Bobby was sprawled on the overstuffed sofa in the living room, a box of crackers on the table in front of him, watching a ballgame on television, Barney at his feet. The Lab got up as Matt came in, gave him a swift, enthusiastic greeting, and went back to monitoring Bob's hand-to-mouth motion. Bob held up a warning finger. "USC, Arizona, flag on the play. Oh, damn. USC's offside." He clicked off the set.

Bobby tossed Barney a Ritz and swung his feet to the floor. "You've got to find a new hiding place for the house key. That flowerpot's history."

Matt threw his briefcase onto the kitchen counter. The key had always been kept in a flowerpot. "I'll get a new one."

"And get the fence fixed while you're at it. You're totally exposed to the street, your neighbors are never here and this place is barely more than a shack. A quick push on the kitchen door, and you're cleaned out in minutes."

"You try getting anything done. Half of Malibu's in line ahead of me."

"What about one of your own work crews?"

"Ned would have a coronary. Leases are signed and we're getting the Contessa project ready for occupancy. Anyway, Barney would take the hand off anyone coming in here."

"Okay, that's my community outreach for the week," Bobby said.

Matt filled Barney's bowl, took a bottle of water from the fridge. He crossed to the living room, dropped into an armchair, propped his feet on the coffee table. "So, okay, what's happened that's so all-fired important?"

Bob leaned forward, elbows on his knees. "A body's been

found up on Encinal Canyon Road. A girl, maybe fourteen, fifteen. White."

Matt knew what Bobby was going to tell him, but he didn't want to hear it. A fourteen year old. Just a kid herself. "Didn't Encinal burn out?"

"No, not all the way down to the beach. Anyway, she wasn't in the fire area. She was by the side of the road, and she was covered in wildflowers. A fire crew checking hotspots found her."

"Flowers? Someone must have cared about her."

"Or some sick bastard thought it was a cute touch."

"How'd she die, Bobby?"

"Until we get an autopsy report, it's just guesswork. She's been badly abused at some time, but the scars are old. Marks on her breasts as if she'd been burned by cigars, that sort of thing. Poor kid had a short and brutal life, but whoever put her on the side of the road wanted her found. She was dressed in some expensive threads, baggy silk pants, a matching top and a shirt. The pants were blood-soaked, but someone had tried to clean her up. My guess is that she gave birth then hemorrhaged out."

"So that's the mother."

Bobby shrugged. "Putting two and two together, that's my guess. Homicide's got it. So far her description doesn't match any missing person on file in Los Angeles County. They've sent it to Sacramento, see if they get any hits statewide. I thought you'd be interested."

"What'll happen if they don't get anything?"

"Nothing much. No identifying marks on her or the baby, no way to find out who they were."

"What about dental records?"

"Sure, but not everyone visits a dentist. And anyway, there's no national database for teeth. All we can do is find out if they're related. After that, there's nowhere to go." Bobby dropped another cracker for Barney. "Don't try to get that baby released to you, Matt. Let it drop."

"It's too late, I told you. I called the coroner this morning." Matt got up, put his empty glass in the sink. "I'm going out to eat. Sylvie still on late duty?"

"Yeah, all this week. You want to take this seriously, buddy."

"I am taking it seriously, but what do you want me to do? I've already called the coroner's office. They have my name, my address, my phone number. They didn't ask for my social security number, or they'd have that, too. So, you want to go eat?"

Bob let out a long breath. "Okay. Usual place?"

Matt had been thinking of Granita for a change, Wolfgang Puck's restaurant at the top of the road, but the prices were pretty rich for a deputy sheriff with a Malibu mortgage, even with two salaries coming in. Bob would agree if he suggested it, then insist on carrying his weight.

"Sure. Googie's Coffee Shop in five."

CHAPTER 5

7:00 a.m. on a Friday morning, and traffic on the I-10 from Santa Monica to downtown was moving steadily. In another hour, it would be gridlock. Matt listened to Coltrane, and restrained the impulse to jockey the Range Rover from lane to lane. He got off the freeway at 9th Street, and stopped to pick up a couple of caffe grandes at the Starbucks by Macy's—he knew better than to risk the coffee on a construction job, which tasted as if it were made with iron filings, guaranteed to burn a hole in the lining of the stomach.

By 7:30 he was at the Contessa, four hundred low-rise luxury apartments on what used to be a used-car lot before the neighborhood got too run-down even for clunkers. Swimming pools, tennis courts, running track, gym, all the bells and whistles, heavily landscaped, an urban refuge, and close to major freeways and the Staples Center. The city was jubilant, already counting on the tax base to revitalize the surrounding area. Lowell Brothers was gambling the company shirt on the project, their first venture into new construction, but so far it looked good. Ned had negotiated leases with both teams that called the Staples Center home, NBA basketball and NHL hockey, the Lakers and the Kings.

Half a dozen trucks loaded with large boxed jacaranda trees were lined up on Bixel Street outside the Contessa. By the time the job was finished, a hundred prime specimens would be in the ground.

"Good morning, Ben." Matt handed Ben Pressman, the landscape architect, a container of coffee, popped the lid on his own and took a sip. He and Ben circled the trucks, checking out the jacarandas.

"Pretty nice, huh?" Ben said.

"Yeah. Not bad, Ben." He and Pressman had personally selected each one, shopping half a dozen tree farms to get what they wanted. "Let's get them in the ground."

He stayed on through the morning, ate enchiladas with the Hispanic work crew gathered around Roxanne's Hot Lunch, the roach wagon that made the rounds of downtown construction sites.

It was almost four when he got back to the office in Brentwood.

Two men, flipping without much interest through magazines devoted to the construction business, looked up as he walked in. Matt raised an inquiring eyebrow at Marni behind her desk in the front office.

"These gentlemen are waiting to see you, Matt. They're from the sheriff's department."

The men replaced the magazines on the table, got to their feet. The elder of the two said, "Mr. Lowell? I'm Detective Jim Barstow. My partner, Detective Eduardo Flores."

Matt glanced at the proffered shields, noted the nicotine-stained fingers and the smell of tobacco that clung to the two men. He shook hands with each in turn, conscious of Marni's ears straining to hear every word, and ushered them into the office. Ned, frowning at the computer screen on his own side of the partners' desk, looked up as Matt introduced the detectives. They refused coffee. Matt settled himself behind his desk, indicated a couple of chairs on the other side.

"So, what can I do for you?"

"Just a few questions. You are the Matthew Lowell who found the child on the beach, is that right?" Barstow asked. Late forties, thinning fair hair, deep set blue eyes. Slim, sharp tailoring.

Not much got past him, Matt guessed. "Yes. During the fire."

"That would be last Monday?"

"Yes. Monday."

"She was alive when you found her?"

Matt nodded. "Yes."

"About what time of day was that, Mr. Lowell?"

"Sometime between four and five. It's hard to say exactly. The smoke from the fire was black and covered the entire sky, so it was dusk long before the sun started going down. And sunset these days is at five. So I can't say for sure. I didn't look at my watch."

Barstow's partner gave a half smile. He'd caught the sarcasm. Flores was in his early forties, bulky but not fat, an ungainly nose away from being darkly handsome.

"Well, that's close enough for now," Barstow said. "Were you working in Malibu on Monday?"

"No, I was here, but I've lived in Malibu all my life and I know how fast a brushfire moves in a Santa Ana wind. I had horses in Ramirez Canyon and was worried about getting them out. And my dog was locked inside my house."

"That's the house on Malibu Road?" Barstow asked. He produced a small notebook from the inside pocket on his jacket.

Matt nodded. "That's right."

"You say you found the baby several miles north of that location between four and five o'clock. By noon the entire area had been evacuated, the highway was closed in both directions from Topanga Canyon in the south, and Trancas Canyon in the north. How was it you managed to be on that particular part of the beach at that particular time? Can you explain that?"

"I drove—"

"Wait a minute," Ned said. "What is this? An interrogation? He's already reported this to—"

"It's okay, Ned, let me handle it," Matt said. He held a tight rein on his irritation. Ned could be a pain sometimes with his big brother concern. Ginn thought it was guilt because Ned had been at Wharton in Philadelphia when their mother was killed, and had gone back to school the day after she was buried, leaving Matt alone with their father in a house that contained only shadows where she had been.

"You're right," he said to Barstow. "The Pacific Coast Highway was closed when I got to Topanga Canyon."

"What time was that?"

"About two, two-thirty."

Barstow made a note on his pad. He looked up, nodded for Matt to continue.

"I turned around and went back to the Santa Monica Freeway, took the 405 north across the Sepulveda Pass to the 101 in the San Fernando Valley." Deliberately, Matt went through every detail of the long circuitous route back to Malibu. "The 101 west was pretty clogged because of fire closures, but I was able to make it to Las Posas Road below Oxnard. I turned off there and drove toward the ocean through the berry fields and came down the PCH that way."

Barstow flipped through the pages of his notebook.

"On your way down the PCH you had to pass Encinal Canyon, right?"

Matt felt his gut clench. "Yes."

"Did you drive up into Encinal Canyon?"

"Of course not. I was trying to get home."

"And the Pacific Coast Highway was already closed at Trancas Canyon when you got there?"

"That's right. They were pretty busy in the market parking lot, getting a convoy together to go over the Kanan Dume Road while it was still open. It wasn't difficult to drive around the roadblock."

"What were you driving?"

"I had a pickup and a horse trailer."

Flores spoke for the first time. "Do you usually commute to work here in Brentwood with a horse trailer, Mr. Lowell?"

"No. I picked it up at Malibu Riding Club on Pacific Coast Highway."

"That's just before Encinal Canyon, is that right?"

"Yes." The enchiladas he'd eaten at lunch suddenly felt like a lead weight in his stomach. They thought he had used the trailer to transport the body of the dead girl.

"Why didn't you take the Kanan Dume Road from the 101? Why go all the way up to Las Posas?"

"I wasn't sure Kanan Dume was open. I didn't want to run into another roadblock and have to turn back. I didn't have that kind of time."

"Are you saying that in the middle of a fire, an equestrian center loaned you a pickup and horse trailer? I would've thought they'd need vehicles like that to evacuate their own animals."

"The truck and trailer didn't belong to the riding club, they belonged to me. I boarded my horses there until a couple of weeks before the fire. I left some tack and the pickup and trailer there until I could pick them up."

"Where are they now, this pickup and trailer?"

"At A-1 Auto Wrecking in Oxnard."

Barstow raised his eyebrows. "What happened to them?"

Matt held on to his temper. What did this bozo think happened to them in the middle of a goddamn fire? "I was trying to get into Ramirez Canyon at Paradise Cove but the gates to the tunnel under the road were closed. The fire came through the tunnel, caught the trailer and pickup. I made a run for it to the Cove restaurant. The trailer and pickup are a total loss. I had to have them towed."

Barstow continued making notes. "I see. What happened then?"

"I got some water from the restaurant, and started south along the beach. It's about seven miles to my place from the Cove. I was more than halfway there, just past the Edwards estate, when I spotted what looked like a downed pelican lying near the water. I got closer, and saw it was a baby."

"And the baby was alive when you picked it up?"

Matt had to force himself not to look away. "Yes. I thought I just said that."

"No, you didn't. So then?"

"I felt a faint pulse. I wrapped her in my shirt and went back to some stairs that I'd seen still standing. I thought maybe I could get some help there, but when I got back the stairs had burned and the wind had blown them apart, so I turned around and continued toward home."

"It didn't occur to you to go back to the restaurant?"

"Of course it did, but what for? Fire blocked the road, the restaurant was empty, no one was coming, no fire crews. Plus I was more than halfway home."

"When did you realize she was dead?"

"When I got home. I put her on the couch. She seemed cold. I tried to feel a pulse and couldn't. I tried to give her CPR, holding her nose and breathing into her mouth, but it was too late. She was dead." He'd been reliving that moment over and over ever since.

"You've got a bandage on your arm, Mr. Lowell. What happened?" Flores asked this question. Matt guessed they were taking turns.

Instinctively, Matt looked down at his wrist. He'd dropped by his doctor's office, Phil had put a couple of stitches in, and covered it with gauze and a Band-Aid. That was the day after the fire.

"I broke a window at the restaurant to get some water and I guess I cut it. I didn't notice it until later."

"You didn't notice a cut that was bad enough to need stitches and bandaging?"

"A hell of a lot more was going on then than a cut on my arm, Detective Flores. Half of Malibu was on fire."

Flores nodded and gave him that thin smile again. "So is that your blood on the blue shirt the baby was wrapped in?"

"Yes."

"So why didn't you get help for this baby right away?"

"Where? It was in the middle of a wildfire. The phones were down. I'd dropped my cell on the beach. Where was I supposed to find help?"

"You could've taken her to the Civic Center there in Malibu, couldn't you?"

"She was already dead, and flames were coming over the ridge. What would have been the point of attempting that?" He wanted to ask if this guy had ever been caught in a firestorm, but the answer was obvious. He hadn't.

"You've shown an interest in claiming this baby, Mr. Lowell. Why is that?" Barstow asked.

Out of his peripheral vision, Matt saw Ned open his mouth, then close it without speaking. He hadn't told Ned what he intended.

"No reason. I just thought… I didn't like the idea that she might be cut up for the purpose of training doctors."

"Who told you that would happen?"

"Doesn't it?"

Barstow shrugged. "A young woman was found yesterday morning on Encinal Canyon Road. It's possible she was the mother."

"Really?"

"You don't sound too surprised. Did you know this girl?"

"Know her? No, I didn't know her. I would've told you if I knew her. Look, I found a child on the beach in the middle of a wildfire. I did the best I could to keep her alive. I feel terrible that I wasn't able to, but I got in touch with the authorities as soon as I could, which was around midnight. After I'd spent hours fighting to save my house. I thought it would be the right thing to do to give her a burial. Where are you going with this?"

Flores joined the conversation. "Why do you feel so threatened by these questions?"

"I don't feel threatened, Mr. Flores." Matt made a conscious effort to relax. Flores was right, he sounded defensive. "I just don't understand why you're talking to me about a young girl found dead in Encinal."

"Well, the spot in Encinal is not too far from where you said you picked up the child on the beach. You've shown quite an interest in that baby. We're just trying to do our job, get to the bottom of who knew what and when they knew it," Flores said.

Matt held his eyes. They were a mid-brown, the sort of brown usually described as warm. But these were as cold as any Matt had seen, and the slight smile hovering around Flores' tight lips didn't help.

"Well," he said, "if I can help you do that, of course I will. Anyway, are you sure the girl you found was the mother?"

Neither man responded. It was clear they were not here to answer questions, just ask them.

"Would you be willing to give a sample for DNA testing, Mr. Lowell?" Flores asked. "Just for the record."

"Now wait a minute," Ned said. "Just you guys wait a minute here—"

"It's okay, Ned," Matt said. He turned to Barstow. "Why are you asking me to do that?"

"There's nothing to it, Mr. Lowell, nothing invasive," Barstow said. "A swab, some saliva, that's all."

"You haven't answered the question," Ned said. "Is he suspected of some crime?"

"We don't know that a crime has been committed, Mr. Lowell. This is just routine."

Matt sat back and let Ned run with it. He'd seen Ned's face and knew better than to start an argument with him in front of a couple of detectives.

"Routine, bullshit," Ned said. "What happens to that sample afterward? It's kept on record, right? So my brother, who has done absolutely nothing except behave like a model citizen, now has his DNA on record in a police file connected to some unknown girl's death?"

Flores shook his head. "The sample will be destroyed."

"Come on," Ned said. "We're supposed to trust the police department that screwed up the blood evidence in the O.J. Simpson case?"

Barstow turned to Matt. "We have your shirt, Mr. Lowell, and we don't need your permission to test it."

"Then why are you asking for saliva?"

"Well, cooperation would count in your favor—"

Ned was on his feet. "What are you talking about, in his favor? Is he being accused of something?"

"No. Well. Thank you, we'll be in touch. If you remember anything else, give us a call." Barstow produced a small leather cardholder, removed a business card and placed it on Matt's desk. He glanced at Flores, and both detectives rose. "And we're the sheriff's department, not LAPD. Just so you know. Anyway, thanks for your time." At the door, Barstow turned. "Your horses get out okay?"

"Yes, thanks," Matt answered.

Barstow nodded and offered a polite smile. The two detectives left the room, leaving behind a faint trail of stale cigarette smoke, and the unspoken words hanging in the air.

They suspected him of murder.

CHAPTER 6

Matt turned off his laptop and pushed back from his desk in the corner of the living room. It was no good. He couldn't work. It seemed as if he'd been going over the same set of drawings for the last three hours. All he could think of was the conversation with the detectives and the two creatures who'd somehow fallen into the middle of his life, the baby who had died in his arms, and the young girl who may or may not be the baby's mother.

He got to his feet, poured another cup of coffee, his third that morning, took it to the window. Rays from the sun pierced the bottom of the mounting gray-and-white thunderclouds, and sparkled in large intermittent coins of light on the water. The temperature had dropped dramatically since the fire, and rain was in the forecast.

A flight of California brown pelicans swept low, wingtips skimming the top of the waves. Matt followed their glide with his eyes until they disappeared over the water. The pelicans were making a comeback after the DDT disaster in the seventies that had damn near wiped them out.

He picked up the phone, punched out the number for the animal shelter in Agoura, identified himself to the woman who answered, described his two horses, the small gentle Andalusian mare he'd bought for Ginn, his own buckskin quarterhorse gelding, and asked how soon he could pick them up.

"The sooner the better," she said. "We're like Noah's ark over here. If you can tell me what time you'll be here, I'll have them brought in from the pasture."

"I have to make a couple of calls, see if I can borrow a trailer. Probably be around one, is that okay?"

"Sure. See you then," she said and hung up.

Margie Little's place had been burned out, so he called the Malibu Riding Club, agreed to pay double the usual boarding fee—the stable manager made sure he was aware she was doing him a favor, that space was tight after the fire, and he had, after all, removed his horses from the club for no reason she had been able to fathom. But as a courtesy, he could leave his Range Rover at the club, use one of their trailers and a pickup to get his horses from Agoura. If he were still a member, she'd waive the rental fee, but since he wasn't, of course, there would be a charge.

He loaded Barney into the Range Rover and took the Pacific Coast Highway north. The roadblocks at Topanga and Trancas had been removed, but traffic was still sparse. By tomorrow, if the rain held off, Sunday drivers would be out in force inspecting the damage—the chimneys still standing surrounded by rubble, the blackened beams from collapsed roofs, the burned-out armchairs and sofas that had once enclosed celebrity bottoms.

He slowed at the sign for Encinal Canyon Road. The girl's body had been found less than a mile from the PCH. On impulse, he turned right onto the canyon road, a tortuous two-lane ribbon of asphalt that switchbacked across the Santa Monica Mountains down into the San Fernando Valley on the other side.

A quarter mile up the narrow gorge was a different world. The erratic wind-driven fire had skipped the entire lower canyon.

Sycamores were still in fall yellows and russets, branching over the roadside tangle of willow and toyon and wild tobacco.

For Matt, the Santa Monica Mountains with their latticework of canyons and ravines were as much a part of Malibu as the ocean. When they were kids, he and Bobby Eckhart had camped all over these hills. They'd seen bobcats and mountain lions, rattlesnakes and redtailed hawks, even eagles soaring above bare rocky crags. They'd found traces of Chumash Indian pictographs in caves, and they knew where the virgin creeks were that ran all year, tumbling over rocks into pools deep enough to swim in. They'd also seen their share of abandoned vehicles and rusted-out discarded appliances. They'd never seen an abandoned body, but the canyons of Los Angeles were notorious for all kinds of murder and mayhem and they'd heard the stories.

Matt pulled into the clearing in front of the wide metal gates to the old archery range. According to Bobby, the dead teenager had been found about three hundred feet beyond this point.

He left Barney in the Range Rover—there was no shoulder to speak of, and the edge dropped off sharply on the creek side, dangerous if a vehicle hurtled around a curve, too many people used these mountain roads as raceways. Barney would be safer locked up. Matt crossed the road and walked toward a strip of yellow plastic police tape sagging between a couple of coastal oaks.

That was all there was to mark the place. There should be more, Matt thought. But what? Maybe crime scene tape's as good as anything. Maybe it doesn't really matter. But he couldn't shake the barren feeling he had standing in this empty spot along the road.

On the ground at his feet he noticed a scattering of desiccated wildflowers. He knew them from Boy Scouts, yellow tree tobacco, white virgin's bower, red California fuschia, purple rosemary. Bobby had told him the body had been covered in flowers. He sat on his heels, picked up a spray of canyon sunflower, held it to his nose, breathed in the faint scent. He twirled the spray gently in his fingers, then realized there was moisture on his skin. Sap from the stem.

The flowers in his hand were fresh. He looked around. The road was empty, quiet.

He stood and peered over the edge of the steep cliffside that fell off down to the creek. His eye caught a flash of blue. He squinted, made out a crouched form hidden in a tangle of toyon and manzanita.

"Hey!" he called. "Can I talk to you?"

The figure bolted upright, plunged through the brush in a wild crashing descent.

"Wait a minute."

Matt started after him, grabbing branches, using his boot heels as a brake, half sliding, half running.

The flash of blue disappeared, reappeared and disappeared again. Part way down, another figure, long straight brown hair, broke cover and took off headlong down the hillside.

Girls, he thought. A couple of girls. He hit the canyon bottom, raced after the two of them toward the dry creek bed. They jumped from rock to rock, scrambled up the other bank.

Matt followed across the creek, leaping the same boulders. He stopped short as the figure in blue suddenly turned in a small clearing in front of a grove of wild walnut trees, blocking Matt's way, teeth bared in a snarl, eyes blazing and wild. With a jolt, Matt realized he was looking at not a girl but a teenaged boy. He was an astonishing apparition in blue silk shirt, torn and soot stained, an open blue velvet vest, matching blue velvet pants, worn tight, the knees ripped. He'd armed himself with a long, heavy stick, and stood protectively in front of four young girls. They appeared to be no older than sixteen, and white, except for a black child who was maybe ten.

Matt held up his hands. "I'm sorry. I didn't mean to frighten you. I'm not here to hurt you. I just want to talk to you."

The boy lifted his chin, fixed fierce narrowed eyes on Matt.

He was trembling, Matt saw, but not from fear. This kid would kill if he had the chance.

Matt looked at the girls huddled together under the walnut trees, a bizarre little group, dressed in a strange assortment of garments in brilliant parrot colors, green, yellow, scarlet. Torso-hugging, skinny strapped tops, silky loose-fitting pants. The fabric looked rich, heavy silk, torn and stained. Their feet were clad in matching soft leather boots. They could have been a circus troop still in costume.

"What are you doing here?" They were sure not on a camping trip, not in that gear. They all had sun-damaged skin, huge welts on arms and chests caused by the poison oak that grew all over these mountains. Their lips were dry, cracked and bleeding.

He looked at each girl in turn. Their faces were filthy with mud and ash, their bodies shivering in the cool air of the canyon, even cooler on a day like this with rain clouds hanging low. They looked traumatized. No one spoke.

"Okay, you don't have to talk to me. But you're going to have to talk to someone. A girl was found up on the road. Did you know her?"

His questions were greeted with silence.

"Who are you? How long have you been here in the canyon?"

Every eye was locked on Matt, watching his every move, the girls looking as if they were ready to run. Or maybe fight. They stared at him, no glimmer of understanding in their eyes. They either didn't understand English, or they were deaf. Matt touched his fingers to his cheeks and arms, made small circling motions and then pointed to the group's faces and bare arms.

"Poison oak," he said slowly. "You need to have that treated. I've got salve in my car. And water, you look like you need some water." No one moved and Matt said, "Look, I want to help. Why are you here?" He looked around at the canyon. "You shouldn't be here dressed like that. The weather is going to change, it's going to rain and turn colder."

One of the girls started to cry. She appeared to be the oldest, the longhaired girl he'd been chasing.

Matt took off his denim jacket, held it out to her.

"Come on, you need it. It will protect you." He patted his own shoulders to show her what he meant.

The girl moved to reach for it. The boy spoke sharply.

In spite of her distress, the girl responded just as sharply. Nothing wrong with their hearing, Matt thought. For a moment, they argued in a language he had never heard before.

The girl accepted the jacket and said something to him. Matt thought she was asking a question. It could be English, but the accent was so heavy he couldn't make it out.

He shook his head. "I'm sorry. Please, speak slowly." He watched her lips. It sounded as if she were saying "eye eeder."

"Eye eeder." Her voice broke on a sob. "Eye eeder." The boy yelled at her. The other three girls started to cry.

"Eye eeder?" Matt started to shake his head, then realized she was saying a name. Matt gestured toward her. "Your name is Aida?"

She shook her head.

"She was the girl on the road?"

In a soft voice, she answered, "Yes."

Her eyes darted toward the boy. Screaming, he lunged at her, the heavy stick raised. Matt grabbed him before he could strike, shook the menacing club out of his hand, spun him around so that the boy's back was against his chest. Holding him was like trying to control an octopus, limbs everywhere. The kid was frantic, explosive, strong beyond his slight frame. It took a few minutes before Matt was able to pin both arms to his sides and swing him off his feet. Gradually the boy stopped struggling.

"Listen," Matt said against his ear. "I'm not going to hurt you, any of you. A girl died. Tell me how she died."

"You bring police," the boy said.

He could speak English. Now maybe they could get some-where. "No one's going to bring in the police, so you just relax, all right?" The boy said nothing. "Okay?" Matt said again. "I'm going to let you down now. Just stay quiet, nothing is going to happen to you."

It was a long time coming but finally the boy nodded. Carefully Matt allowed the boy's feet to touch the ground and as soon as he thought the kid would stay put, released him. The boy turned quickly. Tears of rage wet his eyes.

"You're a good man," Matt said. "You're okay. What is your name?"

The boy clenched his lips together as if to prevent Matt from seeing that they were trembling.

"Hasan." The older girl answered for him, and the boy spat what sounded like a curse.

Matt looked at him in surprise. The Arabs Matt had met or seen were dark-eyed, dark-haired, olive-skinned. This Arabic boy was blue-eyed, had dark blond hair, neat small features. Matt kept his eyes on the boy. "That's you? Hasan?"

The boy did not answer.

"Okay," Matt said. "Hasan. Good. And Aida was the girl who died. How did Aida die?"

No answer.

He tried a different question. "Where do you come from?"

The older girl said an indecipherable word. She pointed to herself and the two other white girls. She repeated the word. Matt still couldn't understand her.

Matt looked more closely at the little black girl. "What about you?" he asked gently. "Where do you come from?"

The child refused to meet his eyes, and the older girl, the only one who had so far spoken, put an arm around her protectively.

"Africa," she said. "She from Africa."

CHAPTER 7

Matt took off the flannel shirt he had on over his T-shirt and stepped forward to wrap it around the child. All he could see was the top of her small dark head. She flinched as he touched her, and the older girl murmured a crooning sound of comfort. She took the shirt from Matt's hand, knelt and wrapped it around the African child's body.

"What's happened to her?" he asked softly. And to the rest of you, but he left those words unsaid. What kind of disaster had brought this strange band into Encinal Canyon?

Darting fearful looks at Matt, the girls exchanged a few words among themselves, until Hasan spoke sharply, driving them back into silence.

"She want mama," the boy said.

Yes, Matt thought, of course she does. Matt had the sudden image of himself at that same age, watching his mother's flower-blanketed coffin being carried from St. Aidan's Church. He took a breath, and the image faded, leaving him feeling as if he had been hit by a two-by-four.

He fumbled in his pants pocket for the energy bar he always kept handy and offered it to the child, but she would not look up. He passed it to the older girl, who unwrapped it, lifted the child's hand, and pressed her fingers around it until she was sure it would not fall from the child's grasp. The child broke off a corner, put it into her mouth and handed the rest back. The older girl divided it up, handing a fragment to each of the others, including Hasan who ignored the piece she held out to him. After a moment, she gave it to the little one.

"This little girl needs help," Matt said. "All of you need help. I will take you to my house, get you some food and clothes." He looked at Hasan, making a point of including him. "We will talk, and we will decide what to do."

"Kanita," the older girl said. She pointed to herself. "Kanita," she said again. She then pointed to Matt.

More progress, he thought. They were communicating. "You are Kanita." He enunciated each word carefully. "I am Matt." He glanced at the closed, hard face of the boy, and turned back to the girl. "Kanita, you cannot stay here." He pointed to the sky, gestured rain with his hands, hoping she understood. "Rain. Rain is coming. You must get shelter. Come with me. I'll get help." And maybe these kids could tell the authorities what they knew about the dead girl, Matt thought, and remove the cloud of suspicion hanging over his head.

Kanita slid a nervous yet defiant look at Hasan then beckoned to Matt and started toward a cluster of large granite boulders. Matt glanced at the boy, then went after her. She led him between the rocks and into a sheltered crawlspace created by a tangle of roots and the limbs of canyon oak trees. Matt peered inside.

A slight solitary figure lay motionless on the ground. Also a teenager, she was dressed similarly to the others, in a beaded tank top and gauzy loose-fitting lavender pants. She lay on a makeshift bed of brown paper grocery sacks spread out on the bare ground.

Matt's throat tightened and he fought back a wave of panic. Another dead girl? He crawled into the shelter and touched the girl's hand, and started to breathe again. Her skin was an unhealthy grayish white and clammy, but warm, maybe too warm. Her eyes were closed, her face framed by a mass of dirt-encrusted black hair tangled with bits of leaves and twigs.

"How long has she been like this?"

Kanita frowned and he repeated the question slowly.

"Today, yesterday, tomorrow." Kanita shrugged as if an explanation of time was beyond her.

He patted the unconscious girl's hand, hoping to rouse her. He'd have to carry her out and she would be a dead weight to pick up. He turned to Kanita. "What's her name?"

Kanita shook her head. Matt pointed to himself, to Kanita, repeating their names as he did so. Then he indicated the girl. Kanita patted her mouth, pointed to the girl and shook her head again.

This was getting them nowhere. Matt slid an arm around the girl to lift her into a sitting position.

The girl opened her eyes, deep black eyes that widened in terror at the sight of him. She shoved hard at his chest, scrabbled to get away but managed only a few yards. A long high-pitched keening ripped from her throat.

The skin on the back of Matt's neck shuddered at the sound. "It's okay. You're okay." He managed to quell the instinct to raise the pitch of his own voice and kept his tone low and reassuring. "I'm not going to hurt you. It's okay."

Matt quickly ran through his limited options. The girl needed medical treatment. He could go for help, but as as soon as Matt was out of sight, the boy would be gone, dragging the girls with him. And the Santa Monica Mountains were wild enough to swallow up anyone who didn't want to be found. These kids were a line to the dead girl, and if she were the mother, to the dead newborn. He could not lose track of them.

Kanita was speaking softly to the sick girl, insistently, the same words over and over, in the same unrecognizable language. Kanita held her until she quieted and her agitation softened into a rhythmic rocking motion.

"No immigration. No police," Kanita said suddenly as if reading Matt's mind. "No immigration, no police," she said again, repeating the universally understood words.

"Okay, right, no immigration."

"No police."

Matt smiled at her. Brave girl, he thought. Kids shouldn't have to be this scared. He knew there were children in the world who lived in daily fear, including a primal fear of the authorities, but he'd never seen it up close and raw.

"No police," he conceded. "No immigration."

The sick girl continued lying quietly in Kanita's arms. If he wanted to learn anything more from the older girl, now was the time to ask, with Hasan out of earshot. He leaned toward her. "What happened to Aida?"

Kanita shook her head. "She die."

"A baby, then die?"

Kanita's eyes stared unblinkingly into Matt's before sliding to a point over his shoulder. He turned his head. Hasan stood just feet behind him. Matt hadn't heard a thing, not the crunch of a twig or the rustle of footsteps through leaves. The kid had approached in absolute silence as if trained in guerrilla warfare.

Kanita motioned to Matt to take the girl in her arms, then scrambled to her feet. Eyes lowered, she scurried past the boy and disappeared around the edge of the rocks. With Hasan watching, Matt put an arm around the limp body, another under her knees and maneuvered her out of the shelter and into the open.

"I'm taking her to a doctor," Matt said the boy. "I want you all to come with me."

The boy stood squarely in the narrow defile between the boulders, barring the way.

"If Aida died after giving birth, Hasan, I promise you won't get into any trouble. It wasn't your fault, man." Matt wasn't sure about the legalities of child abandonment—hell, he wasn't sure about anything anymore—but that would have to wait. "If you come with me, I'll explain what happened. I'll get you all the help you need."

Hasan stood unmoving.

"Okay, your call," Matt said.

He squeezed past the rigid figure, made his way back along the path, into the clearing. If they were illegal, they'd need a lawyer, child services, some kind of help. He could feel how tired they were, how much they wanted some relief, someone to care for them.

"Tell them it's going to be okay, Kanita." Although he wasn't sure himself exactly how. "Tell them they should come with me now."

The slight, slim figure of Hasan appeared in the clearing. His voice, filled with the biting power of rage, swept over the small group of girls.

Matt looked at Kanita. "What did he say?"

She gestured to the girl in Matt's arms. "Okay, she go."

"What about you and the others?"

She shook her head.

"Hasan, rain is coming. Let them come with me, man."

The boy stared without speaking, hatred seeming to emanate from every part of his body.

Matt could feel the girl becoming heavier. He'd hit a dead end, at least for now.

"I'll be back with food." He included Hasan in his glance. "No police, no immigration. Stay here. We'll talk. We'll work it out, whatever has happened. Whatever it is, Hasan, it can be fixed."

No one spoke.

One of the older girls put an arm around the ten-year-old and drew her closer.

At least that was something, Matt thought. He turned to go.

CHAPTER 8

As soon as they were out of the canyon, Matt picked up his cell phone, tapped out Phil Halliburton's private number. He threw a quick glance at the girl, wondering why Hasan had let her go with only a token show of obstruction, unlike the others who needed help almost as urgently. Her eyes closed, she was still leaning against the door of the Range Rover, covered by the blanket he kept in the back for Barney.

"Phil, it's Matt."

"Hey, Matt, how are you doing? And that's strictly a social question. If you have symptoms, take two aspirins and call the office on Monday. Whoops, I forgot. How's the arm?"

Matt dispensed with a laugh at Phil's standard joke. He'd known Halliburton since Phil opened his practice in internal medicine in Malibu ten years ago. Their relationship was mainly social, but Halliburton was the guy he saw on the rare occasions he needed a doctor.

"It's okay, thanks. Phil, can you meet me at my house? I need some help."

"What's up?"

"I can't say right now. I'll explain when you get there."

"If it's a medical emergency, Matt, really, you're better off calling 911. The paramedics have everything at their fingertips. All I've got is my little black bag."

"No, I need a private doctor. Can you make it?"

A moment of silence. "You're being very mysterious. Annie and I have plans for tonight."

"Phil, this won't take long. Please."

Another silence. Matt waited him out.

"Okay, but this had better be good."

"Bring the black bag. I owe you one, Phil."

He hung up then called the Agoura shelter to tell them something had come up, he'd have to reschedule a time to pick up his two horses. Ten minutes later he drove into his garage. The girl had not moved since he had placed her in the seat and her eyes were still closed. He got out, opened the tailgate for Barney. Before he could go around to the passenger door, the girl slammed it open and was out of the garage, across the road, narrowly missing a passing car.

Shouting at Barney to stay, Matt tore after her. He dragged her off the bank, scooped her against his chest, started back across the street. A few houses away the car had slowed almost to a stop. He put his mouth to the girl's ear, the words soothing and simple. "It's okay. It's okay."

Matt crossed the road without looking in the direction of the car, the picture, he hoped, of a young father and his playful teenager, their ecstatic Labrador jumping around them in greeting. He ran along the deck by the side of the house, got the kitchen door open, kicked it closed behind him, and set the girl on her feet.

She backed away, dark hair tangled with leaves and twigs hanging in her eyes, lips bared in a snarl. Dressed as she was in flimsy silk she had to be freezing.

Matt held his hands out to the side. "It's okay, you're safe here. I'm not going to hurt you. A doctor is coming, you understand, a doctor?" Keeping his distance, he went to the hall closet, pulled out a blanket, held it out to her. "Put this around you."

She kept her eyes on him without moving and he tossed the blanket on the back of the sofa that separated the living room from the kitchen. He turned the thermostat up to eighty, then knelt and touched a match to the fire. The gas lighter flared, caught the kindling, flames curled around the logs. He went back into the kitchen, filled the kettle, put it on to boil, keeping up a running commentary to reassure her.

"It will be warmer in here soon. Do you like peppermint tea?" He was completely out of his depth.

He picked up the telephone on the kitchen counter, tapped out Ginn's number. His heart hammered in his chest while he waited, then her voice, her real voice, was in his ear.

His mouth was suddenly dry. "Ginn, it's me."

"Matt, I am going to hang up. Goodbye."

"No, don't. Ginn, listen. Please. I need help—"

"Then call your brother, or your father in Palm Springs, or Bobby. Why call me?"

Because I love you. "Because you're a lawyer, and you're the only one who can help."

"Goodbye, Matt."

Speaking quickly to hold her, he said, "I found some kids today, holed up in a canyon."

"What?"

"Kids on their own, fourteen, fifteen, suffering from exposure and covered in poison oak. Illegals, I think. A young boy, five girls, one of them a black kid about ten." He spoke rapidly, trying to convince her before she hung up. "I've got one of the girls here now, and she won't speak. I've got to go back to get the others—"

"Are you crazy? Call the authorities. Call Bobby Eckhart. Do it now, before you get any deeper. Goodbye."

"I can't, Ginn. They're illegals, I promised I wouldn't call the police—" He was speaking to a dial tone.

The kettle was whistling. He rummaged around in the cupboard, found a package of peppermint teabags, dumped a couple in a mug. He covered them with water, spooned in sugar. The girl had not moved. Mug in hand, he started to walk toward her. "Now you sit down and drink this, you'll feel better—"

She exploded into action, made an end run around him, grabbed a knife from the wooden block on the counter. She backed into the far corner of the living room, wedged herself between the built-in bookcases and the wall. She held the long narrow bladed paring knife in front of her with both hands. It looked as dangerous as a shiv.

"Hey, hey, wait a minute," Matt said. He put the mug on the end table, and moved toward her. "You don't need that." Slowly, he held his hand out for the knife. "It's very sharp. Come on, give it to me."

She slashed at him, barely missing his fingers, and he jumped back. He could see the whites of her eyes surrounding the dark iris. She looked like a trapped animal, in shock, ready to kill, ready to die.

Footsteps pounded along the walkway and Matt backed through to the kitchen and opened the door.

"Man, am I glad you're here."

"So, what's up?" Phil Halliburton took off his outer coat, hung it on the coat stand by the door. Early forties, he was tall and slender, well barbered dark hair, the kind of guy who spent time and effort cultivating a polished image. He looked more like a celebrity lawyer than a doctor. He rubbed Barney's ears while trying to keep the Lab away from his dark slacks. "So what's the big mystery?"

"There she is," Matt said.

Halliburton looked at the girl pressed into the angle between bookshelves and wall, then back at Matt. He looked in shock. "Good God, Matt. What's going on?"

"I don't know. I came across a bunch of kids in Encinal. This one was lying on the ground, looking half-dead, so I brought her home and called you."

"You what? A bunch of kids? What kids?"

"I don't know, Phil. Just kids, obviously illegals. It was going to rain, and she looked so sick. I couldn't leave her."

"You kidnapped her?"

"No, I didn't kidnap her. What are you talking about?"

"What else would you call it? Doesn't look as if she came willingly. What's that you've given her?"

"Peppermint tea, with a lot of sugar. I tried to hand it to her and she grabbed the knife."

"Matt, you should have left her there, whoever she is, and called the authorities."

"Yes, well, maybe, but it didn't seem the thing to do at the time."

Halliburton crossed the living room, but stopped when the girl jabbed the knife at him. "What's her name?"

"I don't know. She hasn't said anything." Then Matt remembered the girl Kanita patting her mouth and shaking her head, and he realized why Hasan was willing to let her leave.

"I don't think she can speak."

"Can she hear?"

"Yes, I'm pretty sure she can."

Phil looked from the girl to Matt. "Oh, man, you've got yourself into one hell of a mess here. Well, if I can get the knife away from her, I can give her a shot, calm her down. Then we can figure out where to go from there." Halliburton took another step toward her. The girl pressed her back deeper into the corner and kept the knife pointed toward him. "Come on, honey, put down the knife," he said firmly. He moved closer.

Her eyes locked on his, the girl pressed the point of the blade into the soft place beneath her own chin.

"Back off, Phil," Matt said. "She's going to hurt herself."

Halliburton ignored him. "Now, you're not going to do that,

are you, honey? Come on, be a good girl, put the knife on the table."

Matt could see the point pressing deeper into the delicate skin. "Phil, back off, she means it."

"Don't worry, she's bluffing."

The skin broke, blood trickled down the girl's throat.

Matt grabbed Halliburton's arm. "This is not going to work. I'm going to call the sheriff's department."

"No, wait a minute. This kid's in shock. Look at her, her skin's gray, and she's sweating. That's not a fever. Get a bunch of deputies in here slamming about, this could escalate into a tragedy."

His eyes on the girl, Matt said, "You just said—" He stopped as the outside door opened.

Wriggling with joy, his tail waving from side to side, Barney hurled himself against the small, slight figure in the doorway.

Ginn Chang staggered, dropped to her knees, put both arms around him. "Oh, Barns. I love you, too." She buried her face in his neck, as if giving herself time to ease into the room. "I've missed you, Barns. I've missed you so much." She held Barney's head, kissed him between his eyes, then looked up at Matt.

Matt drank her in. "Ginn."

She was wearing a bright red pea coat, a heavy white turtle-neck, jeans, the elegance of her French mother as apparent as the delicate bone structure and bloodlines of her Chinese father. Matt's mouth was suddenly dry, his heart bumped unevenly. She hadn't been here for ten months, the longest ten months of his life and he hadn't heard her light step along the deck. He couldn't see her fabulous hair, it was pushed under a red woolen watchcap—unless she'd had it cut off, an awful thought. She looked wonderful. "I didn't think you'd come."

"Well, here I am. What did I interrupt?" Ginn got to her feet, took off the hat, freeing a shoulder length mass of shining black hair. She shook her head, removed the coat, threw it on the back of a kitchen chair. She looked at the girl, took in the knife. Her eyebrows shot up. "What's going on here?"

"This is the girl I told you about on the phone."

"No kidding. What's she doing with a knife?"

"She grabbed it when I tried to hand her a cup of tea."

"He was just explaining to me how he found her in the canyon and decided to bring her home because she was sick," Phil said. "Good to see you, Ginn."

"You, too, Phil." Her tone was less than convincing. Matt knew she'd never had the same regard for Phil that he had. As far as she was concerned, Phil was just one more guy who wanted everything but marriage, and was breaking Annie Lautner's heart in the process. Matt felt his face flush as she turned back to him. "Did you call Bobby?"

"No," Matt said. He was beginning to realize how crazy all this sounded. "I found this kid lying on the ground in Encinal. There were several others, and they were all so terrified I promised I wouldn't contact the police."

Ginn glanced at the girl. "She looks pretty bad." She started across the room, the dog following. The girl's black eyes darted from the men to Ginn, and the point of the knife pressed deeper into the soft spot beneath her chin. Beads of fresh blood oozed from the wound. Ginn stopped well short, and dropped to sit cross-legged on the floor, eye-level with the girl. Barney leaned against her and Ginn put an arm over him and drew him closer.

She smiled and said gently, "You look very tired. Why don't I make you something to eat, and then we'll talk. No one is going to hurt you, sweetie."

The girl's dark eyes swept across the two men, then came back to Ginn. The hand holding the knife was shaking.

Ginn picked up the mug, put it to her nose and inhaled. She smiled. "Nice. Peppermint. Have some." She held it out. The girl shrunk back. Ginn sipped the tea. "Mmm. Good." Slowly, carefully, she pulled the small end table within the girl's reach, replaced the mug and got to her feet. "Have you got any eggs, Matt?"

"Yes, sure."

"This girl is in shock, suicidal, probably psychotic. Eggs won't cure that," Halliburton said.

"Can't hurt. Why don't you two go sit at the kitchen table while I fix something for her to eat. Give her some space."

Ginn moved around easily in the kitchen that had been hers for five years. She scrambled eggs, toasted bread, put oatmeal cookies on a plate, warmed milk. She placed the food on a tray, carried it over to the table and put it down. As if the last of her strength was deserting her, the girl had leaned her back against the wall. Even with both hands wrapped around the handle of the knife, she was only just managing to keep it upright, the shaking point at her throat.

Tail waving, Barney followed the tray. Trained to ignore any food unless invited, he nuzzled the girl, then licked her face. The knife wavered, the girl sagged against him and the same thin, terrible moans Matt had first heard in the canyon seemed wrenched from her throat. The sound arrowed straight into his heart.

Ginn knelt in front of her and slowly reached for the knife. She covered the girl's hand with her own, holding it until the small fingers relaxed the knife into her hand. Barney licked the girl's face anxiously and she put her arms around him, burying her head in his shoulder.

Briefly, Ginn touched the girl's dirty, tangled hair, then reached for the blanket on the back of the couch and draped it over her shoulders. The girl's face was hidden in Barney's coat, but the moans were turning into sobs. Ginn passed her fingers briefly over her eyes before standing up slowly to rejoin the two men at the kitchen table.

"Now what?" Matt said softly.

Phil got his bag, broke open a sealed sterile syringe, selected a vial, drew the colorless liquid into the syringe.

"The first thing is to quiet her down, give her some relief from all that anxiety. It will also give me a chance to examine her. Something's caused all this."

"Leave her alone, Phil," Ginn said. "Just let her cry."

"So, you're a doctor now, Genevieve?" Halliburton asked pleasantly.

"It just seems common sense, that's all. Look at her."

The girl had her arms around Barney, her head resting on him. The dog sat quietly, his eyes on the plate of food. "I'd use a knife, too, if some strange guy came at me with a needle, wouldn't you? Sit down, I'll make some tea."

Matt smiled to himself. Ginn's response to most crises was tea. The canister she had left when she moved out was still full of some blend she had sent to her from Canada.

Phil replaced the syringe and vial, and closed his bag. "That little girl is suffering from exposure, dehydration and hysteria. She's suicidal and should be in a hospital."

"How can I send her to a hospital?" Matt said. "Who am I going to say she is? I don't know her name or anything about her. I can't answer any questions. How long could we get away with it if I made up something?"

"Maybe she's a runaway and she's got parents searching for her, frantic with worry. Did you think about that?"

"Phil, does she look like a runaway to you, with a loving family somewhere? They're not runaways, these kids, not unless they've run away from a circus. They were all dressed in these bizarre outfits. One little kid was black, Phil. Ten years old and African. And not African-American, from some place in Africa. God knows what language she speaks. And it's going to rain."

Matt looked out the window. The sky was heavy with cloud and a band of rain moved across the horizon. Ginn put a mug in front of him, handed the other to Halliburton, and took a chair from which she could keep an eye on Barney and the girl. With her head, Ginn motioned for Matt to look, and he turned. The girl was kneeling in front of the little table, shoveling food into her mouth, with Barney at her side following each bite. Smiling, Matt held Ginn's eyes, sharing a moment of pleasure with her for the first time in almost a year.

"I really don't understand what's going on here, Matt." Halliburton had not picked up on the moment. "What were you doing in Encinal in the first place? Isn't that where a girl's body was found couple of days ago?"

"What body?" Ginn asked.

"You don't know about that? A girl was found dead by the side of the road," Halliburton said. "Do you think this girl, these kids, could be tied up somehow with that?"

"I don't know. Could be." Matt looked at Ginn. "During the fire, I had to come home along the beach. Just past the Edwards old house, I found a baby, maybe a couple of hours old. When I got her here, she was dead. The girl they found might be her mother."

"Oh, Matt! Oh, my God!"

"You didn't tell me about that when you came to get stitched up," Phil said.

Shrugging in dismissal, Matt showed Ginn the Band-Aid covering the wound on his wrist. "I must have cut it breaking a window at Jimmy's. Phil put a couple of stitches in. Anyway, a couple of sheriff's detectives came to see me about the baby and they told me a girl's body had been found, covered in wildflowers, so I went to have a look at the place for myself. I saw these kids but when I called out, they ran, so I followed them. Five girls and a boy. One of the girls spoke a few words of English, really a few words, I could barely understand her. It was very strange, they seemed to be completely dominated by the boy."

"If they're that scared, you'd think they'd put distance between themselves and the place where a body was found, not hang around like that," Phil said.

"That's what I thought." Matt got to his feet. "First I'm going to get some clothes together for them and then I'm going to try to bring them back with me. Their clothes were barely covering them, and it's cold out there now." He nodded toward the girl. "I had to wrap that one in Barney's blanket."

"You're planning to keep five, six kids here?" Halliburton looked around the combined kitchen, dining room, living room. "Besides the little detail that it's illegal, this whole place is smaller than my foyer."

"I'll think of something. Phil, can you stay here with Ginn for about an hour?"

Halliburton held up a warning hand. "Sorry. I've done all I'm going to do. I was never here, I don't know anything about illegal kids. Annie and I are going out to dinner." He got up, took his coat from the stand, shrugged into it. "This girl needs care and she should be watched." He picked up his bag. "Plenty of fluids, light nourishing food, bed rest. Lock away the knives. Good seeing you, Ginn." He closed the door firmly behind him.

"Good seeing you, too, Phil," Ginn said to the closed door. The retreating footsteps faded. "So what are you going to do with a bunch of illegal kids you can't communicate with?"

"I don't know." Matt hesitated, then said, "Would you feel safe staying alone with her? I won't be gone long."

"You're really going to bring them here?"

"If you've got a better suggestion, God knows I'm open to it."

Ginn shook her head. "All right, I'll stay, but I'll have to make a call. I had plans, too."

"Oh. Okay, I'll leave you to it, then."

Matt went into the small spare bedroom. Of course she was dating, he should have expected that. But right now she was here, with him. That was something. He opened the closet, pulled out skis and poles, tennis racquets, a couple of baseball bats and mitts, and threw them on the bed so that he could get at the shelves of old winter clothes, some of it his, some of it Ginn had left behind when she moved out. Her sweats were small enough for the girls to wear, Hasan, too, come to that. He was so slight he was hardly there. A tough little bastard, though, a fighter. Matt cleared a shelf, dumped the clothes into a black canvas bag.

Then he felt Ginn behind him. Matt breathed in the scent she always wore, maybe from the giant bottle he'd put in her stocking last Christmas with a card from Barney... Not last Christmas. Last Christmas was the first without her in five years. Last Christmas he'd skied in Davos and fucked his brains out with some Italian girl whose name he didn't even remember.

"I raided the refrigerator. You haven't got much, just some cheese and bread and some apples. I put in water as well." Ginn handed him a plastic bin liner. "I tried to get her into bed but she wouldn't go. She's lying down on the couch, so that's something. I had to let Barney get up on the couch with her."

Matt gave a small laugh. "Bet that was hard."

"You know Barns. Matt, do you think Phil will go to the sheriff?"

"Come on. I know he's not your favorite, but he wouldn't do that." He packed in another load, fastened the bag and stood. "Okay, now you've got my cell phone number, Bobby's is on speed dial on the kitchen phone and in the bedroom. If she gets violent or threatens you, just run. You leave her, or you let her go if that's what she wants. Don't try to stop her. Promise me."

"Matt, she's not going to do anything like that."

"Ginn, please, just do as I ask. Promise me."

"Okay. I promise. But don't worry, I've got Barney."

Matt picked up the bag. "Back in an hour."

CHAPTER 9

Using the bag as a brake, Matt half slid, half slithered down into the canyon. The heavy moisture of late afternoon intensified the foul stink of the burn being drawn toward the ocean.

"Kanita!" His voice came back at him. His stomach was heavy with the weight of anxiety. "Hasan!" He hefted the bag, made his way to the piled rocks and trees where he had left them, his boots sliding on wet rock. He stood by the boulders, yelled again, listened to the silence resonate. He dumped the bag, walked the immediate area, then widened the search, calling, scanning the ground for footprints, but the leaf-strewn ground gave up nothing but the wrapper from the energy bar he'd given the child.

Hasan had herded them away, and they could be anywhere by now. Images flipped through his mind, the girls crying, the little group huddling together for comfort—and the child, her face filled with bewilderment and terror. She was about the same age he'd been when his mother died. He knew the bewilderment, but he'd never experienced the kind of terror he'd seen on that little girl's face.

He returned to where he'd left the canvas carryall, took out his wallet, tucked every bill he had into a side pocket, not much, five twenties, a ten and some singles. He carried the bag to the little shelter under the trees, knelt to shove it way back into the darkest patch of tangled branches. He stood and looked around. He'd done all he could. So why did he feel so lousy?

The headlights on the Range Rover picked up Ginn's silver BMW, then swept across a new black Mercedes 500 parked just beyond it. Matt drove into the garage, turned off the ignition, walked along the side deck. Ginn had put on the beach lights, illuminating the sand in front of the house, and the curl of the waves hitting the beach. She always used to do that when he worked late.

He opened the door. "Sorry it took so long," he called out.

"It's okay, Phil kept me company," Ginn said. She came into the kitchen, looked over his shoulder. "Where are they?"

"They weren't there. I left the stuff under a tree." Matt hung up his coat and glanced at Halliburton. "I thought you had a dinner date with Annie."

Phil shrugged. "I cancelled. I couldn't leave you alone with this."

A surprisingly kind gesture. He and Phil were not that close. "Thanks. Where is she?" He looked at the sofa, then at Ginn. "Where's Barney?"

"I managed to persuade her to get into bed. Barney's with her, she seems to feel better when he's there. I think she's sleeping. Phil, can I get you a fresh drink?"

"Sure, thanks."

Ginn reached into the cupboard for glasses, mixed the drinks, put a vodka and tonic on the coffee table in front of Phil, handed the other glass to Matt, then poured a glass of Chardonnay for herself. Matt wondered if she realized she had not asked him what he wanted, she'd just fallen into their old end of the day routine, Laphroaig and water for him, white wine for her.

Matt swirled the liquid in his glass. His breath felt heavy, his very bones felt as if they were made of lead. "I think I'm going to have to call Bobby Eckhart."

"We've already been through that. It's not an option," Ginn said. "Bobby would have to report it. She'd be taken into custody right away."

Matt got up, walked around the sofa, looked out the window. The horizon had closed in, as if a gray curtain had dropped fifty yards out. The forecast said rain would move onshore sometime during the night but it looked as if it was already here. "Phil, can you get me a nurse, twenty-four-hour care?"

"You mean, live in? Here?" Phil asked.

"Well, I can't leave her, I can't take her to the hospital, what else is there?"

"Well, I suppose I could take her home with me," Phil said slowly. "My housekeeper Lupe was illegal herself before the amnesty."

"What about Annie?" Matt asked.

"What about her? We don't live together. Besides, it's only until you find another solution."

Matt felt a flood of relief. "I'll start with an immigration lawyer tomorrow."

Phil looked at his watch. "I've got to get going. You got something to put on her? I can't take her out dressed like that."

"There's still some of Ginn's stuff in the closet."

"I'll get it." Ginn got up, disappeared into the small guest bedroom.

As soon as she'd left, Phil opened his medical bag. "I'm going to have to give her that shot, Matt. I won't be able to deal with her in the car if she's hysterical."

"No, I'm with Ginn on this. You saw how she was."

"That's precisely the point. A shot of Valium and there's no danger of it happening again." Halliburton opened the bedroom door.

The girl's shriek brought Ginn hurtling through the doorway. She dropped a pile of clothes to the floor, shot across the room.

"What are you doing?" She saw the syringe in Halliburton's hand. "It's the needle, she's frightened of the needle."

"It's hysteria, Ginn. In two minutes, she's going to be okay."

"No, she's not," Ginn said. "She's terrified."

The girl was curled into the fetal position, her shrieks replaced by the awful mewling of terror.

"This is not the first hysterical teenager I've treated. It's just Valium, for God's sake."

"You're not giving her anything. You guys get out," Ginn said. "Go on. I'll sit with her. She's not going anywhere."

"Ginn, this is a medical problem," Phil said. "It's hysteria, pure and simple."

Ginn shot him a look that would have withered fruit on the trees. "Got it. Thanks, Phil. Leave Barney here when you go."

Matt hustled Phil out the door, pulled it closed behind them. He was more shaken than he wanted to admit. "I can't take her like this, I'm sorry," Phil said. "I can call in a psych nurse I know. He's experienced, does only celebrity cases. He's not cheap, but he can be trusted. At least until you get some advice from a lawyer."

"Okay, thanks, but I don't want anyone else knowing about this."

"Matt, half the maids and gardeners you see working in Malibu are illegal. Nobody gives a damn."

"I wish to God I'd left that baby where it was and kept on running."

As he said the words, Matt knew it was not true. What he wished was that he'd grabbed Barney, then gone on to find help, instead of worrying about the house because it was his mother's. What a screwed up decision.

Both men turned as Ginn came into the room. "She's quiet as long as Barns is with her."

"Phil knows a psych nurse who can keep his mouth shut," Matt said. "I think that's the best thing."

"Matt, don't you guys get it? It's men she's scared of." Ginn picked up the pile of sweats she had dropped. "I'm going to take her home with me."

"That's a nice charitable thought, but it's not wise," Phil said. "She's a danger to herself, and she could be a danger to you whether she's acting out right now or not."

"A chance I'll have to take, I guess."

"Ginn, you can't take her with you to work every day any more than I can," Matt argued. Ginn was a trial lawyer with a busy office.

"I don't intend to. Unless I'm in court, I can work at home, and my mother will come and stay."

"Be sensible, Ginn. How can she do that?" Ginn's mother worked as a translator, mostly books from French into English, English into French. She was considered one of the best in her field.

"She's between jobs right now. Anyway, since Daddy died, she needs someone to take care of. It'll be good for them both."

"You can't let her do this, Matt," Phil said. "I'm telling you, the girl could be dangerous."

"You try stopping her. This is Ginn Chang you're talking about." In Mandarin, the word Ginn meant energy, her father's choice for her name. It suited her in every way.

Ginn smiled sweetly. "We'll stay here tonight, leave in the morning." She closed the bedroom door behind her.

"Well, that takes care of that," Matt said. He was embarrassed at the surge of joy he felt. She was back in his life. Ginn was back, at least for tonight.

"This is a lousy idea. Next time you find a girl in some canyon, please, call someone else." Phil picked up his bag and let himself out.

Matt stared out of the window. The rain was starting in earnest. Tonight, the creeks would start to run. He imagined the mud, the dripping stands of poison oak. Those kids were already dropping with exhaustion, especially the youngest one, the little black kid. He picked up the early edition of the *New York Times* and took it into the living room, scanning the pages of the real estate section without taking anything in. Ginn emerged from the bedroom.

"I think Barns has to go out."

"I'll take him." Matt picked up a handful of paper towels and a plastic bag from the stash he kept by the door, took the dog down to the beach, waited impatiently while, impervious to the rain, Barney poked around leisurely to find the right spot. He cleaned up, ran the dog back upstairs, rubbed the sand from his belly and feet with his old beach towel, then let him into the house and filled his bowl.

Ginn was at the stove. "I'm warming up some corn chowder. There is enough for you if you want it."

Matt washed his hands at the sink, dried them on a paper towel. In the small confines of the kitchen, he could feel the warmth of her body, smell her scent, had to fight the impulse to bury his face in the amazing hair that looked like black silk.

"Don't worry about me, Ginn. I can get something for myself."

"That's right. You don't need anyone, do you?"

"That's not what I said." Somehow he managed not to wrap his arms around her, pull her body against his. "I need you."

"No, you don't." Ginn poured the soup into bowls, picked up the tray.

"I'll take that."

"I can manage, thanks." Matt bit back a retort as Ginn said, "You can open the door for me, though."

The girl was sitting up, the blanket tucked up to her chin, her forehead resting on her knees. Matt realized he had not seen her eyes since she had stared at him, ready to kill. The television was tuned to a cartoon channel with the sound off. Barney jumped up onto the bed as if he'd been sleeping there all his life and settled beside her. A small hand reached to touch him and the Lab's ribs expanded in a huge sigh of contentment.

"Call me if you need me, Ginn," Matt said softly. He wondered if she, too, was thinking of the nights they had slept in that room together.

"Good night, Matt."

CHAPTER 10

Matt shot upright, onto his feet in the same motion. It sounded as if Barney was losing his mind. Cursing, he stumbled over a pile of skis and poles, got himself disentangled, ran to the master bedroom. It was dark, but he could make out the girl sitting up in the bed, with Ginn by her side, holding her hand. Barney was at the curtained window, barking.

"Someone's outside," Ginn said urgently. Her voice was shaky. "I saw him through the window. It's pouring out there, who could it be?"

"Probably just some guy looking for an easy score after the fire. Hold on to Barney, I don't want him attacking anyone."

Matt returned quickly to the guest bedroom, pulled on sweatpants and shirt, and started across the living room then went back to get one of the baseball bats. He opened the kitchen door, ran along the side of the house toward the burned-out front garden. Rain was bucketing down, half blinding him. The automatic light hanging tenuously from a wire on the garage roof flickered briefly before dying altogether, deepening the murk. He could see no one. Maybe Ginn had been mistaken. But not Barney. Barns sure wouldn't bark like that unless he had cause.

Without warning, a figure rounded the corner of the house, slammed into him, shoving him backward until his spine hit the wooden rail of the deck. Bare feet sliding on the slick wood, Matt grappled with the intruder, the bat useless without space enough to use it. The rail groaned, the old wood bowing dangerously. Matt had an image of the boulder-strewn beach twenty feet below, and brought up a knee, managed to slam it into the guy's crotch. The guy screamed, spraying foul garlicky saliva into Matt's face, doubled over and staggered back.

It was the space Matt needed.

Without time to line it up, the swing was wild, he'd aimed for the head, and struck a shoulder, but it was a lucky hit. A gun dropped from the intruder's hand, clattered across the deck. Matt dove for it, scooped it up, slammed it against the guy's ear. He fell as if he'd been hit by a freight train. Matt knelt and turned him over. Swarthy, rain-soaked black curly hair growing low on his forehead, full mustache. Medium height, solid build. Not Hispanic.

A shiver of motion from heavy footsteps ran through the sodden wood beneath Matt's feet, a voice shouted, the words unintelligible.

Matt's belly clenched. There were two of them. If the guy at his feet was armed, the other probably was, too.

Matt hit the deck behind the prostrate body of the guy he'd just axed. Shots raked the spot he'd occupied a microsecond earlier.

A couple of looters would have gone for the beachfront mansions flanking his tiny gray wooden shack of a house. So who the hell were these guys?

His heart hammering as if about to leap out of his chest, Matt inched his way toward the edge of the building. Another wave of movement shivered through the sodden deck and he stopped.

Without bothering to check to see if he'd killed Matt, or

whether his partner was dead or wounded, the second man was running back to the other side of the house.

Matt jumped to his feet, raced along the front wall facing onto the burned-out garden, past the curtained bedroom windows. The crash of the surf, the rain pounding the deck masked all other sound, but he stopped at the far corner to take a couple of deep breaths, then peered along the narrow walk.

The figure was only slightly darker than his surroundings, but it was enough. The bastard was trying to open the side door to the house—the door across from the kitchen. The door that was kept locked and had a couch set in front of it.

He'd been going to the firing range with Bobby Eckhart, and without conscious thought, Bobby's instructions kicked in. Matt stepped out onto the clear walkway, raised the weapon, cupped his right hand with his left, squeezed off a shot.

And missed.

In one swift motion, the guy straightened, turned and fired. Matt pressed his back against the wall as the burnt husk of the lemon tree that used to shade the front garden exploded into charred fragments. Adrenaline pumping hard, Matt raced back the way he'd come. In this weather, he could circle the house without being heard, surprise the bastard from behind.

Matt turned the corner, found the son of a bitch he'd put down only minutes ago was struggling back onto his feet. Before Matt could react, Barney hurtled out of the kitchen door, along the walk, thudded into the guy's chest. The man stumbled back, caught his heel in an uneven paving stone at the edge of the patio, lost his footing. Screaming, he went down with Barney riding him to the ground, his teeth slashing through flesh as he fought to get at the invader's throat.

He must not have closed the door securely, Matt thought. Barney had muscled it open. Suddenly terrified Barney would get shot, Matt lunged at the dog, somehow managed to drag him off. Barney's bleeding victim stumbled to his feet, then out into the road as the censor lights next door went on, flooding the driveway of the three-story monster with brilliance. Like a freeze frame in black and white, the light caught the running figure of the other attacker halfway across Matt's exposed patio.

Matt fired, but even in midday sun, he wouldn't be able to hit a moving target. At night, in driving rain, holding Barney's collar, it was a gesture, but a gesture he had to make.

An engine roared to life, an SUV careened past the house driving north toward the coast highway. Matt released Barney and ran into the road, but the red tail lights wavered in the rain, and the vehicle was too far away for him to see the license plate. Matt turned and herded the Lab ahead of him into the dark kitchen. Between them, they had done some damage, he and Barns, but it was over.

Ginn turned on a lamp at the end of the couch. "Matt, are you all right? They tried to kill you. Are you all right?"

"Yes, I'm okay. They're gone. There were two of them. They won't come back." Matt spoke with more confidence than he felt. "Turn that light off, Ginn."

"The girl's very frightened, Matt. We're both frightened."

"It's okay, they're gone. Turn off the light and keep your voice down. I don't think either the Connollys or the Madsens are home, but if they are and someone reports gunfire, the sheriff will be here in a few minutes." Ginn knew the score. She didn't need to be told that with the level of political power and the celebrity of many of its residents, response in Malibu was immediate, unlike the rest of Los Angeles. "We have to look as if we're asleep. It's 3:00 a.m., we didn't hear anything, we don't know anything." He put the gun on the table.

"What's that?"

"It's a Glock. One of the guys dropped it. I'll keep it under the pillow tonight."

"Oh, my God." She looked at him, horrified. "Do you know how to use it?"

"Well, I've been to the range with Bobby a few times, but I'm no marksman." The weapon was gray, light in weight. Bobby told him at the range a Glock like this was virtually indestructible, lightweight, constructed of a synthetic that was stronger than steel.

Speechless, Ginn turned off the lamp then went into the bedroom. Matt could hear the reassuring murmur of her voice, but no sound from the girl. It seemed odd that she moaned in terror when anyone tried to help her, but took gunfire in her stride.

His own heartbeat was slowing, but his hands seemed to have a life of their own and the icy calm he'd felt had been replaced by waves of nausea. Probably something to do with the adrenaline.

Matt ran his hands over Barney, made sure the blood on his yellow coat was not his blood, then got a towel to rub him dry—he was soaked and still high with excitement. "You did good, buddy."

"Who were they?" Ginn left the bedroom door open and came back into the room.

"I don't know." Matt gave Barney a biscuit, then took a bottle of water from the refrigerator, twisted the top and drank it down. He felt as if in the last few minutes he had sweated every spare drop of moisture out of his body. "Not your regular thieves looking for an easy score, that's for sure."

"Do you think this is about the girl?"

"If it is, why not knock on the door at a reasonable hour and ask about her? Why mount a midnight raid? It sure doesn't make me inclined to give her up to a couple of thugs."

Ginn flashed a sudden grin. "Sir Galahad."

His heart jumped. "That's me. I don't know what this is about, but whatever it is, there's nothing we can do tonight. We'll talk in the morning. Go back to bed now in case the sheriff arrives." He smiled back at her. "Unless you're tired of the armchair and want to share the spare bed with me?"

"You wish."

Matt kept the gun under the pillow, but the rest of the night was uneventful. No visit from the cops.

At 6:00, he was in the kitchen spooning French roast into the coffeemaker. He filled it with water, turned it on, and retrieved a flashlight from under the sink.

He stepped outside, making sure the door was closed securely behind him this time. The heavy rain had settled into a steady soaking drizzle, and the predawn sky was even darker than it had been at three. He switched on the flashlight, played the beam over the walkway. Just outside the garage, the light struck what he was looking for, a bullet casing. He picked it up, circled the house, found two more outside the side door. He continued to search, but that was it. He thought there had been more shots fired, the gunman must have gathered the rest. Just as well neither of his neighbors, the Connollys in their three-story pile of stark white cubes to the north, or the Madsens in their two-story English mock Tudor to the south, had been using their weekend getaway mansions. No one knew of last night's visit.

He crossed the patio, stood in the road and looked both ways. As far as he could see in each direction it was empty of cars. This close to the ocean, people tended to park inside their garages to protect the paintwork from corrosive salt spray.

Light from the kitchen door spilled across the deck, Ginn's frightened voice reached him. "Matt, are you out there?"

"Yes, I'm here." Matt returned to the house. "I was looking for these in case Bobby or anyone else saw them and starts to ask questions I don't want to answer. You know how persistent Bobby can be." Matt opened his palm, showed Ginn the brass casings, then dropped them into a kitchen drawer. "I don't think there are any more, I got them all."

He didn't want to frighten her, but his guess was that the gunmen were professionals. If there were any more casings, they would have picked them up so that there was nothing to trace if he went to the police.

He couldn't believe he was suddenly considering such things. Where had his life gone?

Ginn started back toward the bedroom. "I'm going to get her up and get her out of here."

"Ginn, I'm sorry but she's not going with you. Whatever this is, I'll figure it out. I don't want you involved."

"What did you say?" Ginn came back to face him. "Why do you have to do everything alone?"

"I don't. I called you, didn't I?"

"You know what I mean. This is just like you, this attitude. You can't let Bobby know about any of this. You certainly can't confide in Ned, he'd have a foot stamping fit, and I don't blame him, he's got kids to think of. So what are you going to do, Matt? Go it alone?"

"No, I'm going to call Phil."

"Oh, great. Dr. Phil with his needles and his psych nurse. Forget it. She's coming with me." Ginn closed the bedroom door firmly behind her.

Ginn stood for a moment by the bed. Lank, dirty hair had blackened the pillow, but the sleeping girl looked more like a child than a teenager. A child with dark smudges under eyes that were those of a woman who had seen too much and hurt too much.

Ginn tucked the duvet closer around the slight body—a few more minutes wouldn't make much difference. She and Matt had started the day on the wrong foot. How much of her anger was about this kid and gunmen and fear, and how much about loving him and the pain that brought? She went back to the living room.

Matt was silhouetted against the window, drinking his coffee. The ocean was just becoming visible, a hammered pewter, the white choppy waves blown apart before they could reach the beach, although great chunks had been gouged out of the sand during the night.

"Hey," Ginn said softly. "I'm sorry. Let's start over."

Matt turned. His dark blue eyes studied her and she found herself suddenly wanting to go to him and put her head on his chest.

"You always keep the house too cold at night. It's freezing in here."

"Yes, I know, I'm sorry. I've turned up the heat."

He went into the kitchen, filled a mug and handed it to her. Ginn held it with both hands, breathed in deeply before taking a gulp.

"Did you get any sleep?" he asked.

"Not much. Did you?"

Matt shook his head.

"I'll wake her in a minute and we'll get going. My mom will be there early. Don't worry, Matt."

"No, I mean it, Ginn. It's too dangerous for you to take her with you."

"We've got to get her out of here. If I take her home with me, you're free to find out what's going on. You can't do everything, Matt." She looked out of the window. "We'll leave before it gets too light. If anyone follows, I'll come back. Go take Barns out while I get our little girl up."

"No, he can wait."

"Matt, he can't. Take him out. I'll be here when you get back."

"Okay, I'll be just a few minutes."

Ginn stood at the window, watching them run along the edge of the tide, the dog barking as the gulls rose, a wheeling undulation of gray and white. Her heart felt as if it was overflowing with pain. He loved her, she had never had any doubt about that. Loved her still, it was clear every time he looked at her.

So why couldn't he take the next logical step?

CHAPTER 11

Ginn turned into Hurricane Court, the fancy name for the alley behind her house on Hurricane Street. She'd been lucky to find a house she could afford on one of Venice's walk streets, with front gardens facing each other across a narrow central lane only wide enough for foot traffic, and the beach at the end.

Matt had insisted on following her home. At this time of the morning, not yet seven on a Sunday, few cars were on the road, so it had been easy to see that no one had followed them. She pressed the opener attached to the visor, drove into the empty garage, killed the engine and waited until Matt parked the Range Rover beside her silver BMW before lowering the garage door.

She turned in her seat and smiled at the girl sitting beside her. She had Matt's navy blue terry cloth robe clutched around her over the torn silk top and pants she had so far refused to take off. "Come on, honey, we're going to get you into a long, hot bath with loads of sweet, smelly bubbles."

The girl remained still, staring straight ahead as if too fearful to examine her new surroundings. In fact, she gave no indication she had even heard. Since the episode with the knife, she had not once made eye contact with either of them, Ginn or Matt. Only with Barney.

"Come on, sweetie," Ginn said again. She waited for a moment, then got out, looked over the top of the car at Matt. "Now what?" In Malibu, the kid had walked out to the car under her own steam.

"Well, I can always carry her inside." Matt went around the Range Rover, opened the back for Barney. As if this was his regular routine instead of a first time visit, the dog trotted over and waited at the door that led from the garage into the house.

The girl followed him with her eyes. Then without being urged, she got out of the car, crossed the garage to stand at his side.

"Look at that. Wasn't there a dog in *Peter Pan* who took care of boys who didn't want to grow up?" Ginn asked. "Old Barns is the perfect dog for you, Matt."

"Her name was Nana. She took care of Wendy and was very suspicious of Peter Pan," Matt answered. "But you're right about Barns being the perfect dog for me. You gave him to me, Ginn."

Ginn slid a key into the lock, and ushered the girl inside.

Matt followed and looked around the kitchen. "You've done a great job with this house, opening it up so we can see its bones. And I like what you've done with the windows."

"Thanks." Ginn didn't mention that she'd seen him walk by a dozen times during construction. She'd bought the small nondescript house right after they'd broken up, had a second story built on part of it, the ceilings opened to wooden beams. She'd had long narrow windows cut to frame the palm trees outside so that they were like paintings in constant movement. She had put in dark hardwood floors and extended the kitchen, adding a small bay out into the enclosed garden. Pebble paths wound past a small Japanese black pine sheltering a group of three carefully placed gray boulders, and the fences were hidden by black bamboo that rustled in the sea breeze that came up in the afternoons. It wasn't on a million-dollar beach in Malibu, but it was her own calm space and for months it had been therapy, the only thing that had kept her from falling apart, or running back to him.

"I'm going to try to get her into a bath. You don't have to stay. My mother will be here soon."

"I'm not leaving you alone with her."

Ginn took the girl's unresisting hand. "Okay, cereal's in the cupboard, coffee on the shelf by the pressier, eggs in the fridge. We'll be down in a while, and you can make us breakfast. Come on, Barns."

Barney trotted toward the front of the house, past the living room on the left and up the stairs. He stopped on the landing to see which way he should go, his tongue hanging, a grin on his face. Ginn drew the girl with her along the upper hallway, opened the door to the little spare bedroom that overlooked the garden and ushered the girl inside.

"This is your room." A wide Chinese screen of ibis and fishing cormorants hung above twin rosewood beds. The colors in the screen were echoed in the soft celadon bedspreads and darker green chair and ottoman. An old Chinese chest was a gift from her parents's house, as were the antique tables on either side of the beds. "You will be safe here."

Ginn crossed the room to the bathroom, turned on the taps over the claw-footed tub and poured in a liberal amount of vanilla-scented bath gel and then returned to the bedroom. The girl had moved to look out of the window, for the first time showing interest in something other than Barney. Ginn stood behind her, and pointed over the tops of the surrounding houses to the Ferris wheel on the Santa Monica pier.

"See that? It's called a Ferris wheel—it's very pretty at night all lit up." Although the girl didn't seem to understand a word being said, Ginn hoped that the sound of a soft voice would be reassuring. "As soon as you feel like it, we'll go and take a ride. Come on, honey, let's get you cleaned up."

Her eyes lowered, the girl allowed Ginn to draw her toward the bathroom. Moving slowly so as not to spook her—although she had already made sure there were no nail files and scissors visible—Ginn slipped the robe from her shoulders, gently pulled the filthy tank top over her head, then snapped at the waist of the awful purple harem pants to indicate that she should remove them herself. The bathroom was filling with steam and Ginn bent to swirl the scented water, laughing and flicking suds at Barney, watching out of the corner of her eye until she saw that the girl was nude. She was small with a slim body that was not that of a child, but not yet mature. The girl turned to pick up the sponge from where Ginn had placed it on the white tile counter.

Somehow, Ginn managed not to gasp. Her narrow back was covered in fading bruises, long yellowish marks, maybe from a belt, certainly made by a weapon of some kind. But worse were the scars on her buttocks and the backs of her legs. At some time in the not too distant past someone had ground lighted cigars and cigarettes into her skin.

Ginn sank onto a bath stool by the tub. "Who did this to you?" She put a gentle finger onto a large round scar. The girl jumped as if being burned again. "I'm sorry," Ginn said quickly. "It's okay, sweetie. Get into the tub." The girl lowered herself into the water, leaned back and closed her eyes. Tears forced from beneath her eyelids coursed down her cheeks.

"Bobby Eckhart said the girl found in Encinal had the same kind of marks on her," Matt said. Ginn had just told him what she'd seen. Before he could say more, his cell phone rang.

"Better answer it." Ginn filled a mug with coffee and leaned against the countertop.

In his ear, Phil Halliburton's voice said, "So you survived the night. How's the patient?"

Matt thought about one of his dad's bits of advice, "never tell anyone anything they don't need to know," so he did not mention the nocturnal visitors with guns. There was no point in frightening Halliburton into going to the authorities.

"Apart from scars all over her, she's fine."

"What kind of scars?"

"The same kind the dead girl in Encinal had on her, cigar burns."

A beat of silence, then, "Matt, I didn't want to say this in front of Ginn, but you do realize her mother might scare this kid? She could well send her over the top again."

"Ginn's mother? What do you mean?"

"Well, you know...does she speak English, or Cantonese or what?"

"This kid doesn't speak at all so what difference does it make?" Matt asked.

"Come on, Matt, you know what I mean. A little Chinese woman fussing around."

"I'm going to pretend I didn't hear that. But for the record, Phil, Ginn's father was an eminent American economist who represented this country at some U.N. mission in Geneva where her mother was an interpreter. Gabrielle Chang is French, but thanks for the concern." He looked at Ginn and she sighed and rolled her eyes. This was not the first time she had heard this conversation.

Phil picked up on Matt's tone. "Okay, don't make me out to be some redneck, it occurred to me and I had to mention it. I'm a doctor and my concern is for the girl's welfare. And I still recommend a nurse."

Matt glanced at Ginn. "Yes, well, I'll have to get back to you on that." Goodbyes said, he shrugged. "Good old Phil."

The front door opened, high heels beat a tattoo on the bamboo floor of the hall, a voice called Ginn's name. A tall slender woman entered the kitchen, hazel eyes moving from Ginn to Matt to the girl sitting at the table and back to Matt.

"Matt! How lovely to see you." The words were warm, the tone wary. Gabrielle Chang glanced at her daughter.

"Hi, Gabby." Matt went over to her and took her hand. Forty years in the United States and still she managed to be very French. Dark shoulder-length hair, pale skin, dressed as usual in black, narrow skirt and high-heeled boots, cashmere shawl thrown casually over a sweater, gold at her ears and around one wrist. He had often wondered how the scholarly Dr. Chang had managed to capture a woman like Gabrielle Boulez, but they had been devoted to each other. "You're as beautiful as ever."

"Thank you, *cheri*. You, too." She kissed him on both cheeks, and handed him the woven peasant's basket she was carrying. "Croissant for breakfast, and some good butter and jam not from the supermarket." She looked again at the girl. "Who have we here?"

Dressed in Ginn's pink sweats, her hair clean and pulled up into a ponytail, the girl looked young and vulnerable. Her face was heart shaped, with long dark eyes that tipped slightly at the corners and wide, high cheekbones. Unnaturally pale, the dark smudges under her eyes were even more evident now that her face was scrubbed and shiny.

"Well, we don't quite know, Mom," Ginn said. "We'll explain over breakfast."

CHAPTER 12

At 10:30 a.m. Matt was at the office of the Malibu Equestrian Center picking up the keys for the pickup and trailer he'd arranged to borrow the day before. He threw his old saddles into the trailer, chose a moment when no one was around to retrieve the Glock from the glove compartment of the Range Rover, shoved it in his belt and quickly covered it with his denim jacket. Damn thing pressed uncomfortably into his belly, but after last night, it was good to know he had something more than horseshoes to throw back if they came after him again. The clip was still full, he'd checked before he left home.

When he got to the Agoura animal shelter on the other side of the Santa Monica Mountains, he found that both of his horses had been sent back to the pasture when he'd failed to arrive as he had promised. By the time he'd brought them in, curried and saddled his quarter horse gelding, loaded both horses, made a generous donation, eaten a quick sandwich at a coffee shop, and driven back over the Kanan Dume Road, it was past two in the afternoon. He was getting started a lot later than he'd hoped.

He parked in front of the archery range on Encinal, then backed the saddled buckskin out of the trailer into hock deep mud that had been churned since last night's rain by tire tracks and booted feet, swung into the saddle. Automatically he whistled for Barney before remembering he'd left the Lab with Ginn.

The quarter horse made easy work of the steep muddy bank down into the canyon. Matt followed the path he'd taken before across the creek. At the little walnut grove, he dismounted and crawled into the small shelter beneath the trees. The canvas bag was gone. Nothing remained so it had been taken by human hand—animals would simply have torn it open, scattering the contents. The kids had probably found it—he'd pushed it deep into shadow, and there was nothing in a burned canyon to attract casual hikers, especially in this kind of weather. He knew the truth was that he wanted to believe they now had warm clothes, and a little cash.

He remounted, rode on into the canyon until he left the verdant mouth of the creek, and entered the burn, riding through a moonscape of charred trees and barren rock. The only sounds were Buck's iron-shod feet, the creak of leather. No birdsong, no rustle of leaves, no sound of distant human voices. In the silence, the weight of the Glock in his belt was reassuring.

Matt scanned the blackened hillsides for flashes of color, although he had no real hope of finding them. Only the image of the frightened child, flinching at his touch, drew him on. A bright spot was a pair of coyotes trotting single file along an old deer path visible now because the surrounding vegetation was gone. They were singed and tattered, but surviving. An hour later, he saw a couple of crows; throughout what seemed to be a very long few hours these were the only signs of life.

The sun dropped below the western ridge, the shadows on the canyon walls deepened, and he realized that he had to turn back, or he would spend the last hour riding in the dark.

At the walnut grove he dismounted, retrieved an envelope with a couple hundred dollars in twenties from an inside pocket, made his way to the little tangle of boulders and roots where he'd left the bag. He knelt and looked around for a place to hide the envelope in plain sight, somewhere not obvious to a passerby but if the kids came back and took shelter again, where they would certainly find it. A remnant of one of the brown paper sacks that had covered the bare earth was crumpled in the far recesses of the little shelter. Matt crawled inside, pushed the envelope beneath a couple of large rocks, careful to leave a corner of the envelope visible, then gathered up the paper to take it out and dispose of it. As he did so, his eye caught part of the red logo. It was torn down the middle but the picture was familiar. He smoothed it out and the form of a curvaceous female appeared. She had the tail of a fish and reclined on a rock. Beneath in large red letters were the words "The Mermaid."

The Mermaid. Matt sat back on his heels. He hadn't been there for years, but when he and Bobby were kids, it had been their home away from home.

As usual, the café's lot was crowded—directly across the Pacific Coast Highway was one of the best surfing beaches in southern California. The lot to the side of the one-story clapboard building was filled with an assortment of vehicles, most of them carrying racks and boards, but the concrete apron in front was lined with a dozen chopped-down Harleys.

On his way, Matt had stopped to unload the horses and return the trailer to Malibu Equestrian Center. He'd picked up the Range Rover, so he managed to squeeze into a narrow spot next to an ancient Honda Civic. He took the four wooden steps in two strides and made his way across the covered wooden deck. Colorful wet suits hung over the porch rail, every inch of space was taken up by surfboards propped against the wall. Some of the kids still wore their suits—more girls seemed to be surfing than in his day—boys and girls alike shiny as seals, although there were plenty of baggies and tank tops that barely covered their bodies and certainly gave no warmth. They had to be freezing out there.

He was getting old, Matt thought. Only yesterday it seemed he'd been one of these kids—the Mermaid had been a local landmark long before he was born—talking about radical boards and radical waves, arguing the merits of this wax or that wax, but thinking about sex, who would and how to score. He'd never thought about being cold, either.

Matt pushed through the swinging doors into a blast of noise. At first glance, the place hadn't changed since the last time he'd been there, ten, twelve, years ago. A small grocery to the left, shelves of candy and chips and cookies, cold cases with juice and beer and soft drinks, and in the café itself scarred wooden tables and an assortment of chairs picked up at garage sales, the décor a few fishing nets and glass floats hanging from the rafters.

The difference was in the clientele. Instead of a bunch of teenaged surfers, tattooed bikers in leathers and headbands lounged at tables loaded with bottles, metal-tipped boots propped on chairs. A couple of mamas danced in front of the jukebox, flabby white arms writhing above their heads, hips pumping, shrieking with laughter as they evaded the grope of a biker with a face hidden by a rough grizzled beard. A lurid tattooed snake writhed around one arm, disappeared under the leather vest covering his bare torso, reappeared on the other arm, its head and spitting tongue spread over his hand.

The feral stink of male sweat, greasy hair and unwashed bodies, motor oil and cigarette smoke mingled with the smell of frying hamburgers and tuna fish sandwiches.

Tommy Aguilar, the owner and a legend in the surfing world, was at his usual spot, flipping burgers.

Matt walked between the tables, feeling the hostility from the eyes appraising him from hair to boots, daring him to ask someone to move to allow him to pass. He slid onto a seat at the counter, glad he'd had the sense to leave the Glock in the glove compartment—he sure wouldn't want Tommy's new customers to read the weight in his jacket as the badge of an undercover narc. At the other end of the counter, a young man in salt-stained cutoffs waited for his order, eyes glued to Tommy's back, carefully avoiding even the appearance of watching the girls dancing.

"How you doing, Tommy?" Matt said. "Got through the fire okay, I see."

"Hi, dude," Tommy responded without turning around to see who spoke. His bleached hair was tied back in a ponytail and he wore his working ensemble, baggies, Hawaiian shirt, rubber flip-flops. The biceps on his right arm, the muscles on his calf and what could be seen of the rest of his right leg not covered by the loose shorts, were severely damaged, the visible teeth marks evidence of a close encounter with a great white off Bondi Beach in Australia. "Yeah, fire passed us right by."

"Still surfing, Tommy?" Matt asked.

"Sure, man, when the big ones roll in." Tommy slid a plastic basket containing the burger and fries down the counter, called out a number. The young man picked up his order, hurried outside. Aguilar turned to Matt. "So what's your pleasure, my friend?" He stopped. A slow smile spread to his dark eyes. "Hey, Mattie. Matt Lowell, long time no see." He reached a hand across the counter. "So how they hanging, Matt? Hear you're a big-time business man now."

"Wouldn't say that, Tommy. Doing okay, though."

"Yeah, that's what Bobby Eckhart tells me. What's it to be, hamburger all the trimmings? Root beer, right?"

Matt laughed. "That's it."

"On the house, dude. Jesus, it's good to see you. Still surfing?"

"Like you say, only when the big ones roll in."

Tommy slid his eyes past the bikers and looked out at the youngsters crowding the front porch. "Yeah, we had the best of it, man. Too many amateurs out there now, have to fight to get a wave. I'm too old for that shit."

"Well, I hear you've been flying out every couple months, finding yourself a radical wave or two in the islands."

Tommy placed a can of root beer on the counter. "That Eckhart. Regular two-way radio."

"So where's the action been lately?"

They talked surfing while Tommy cooked. Twenty years ago, Tommy had been the idol of every surfer on the west coast. He'd made his bones on the North Shore of Hawaii, competed professionally worldwide until the close encounter brought his career to an end and he bought the Mermaid.

Matt threw a glance at a table of bikers, found it thrown back by a guy with greasy dreadlocks. Two-fifty at least, not all of it blubber. Their leathers identified them as "Sons of Satan." No argument from me, Matt thought.

He lowered his voice. "How long have they been coming around, Tommy? Pretty rough trade for this place."

Tommy matched his tone. "They've always been up and down the PCH, stopping in for a beer, a sandwich. That's all they do, man, then they move on."

"They look very comfortable."

Tommy shrugged. "They got the weight, dude."

"They dealing here?"

Tommy's eyes darted around the café. "Shit, man, what kind of question is that? I don't know what they do, I don't want to know."

Matt swiveled to look out at the crowded deck. One of the bikers, thin mousy hair straggling from a leather headband, was on the porch, huddled with half a dozen of the boys. "Not lacking in customers, anyway. Lambs to the slaughter out there."

Tommy followed his eyes. "You know how it is. Kids come in from somewhere, Kansas, North Dakota, some shit state with no water within a thousand miles, think they're gonna live the good life on the beach in California."

"How many develop a habit and end up doing whatever it takes to support it? Ever think of that?"

Tommy raised his eyebrows. "You did your thing, dude, got over it no trouble."

"We never got into anything heavier than Mexican." He and Bobby had seen too many of their buddies too wasted even to paddle out. The death toll had been high enough to scare them clean. "These guys are into a lot of nasty stuff—crystal, Ecstasy, K. They're bad news, Tommy."

"Yeah, well, no one's stopping these kids from going home, or maybe, God forbid, getting a job and a straight life. Listen, I slip them leftovers, pay them to do a few chores when I can, but I'm not their mother."

Matt wiped his mouth with a paper napkin, dropped it on his plate. "You hear about the kid found up on Encinal?"

"Yeah. Too bad about that."

"There was a dead baby on the beach, too. Did you hear about that?"

"Matt, Jesus. You're a fountain of good news. Don't see you for ten years, and here you turn up asking questions about dead kids."

"Just thought you might have heard something. I found that baby, Tom. On the beach."

"That must have been a shock." Tommy looked across at the skinny girl still dancing in her own world, still laughing at God knows what. The other mama had been caught by the snakeman. He had the head of the snake deep inside the front of her jeans and was grinning and jerking her upward with each beat from the juke as if she was a rag doll. She didn't look too happy.

"So, Tommy, what's the word?"

"Matt, I cook burgers and fries here. I keep my head down, and keep out of trouble. Get my drift?"

"You used to know everything that went on along this coast."

"Times change, wise man changes with them."

"Sounds like you got that from a fortune cookie. You ever see a pregnant girl around here?"

"Pregnant? No, can't say I've seen anyone pregnant. Not pregnant that you'd notice anyway. You want another root beer?" Tommy picked up the paper plate, turned to reach into the refrigerator behind him.

"No, thanks. Still working on this one. I hear that girl was a mess, Tommy."

"What girl?"

"The one who died. You don't think she could have been hanging out here?"

"No. I just said that. No pregnant girls around here," Aguilar said. "I told the sheriff already, and now I'm telling you. I never saw any pregnant girl. I keep my head down, my mouth shut, and I keep out of trouble that way." He glanced over Matt's shoulder. "I gotta go. Hey, next time they rip in from Hawaii, grab your board and we'll go out, show these kids how it's done, okay?"

"Yeah, sure, Tommy. Sounds good," Matt said. He reached for the bill.

"Like I said, on the house, dude," Tommy said.

Matt got to his feet, and Tommy motioned him to lean closer. "You're asking a lot of questions. Let it go. This is not like old times. Questions could cause you a shitload of trouble."

"Okay, just one more thing. I ran into some youngsters sleeping rough in Encinal. They didn't speak English, they had no warm clothes. But they did have food from here. You remember seeing a group like that?"

"Matt, what is it with you? A bunch of illegals sleeping rough and that's a surprise? Christ, the goddamn state would fall apart without the illegals."

"Hey, Tommy," a voice yelled. "Get your ass over here."

Tommy's still muscular body stiffened. He flipped up a hinged portion of the counter. Matt held his arm. "I'm not talking about Hispanic boys looking for work. These are very young, four girls fourteen or fifteen maybe, and a boy. They look European, but one of them is African. A little kid, Tommy, maybe ten years old. And not African-American, straight from Africa."

"So it's an international scout troop. What do you want from me?"

A nerve under Aguilar's right eye twitched. He put up a hand to smooth his hair so that he could touch his eye in passing.

Matt held his eyes, daring him to look away. "You always were a bum liar, Tommy. You've seen them."

"No, man, I haven't. I gotta go."

"I think you know what I'm talking about, Tom." Matt lowered his voice even farther. He gestured toward the bikers with his head. "These guys got something going back in the canyons?"

Tommy matched his tone. "If you're talking meth labs, try Chatsworth or Palmdale."

"What about a plantation?"

Tommy shot an uneasy glance over Matt's shoulder and leaned forward. "Christ sake, Matt. I don't know anything about shit like that, man."

"Okay. If you see a blond kid in blue velvet pants and a bunch of girls in some kind of silk stuff, give me a call." He wrote his number on a paper napkin, held it out.

"Silk stuff and blue velvet? And you think they're pack mules?" Tommy snorted, but he picked up the napkin, tucked it into the pocket of his Hawaiian shirt. "What's this got to do with you, anyway?"

"Nothing. Just curious."

"Tommy!" the same voice yelled. "You getting your sorry fucking ass here before we fucking die of thirst, or do I got to drag it over?"

Matt held Tommy's eyes. "How long have people been talking to you like that?"

Tommy looked away, embarrassed. "Yeah, well, it ain't like the old days, dude, that's for sure. I got to get back to work."

Matt watched him limp over to the table, collect a bunch of empties, share a laugh with the customers. He finished his root beer, crushed the can like he did when he was a kid, and dropped it in the trash can at the end of the counter. He crossed the room, carefully avoiding eye contact with anyone, pushed open the doors and stepped outside.

On the other side of the road, a glittering silver gilt path arrowed across the Pacific, the sun was sinking below the horizon, and the gathering clouds were a brilliant palette of color, turquoise, lavender, purple, apple green. The sleek gray bodies of a pod of dolphins broached and Matt took a deep breath. This was it. This was why he was willing to fight the traffic on the PCH twice a day, suffer the fires and floods that kept Malibu in the news.

As he turned out of the parking lot, he picked up the cell phone, called Bobby's number at home.

"Hey, Bobby," he said when Eckhart answered. "I just left the Mermaid. You guys check out the action in there lately?"

"You mean the Satans?"

"That's what I mean. They are a major presence, Bob."

"We keep an eye on the Mermaid. Never had a reason to roust the place."

"I saw them dealing."

"Did you see money and product pass hands? Did you even see the product?"

Matt expelled an impatient breath. "Not exactly, but I could make a hell of an educated guess."

"I'm not saying it doesn't go on, Matt, I'm saying they are very careful. I drop by occasionally, have a chat with Tommy. He's never complained about them."

"They're paying him off, Bobby."

"Probably. Now just prove it."

"You think they had anything to do with that girl's death?"

"Oh, yeah, Matt. Sure. I can see them now, the Sons of Satan, picking flowers, dropping them gently over her, making a little bouquet for her to clutch in her cold dead hands. A touching picture."

"Have your guys been searching the canyon where the girl was found?"

"I don't know, maybe. I'm off duty. Why?"

"I was up there and saw some tire tracks. I read where a biker gang called the Bandidos had a plantation that was raided last week down near San Diego. They'd hand carried enough material, piping and fertilizer and water to grow fifty thousand plants to a height of six feet. I wondered if these guys have something similar going on."

"Not likely. The sheriff's department makes regular sweeps over these mountains by helicopter. If our guys missed anything, the fire sure as hell didn't. Don't mess with bikers, Matt, you're out of your depth there."

"As long as you're on the job, buddy."

"Rest easy. We're here to protect and serve."

"Wasn't that the name of a cookbook?"

Bobby was laughing when he hung up.

CHAPTER 13

With two lanes and a 25-mile-per-hour speed limit, it was easy to watch the rearview. Behind him, Malibu Road was empty and when he got home, no cars were parked anywhere near the house. Just the same, he kept the Glock in his hand as he walked along the deck toward the door. It was a hell of a thing, he thought, that he had to be armed before entering his own home.

Halfway down, he stopped. The kitchen door was wide open. He slid the safety off the Glock and flattened against the wall. His heart rate in overdrive, he inched his way toward the door, the sound of his boots on the deck clearly audible, though he knew that was probably only to his own ears. The surf was still heavy with the passing storm, nothing could be heard over the crash of the waves. He took a breath, reached inside the door and flipped the light switch.

Nothing happened. No shots, no voice, no response of any kind.

Matt walked inside. Quickly, he checked each room, but the house was empty. The only sign that someone had been there was the open door with the key from under the flowerpot still in the lock. And the knife driven deep into the kitchen table.

It was one of his own, the large butcher knife with a twelve-inch blade from the set in the wooden block on the counter. The same block from which the girl had grabbed her weapon.

He poured a drink and stared at the knife, considering what to do. Calling the police was out of the question, but maybe at some time in the future, it would be useful as evidence, of what he didn't know, but it seemed a good idea to keep it. He got a kitchen towel and pried the knife out of the wood, careful not to get his own prints on it, then wrapped it in the towel, put it into a Ziploc bag. He added the bullet casings from the drawer, then dropped the plastic bag behind a stack of bath towels in the linen closet. That done, it seemed a good idea to shove the block and the rest of the knives out of sight under the sink. He never used them anyway.

He picked up the phone, called Ginn and got the familiar recording. Alarmed, he said, "Ginn, call me right back, or in thirty minutes, I'll be knocking on your door."

He'd barely hung up when the phone rang. He grabbed it.

"Okay, Galahad, everything's fine," Ginn's voice said.

"You see anyone prowling around?"

"No. Where are you?"

"I'm at home."

"You're not going to stay there tonight, are you? It's not safe."

He wished he felt more certain, but he said, "Don't worry, I've got the Glock, and I'm pretty handy with a baseball bat."

While dealing with the knife, he'd given it a lot of thought. If they'd come for the girl, and he couldn't think of any other reason for an attack in the middle of the night, they, whoever they were, would likely think they had scared him enough to either let her go, or turn her over to the authorities. Although Ginn's car had been in his garage last night, before going to bed he'd thrown a tarp over it to protect it from the salt in the air, so there was a good chance they had not known she was here; the curtains were drawn and the lights in the house had been off so they could not have seen her. He felt fairly certain no one had followed them to her house this morning.

If he went into hiding, they might just assume he had the girl with him and keep looking, broadening the search, maybe even to Ned and his family, ultimately to Ginn. Last night, the bastards had been willing to kill him to get this kid, so going into hiding meant he'd have to drop out of sight completely, just disappear. Even the thought pissed him off.

On the other hand, if he went about his life normally, if they were watching, with any luck, they'd assume he'd extricated himself from the problem. It sounded reasonable. It also sounded risky, but it was a risk he had to take.

"You are so stubborn," Ginn said. "Please don't stay there tonight. Go to a hotel."

"I've thought it through, Ginn, and staying here makes the most sense. So how's the day been?"

Ginn allowed a few seconds to pass in silence. When she spoke, her voice was cold. She knew he had changed the subject, something she said he had a habit of doing to avoid discussion.

"Okay. Right now she and my mom are sitting together on the couch watching a video of *The Princess Diaries*, and Gabby's describing the action."

Matt laughed. "Has she spoken?"

"No, but I have the feeling she understands. My mom has been speaking to her in French."

"The kid's French?" Matt asked, astounded.

"I don't know, Matt. I just think she understands what my mom is saying, at least sometimes. We'll see."

"Your mother speaks several other languages, doesn't she?"

"You mean other than Mandarin?"

Matt laughed again. "You try her with that?"

"Sure. No response."

He could hear the amusement in her voice and his heart lifted. They were having a normal conversation.

"What happened in the canyon?" Ginn asked.

"The bag was gone. There was no trace of them, but I did find some paper sacks from the Mermaid. I dropped by there, but Tommy Aguilar says he's never seen them." He gave her a brief summary of the conversation with Aguilar.

"Do you believe him?"

"No, but I don't know what else I can do without bringing the cops in. I'll start with the immigration lawyer tomorrow first thing, and go from there."

"I'll handle the immigration lawyer if you like. I'll have the bills sent to you, and keep you current on what's happening."

"Sure, thanks. That would be great, Ginn, a great help." Matt spoke casually, more casually than he felt. For the first time since she'd left, they were talking and laughing together. Anything seemed possible.

Ginn seemed to pick up on his thoughts. "Don't read anything into this. Nothing's changed between us. This is about the girl. I'd like to see it through until she's safe."

"Yes, okay, I understand. I'm just grateful for the help, Ginn. Thanks."

"Got to go. Good night." When he hung up, the house seemed emptier. Even her disembodied voice in his ear was better than no connection at all.

A shower took three minutes—the Glock within easy reach on the countertop—then he took his drink into the bedroom he'd shared with her. The bed was grim, the pale green sheets Ginn had chosen last year rumpled and black from the girl and sandy from Barney. He got a pillow from the spare bedroom, pulled off the comforter and dropped them both on the sofa in the living room, retrieved his book from the bedside table—TV was out of the question, he had to be able to hear every outside noise, difficult enough with the ocean pounding away. He put the Glock on the coffee table, opened the book to where he'd left off, read and reread the same paragraph, trying to make sense of the words.

Finally, he gave up, turned off the light, and listened to the creak of the deck as it moved with every wave that hit the sand.

CHAPTER 14

Matt cut his early morning run short, turning back before he got to Corral Beach, the exposed stretch of public beach at the end of Malibu Road, instead of continuing around the bay toward Point Dume as he and Barney usually did. He'd thought about cutting the run altogether, but he'd spent the night half awake and half asleep, starting at imagined footsteps and was as pissed off at himself as at whoever "they" were. He needed fresh air, he needed exercise, and he was damned if anything, including his own hovering anxiety, was going to prevent him from working the tension out of his body. If he was going to behave as if nothing was amiss in his world, the time to start was now. That included the Glock. He'd felt ridiculous with it dragging down the pocket of his sweats, so he'd left it on the kitchen table.

So now he felt vulnerable. The illusion of being safe as long as houses blocked access to the beach, was just that, an illusion, especially since four of those houses had recently burned down to their foundations. He picked up his pace, and was glad to jog across the beach to his own stairs.

During the night, the tide had washed around the pilings, but he took the time to search the beach anyway. The casings, if they had been there, were gone, swept out to sea, or buried under the sand brought in by the tide.

He picked up the newspaper in the front of the house, casually glancing both ways along the road as he did so. He checked the mailbox, riffled through Saturday's mail as he walked back down the deck—the very picture of a man with nothing to hide.

He showered, dressed, poured his second cup of coffee of the morning. His eye fell on a picture in the Surfside News—Jimmy McPhee outside the Cove. The headline read "Popular Beach Restaurant Robbed."

> The Cove Restaurant, owned and operated by long time Malibu resident, Jimmy McPhee, came through the fire unscathed only to be robbed sometime in the early hours of Friday. Daytime manager, Maria Alvarez, arriving at 6:00 a.m. to open up for the breakfast trade, discovered that entry had been made through a window in the kitchen door, broken during the fire and since boarded up.

Matt ran his eyes over the rest of the article. Food stolen, cash from a petty cash drawer, less than a hundred dollars. According to the sheriff's department spokesman, the strangest aspect of the break-in was the condition of the restaurant's restrooms. Soap containers were empty, wet dishtowels folded and left in a neat pile. "We are surmising that more than one person left the Cove cleaner than when they arrived."

Maybe that answered the question of whether the kids were still around. Matt picked up his laptop, locked the door behind him, backed the Range Rover out into Malibu Road, turned east to the Pacific Coast Highway and his Brentwood office.

He punched out McPhee's number, switched to the speaker phone. The trip into town at this time of day, referred to locally as the Malibu to L.A. road race, meant driving straight into the sun as the PCH followed the curve of the Santa Monica Bay. He needed both hands on the wheel to avoid aging tycoons in powerful sports cars, none of whom were inclined to give any quarter.

"The Cove. McPhee."

"Jim, this is Matt. Read about your trouble at the Cove. Are you okay?"

"Oh, yeah, Matt, thanks. Gave Maria a bit of a shock, but nothing much was taken. Few dollars in a cash box and some food. And the .38 I kept by the register is gone."

"Any idea who did it?"

"Cops say transients living rough."

Matt noted the doubt in Jimmy's voice. "That's not what you think, though."

"Well, cops say your transients usually have the urge to mess things up, maybe shit somewhere like animals leaving their mark. That sure wasn't the case here. The johns looked as if whoever it was had bathed in the sinks. They used all the dishtowels from the kitchen to dry off and left them folded up in a neat stack. That sound like transients to you?"

"So what do you think happened?"

"I don't know." His tone became firmer. "Probably the cops are right."

"What's wrong, Jimmy?"

"Pissed off is all."

Matt laughed. "Maria didn't see anyone?"

"No, thank God. They were long gone before she arrived."

"Well, if she does remember seeing who it was, let me know, okay?"

"Now who are you thinking she saw? What's so important?"

"Hey, you're breaking up," Matt said. "Talk to you later."

He slammed on the brake, swore as a Ferrari swerved into his lane with inches to spare, the driver's gray ponytail flapping in the slipstream. Without turning his head, his young blond companion waggled his fingers in apology.

By seven-thirty he was at his desk. This was his favorite time of the working day, the quiet before anyone arrived, and the bus-tle began. He started on his e-mail and was deep into paperwork when Marni came in with a cup of coffee.

"Good morning, Matt. Dave Landau's here."

"Hi, Marni. Already?"

"His appointment was at nine-fifteen, and it's now nine-thirty. This time traffic was heavy." She raised her eyebrows. Landau was never on time and always had an excuse. "I gave him coffee and put him in the drafting room. Benny Pressman is coming at 10:30, and Eddie Kanaka from Susan Dean's office will be here at 11:30, so don't let Dave hang you up. You know how he is."

Smiling, Matt nodded. "Okay, boss." He picked up his coffee, walked into the drafting room. Landau already had the structural schematics for the Brickyard project spread across a table. In a year or so from now, derelict warehouses along the old Pacific railroad track downtown would be a mixture of artisan studios and low cost housing units.

"So what have you got for me, Dave?"

The morning passed swiftly, everyone in and out, their business completed within the time scheduled for each meeting. As he walked back into his office, Marni's voice came from the intercom on his desk.

"Matt, Jake Broagan on line one."

He dropped into his chair and picked up the phone. "Hey, Jake, what's up?"

"Happened to be in the neighborhood and wondered if you're free for lunch."

Matt glanced at his watch. It was the last thing he wanted but his business world ticked on in spite of what was happening in the rest of his life. "Sure. How about Berty's on San Vicente, fifteen minutes? Suit you?"

"Yes, great. See you there."

Matt hung up, picked up his jacket. "Jake Broagan," he said to Ned. "Wonder what he wants. Be back in an hour or so."

As he passed Marni's desk, he asked her to call the restaurant to keep a table open, and let them know Broagan would be there in case Jake arrived first. He ran down the outside stairs into a clear autumn day, walked the half a dozen blocks to the restaurant.

Jake waved from a booth at the back. Matt slid in beside him without shaking hands. They'd known each other since they were kids and the Broagans had a second home in the Malibu Colony. They'd both gone to Georgetown, Jake a senior and a face from home when Matt had been a freshman. They'd never been close, but since they were in the same business and knew a lot of people in common, their paths crossed fairly often, and that passed for friendship.

"You're looking good, Matt."

"You, too," Matt said.

In fact, Jake looked better now than he had when they'd been students. His sandy hair was now cut short, his olive green eyes were clear, and he looked as if he spent time on the tennis court. Jake had had a longstanding reputation as a woman chaser. Even in college, his parties were notorious for being wild, a lot of local girls and tattooed guys with pumped muscles whose main contribution seemed to be standing around being street tough. Matt had been to couple of them, after that he'd begged off.

"Have you ordered?" Matt asked.

"Not yet," Jake picked up the menu. "What's good?"

"Everything, if you like French food. I usually keep it simple and go for a steak."

"Suits me."

They ordered, refused drinks from the bar, settled on some fancy French water.

"So how you doing, Matt?"

"Good. You?"

"Couldn't be better."

"How's Gena?" Matt asked.

"Still shopping. No," Jake laughed, "she's terrific, thanks. The girls, too. I swung by the Contessa project the other day. Looks impressive."

"Fifty percent pre-leased. We start moving tenants in at the end of the week," Matt said.

"That's great. I'd like a tour sometime."

"Just let me know and I'll take you around."

They talked generally until the waiter arrived with the food. "Hot plates, gentlemen. Can I get you anything else? No? Then *bon appetit.*" He moved away.

Matt cut into his steak. "So what's on your mind, Jake?"

"Hey, can't I call an old pal for lunch without having something on my mind?"

"Sure. What's on your mind?"

Jake laughed and reached for a bread stick. "Money. It's that time of year when I come around with the begging bowl. Can I put your firm down for twenty-five? My father would be thrilled."

Puzzled for a moment, Matt frowned. Jake was speaking in tongues. Then light dawned and he laughed. "You can be clearer than that. You're collecting for Hannah's House." Back in the early fifties, Nate Broagan had founded a home for orphaned Jewish children and for women who had lost their families in the Holocaust. Five years ago when he lost his wife, he'd changed the home's name to Hannah's House in her honor.

"How is your father?"

"You know what they say about my old man." Jake broke a roll and reached for the butter. "The stuff of legends." He spaced each word carefully.

Matt nodded without comment. Jake had had trouble enough in his life measuring up to a legend. "Jog my memory. What did we contribute last year?"

"Now what sort of question is that? Are you going to make me work for this? Come on, you guys have had a damn good year. Share the largesse, it'll make you feel good."

Matt laughed. He knew exactly how much the firm had contributed. "I don't know, Jake. Twenty thousand is a lot of money for a couple of poor Episcopalians."

"That's why I'm giving you a break. You won't even miss it. Anyway, Hannah's House is strictly ecumenical now, all colors, creeds, races, religions. Have I left anything out? Ah, yes, gender. So, can I tell the old man Lowell Brothers went to twenty-five?"

"I'll have to talk to my partner."

"Okay, but don't disappoint him, Matt. He's an old man and he's very fond of you boys."

Matt laughed again. "Jake, he wouldn't recognize us in a lineup."

"You'd be surprised. He knows exactly who you are. Talking about a lineup, what's this I hear about you and a dead baby and a murdered girl?" Jake sliced his own steak, carried his loaded fork to his mouth.

Matt sat back and looked at him. "Who told you the girl was murdered?"

"You mean she wasn't?"

"If we're talking about the same girl, the one found in Encinal, no, as far as I know, she wasn't. Who told you she was?"

"I don't know, seemed common knowledge. Gena and I were out in Malibu at the Howes yesterday, you know Babs and Ferdie Howe on La Costa Beach. The fire came nowhere close to their place, but any excuse for a party is a good excuse with them. This one was to celebrate not getting burned out. Anyway, people talked about it, you know how it is, the other guy's misfortune is always a good topic."

Matt shook his head. "Bonehead gossip. What happened was I found a baby." He went through the story one more time. "Then the girl was found up on Encinal. I don't think the autopsy report on her is back yet, but if she'd just given birth, it makes sense the baby was hers."

Jake grimaced. "That must have been a hell of a thing, finding a baby. What happens to a child like that? Would they do an autopsy on an infant, DNA, that kind of thing?"

"I don't know, but I'm arranging for this one to have a proper burial." He hesitated, almost ashamed of what he was thinking, then asked, "Was Phil Halliburton there?"

"Yeah, he and Annie." Jake laughed. "She's a wild one, that girl."

"How would you know? No, don't tell me. I don't even want to guess."

Jake grinned, and looked at his watch. "You want dessert?"

Matt shook his head and Jake beckoned the waiter. "This one's on me. And thanks for the donation. No kidding, Matt. The foundation means as much to the old man today as it did when he started it. More, I think."

While he was signing his name on the bill, Jake said, "You still carrying a torch for Ginn Chang?"

"Sure. Everyone who knows her carries a torch for Ginn."

"You see anything of her now?"

"No, not lately. Not since we broke up."

Jake used to drop by the beach house often when he and Ginn were together, usually unannounced, always alone. He'd heard through the grapevine that Jake had called her right after they separated. By all reports, he got short shrift.

"You let the good one get away there, champ," Jake said. "She still with the same law firm?"

"Jake, if you've got any ideas about Ginn, forget it. She won't go for a married man." And certainly not someone with Jake's reputation, though he kept that thought to himself.

"Come on, what are you, her social secretary? I'm just inquiring about an old friend, nothing but innocence on my mind."

"If you say so, Quickdraw, and I'm just dropping a friendly warning."

Jake shot him a glance, then laughed. "Quickdraw. Haven't heard that in a while. You know, if I did half the stuff people say I do, Gena would have my balls in a basket."

"Now why do I have difficulty believing that?"

"Hey, you seen anything in the papers lately?"

"When have I seen anything you've done in the papers?"

Brawls, trashed hotel rooms, car wrecks, even one in which it was rumored a girl died and her family was paid off. Erik Hoffmann, Nathan Broagan's right-hand man always managed to keep Jake's escapades from his father, and his name out of the media. Jake had always said that Hoffmann was more of a father than Nate had ever been. Matt had serious doubts about that.

Jake grinned. "Matt, I am a reformed character. You'll see one day, marriage and fatherhood changes a guy."

While they waited on the sidewalk for the valet to bring Jake's car, Jake said seriously, "Talking about warnings, Matt, you want to plug the rumors about this Malibu situation before it gets out of hand. You know how people are, they love a scandal."

"They'll lose interest as soon as some actor's arrested for peeing in public. It won't last."

"Maybe, but Chet Barnes of Bankorp was there. If it were my banker listening to rumors that I was involved with some kid's death like that, I'd sure be concerned." His midnight blue Bentley drew up to the curb, and Jake went around to take the driver's seat. "See you Friday night. Bring Ginn." He laughed and slid behind the wheel.

Matt waved, watched the Bentley pull smoothly away from the curb and merge into traffic, and made a mental note to ask Marni where he was supposed to be on Friday. Before returning to the office, he crossed the street to Dutton's, L.A.'s best independent bookstore, to pick up the latest batch of books they were holding for him. TV had never held much interest beyond the news, and since Ginn left he'd discovered some good mystery writers—John Dunning, Alan Furst, Ross Thomas—whose books helped to fill the empty hours without her.

In the office, he dumped the books on his desk, dropped into his chair. Ned glanced over at him. "So what did he want?"

"A donation for Hannah's House. Twenty-five thousand, five more than last year."

Ned whistled. "What did you tell him?"

"That I'd ask my partner. I think we should do it. It comes off our taxes. Everyone wins. Okay with you?"

"Yeah, okay, what the hell, it's a good cause. Anything else?"

For a second Matt considered whether he should burden Ned with Jake's comments about Chet Barnes, then decided he had no choice. Ned's part of the business was finding and negotiating the financing for the deals Matt found and nurtured to completion. He dealt with the bankers every day. If he didn't know, he could be blindsided.

"Well, he and Gena were at a party in Malibu yesterday at the Howes', you know them, live on La Costa. Seems I was a topic of conversation. Rumors are flying that I'm involved in some way in that girl's death. He said that Chet Barnes was there and heard it all."

"Chet Barnes?" Ned looked at him with alarm.

"Don't sweat it, Ned. All bankers care about is the bottom line."

"Yes, but you're fifty percent of this firm. If you're in trouble, we're in trouble."

"I'm not in trouble," Matt said.

He picked up the note Marni had left on his desk.

Detective Jim Barstow of the sheriff's department. Call back.

CHAPTER 15

Jim Barstow crossed the waiting room of the Lost Hills sheriff's substation, hand outstretched in greeting. "Thanks for coming, Mr. Lowell."

Matt gave the proffered hand a brief, hard shake. "My pleasure" certainly did not fit his mood. "Did I have a choice?" was more like it but Barstow had made it plain he did not when he'd suggested Matt come into the homicide detective's headquarters in the City of Commerce on Tuesday afternoon. After some discussion, they'd settled on 9:00 a.m. Wednesday at Lost Hills, the substation that covered Malibu. Matt had arrived right on time but they'd kept him waiting, alone with his thoughts, and his conscience, for half an hour.

He settled on a simple, "Good morning."

"Sorry to keep you waiting," Barstow said. He indicated the door from which he had just emerged. "We can use this room. You remember my partner, Detective Flores?"

"Sure. Good morning," Matt said again.

"Mr. Lowell." Flores nodded without rising from his chair.

Matt felt a twinge of relief. He'd half expected the dingy interview room from police dramas on television with beat-up metal furniture and a one-way mirror. This room was a simple office, dark gray industrial carpet, a wooden desk, chairs, the flags of the United States and California. "Well, I'm glad you suggested meeting here this morning, Mr. Lowell. A nice drive out once you get past Woodland Hills. Very pretty country around here," Barstow said. He indicated a chair. "Can I get you some coffee?"

Matt glanced at his watch, although he knew the time. He'd been checking the clock above the desk in the waiting room every five minutes since nine. "No, thank you. I've been waiting half an hour, so maybe we could get to the point. What is this about?"

"Well, it's the young girl found in Encinal Canyon last week. We're operating on the assumption that the two deaths are connected, the baby you found and this young woman." Barstow paused as if waiting for Matt to respond.

Matt nodded. "I see."

Flores took over. "We hear you've been asking quite a few questions around Malibu, Mr. Lowell. That interests us."

Matt tried not to look as surprised as he felt. He kept his voice low-key, his tone pleasant. "Have you got my personal life under scrutiny, Mr. Flores?"

Flores smiled. For a smoker, his teeth were surprisingly white. "It's Detective Flores. No, your personal life is no concern of ours. Except when it crosses an open case."

"And has it?"

"You tell us. A baby dies. You start asking questions about the girl who was found dead, and you claim to have seen a bunch of kids down in the canyon, close to where this girl was found. You want to tell us about that?"

For a second, he stopped breathing. Only Halliburton, Ginn and Tommy Aguilar knew he'd seen those kids. So how in God's name did the police find out? Possibilities caromed around his brain—Ginn was a lawyer, an officer of the court, harboring a girl who was probably an illegal alien. He'd involved Phil Halliburton, then promised to keep his name out of it. Both were professionals with a lot to lose. It had to be Tommy. Thank God he had not dragged Bobby into this.

"Who says I've been asking questions?"

"Haven't you?"

Choosing his words carefully, Matt said, "You must be talking about the conversation I had with Tommy Aguilar. Tommy is an old surfing buddy and when I stopped off at the Mermaid for a burger, I told him about the baby I'd found on the beach during the fire. The dead girl came up in the course of conversation. Malibu's a small town, everyone knows that a body was found. That's all."

Flores kept a pair of dark unblinking eyes locked on him. Matt restrained the urge to cross his legs, scratch his ear, shift his weight in the chair. The guy was unnerving.

Barstow said, "We're interested in whatever you saw down in that canyon."

Matt frowned, shook his head again, as if puzzled. "I don't know what you could be referring to. I didn't see anything."

His heart rate had picked up. He'd crossed the line and there was no going back. Lying to the police was probably a punishable offense, obstruction of justice or something like that. But so was harboring an illegal alien who very likely knew something about a dead girl. And being a party to such knowledge and not reporting it. Or maybe lawyer-client and patient-doctor privilege applied and by lying he had truly screwed things up. He felt needles of sweat breaking out on his chest.

"You took a trail ride down in that canyon even though it's burned out? Can't be much of a place for pleasure riding. Why Encinal Canyon, Mr. Lowell?" Flores asked.

He hadn't told Tommy he'd been riding. Or had he?

"I grew up in Malibu, and I ride all the time. I have since I was a kid. Right now, there's fire damage all over the mountains, but the mouth of Encinal escaped. It's just a place, nothing significant."

"So you just happened to choose an area below where a girl's body was found?"

Matt fought the urge to swallow. He was digging himself deeper into this story. Why hadn't he just said he was curious? "I never even gave that a thought."

"And the mysterious youngsters?"

"None that I saw. But as Tommy Aguilar can tell you, there are encampments of illegal laborers all over those hills and canyons."

"But not in Encinal Canyon last Sunday?"

"Well, sure, there could be, but I didn't see any."

"We'll find them if they're there, but anything you can tell us would be very useful."

Matt ran his mind quickly over the area. He'd found nothing that could be connected with a death and he certainly would have noticed. He'd picked up the torn remnants of the paper sacks that had covered the girl, brought them out and disposed of them, something he often did when he came across discarded trash. He'd known those mountains all his life. It was a thing with him, he felt it personally when they were treated as a garbage dump. "I wish I could help. I'm sorry."

"What about seeing someone wearing blue velvet pants?"

Matt shook his head slowly. Tommy hadn't kept anything back. "It's pretty tangled undergrowth down there, a lot of poison oak, poison sumac and ivy. A place for denim, not blue velvet pants, detective."

Barstow looked at his partner. "Anything you want to add, Ed?"

Flores linked his hands across his flat stomach and leaned back. "Just let's see what we're talking about here. You found a baby, you say on the beach, but the child dies before you could get help. Later, you rode into a canyon below the point where the body of a young girl was found, possibly the mother. We can put that down to natural curiosity, Mr. Lowell, the looky loo syndrome, a common response to disaster. But what's disturbing is that we get word that you saw a number of people down there who may have information that could help with the inquiry, and you are now saying that you did not. You're sure about that?"

"Yes."

"My mistake. You didn't strike me as the kind of guy who'd get off on inventing a story like that."

"I'm not."

"Our informant must be mistaken then," Flores said. He glanced at Barstow and shrugged.

"I guess that's all," Barstow said. "Get in touch with us if you remember anything you think would help our investigation, Mr. Lowell. Thanks for your time."

"Sorry I couldn't be of more help." Matt rose to his feet, shook hands and started to leave.

"Oh, by the way," Flores said, "our boss, Captain Singleton, said to tell you the baby will be released to a group called the Garden of Angels for burial."

Matt turned. "I thought abandoned babies went to medical research."

"I don't know how you got that impression. Unknown newborns are released to this charitable organization, Garden of Angels. They take them for burial in a cemetery out in Riverside."

"What about the mother?" Matt asked.

"If she is the mother. The tests will take some time before they're complete."

"So will the coroner keep her body until then?"

"No, there's no room down at the morgue for that," Flores said. "Once we've got the tissue samples we need, and the autopsy report, she'll be disposed of at state expense."

And the baby will be buried alone, without her mother. "They should be together."

"Sure, but that won't happen."

Matt heard himself say, "Would there be any objection if I arranged for them to be buried together?"

Flores shrugged. "I guess it would save the state the couple of dimes they'd spend on it."

Matt tried to remember what had happened with his mother. His dad had called a funeral home. "Okay. I'll have a mortuary get in touch with the coroner."

"We'll have to send it up through channels to see what Singleton has to say. Better wait until you hear from us," Barstow said. "As soon as the autopsy reports are in, we'll give the coroner's office a call, and tell them to release the bodies to you. How's that?"

"Okay. Thanks."

"No problem," Barstow said. "Have a nice day."

Matt turned out of the parking lot onto Agoura Road parallel to the Ventura Freeway. He felt as if he'd taken a beating. Why the hell had he offered to bury the girl as well? He punched in the number of his office.

"Anything urgent?" he asked when Marni answered.

"Nothing that can't wait. Just a minute. Yes, Susan Dean called. She's had to go to New York, but she should be back in time for the fund-raiser on Friday night. If her Friday meeting runs late, she may have to catch a later flight but worst case, you'll miss part of the cocktail hour. She left a couple of numbers where you can reach her, her New York office and the hotel where she's staying."

So that was where he was supposed to be on Friday night— the fund-raiser to benefit the cultural life of the city, the Music Center and the Los Angeles Opera Association, the L.A. Theater, a lot of lesser organizations. The affair had been driven from his mind. So had Susan Dean, come to that. He felt a twinge of guilt. Susan was talented, good-looking, passionate about old buildings and a partner in the architectural firm they used. She deserved better than a guy who was still hung up on another woman.

"Okay, thanks. I'll call her from home later." He glanced in his rearview at a black and white, light bar flashing. "Damn. Got to go. I'm getting a ticket."

He disconnected, slowly pulled over and stopped. He lowered the window, then placed his hands at ten o'clock and two o'clock on the steering wheel, plainly in sight, and stared straight ahead. The first rule his dad had drummed into him when he'd passed his driving test—when dealing with law enforcement, always keep your hands visible.

The deputy leaned against the window. "Driving at the speed limit, never straying over the line, observing stop signs. Sir, in California those are ticketable offenses. But I can be bribed."

Matt looked up. "What will it take, officer?"

Bobby Eckhart laughed. "A cup of coffee should cover it. I'm due for a break."

"Sure. The Koffee Korner?"

"See you there."

Bar lights off, Bobby pulled around him, and led the way to the Korner, a pit stop for north- and southbound travelers for years before the freeway was built and cut off the customers.

Matt parked by the patrol car and followed Bobby inside. The coffee shop looked exactly what it was, a leftover from the sixties; alternating avocado and burnt orange Naugahyde booths, vinyl floor worn thin by the pounding of untold thousands of feet, domed cake stands on a counter top that had not been changed in thirty years. The air smelled sweetly of butter and pancakes and maple syrup.

The two men slid into a booth overlooking the freeway a hundred feet away on the other side of the chain-link fence. Without asking, a waitress with the same well worn, welcoming patina as the restaurant, turned over the two thick ceramic mugs already on the table and filled them with coffee. Bobby put an arm around her ample middle.

"Rosie, put me out of my misery and let me take you away from all this."

Rosie smiled at Matt. "You know this guy?"

"Grew up together."

"Lucky you. What's your pleasure, gentlemen?"

They each ordered coffee. "And a nice muffin," Bobby said. "Surprise me." As soon as Rosie left, Bobby said, "What are you doing out here this time of day? Don't you work anymore?"

"Barstow and Flores had me in for questioning."

Bobby's eyebrows rose. "What's their problem?"

"Someone told them I'd been at the Mermaid asking questions."

Bobby snorted. "Don't tell me they're interested in the Sons of Satan for that girl."

"I don't think so."

Rosie placed a plate bearing a muffin on the table. "Bran. Keep you regular. Get you anything else?"

Bobby smiled up at her. "Only you, Rosie, and you won't have me."

Rosie laughed and topped their mugs. Bobby watched as she took the coffeepot to the next table, then said, "Why are you surprised they brought you in, Matt? Don't you realize that going around asking questions draws attention to you? I know a baby died, I know it bothers you, but why the hell are you poking around asking questions? They have to at least wonder why you're so interested and if they turn up nothing else, they'll try to shake your tree. Just let it go, Matt. You didn't kill that baby, whoever left it there on the beach did that. It's not your fault, and it sure as hell isn't your business."

Matt stirred his coffee, placed the spoon carefully on a napkin. "I was down in Encinal with Buck on Sunday. I found some paper sacks from Tommy's place, that's why I went to ask Tommy if he knew anything."

"Paper sacks? What the hell are you talking about? Someone had a picnic and left trash behind? Or do you think that girl bled out on paper sacks from the Mermaid?"

"No, there was no sign of blood. Bob, how long have we known each?"

"I don't know. We lived across the road from each other on Zumirez Drive when we were three or something. So that's thirty-three years. Why?"

"I saw a bunch of kids in Encinal. That's why I went to talk to Tommy. I wanted to know if he'd seen them because I think the dead girl had been with them. Barstow and Flores asked me if I'd seen anyone and I told them that I hadn't. But I think they know that I was lying."

"You lied?" Bobby leaned forward as if about to climb over the table. "You lied to a couple of homicide dicks? Matt, honest to God, you need your brain examined. Shit! Who told them you were asking questions?"

"It had to be Tommy Aguilar. There wasn't anyone else there."

Bobby put the mug to his lips, lowered it without drinking. He shook his head. "Buddy, you've done some pretty dumb-ass things in your life, but I do believe this comes close to topping the list. What makes you think these kids you saw had anything to do with the dead girl?"

"They wore the same kind of skimpy, silky stuff you said she was wearing for one thing. Plus they were right there where her body was found. What more do you want? They're gone, anyway. I took Buck down to look for them."

"Well, they're going to make quite an impression wandering up and down Malibu freezing their asses off dressed like that in November with the rainy season coming on. They'll get picked up in no time."

"They're not dressed like that anymore. I left clothes for them."

"Oh, great. This is getting better and better. If they are picked up and they identify you as their benefactor, what then?"

"Giving clothes to needy kids is against the law?"

"No, but lying to the law investigating a homicide is."

"You mean this is a murder investigation?"

"It's a homicide investigation, Matt. A death in unusual circumstances is treated as a homicide until the cause of death can be established. I don't think this girl was killed. I think she died from complications of having a baby on the beach. If you don't know any more than you're saying, you just lied for no reason. Jesus, Matt."

"Yeah, I know. I know, Bob." He wanted to tell him about the girl he'd brought home, but to ask him to keep silent about it would be asking him to put his career in jeopardy. "I don't want to ask you to do anything that would put your job on the line, but is it possible for you to keep an ear to the ground so that I'm not blindsided? I don't want to be surprised by the SWAT team battering the door down one morning in the dawn's early light."

"I'm just a humble road warrior, buddy." Bobby shook his head. "Still, the girl was picked up on my patch so it won't be too strange for me to keep in touch with the investigation, not with a baby involved. Yeah, okay. Don't worry. But for God's sake, Matt, leave it alone."

"I will as soon as I can. They said they'd release the bodies to me to be buried together."

"Bodies? You said bodies, plural?"

Matt nodded. Bobby opened his mouth, changed his mind, and closed it without speaking.

"Yeah, okay," Matt said. He stirred the cold coffee. "You think it's about my mother. That's what Ginn would say." Ginn thought everything was about his mother leaving him when he was ten. It didn't seem to register with her that he understood that his mother did not abandon him. She was just killed on her way home from the store with ice cream by a drunk in a sports car. Just another summertime fatality on the PCH. "But after they're buried, I'm through."

"You hope." Bobby looked at his watch. "Gotta go or they'll send out a search party. Leave a nice tip for Rosie, she's got a sick husband." He slid out of the booth, started toward the door, then returned. "Have you heard from Ginn lately?"

"No." He couldn't tell Bobby he was talking to her daily now. "Why?"

"She kept in touch with Sylvie during the fire to make sure

you and Barney and the horses were okay. I'm sworn to secrecy, but what the hell. You might need a lawyer sometime soon, and she's a good one. Just a thought." He turned, called a goodbye to Rosie, and was out the door.

At six Matt drove into his garage, got the Glock from the glove compartment. It was too dark to check the road, but he was making a point now of watching his back, so at least he was pretty sure he had not been followed home. He riffled through the usual junk in the mailbox, dropped catalogues and coupons into the recycle bin. The house was bleak, cold and lifeless. With Barney around, he'd been getting used to it, but Ginn's lingering energy made it seem emptier than ever. He got a bottle of water, drank it standing at the kitchen counter waiting for the toaster oven to tell him dinner was ready. He was cruising the channels, eating warmed-over pizza when the phone rang.

"Matt, it's me, Tommy. Those kids you were asking about? They're here."

CHAPTER 16

The Mermaid parking lot was empty. Matt parked in front, ran up the steps, burst through the doors. He scanned the room—no one at the tables or the pinball machine, the place was devoid of customers. He checked the little grocery, found it closed for business. He went back to the restaurant and banged on the counter.

"Tommy! You back there?"

"Hey, dude, I'm coming." Tommy emerged from the door to the kitchen. "They're gone, man."

"Why didn't you hold them until I got here?"

"You mean, tie them to chairs or something? They're gone, man. That's it."

"You're sure it was them?"

"Skinny blond kid, a bunch of girls who did what he told them. Foreign language. It was them. I'd seen them before, I just didn't want to get into it, not with the kind of customers here on Sunday."

Matt started toward the door. "I'm going to take a look along the highway, maybe they're hitching a ride somewhere."

"They're not thumbing, man, they're hanging around. You won't find them now."

"I'll check out back."

Matt ran outside, got in the Range Rover and turned on the headlights. He inched the big vehicle along so that light could penetrate the trees behind the building. They were nowhere around the restaurant and he had just come from the south. If they were walking along the shoulder of the PCH in the middle of nowhere in the dark, the headlights would have picked them up. He turned north, drove slowly, peering into the darkness, sweeping his eyes from one side of the highway to the other. The Coast Highway was flanked by ocean to the west, and pitch-black canyons and hills to the east. Tommy was right, there was no way to find them, they could melt into this country with no problem.

He swung a U-turn and drove back to the Mermaid.

He took a seat at the counter. "Why didn't you tell me you'd seen those kids when I asked you on Sunday?"

"Wait a minute." Tommy went to the front door, and locked it. He flipped a switch to turn off the outside lights then limped back behind the counter. "Lousy business tonight anyway."

He produced a couple of glasses and a bottle of bourbon from under the counter, poured a healthy slug into each glass, shoved one across to Matt.

"I like my life. You know? I told you, I surf when I want, I got dough, things are okay. That don't mean I don't know what goes on around here, man. But you gotta understand, who pays who for what, and how they pay, sex, cash, boys, girls, not my business, dude. This was different. These kids were not into dope. They were fucking the Satans for a takeout hamburger and those sons of bitches were laughing about it. They thought it was funny to take turns fucking a hungry little girl up against the wall for a burger they threw on the ground for her to grovel for. Jesus, just about turned my stomach. You think I was going to talk about that with the Satans around?"

"How long was that going on?"

"The boy appeared the day after the fire. I saw him rooting around in the Dumpster. The girls came later. Looked like two of them maybe took turns out there, but it was hard to tell them apart."

"You didn't think to feed them, Tommy?" Matt asked.

"Dude, I'm running a business here, I can't afford to give away the store." Tommy rubbed a hand hard over his mouth and avoided Matt's eyes. "Besides, I didn't know what was going on for a couple of days, and I got the fucking Satans breathing down my neck. Then you appear. Anyway, they've got money now. Couple of times they've been here since, they paid for hamburgers and milk and cookies. And they're not dressed in the tits and ass gear they were wearing before. They got clothes from somewhere."

"What about the boy? What was he doing when this was going on?"

"After the first time at the Dumpster I never saw him again until tonight. And I saw the little black kid tonight for the first time, too. They seemed to be taking care of her okay."

"He was here with them?"

Tommy nodded his head. "Yes. The girls waited for the hamburgers right there where you're sitting. He stood at the end of the counter there, watching me. That's one spooky kid."

Matt took a sip of the Jim Beam, let it trickle down his throat. "The sheriff had me in this morning about the dead girl dumped in Encinal. They knew I'd been asking questions about these kids. You tell the sheriff what you've just told me?"

"You think I'm crazy? I tell you, I got a good life, I want to keep it. I do not talk about the Satans. Period."

"But you told the sheriff I'd been asking questions about these kids."

"Matt, I don't talk to no one about nothing. I'm a model citizen, dude, pay my taxes, that shit, have a chat with Bobby when he comes around, but I don't volunteer anything to the law.

They ask, I answer. So, they call you in, it didn't come from me. But I gotta tell you, you ain't the only one interested in these kids. Big dude was in here asking right after you left on Sunday."

"Who was he?"

"Never said, I didn't ask."

"What did he look like?"

"I told you, big dude. Mustache, looked like he'd been in a fight, face banged up, bandage on both arms. He came back again couple days later—"

"What day, exactly?"

"Yesterday. I didn't tell him anything then, either."

"What did he say exactly, Tommy?"

Tommy snorted. "I just told you, dude. Seen any young kids around here. Said they took off from some teenage drug rehab place for the rich and famous during the fire. Said their parents were pissing blood. Like that. Had a beer and left. Heard he was checking all along the coast."

"You tell the sheriff about it?"

"Matt, you listening to what I'm saying here?" Tommy spoke slowly, dropping each word carefully. "If the sheriff asks a question, I answer. They don't, I don't. Simple. Got it, dude?"

"Yes, right." Matt drained his glass. "Thanks for the drink. And the call, Tommy, I appreciate it. If the kids come back, I'd still like to talk to them."

Tommy picked up the glasses, dumped them into the sink, swiped a blue cloth across the counter without answering.

"Okay, Tom?"

"Have to be a night like this, dude, no customers. That don't happen often."

Matt waited for him to continue, but he didn't. Matt got the message. Tonight Tommy had squared himself with his conscience. He'd gone as far as he was going to go.

* * *

When Matt returned home, the red light was flashing on the telephone. Two messages, neither from Ginn. He talked to Phil Halliburton first.

"I've got a psych nurse lined up, Matt. Very discreet woman with a lot of experience."

"I think we'd better hold off on that," Matt said. "If Ginn needs help, she'll let me know, and she hasn't."

"Give me Ginn's number, I'll talk to her."

"No need. Phil. Did you mention any of this at that party at the Howes' place on Sunday?"

"Are you crazy? Why would I do that?"

"Apparently, my name's being linked to the dead girl. Jake Broagan said it came up at that party at the Howes'. You hear anything?"

"Nothing while I was around. Anyway, rest assured I don't talk about my patients, especially the illegal ones."

"Do you know of any drug rehab place for rich teenagers around here?"

"Malibu's the fashionable destination for high-end addicts who can afford thirty thou a month and up, but I don't know of any place that specializes in teenagers. Why?"

"Someone is looking for the kids who were holed up in Encinal." Matt gave him the highlights of the conversation he'd just had with Tommy Aguilar, and the interview at Lost Hills. "The cops don't know anything about you or Ginn, and I don't know who this guy is poking around. I'd feel a whole lot better if you forget you ever came over here last Saturday, Phil."

"You and me both. If you hear anything I should know, give me a call."

When they'd hung up, Matt returned Susan Dean's call from her hotel in New York. She wasn't in her room and he left word that he'd call her on Friday to check her flight. They could decide then what time he'd pick her up for the fund-raiser.

He hung up and grabbed up his car keys. At night, traffic into town was light, he made it into Santa Monica in twenty-five minutes, although it was impossible to keep track of the headlights in his rearview, so to be safe, he took a few turns before heading for Hurricane Court. He parked against Ginn's back fence, then walked down the alley, along Pacific, into the narrow walk street. In front of Ginn's home, he stopped for a moment. Drapes were drawn, but he could see the glow of lights in every room. He walked up the brick path to the front door and rang the bell. He waited and rang again, then pressed his face to the door. "Ginn. It's Matt."

The outside light snapped on. The door opened.

"Hey, what are you doing here?" Ginn looked over his shoulder as if checking to see if he was alone.

"Just wanted to see you, maybe take Barney for a run."

Tail lashing from side to side in welcome, Barney pushed his way out of the house. Matt bent to scratch his ears, and grinned at her. "Come on, Ginn, ask me in."

Ginn widened the door. "They're in the kitchen. I just got home from work."

"You keep late hours," Matt commented. He closed the door and followed her down the hall. The air was warm, suffused with the subtle scent of chrysanthemums, Ginn's favorite flower for this time of year. He knew she'd make regular trips down to the flower mart and buy them by the armload so that she could have vases all over the house, spider mums in bronze and russet, autumn colors. He missed that.

Gabrielle sat at the table set in the nook of the bay window the young girl kneeling by her side, intent on holding an ice pack to Gabby's knee. Her hair was pulled away from her face and fastened with a green ribbon that matched her sweater. She looked as cute as any American teenager, Matt thought. Then she looked up and caught sight of him. Immediately, her face crumpled. Large black eyes darted from Gabby to Ginn to Matt. The ice pack fell from her hand, she backed into the corner of the room, the awful whimpering sound issuing from her throat.

"This is the first time she's done that since she's been here," Ginn said.

"While she's awake, anyway." Gabby started to get up.

Motioning her to stay where she was, Ginn hurried over to the girl, knelt close without touching her. She spoke in a calm even voice, repeating the same words and phrases. "It's all right, honey. It's all right. There's nothing to be afraid of. It's Matt. You know Matt. It's all right, honey."

Feeling helpless Matt hovered in the doorway, careful to keep his eyes away from the girl, surprised at how much it hurt to see this young kid so terrified, and know that it was of him. He looked at Gabby without really seeing her, and said the first words that came into his head.

"How are you doing, Gabby?"

Gabby picked up the ice pack from where the girl had dropped it. Her eyes on the two girls, she said, "A bit bruised, that's all. But Sophie is fine."

He snapped back into the moment and realized what he was looking at: Gabby with an ice pack on her knees. "What's happened?"

Gabrielle looked at him. "Oh, I thought that's why you were here."

"I didn't call him, Mom," Ginn said.

"Oh," Gabrielle said. "Some fool out driving when he should be out taking lessons nearly ran us down. I pushed Sophie out of the way, but I slipped on the curb, and here, you see? I grazed my knees."

"Sophie? That's her name? Sophie?"

Gabrielle gave a slight, Gallic movement of her shoulders. "She hasn't spoken yet, but we have to call her something."

"What happened exactly?"

"Well, there it was, no doubt rushing to get somewhere completely unimportant." She hitched her narrow skirt, offered her torn black hose and grazed knees for Matt's inspection. "He didn't even stop to ask if we were all right."

"What sort of car, Gabby?"

The sounds from the corner were diminishing. Gabby looked at him, and shrugged. "A car. A black car. I saw him, who would think the idiot driver would not see us? Then just before it would have hit us, he noticed other people existed in the world, and he swerved. Idiot! I pushed Sophie, I stumbled on the curb." She made a small sound of disgust.

"Where was this?"

"Right here. Right on Pacific Avenue as we came out of our little street."

He wanted to ask what they were doing out at night, and was trying to frame the question without either alarming her or sounding accusatory when Gabby volunteered the answer.

"Sophie does not feel safe outside, so we do not go out during the day, you understand, and we keep the blinds drawn." She spoke as if it were the most normal thing in the world to live in a darkened house a block from the beach and not to venture out during daylight hours. "Tonight was to be our first little excursion. A walk to the video store, and if that went well, a visit to the ice cream parlor on Main. Then this happened. Idiot man ruined our evening."

"The driver was a man, you're sure?"

"Yes, a man. Definitely."

"Did you notice anything about him, a mustache, or his face?"

"No, a car swerved. I didn't see his face. I saw only Sophie. I pushed her, I fell. Poor child, she lives in terror. Every night it's the same, these nightmares." Gabby glanced at the two girls. "Excuse me, Matt." She got up, crossed the room and sat on the floor. Unlike Ginn, she did not hesitate to pull Sophie's rigid body into her arms. Gradually, the girl relaxed against her and Gabby started to rock gently, murmuring softly to her in French. Ginn rose, left Sophie to her mother, and returned to the table.

Matt touched Ginn's arm. "Walk out with me." He threw a farewell wave to Gabby over the girl's head and drew Ginn along the hall, into the front main room. Ginn pointed to a low cinnamon-colored couch, and switched on a floor lamp, then knelt in front of the fireplace and put a match to the gas bar. Flames licked around the realistic looking logs, artificial ashes glowed red. She sat back in the armchair facing the couch.

"I made some calls and we were right not to get the INS involved. It would be a bleak outlook. She'd go into the system while they try to find out more about her. We know that she can speak because she calls out in her nightmares, it could be a Slavic language. Gabby called a woman she knows, another translator who is an expert in Slavic languages, and she's waiting to hear back. Maybe if we give Sophie some time and some peace, she'll feel safe enough to trust us and we can find out about her background ourselves. That way we can take an informed case to an immigration attorney. Is that okay with you?"

"Yes, that sounds good." Anything Ginn Chang wanted to do was okay with him. "I was at the Mermaid tonight. The other kids were there buying hamburgers. Tommy called me but by the time I got there, they were gone. Then he admitted he had seen them before, but I'd already guessed that anyway. He said one or two of the older girls had been trading with the bikers that hang out there now. Sex for food." He didn't go into the horrifying details Tommy had laid out for him.

"Oh, Matt, this is getting more awful by the day. Did Tommy say he would call you if he sees them again?"

"No. He called tonight because his conscience was bothering him, but I don't think he will again. Tonight at least, they had money to pay for their hamburgers. They must have found the cash I left them, so for now no one has to trade sex to eat. Tommy also told me someone is looking for them. He told Tommy they're runaways from a high-end drug treatment place for teenagers."

"Do you believe that?"

Matt shook his head. "From Tommy's description, he sounds like the same guy Barney attacked. Anyway, I plan to keep on top of our friend Tommy, see what turns up. The other thing is that I saw Flores and Barstow this morning." He ran the gist of his morning by her.

Ginn eyes widened, her eyebrows rose. "You lied to the police?"

Matt shrugged. Ginn was a trial lawyer and he didn't want to go there. What he wanted was to tell her he knew she'd called Sylvie Eckhart during the fire, but that would get Bobby in trouble with his wife. He got to his feet. Ginn rose with him and walked across the room, along the hall to the front door.

"Matt, when you are dealing with the police, remember they are trying to make a case. You have to consider every word because that's exactly what they are doing."

Suddenly, he couldn't bear to leave her. He put up a hand and ran a strand of her hair through his fingers.

Ginn stepped back. "Don't. Don't do that."

"Ginn, I miss you, I can't believe—"

She cut him off. "Matt, we've been over this. We don't want the same things in life, nothing's changed."

"Yes, it has. Really, we could—"

"No. We can't. And if you're going to keep on about it, then we can't even do this together."

"All right, I won't keep on." He knew if he pressed her, the thaw that was just starting would freeze over. "Be careful, Ginn. Lock the doors, keep the outside lights on."

"No one knows she's here, Matt. Stop worrying."

"I do worry. I don't think what happened tonight to Gabby was an accident."

"Of course it was. Everyone in Los Angeles drives as if they're the only people of the road. Listen to me. Only three people know she's here, and we are not talking. Good night." She opened the front door, leaving him no choice but to leave. He touched her face briefly with one finger and went through the door, then stood for a moment on the porch listening to her footsteps retreating along the hallway.

He walked through the alley to the Range Rover, trying to convince himself that their narrow escape tonight was just coincidence.

Somehow, though, he was unable to shake an ever deepening sense of anxiety.

The scream of sirens brought Matt upright out of a restless sleep. His waking thought was fire. He jumped out of bed, pulled on jeans, saw the Glock on the bedside table and grabbed it up before running out onto the deck.

The moon was high, the sky clearing. The air was cold but free of smoke, and there was no glow of flames. From where he stood, Matt could see the flashing light bars, the sheriff's response team going north on the Pacific Coast Highway. It had to be a major event, four cars with sirens making a hell of a din.

Matt glanced at his watch, saw that it was six-fifteen and time to get the day going anyway. He picked up the *Wall Street Journal* and *Los Angeles Times* from where they'd landed under the rear wheel of the Range Rover and checked the road in both directions. Half an hour later, he was at the kitchen counter, coffee cup in hand as he skimmed the headlines.

He heard hurried footsteps coming along the side of the house and reached for the Glock then saw Bobby Eckhart passing the kitchen window. He had just enough time to shove the weapon under the newspaper before Bobby banged once on the door as he opened it.

"Hey, Bobby. What are you doing here?" Matt reached for another mug. "You smell the coffee from the highway?"

"Tommy Aguilar's dead."

Matt felt his face go rigid with shock. "But I just saw him, I visited with him. When?"

"Some time last night. I've only got a minute, I wanted to let you know myself."

Bobby looked exactly as Matt felt, shattered. "How did it happen?"

"Someone stuck a knife in his belly."

"What? Oh, God."

"We just found him. Someone called, didn't leave a name, said he'd stopped at the Mermaid for coffee and Tommy was dead. When we got there, the place was wide open. We found Tommy behind the counter. He was shot in the head, and then they shoved a knife in his belly. Can you imagine doing that to old Tommy?" Bobby's voice roughened. "You remember how he used to look? You ever see anyone more graceful on a wave? He had the style, the feeling for the way the curl would break. Last couple of years, you'd never know it was the same guy… It was like he'd sold his soul."

Matt swallowed. His stomach roiled with the coffee he'd just drunk, and his mind whirled with questions. Should he tell Bobby about the girl Sophie, the attack on the house, the break-in, the knife he'd hidden behind the towels in the closet, the guy asking about kids from a rehab? The guy Tommy said looked as if he'd been in a fight? How could he mention any of it without dragging Bobby into the quagmire, without further implicating Ginn. He filled the mug and shoved it across the counter. "Who did it? You got any idea?"

Bobby shook his head. "Someone who wanted to get up real close that's for sure. A knife is a personal kind of weapon, the killer gets off on the feel of it going in. They're pulling in the Satans, see what they know. I warned you these were bad people, we've just never been able to pin anything on them."

They were silent for a moment, nothing to say, no questions to ask.

"He was a hell of a surfer in his day, wasn't he, old Tommy? I've got to go." Bobby took a gulp of the coffee, slammed down the mug, pulled the door closed behind him.

Matt stared out of the window, seeing Tommy as he used to be, radical, beyond fearless, the best of the big surf chasers.

Now he was dead, a knife in his belly. He couldn't get his brain around it.

CHAPTER 17

Matt struggled with his black tie, wondering why he hadn't got himself an elastic snap-on. Ginn had been with him when he'd bought the damn suit, and she'd always tied it for him, made it look easy to get a perfect bow. He should have gone out and bought one of those Italian suits that didn't need a tucked shirt and bow tie, but that would have meant stores and tailors and fittings, which was why he was stuck with the same damn bow tie and the same damn suit. Time was pressing on, he had to be at Susan's in less than an hour.

He pulled off the tie, and was starting again when he felt the weight of heavy feet rippling through the wooden deck. The Glock was close at hand and he picked it up, flipped the bedroom light off, went to the window and twitched the drape. Damn thing was becoming his new best friend. The outside light on the garage flickered on as two men passed through the beam.

Astonished, he recognized Barstow and Flores. At seven on a Friday evening? At his home?

He shoved the Glock under a pillow, pulled the bedroom door closed behind him, crossed the living room and opened the outside door.

Flores had a hand raised to knock. "Mr. Lowell." He dropped the hand.

Barstow peered over the rail at the sand below. Since the attack, Matt kept the beach lights on and the waves sheeted white foam as they retreated with a hiss.

"Nice little place. Surprising to find a little house like this nowadays along here. Beach lots along here must be worth a few bucks."

"Yeah, like millions," Flores said.

Matt found himself trying to fathom the significance of the exchange. Maybe he was supposed to feel guilty because he lived on an expensive piece of beachfront surrounded by multimillion-dollar houses. So what? His house was a thousand-square-foot shack that rattled and shook in a high wind, and even if it didn't, so what?

"Come on in." He left the door open for them to enter, switched on a couple of lamps. He stood in the center of the softly lit room. "What can I do for you?"

"We've caught you at an inconvenient time." Barstow closed the door, took in Matt's black suspenders, the white pintucked shirt, the untied black tie.

"That's okay." Matt remained standing and did not invite them to sit. "What can I do for you?" he repeated.

Flores undid the button on his jacket. Matt caught a glimpse of the butt of the weapon in a holster on his hip. Flores's eyes swept the room as his partner answered.

"The investigations into the death of the child you picked up, and the body of the girl found on Encinal have been terminated," Barstow said.

Matt let out a breath. "I see." So it wasn't about Tommy. So much had happened, he didn't know what to worry about next. "Thanks for coming in person, a phone call would have done.

I'll have the funeral home get in touch with the coroner's office tomorrow. It's too late now." Pointedly, Matt glanced at his watch.

"You don't want to know the cause of death?" Barstow asked.

"Yes, of course. You've got the autopsy report, then?"

"Yeah, we still have them, Mr. Lowell. Both of them."

Something about the phrasing, the tone of voice, the chill from both men, caught Matt's full attention. He looked from Barstow to Flores and back, got nothing from either of them.

"Well, what happened?"

"You mean what caused the girl's death, or what happened to her prior to her death?"

"I'm getting lost here," Matt said. "I mean whatever you want to tell me."

"She hemorrhaged after giving birth and bled out. Must have been a hell of a mess, body holds eight pints of blood and she didn't have much left. Of course, the circumstances of the birth contributed to her death," Barstow said.

"What my partner is saying is that she wasn't killed, as such," Flores said. "She was fucked some time before giving birth, and I do mean fucked, and then they both died. Conveniently died, a young mother and what was probably her baby. Investigation terminated. Someone has just been handed a clean slate. A get-out-of-jail-free card, as they say."

Flores's cop's eyes held Matt's in an unblinking stare. Matt felt the blood rush to his face. His mouth was suddenly dry and he swallowed.

"The word has come through channels to put this one in the cold file, Mr. Lowell. Officially the investigation is over."

"You mean she was raped?"

"Raped and sodomized. Then she gave birth somewhere on the beach the night of the fire and died. Then a child died." Barstow looked around. "That happened right here, I guess. End of story."

"End of story? You mean you're not going to pursue this?"

"That's what we've been told. Our limited resources are to be directed to cases we can solve." Barstow turned to his partner. "Am I quoting that right, Ed? Limited resources for more important cases than a couple of Jane Does?"

"Yeah, Jim, I think you captured the essence," Flores said.

"So we'll never know where she came from or who raped her. Or who covered her with flowers. Someone out there must be very relieved to think we'll never know."

Matt went into the kitchen, took down a bottle of single malt from the cupboard. "Sit down. You want a drink? Scotch?"

"No, thanks," Flores said. "Not right now."

Matt heard the words and caught the meaning. Flores was saying he was careful about with whom he drank. Or maybe he was reading too much into this, too. Maybe the guy just didn't want a drink.

"But you go ahead. You look a bit pale and you've got a big evening in front of you. Nice suit, by the way," Barstow said. Both detectives remained standing.

Matt poured a couple of fingers of scotch, splashed in some soda water he took from the fridge, went back to the living room. The phone rang, and he looked at it numbly, without really seeing it. Rape. Sodomy. Of a teenaged girl. Things you read about in newspapers, felt a brief pang of horror about, then went on about your day. Now these horrors were real.

"You want to take that, Matt?" Flores said. "We can wait."

Matt looked at him. "No, I'll pick it up later." If it was Ginn, now was not the time to be talking to her and there was no one else he cared to talk to. The ringing stopped and he put the glass down without drinking. "Look, why are you here when you could have called? I found a baby. I offered to have the mortuary call and arrange a funeral for the baby and her mother. There's nothing for you to attach to that. But I get the feeling there's something on your mind you're not saying."

"Well, look at it from our point of view," Flores said. "One," he held up his left thumb. "We have no one else to talk to and, two," his forefinger came up, "we know you've lied to us. Besides that, for a single young guy, lot of money, busy with a career, the good life, dating a lot of different women, you've shown more than a usual amount of interest in this case. So—" he smacked the third finger, continued with the fourth and fifth, started on the other hand "—you've lied, you're rich, your company pays a lot of taxes in this city, you are influential enough downtown to have the ear of people who count. Then, wham—" he clapped his hands together "—the word trickles down through channels to close this one out, someone high up, who the hell knows where it started, the mayor's office, some tame county supervisor someone's got in his pocket. Hell, right in our own department for all we know. You know how that works, campaign contributions, people have to run for reelection. So, you can see how my partner and I would find that interesting, can't you, Matt?"

Matt let out a heavy breath. "That's a hell of a reach. Why do I feel that no matter what I say, I'm going to get deeper into something I don't know anything about?"

Flores shrugged. "Hey, don't sweat it. The case is closed. No, as a courtesy my partner and I dropped by on our own time to give you some news. We came to tell you personally that the bodies of the two Jane Does you have shown considerable interest in have disappeared."

"What?"

"That's right," Barstow said. "The bodies can't be released to you for burial. No one can find them, no one knows what happened to them. They have disappeared as if they never existed and the cases have been closed."

"Thing is, we both have daughters around the same age as this young girl," Flores said. "Fourteen and fifteen, so you can see it won't be easy for us to let go of this case—"

Matt's blood was pounding in his head. "Wait a minute, you are just way out of line with this."

"With what?"

"You are making it sound as if you think I had something to do with this."

"Did you?"

"No, I didn't."

"Then relax, you've got nothing to worry about. Well, we've got a long drive back and you look as if you have a pleasant evening ahead of you. We won't keep you any longer. Have a good time tonight, Matt."

Neither man offered to shake hands as they had at the end of the previous meetings. Matt opened the door, stood back to let them out. The slight stir in the air was too light to be called a breeze, but it was onshore so the stink of the fire no longer swept down from the denuded hills—the scent was fresh and sweet, with a tang of salt.

Matt breathed deeply, and watched their retreating figures. What they had just said was that they were not going to let it go. But what was the worst he had done? He'd lied to protect innocent friends, he had not reported an attack on the house, and he had not volunteered what he knew about an unknown guy looking for teenaged escapees from a rehab. But Tommy said the Mermaid wasn't the only place the guy had been asking questions, and they could find that out easily enough.

But he knew what he had really done was more complex than that. He'd given refuge to an illegal alien, a girl who had to know something about two deaths that were of deep concern to the cops who'd just left.

CHAPTER 18

The line of cars moved quickly. Matt handed the keys to the valet, and turned to help Susan Dean negotiate an exit from the Range Rover. She slid him a smile as she hiked her dress, revealing a long slender leg, and felt for the ground with a high-heeled jeweled sandal. In boots and jeans and her gold-painted hard hat with the word "Architect" blazoned across the front, Susan Dean was an eye-catching woman. In a black dress that clung to her like a glove, green eyes made up to look even larger, her red hair tumbling around her shoulders, she could stop traffic.

As he'd feared, Matt had arrived at Susan's almost an hour late and was embarrassed to find she had prepared caviar and toast points, and had champagne ready for him to open. She'd shrugged, and brushed aside his apology with a comment about L.A.'s traffic getting worse. He had not contradicted her. What could he say? "No, it wasn't the traffic. I had a visit from a couple of homicide detectives who seem to think I might be a killer."

She did not even know he had found a dying baby during the fire. It was not something he wanted to talk about, except maybe to Ginn.

Golf carts were running guests up to the house, disappearing, returning empty for the few late comers. According to Julie, an avid reader of the society pages, this one event held annually at the Broagan estate and underwritten by Broagan Enterprises generated over a million dollars every year for the Music Center and the Los Angeles Opera and other small theaters important to Los Angeles cultural life. People came from all over the country to see and be seen.

They took the next cart. The drive was steep, the driver enthusiastic, wheeling the little cart around the curves and up the hill, rumbling over a quarter-mile of cobblestones, flanked by a double avenue of trees twinkling with points of light that emphasized the great manicured emptiness stretching beyond into the darkness.

His dad was right, Matt thought. The most valuable thing money could buy in a crowded world was space. The house came into view—three stories, white columns supporting a portico, wide stone steps. The drive divided around a stylized horse from whose mouth water poured into a series of mosaic pools, then rejoined to form a forecourt.

"Mmm, nice," Susan said. "Your basic French château. When was it built?"

"1913. The estate was laid out when Beverly Hills was bean fields, and Rodeo Drive was a bridle path. Way before even your grandparents were born."

The golf cart passed beneath the portico, came to a stop at a vast green and red striped tent erected over the tennis courts. Red carpets covered a wooden floor laid over the asphalt, chandeliers hung from the center pole, huge urns overflowing fruits and flowers were everywhere.

Matt took a couple of glasses of champagne from a tray offered by a waiter, handed one to Susan. They started down the lines of tables loaded with donated jewelry, sculpture, paintings, cases of wine, French luggage. Matt wondered who would be interested enough in all this stuff to bid for it, and sneaked a look at his watch. Another three hours at least. Dinner, a live auction, dancing. Thank God, Los Angeles was an early town. These affairs usually wrapped up by eleven.

Susan lingered behind a couple looking at a display of bags, soft leather, velvet, crocodile, lizard. Matt's eyes went to the woman who was caressing the bauble in her hand. She was very young, dark-haired, dark-eyed, gorgeous in a deep red satin suit.

Automatically, Matt checked her left hand. She had to be a generation younger than her husband, who was looking down at her as if he couldn't believe his good fortune. She glanced up at him through her lashes and he picked up the pad placed there for bids, scribbled his name, smiling as she made a soft appreciative sound and pulled his head down to kiss him before they moved on.

Susan picked up the item they had admired. "Isn't it lovely?"

"What is it?" Matt asked. It looked like a jeweled box in the shape and color of a tiger. Pretty gaudy, he thought.

"A Judith Leiber evening bag."

Matt picked up the pad, penciled in his name below the signature of the previous bidder, the amount of his own bid and table number.

"Matt! You may actually have to buy that, you know."

"Well, if you like it, I sure hope so." He'd acted impulsively, guilty for being late, for not being in love with her. He caught the eye of the man he'd just outbid.

"Looks like you've just saved me a fortune." The man had a drawl, as if long ago he'd come from the deep South. He was muscular, bulky without being fat, tanned, with sandy hair that was thinning. "Guess I should thank you." He did not look pleased.

"Well, it's for a good cause," Matt responded. He took Susan's arm and pointed. "There's Ned and Julie." As they squirmed through the crowd he whispered in Susan's ear, "I hope she doesn't make him top that bid."

Susan looked back. "She already has, he's signing his name again. Did you see those rubies she was wearing?"

"Oh, hell, I'll go back—"

"No, no. Don't be silly. I don't care."

"Hey, you two, where have you been?" Julie looked at them archly.

Matt dropped a kiss on her cheek. "Making bids. You look lovely, Jule. How are the boys?"

"They're fine. You should come visit," Julie said. "They miss you."

"You mean they miss Barney."

"They miss the beach, too."

Julie widened her dark eyes in the funny little kewpie doll way she had when she wanted something, and he said, "Okay, Jule, I'll call them. Are you bidding on anything, Ned?"

"I'm waiting for the private island. Comes up in the live auction after dinner."

"You're joking," Julie said.

Ned rolled his eyes.

"Who would donate a private island?" Julie asked.

"Someone who needs the tax break," a deep voice said. "Ned. Matt. Good to see you both."

Matt turned and met Erik Hoffmann's ice-blue eyes. Their paths crossed at business functions—Hoffmann was almost as legendary a figure as Nathan Broagan himself—but he was amazed the old man remembered their names. They didn't meet that often.

"Erik," Ned said.

The men shook hands. Hoffmann turned his smile toward the two women, and said to Ned, "Ned, please, introduce me to these lovely ladies."

Smiling, clearly a little awed, Ned complied. "Erik Hoffmann. Erik, my wife, Julie. And I think you may know our architect, Susan Dean."

Matt felt the first tickle of amusement he'd had in a while, watching Julie's expression as Hoffmann raised her hand to his lips, holding her eyes and bending slightly at the waist—the old world patrician exuding a courtly but definitely flirtatious charm. He was an imposing figure for all that he was past eighty, over six feet, more muscle than most guys thirty years younger. His hair was clearly a source of pride—probably once blond, it was now a thick white mane swept back from his forehead, long on the collar. His accent was still heavily German.

Hoffmann turned to Susan, went through the same performance and held on to her hand, smiling. "I know your work. When I was their age," his glance took in Ned and Matt, "I dealt only with men with pencils behind their ears. Things have improved."

Susan laughed. "Mr. Hoffmann. Thank you. I'm flattered."

"You must call me Erik, everyone does. No flattery. You are a good team. I, too, have a love of old buildings. Well, it is good to see you all." He nodded, started to leave, then turned back. He leaned close to Julie, and she swayed forward to hear what he was saying.

"Don't let Ned bid on that island," he whispered. "It's nothing but rocks. No water. Completely useless piece of real estate. I know. I donated it." His laugh was deep and contagious, drawing them into the joke.

"Wow, what a charmer," Julie said when he'd left. "Bet he's broken a few hearts in his time."

"Been married to the same woman for fifty years," Ned said.

"That means he hasn't broken some hearts? And still does, I bet."

"Don't be fooled, he's one of the hard men," Susan said.

"Oh, tell me, I can't wait."

"Not here, Jule," Susan said. "Later."

"Come on, Susie, what do you know? He's fascinating."

Susan shook her head as musical chimes announced dinner

and they joined the crowd exiting the tent, following a lighted gravel path that led to the house.

At the top of the steps, the Broagans, Nathan and his son Jake and daughter-in-law Gena, offered a general welcome as people passed, greeting friends by name, and exchanging air kisses on both cheeks with a few. The old man's evening suit hung on his bony shoulders and he looked frail and tired. Jake's smile was tense and fixed—the distance between the two men was only inches, but their body language spoke of miles.

Matt took Susan's arm, put his mouth close to her ear. "Let's just nod and smile."

The candlelit foyer had more square footage than Matt's entire house including his garage. In the main salons on either side, recessed spotlights picked out a few pieces of the famous Broagan collection of post-impressionists. Guests lingered as if in a museum before going on, through the foyer, and down outside steps into a white tented enclosure behind the house, filled with round tables set for the dinner, flowers and white linen, a lot of fine china and silver and sparkling glass.

An orchestra was playing show tunes. They found their table, not far from the dance floor and comfortably close to one of the many outdoor heaters. Three couples were already seated. The men rose to their feet, introduced themselves and their wives, shook hands. Pleasantries over, they went back to their own conversations.

Susan leaned toward Matt and said softly, "Do you think it's true what they say about him?"

Matt followed her eyes. A couple of tables over, Erik Hoffmann was at the center of a group of men a generation younger than he. No one was seated, and everyone was laughing.

"What, that he plays a kick-ass game of tennis?"

Susan glanced at Julie, and lowered her voice farther. "No, you know, that he was a concentration camp guard, and helped Nate and his younger brother to escape just before the end of the war."

"No, it's just one of those rumors, God knows how they get

started. If there had been anything there, *TIME* would have pounced on it."

Matt caught Julie straining to hear what they were saying. "We were talking about the cover story *TIME* did on Broagan last year."

Julie leaned closer. "I missed it. What did it say?"

"His name originally was Natan Broganski," Susan said. "He survived Dachau, the German death camp, came here totally penniless still in his teens, worked his way across the country to Los Angeles and got himself a job as a laborer in the construction industry just as it was throwing up thousands of houses for returning veterans. The story said he worked double shifts, six days a week, but he always spent one day in *shul*. He lived on air, saved every penny, and managed to get enough of a stake together to put a down payment on an old orange grove in the far reaches of the San Fernando Valley. Then he showed his real smarts." Susan grinned. "He got a young architect who was just starting out himself to take a chance and do work for him on spec when every other builder used a draftsman and prewar designs out of a plan book. The architect was the now famous Barnaby Farrell and Broagan Construction made its name by producing his elegant low-cost houses that were so popular, people had to enter lotteries for a chance to buy one. Broagan built thousands of them. Then he built the first Mt. Sinai Hospital, the first high-rise in Los Angeles, and the first Convention Center, and the rest as they say, is history. He has certainly left his mark on this city."

"Wow, that's quite a story," Julie said.

"He's an incredible man. The first year he turned a real profit, he opened a home for Jewish women and children. It's called Hannah's House now. It's the most respected shelter in the city."

"How absolutely wonderful," Julie said. "What a sweet man, I love him." She turned to Ned, her eyes moist. "Did you know all that, Ned, about Nate Broagan? Isn't he awesome?"

Ned's answer was lost in the sound of a riff from the orchestra and a drumroll. Lights dimmed, conversation fell off as a spotlight picked up Nate Broagan making his way to the microphone in the middle of the dance floor. Slightly built, his hair now a few strands of white across a dome of bare pink skin, he looked as if a gentle breeze would blow him off his feet. His voice reedy, he made a brief speech of welcome, introduced some of the political heavyweights—a former president and first lady of the United States, the senior senator from California and her husband, the present governor, the mayor of Los Angeles and their spouses. He urged everyone to have a good time, spend more money than they could afford—hard to imagine in this crowd, he said—and knew when to get off and leave them laughing.

Waiters poured wine and brought the first course, the noise level rose until the skirl of a bagpipe overcame all opposition and a piper in full Highland regalia, kilt, sporran, tartan over one shoulder, marched in. The sound was deafening.

"Be right back," Matt murmured in Susan's ear.

Susan looked at him, laughing. He thought the word she mouthed was, "Coward."

The auctioneer took up position on the stage, the bagpipe became background to the bidding on the first item to be auctioned—a week of grouse shooting at an ancient castle in Scotland. Someone asked about the plumbing, and the crowd broke into laughter.

Matt edged as unobtrusively as possible through the tables, ran up the steps, through the house, and stood for a few minutes admiring the distant view of the towers at Century City shimmering in a light mist that clung to them like a veil of silver. He took a breath, taking the cool moisture of evening into his lungs. Since the fire, he seemed never to get enough moisture, and tonight his chest was even more constricted. The weight of the conversation with Flores and Barstow had settled somewhere around his middle, squeezing his diaphragm.

A whiff of cigar smoke drifted with the sound of voices from a group of men twenty feet away at the edge of the light in the forecourt. Jake Broagan was among them.

"Matt, come on over, meet some people."

Matt walked toward them.

"Jake."

"Do you use these things?" Jake waved the cigar in his fingers.

"No, thanks. Not one of my pleasures," Matt said.

Jake laughed. "What are your pleasures? I've often wondered."

"A question I'm sure keeps you awake at night, Jake."

"See you didn't bring Ginn."

Matt looked at him without answering.

Grinning, Jake said, "Have you met Erik's nephews? Gerhart Hoffmann, Hans Hoffmann, visiting from Germany. This is Matt Lowell." Matt shook the proffered hands of a couple of the men Hoffmann had been laughing with earlier. Both had Erik Hoffmann's height and musculature, his ice-blue eyes. "And Leonid Petrov, Vassily Palinski from Moscow. Matt and I go way back," he said to the two Russians. "Known each other since we were kids."

"Are you visiting Los Angeles, also?" Matt said to the Russians.

"No, we have homes not far from here," Petrov said. "We have much business in Los Angeles."

Palinski puffed on his cigar without answering. Matt nodded. Anything not far from here would be in the multimillion-dollar class, a bit rich for men who looked to be in their mid-twenties at most.

Curious, he asked, "What business are you in?"

"Oh, import, export. That kind of thing."

An awkward silence ensued. Not illegal drugs, Matt guessed, even Jake wouldn't invite drug dealers into his father's house. Maybe arms, legal but dangerous. A whiff of the clandestine clung to them. "Well, if you will excuse me. Glad to have met you. Hans, Gerhart, enjoy your visit. I must get back."

"Don't blame you," Jake said. "I wouldn't leave Susan Dean alone for very long, either. Too bad I'm happily married, I'd give you a run for that one." He laughed, but to Matt's ears, he sounded as if he was going through the motions, doing what he always did, playing to his reputation. The other men looked at him without smiling.

He nodded, crossed the forecourt, aware of the silence behind him as he went up the steps into the house. The bagpipes were gone, the auctioneer was now taking bids for a dinner to be cooked by the most famous chef in the city.

"Just a moment, please," a male voice said. A hand touched his shoulder.

Matt turned. The speaker was tall, thin, unsmiling. The bulge of a weapon under his arm strained the fit of his tuxedo. Matt's gut clenched, and he felt beads of sweat break out across his top lip. The guy was a cop.

He was being arrested in front of five hundred of L.A.'s power elite. For the first time he understood why innocent men ran from the law.

CHAPTER 19

"Mr. Broagan would like to see you." The man nodded toward Nate Broagan seated between the former First Lady and the senior senator from California at a table set close enough to the dance floor for it to be a step away and far enough from the orchestra to make conversation possible.

Broagan caught Matt's eye, raised a hand and beckoned.

Matt felt himself breathe again. "Please tell Mr. Broagan I'll be right there."

He made a detour, explained where he was going to Susan, and shook his head when she asked what Nate wanted.

"I don't know. I'll tell you when I get back."

A minute later, he was standing by the side of a former president of the United States. Not a man he'd voted for, or admired when he was in office, but still, a man who had been President of the United States. He thought of what a kick it would be for his dad when he told him.

"Mr. Broagan, good evening. You wanted to see me?"

Broagan looked up. "Ah, there you are. Mr. President, this young man is Matt Lowell."

Matt found himself shaking hands first with the president, then with the senior senator from California, who, rumor had it, was sounding out support for her own run for the presidency in the next election. He knew the mayor from dealings with the city, nodded and smiled, greeting him by name. He nodded to the other women as he was introduced and wondered again what he was doing there, nodding and smiling at presidents and senators.

Nate pushed back his chair and started to struggle to his feet. Matt hurried to help. Nate leaned heavily on Matt's arm, nodding toward an opening at the back of the tent. When they were a few feet from the table, Matt said softly, "Jake's outside, Mr. Broagan. Shall I send someone for him?"

"If I needed Jake, I would have sent for Jake. Through that door and across the lawn is my office. The Kings are playing tonight at Atlanta. I want to know the score. Now, I'm going to smile and wave, and you're just going to keep going, otherwise we'll never get out of here. Understand?"

Matt smothered an urge to laugh. He followed Broagan's instructions, watching a master at work as people called greetings, received in return a smile, a wave, a word. They traversed the length of the tent without stopping, Matt motioned to a waiter to hold open the canvas "door," and they were outside in minutes.

As soon as the canvas fell back into place behind them, Broagan's step faltered, and the fingers clutching Matt's arm trembled. He took a breath and Matt could hear the wheeze in his lungs. The air was fragrant with a trace of wood smoke, but it had turned very chill, Thanksgiving was only a couple of weeks away. Matt realized again how frail the old man was.

"Are you all right, Mr. Broagan?"

"Of course I'm all right," the old man snapped. "Just across the path there."

His office was a two-story building, at least four thousand square feet, surrounded by trees and draped in Virginia creeper turning color—at this time of year it was already several shades of russet. Beads of lights traced a narrow, curving gravel path flowing like a stream across a perfect lawn. Matt paced his stride to the old man's faltering step.

"How is your father?" Broagan asked.

"My father?"

"Yes, your father. Are you hard of hearing, Matt?"

Matt laughed. "No, sir, I didn't know you knew him."

"Years ago. Fine architect. Is he still working?"

"Yes, but only for us, and only when he feels like it."

"Too bad. Rough and tumble of business keeps you young."

The rough and tumble was exactly what his father loathed. He said the one thing wrong with his chosen profession was the clients. Now that he could afford it, he preferred to fly small airplanes and play golf, do a little pro bono work for his sons and that only when the project interested him.

"Did he remarry?"

"No," Matt said shortly.

Broagan grunted. "Well, next time you talk to him, tell him I asked about him. Give him my best."

"Thank you, I will."

They had reached the brick patio fronting the building. The upper floor was dark, light spilled from the French doors only a few feet away, but Broagan stopped to catch his breath by a granite basin filled with water lilies. At the center was a life-size bronze of a child, a young girl, pouring water from an urn.

"That's very beautiful," Matt said.

"One of my favorites. English. Came from a manor house being sold so that the owner could pay his inheritance tax. Criminal. A family still going after three hundred years, and the damn government destroys their home." He motioned impatiently. "Come on, the door's open."

They crossed the patio to the door. Matt stood back to allow the old man to enter, then followed. Dark wood floor edged an Oriental carpet, a couple of cordovan leather couches faced each other in front of a log fire. An antique desk, the heavy drapes behind it drawn. The room was book-lined, no computers, fax machines, printers. The only evidence of modern technology. A library rather than office, a rich man's retreat.

"The television's in that cabinet. Find the channel while I use the bathroom. When you get to my age, every time you pass running water, you have to pee."

Matt laughed. Broagan seemed to gain strength from being inside his office. He crossed the room easily to a door in the corner, closed it, then reopened it to gesture toward the table between the couches. "That's a single malt from a small distillery I own in Scotland. Couple of fingers for me, no ice. Ice ruins a good whisky. Try it without, you'll see the difference." The door closed.

On the table was a silver tray with a decanter and glasses, ice bucket, linen napkins. Matt poured a couple of drinks, no ice in either glass, although he did not need to be told ice ruined a single malt. The old man must think he lacked an education.

Glass in hand, Matt turned on the power, started to cruise the channels looking for the Kings game. At home he had Malibu cable and the channels were different.

He heard the toilet flush, the door open and the sound of Nate Broagan's voice over running water. "Did you get the score?" The water stopped.

"Not yet."

"Oh, hell, leave it. That's not what I wanted to talk about." Nate came back into the room, indicated a chair, and took his own place behind his desk. "You and your brother sent a nice check for my personal charity. I wanted to thank you personally."

Surprised, Matt said, "That was our pleasure, Mr. Broagan. It's a wonderful organization. My sister-in-law thinks you are a sweet man."

Broagan laughed. He leaned back in his chair, and kept his dark hooded eyes on Matt's face. Matt tried not to fidget under the scrutiny, and wondered what the hell was going on.

"Okay, here's the deal," Broagan said. "I'd like to put your name forward to serve on the board."

Matt stared at him, astounded. His first thought was why him when Ned was the senior by ten years. "Well, that's an unexpected honor, Mr. Broagan. Jake didn't mention a thing about this when we had lunch."

"He doesn't know yet. We'll get to that." Broagan reached for his drink, swirled the amber liquid and breathed in the fragrance, then took a large swallow. "You've been a close friend of Jacob's for a long time."

That is not precisely how Matt would have described their relationship, but he nodded.

Broagan caught his hesitation. "Okay, maybe not that close, but a long time. You can work together. The present Board of Directors is getting old. We certainly do need new blood, younger men, I agree with that." He was continuing a discussion he'd had with someone else. "You met Jacob's friends tonight, the Russians? And Hoffmann's nephews? I'll be frank. I do not want these men involved in Hannah's. Jacob does. If we need new blood there, I'll decide who that will be." He took a breath. His voice became reedy, as if his fires were burning low. "You know, I wish you were closer with my boy, I worry—"

The outside door opened. Jake Broagan's voice said, "Pa, you all right?"

"Don't you ever knock, Jacob? Why shouldn't I be all right?" Broagan answered. "The Kings are in Atlanta, I want to see the score. You were off somewhere with your Russian kleptocrats, so I asked Matt here to help me get through the room. Did you count your fingers and toes when you left them, Jacob?"

"Please, let's not start with that again."

"What? You forget I was born in Poland and I know these people, these Cossacks?"

"You don't know these people. That war was over sixty years ago."

"Sixty years ago, a hundred years ago, we forget our families now, what happened to them?"

Matt stood, careful to keep his eyes from Jake. "If you'll excuse me, maybe I'd better leave—"

"Stay where you are, Matt," Nate said. "We've not finished talking."

Matt nodded. Anyone else and he'd walk out, but the old man had the rights that came with age. He turned his back on the two men, went to the television and picked up the remote. He tried to tune out the voices behind him. Maybe it was true what he'd heard and Jake really was moving to take control of Broagan Enterprises. It was privately held, a billion-dollar company with no shareholders to consult, so Jake could do it, but not without tearing his father apart.

But he wouldn't care about that, Matt realized. For as long as he could remember, Jake's father had been the butt of his jokes, the living legend, an Orthodox Jew with a code of ethics no one could live up to, least of all Jake. He'd spent his life on Nate Broagan's stage, but always with Erik Hoffmann in the wings, bailing him out of the trouble he got into, covering for him, pandering to his whims. And, now, interestingly enough, here were Hoffmann's nephews, moving right into place.

The voices continued. Two more minutes of this and Matt knew he'd have to leave. Jake would always remember he was a witness to this scene.

He clicked past the local news station, realized what he had heard, and went back.

The screen filled with the stark image of a crane bathed in a spotlight, lowering a wrecked car onto the road. In the foreground, the solemn reporter was saying, "Road rage appears to have claimed the life tonight of a well-known Malibu doctor. Dr. Phillip Halliburton was killed after his car, a witness says, was harassed for several miles on this winding road before plunging into the depths of the canyon. His body has been recovered, and now behind me, you can see Dr. Halliburton's Mercedes, being brought up from the bottom of Latigo Canyon."

"Jake," Matt said. "Jake, come look at this."

The old man said, "What are you doing there, Matt? That's not the sports channel."

"What?" Jake said impatiently. "You want the game? Channel 48. Here, let me." He reached over Matt's shoulder for the remote, then said, "Oh, God. Oh, no. Is that Phil Halliburton they're talking about? Oh, my God. I can't believe this."

Jake's face was ashen with shock. Matt thought his own face had to look the same. First Tommy Aguilar, now Phil.

"What's wrong?" Nate Broagan asked. "What is that, Jacob?"

Jake seemed incapable of answering so Matt said, "It's a friend of ours, Mr. Broagan. He's just been killed in Malibu. I have to go."

The old man continued with his questions, Jake's voice was shaky, explaining who Phil was. Matt closed the door behind him. The orchestra had moved on twenty years and was playing disco, the Bee Gees' "Staying Alive" floating through the air. He took the straightest path, across the wet grass, through the canvas door into the tent. Susan's place at the table was empty, as were Ned and Julie's. The only couple still seated was the owner of the vineyard in Santa Ynez who'd introduced himself earlier, and his wife. The man smiled, waved at the crowded floor. "Everyone's dancing."

Matt scanned the dancers, saw the white hair, the tall imposing figure, then Susan, laughing as Erik Hoffmann twirled her, brought her back to him. Matt jostled through the dancers.

"Susan, excuse me."

"Aah, you've come to claim your lady. You should not leave her alone so long." Hoffmann raised Susan's hand to his lips, smiling into her eyes. "Thank you for taking pity on an old man."

"Erik, you will never be an old man."

Hoffmann laughed with her, handed her into Matt's arms, bowed, and turned back to his table. Still laughing, Susan pushed her hair away from her face, looked at Matt. Her smile faded.

"What's the matter? Has something happened?"

Matt took her hand, led her off the dance floor, away from the orchestra, searching for Ned and Julie. He caught Ned's eye, jerked his head in the direction of their table.

"Hey, what's up? Where have you been all this time?" Ned said when they reached it.

"Phil Halliburton's been killed. I have to leave. Can you take Susan home?"

Ned looked confused. "Killed? Phil Halliburton? How do you know?"

"I saw it on television. I was with Nate Broagan in his study, and it was on the news."

"What were you doing in Broagan's study?'

"Ned, I don't know what I was doing there, he wants me on the Board of Hannah's House, but he hadn't got around to the details. I think something else might be going on, but I don't know what it is. The TV was on, I saw that Phil Halliburton had been killed. I have to leave."

"Why? What do you think you can do?"

"I can't go into it now. Can you take Susan—"

"Matt, you are not making any sense—"

"Of course we can take Susan home," Julie said quickly. "Don't worry."

"No, I'll leave with you, Matt," Susan said. "I'd rather do that."

"Susan, I don't want to spoil your evening."

"You won't. You haven't." Susan picked up her bag hanging on the back of her chair.

Matt took her arm and had to restrain himself from rushing her through the tables at a run. They were silent in the golf cart ride down the drive, Matt trying to formulate a story he could tell her and wishing she had stayed with Julie and Ned. He handed his ticket to the parking valet and the kid left in a cart.

Uncomfortable with the silence, Matt said, "I'm sorry to drag you away, Susan. You should have stayed."

"No, it's okay."

The Range Rover swept up. He put a hand under Susan's elbow to help her in—no flash of thigh, or flirtatious glances from lowered lids. Matt took the wheel, turned south on Benedict Canyon Drive. For a few minutes the silence deepened. He crossed Sunset Boulevard, took Beverly down to Wilshire, his eyes on the rearview. As far as he could tell, no one was following. Finally, he said, "Phil Halliburton's death is the second one this week. One of my old surfing buddies was killed the day before yesterday."

"Oh, I'm so sorry, Matt." Susan reached over and placed a hand over his. "Tell me about them."

Matt shook his head. "There's nothing to tell, just two guys I've known for a long time." Her sweetness made him feel even more like a worm. It seemed safer to hold on to her hand, and allow the silence to surround them. He drew into the curb outside her apartment in a small, smart building on El Camino Drive, a block behind the Beverly Wilshire Hotel. He checked the street in both directions as he got out, then walked her through the tree-shrouded patio to her door. Susan disarmed the security alarm, switched on a lamp. The apartment was tranquil and spare, white wood and neutral colors that complemented her vivid coloring.

"Do you want a drink?" She looked at the half-empty bottle of champagne swimming in a silver bucket of melted ice. "A fresh drink, I mean."

"Thank you, Susan, but I'd better get going."

She did not question him. Instead, she put a hand behind his head, drew him down, brushed her lips across his. Matt knew that if he chose to deepen the kiss, she would be receptive. He pulled her close and held her for a moment. "I have to go. I'll call you."

"Okay."

He saw her face, and wished, not for the first time, that he could fall in love with her. She was so much easier to deal with than Ginn.

He drove south on El Camino to Olympic, turned west, jammed on the gas, his eyes returning again and again to the rearview mirror. The image of Phil's car dangling from a flood-lit crane seemed imprinted on his brain. As unlikely as it was that someone would be following him from a fund-raiser in Beverly Hills, he took no chances. He made a sharp left onto Lincoln, another on Pearl, drove fast through the quiet residential neighborhood around Santa Monica College, made sudden turns, doubled back, always with one eye on the rearview. Finally, satisfied he was not followed, he drove to Pacific Avenue, then parked in the alley behind Ginn's house. He retrieved the Glock from the glove compartment, and got out.

His was the only vehicle in the alley. No one lingered in the shadows. On Pacific Avenue, the traffic was moderate, moving steadily. Matt turned into Ginn's street. Lights showed in her windows. No one was about.

The threat was not visible, but his gut told him it was there, somewhere, waiting.

CHAPTER 20

Matt pressed the bell, heard Barney's warning bark and the click of his nails on the hardwood floor as he came toward the door.

"Who is it?" Ginn's voice asked.

"Ginn, it's me. Matt."

The door opened. Ginn wore baggy sweats and big fluffy blue slippers and had pulled her hair into a topknot so that it looked as if it was erupting from the top of her head. She always did that when she worked at home to keep it out of her eyes. She looked about fifteen, Matt thought, instead of thirty-five. Barney shoved past her, thrust his nose into Matt's hand. He bent to ruffle the Lab's ears.

"Hey, boy, I miss you, too."

Ginn swept her eyes over his tux, and grinned. "You left a party to check in with your dog? How sweet is that? Come on in, you can visit with him inside." She left the door for him to close, walked back down the hall.

He closed the door and followed her, Barney at his heels. A computer screen glowed in her small office off to the right, but the family room was empty.

"Where is everyone?"

"Sophie's upstairs asleep and my mom's gone home."

"Gabrielle's not here? Ginn, you promised you would not be here alone."

"Oh, for God's sake, Matt. Gabrielle had to go home and water her plants and check her mail. Tomorrow morning she's having breakfast with the woman I told you about, the expert in Slavic languages, then she'll be back."

Matt went to the television, tuned it to the local news station. The smiling weatherman was pointing at a three-dimensional map. Matt turned off the sound.

"Phil Halliburton was killed tonight."

"Phil Halliburton? No. No. My God, how?" Ginn dropped into a chair. "How did it happen?"

"A traffic accident. I was at a fund-raising dinner at the Broagan's and I happened to see the news. Something's going on. I don't know what it is, but gunmen attack the house, Tommy Aguilar is killed in a bad drug deal with bikers, and now Phil is dead from a traffic accident. Apart from you, they were the only people who knew about those kids I saw. That's too much coincidence for me. Ginn, please, don't argue, not about this. Get some things together, then wake the girl up. You can call Gabby from the car."

"Where are we going?"

"To Bobby's. He's got weapons and he knows how to use them."

Looking alarmed, Ginn said, "Have you told him about her?"

"I'll call him on the way up."

"Bobby will turn her in, he'll have to. Matt, we've been over this. Think about it. No one knows Sophie is with me."

"All I know for sure is that two people who knew about those kids are dead."

"Do you realize what it will do to that girl to be roused out of a deep sleep, bundled into a car and driven away? I am not doing that to her."

The news was over and the TV screen brightened into a sit-com. Matt picked up the remote and clicked it off, then checked the locks on the French doors into the back garden and shot home the dead bolt.

"Okay, I'll stay here tonight."

"No, I don't want you to do that."

"I'm not leaving you alone here tonight, Ginn, so don't waste your breath arguing. First thing tomorrow, I'm calling Bobby."

"And have her taken into custody. Is that okay with you?"

"Maybe she'd be safer. You sure would be."

Ginn took a deep breath and went into her office. She saved the work on her computer, and was staring at the window when Matt entered the room. She did not turn and he stood behind her, pulled her close to his chest, his arms around her body. Nothing else but Ginn mattered.

"What do you see?" he said against her hair.

The black night on the other side of the window threw back their reflection, a small, slim woman wearing sweats, the tall man behind her in a tuxedo.

"A mismatched pair." Ginn moved from his arms. "I'm going to bed. You can make up the couch down here in front of the fire, or if you want, you can use Gabby's room. I'll put fresh linens and a pillow out for you, and leave the door open so you know which room it is. Good night."

Matt linked his hands under his head and stared up at the beams spanning the ceiling. He had not undressed, just removed his coat and tie, the damn fool patent leather evening shoes and cummerbund before lying on the couch. He thought of checking the locks again, but he'd done that already. Twice.

The girl's shrieks pierced the silence. Matt shot to his feet, ran along the hall and up the stairs. Doors were open, the shrieks were now moans, and he followed the murmur of Ginn's voice, low and soothing, coming from the bedroom overlooking the garden. He hovered in the doorway feeling helpless. The girl was sitting up, her eyes wide, staring at some horror only she could see.

Ginn stroked her hair, crooning wordlessly, until the sound stopped. The girl slumped against the pillows, then turned over onto her side. Ginn tucked the duvet around her, covering her shoulders. She ran a hand over Barney's head, urged him closer to the slight body, then drew Matt into the hall, leaving the door open.

"She'll be all right," she whispered. "She wasn't really awake."

"How often does this happen?"

"It's been every night so far."

She wore blue flannel pajamas, her feet were bare. Matt brushed the hair back from her face, and she looked up at him. Matt pulled her closer, expecting her to resist, but she leaned into him and pressed her face into his chest. For a long moment Matt held her, doing his best to be undemanding, but he knew it couldn't last. He felt the stirring of his body, and knew she had to feel it, too. He waited for her to move away. She didn't. Matt touched her lips with his. She responded and he drank her in, the kiss feeling like water to a man dying of thirst.

"Matt…"

"Shhh," he said against her mouth. "Shhhh. I love you. You are everything to me, Ginn."

The door to her bedroom was open, she allowed him to draw her toward it without protest. The streetlamp outside gave just enough light for him to see the buttons on her pajamas, her small perfect breasts as the jacket fell to the floor. Ginn stepped out of her pajama pants, fumbled with the studs on his dress shirt. Matt shrugged the shirt from his shoulders, lifted her onto the bed. He buried his head in her belly, the soft pubic hair brushing his face, breathing in the scent of her body, so familiar, yet strange. It had been so long.

* * *

Ginn stirred and Matt held her closer as if unwilling to let the night end, but a gray dawn was lightening the sky.

"What time is it?"

Matt raised an arm and glanced at his watch. "Six-thirty."

Ginn sat up, eluding Matt's reach as he tried to pull her back into the warmth. She slipped from the bed, crossed the room and put on a robe, the navy blue terry cloth he'd bought for her when he'd bought his own. She picked his clothes up from where he'd left them on the floor and put them on a chair.

"I'll start coffee while you shower. Don't make any noise. Sophie won't wake up for a while."

She felt his eyes on her as she left the room.

Downstairs, she cracked the front door, reached for the newspaper on the porch, then padded down the hall. The family room was bleak in the dark and Ginn lit the gas logs. The flames and glowing artificial ashes gave a semblance of warmth that did nothing to dispel the chill in her heart. She went across to the kitchen area, put on the coffee and reached into the refrigerator for orange juice. She stood with her back against the counter, sipping the juice, remembering when a night like the one just past had brought with it a sense of joy in loving and being loved. This morning she felt as if she had a hangover. Post-coital remorse. Ten months of saying no to herself, no, she wouldn't take his calls, no, she wouldn't drive by his office, no, she wouldn't take a walk along the beach and accidentally run into him. No, no, and no, shot to hell in one night.

Matt entered the room dressed in tuxedo pants, black suspenders over his pintucked shirt, his feet bare—he always looked so handsome in black tie. His hair was damp from the shower and slicked back, his dark blue eyes clear and smiling. Obviously, no problems with a hangover there.

Ginn put a mug of coffee on the table, handed him the newspaper. "I don't see anything about Phil's death—"

Matt caught her hand. "*Mei Hua*." Fragrant Flower, the teasing love name he knew made her smile.

Ginn pulled away from him. "No. I don't want to hear anything like that. I'm sorry I allowed last night to happen. It was wrong of me—"

Matt attempted to put an arm around her and she moved out of his reach. "Wrong? It wasn't wrong. What do you mean by that? We're great together—"

"Yes, we are. In bed. The sex is terrific." Ginn felt she had to get outside, take in some cold air. She went to the door that led into the garden, turned the lock, struggled with the door. Matt reached above her head and released the dead bolt. She jerked the door open, leaving him standing in the doorway as she strode off down the garden to the gate, turned and walked back. When she lived with him, she'd take a run on the beach when she needed to clear her head, but if she tried to do that now, she knew he'd stop her. If they were going to fight this morning, the arena would not be whether or not she went through her garden gate, down the alley to the beach.

She went back to where he stood on the steps watching her pace, brushed past him back into the kitchen. "We've been through all this before, a thousand times. I don't want to go there again. This is not good for either of us. I'll help with Sophie, but on my terms and that means no Bobby. And we are not starting up again, Matt."

"Then what was that last night?"

"A mistake. Do you want marriage and children, Matt? I mean, now, this year, not some time in the distant future?"

"Ginn, you know I love you—"

"Don't. Don't keep saying that. That is not what we're talking about," Ginn said. "I'm sorry about last night, Matt. Sorry for you, sorry for me. It shouldn't have happened. It won't again."

"Ginn, it's not that black and white."

She felt suddenly tired. "Yes, it is. God, Matt. Why is it you refuse to understand?"

"What I understand is that there's an empty place inside me that only you can fill."

She believed him. She believed she was the love of his life. It wasn't enough. She didn't answer. The silence between them lingered. She picked up her coffee mug, put it into the sink.

Matt went back to the couch, slipped his bare feet into his patent leather evening shoes, shoved black silk socks in his pocket.

"I'll go home and change, then I'll call you." He put on his jacket. "Don't walk Barney outside, okay? Let him do what he has to do in the yard."

"All right."

"Promise me not to leave this house or open the door except for Gabby or me."

"Matt, I promise, all right?"

He reached into the pocket of his tuxedo jacket. "I'll leave this with you." He put the Glock on the kitchen table.

Ginn stared at the weapon, gray and ugly. "No, don't. Don't leave that here. I don't need it. I don't know how to use it, and I wouldn't anyway."

"Okay, then keep it because it will make me feel better. All you have to do is point it, and pull the trigger. Don't let the kid see it, though, might give her ideas." Matt grinned at her, but she was unable to smile back. "I'll go out the back gate. Make sure the bolt is in place as soon as I'm in the alley."

Ginn picked up the gun with two fingers, dropped it into the drawer with the table napkins, then followed him down to the gate. As soon as he had slipped through, she closed it and shoved the bolt home, stood listening until she heard the engine of the Range Rover, then walked slowly back to the house.

She felt as if some very delicate scar tissue had been just ripped open.

* * *

Matt bombed north, and by seven-thirty turned onto Malibu Road. Sea mist coated the windscreen, and clung to the hills above the road. He breathed deeply, relishing the moisture and the tang of salt in the air. The newspaper was lodged in the charred remains of the bougainvillea. He grabbed it as he walked past, opened the door into the kitchen. The place was lifeless and dismal in the gray light of morning. If Ginn still lived here, the house would be filled with flowers. Even on the foggiest days she brightened everything. It didn't help that the room stunk of the whisky he had not drunk the night before. He poured it into the sink, sprayed water to wash it down, clicked on the answering machine as he passed to go into the bedroom to change. Only half listening, he heard the same message he'd heard last night as he was walking out to pick up Susan, Julie's voice warning him not to be late. The message ended, another started.

The voice was male. Matt stopped when he realized he was listening to Phil Halliburton. He sounded distraught. Matt rushed back into the living room, hit the replay button. Phil's voice said, "I've just heard about Tommy Aguilar. He was murdered. I got in too deep and I don't even know how it happened. I'm so sorry, so sorry, Matt. I said I'd do it, but I saw her with Gabby and I thought what am I doing? How did I get to this? And I couldn't. I'm through. I'm going to put an end to it." He was suddenly calmer, as if he'd listened to his own words and realized he had come to a decision. "I'm going to do it. I need to talk to you. Call me as soon as you get this."

Heart racing, Matt played the message again, then picked up the phone, hit the button he'd programmed for Bobby Eckhart, counting the rings until Bobby picked up.

"Eckhart."

"It's Matt. Phil Halliburton was killed last night, did you hear?"

"No. I was off duty last night. How?"

"Is Sylvie there?"

"No, she's in San Diego. Her sister's baby came early, she's gone down to help for a couple of weeks. What's this about Halliburton?"

"It was supposed to be a traffic accident, but I don't think it was, Bobby. I think he was murdered. He phoned me last night but I wasn't here. I picked up the message a couple of minutes ago. Can I bring Ginn and a…" Matt hesitated, then said, "friend up to your house today, this morning? Are you on duty today?"

"Not until later. What are you talking about, who would kill Phil Halliburton? What friend?"

"I'll tell you when I get there. Just don't talk to anyone about Phil until I can tell you what I know."

"Are you in trouble?"

"Yes, I think you could say that. Maybe."

Bobby didn't waste time on questions. "Okay, come on up."

"Thanks." Matt disconnected, hit Ginn's number. As soon as she answered, he said, "Ginn, listen to me." He kept his voice calm, but he talked fast before she could interrupt. "When I got home, I had a phone message Phil Halliburton left last night. It was Phil who tried to run down Gabby. He said he wanted to talk to me but then he was killed before we could meet. I want you to get the girl and Barney into the car and drive up to Bobby's. He's expecting you. Make sure you are not followed. I'm starting back down to your place now, but don't wait for me. I'll watch for you on the highway and drive up behind you. Take the Glock with you."

There was a brief silence.

"Okay. I'll get her there."

He took just enough time to change, jeans and a shirt, the first jacket that came to hand from the closet. In ten minutes he was back on the coast highway driving south. Traffic was thicker, but still not heavy. He caught the red light at Sunset Boulevard and the Coast Highway, and spotted Ginn's silver BMW in the opposite lane going north—she hadn't wasted any time getting on the road. He jumped the light, did a U-turn, cutting across an old Honda topped with surfboards, waved an apology as the young driver leaned on the horn and his passenger hung out of the window to flip him the bird. As he settled in behind her, Ginn waved an arm out of the window to let him know she had seen him.

He was close on her tail when she turned up Las Flores Canyon Road. After the turn, he drew onto the grass shoulder and watched out of his side mirror. No one followed, so he gunned the engine, skidded back onto the asphalt. Within minutes of leaving the coast, the road had climbed a thousand feet. A thick gray mist hung in the canyon below, spilling across the road in dense patches. The outline of Ginn's car was barely discernible in the mist, and Matt closed the distance between them fearing she would miss the turn into Bobby's driveway now that the great cedar that used to mark the entrance had gone. Matt went around her, near the top of the hill, found the charred remains of the hundred-year-old cedar and swung into the driveway, tapping his horn to let Bobby know they were there. He got out as Ginn's car crunched over the gravel and came to a stop behind Bobby's Jeep. Barney had his nose pressed to the rear passenger window, and Ginn leaned back to open the door. Barking a greeting, the excited dog leapt out, circled Matt, rushed over to Bobby as he emerged from the house, then made the rounds of the front yard to mark his territory.

"Hi, Ginn." Bobby started toward the BMW. "Who's that you've got there with you?"

Matt intercepted him. "Bobby, hold on a minute."

Bobby stopped and waited for Matt to join him. "What? Who is this kid? What's the mystery?"

Matt called to Ginn to take her time. "Let's go in the house. They'll come in when they're ready." He called Barney knowing it would make it easier for Ginn to persuade Sophie to get out of the car, and follow the Lab inside.

Looking puzzled, Bobby led the way back inside the small

adobe. It had been there for sixty years or more, one of the last originals in the canyon, built when water came from a well, and light from kerosene lanterns. The ceiling was low; a fireplace, handcrafted of smooth rocks brought up from the creek below, dominated one wall and was flanked by shelves filled with books and a collection of Native American baskets and pottery. The house smelled faintly of woodsmoke as it always did, even in those years when wildfires hadn't scourged the hills. Something about the way the fireplace had been built.

Bobby stepped behind the Mexican-tile counter that separated the tiny kitchen from the main room, poured coffee into a couple of mugs. "Okay, so what's this about Phil Halliburton, and who is this girl?" He pushed a mug toward Matt, leaned his back against the sink with the kitchen window behind him framing the steep mountain slope on the other side of the canyon.

Matt perched on a high stool at the counter, spooned sugar into the mug of coffee, stirred, put the spoon on a napkin before answering, considering his words. "I told you I saw some kids where the girl's body was found. Well, what I didn't tell you was that one of the girls was in bad shape, so I took her home with me and called Phil Halliburton."

Bobby came upright. "You what?" As if unable to contain himself, Bobby half turned away, then swung back. "Christ, Matt, where are your brains? First you tell me you've lied to a couple of homicide dicks. Now you're telling me you took a strange kid home with you? A kid who may know something about the death of the girl on Encinal? What were you thinking? Why didn't you take her down to Malibu emergency if you were so damned concerned?"

"Bobby, I wish to God I'd left her there, but I didn't. Let me finish."

He went through the sequence of events, the girl in shock; her illegal status; her obvious terror and the fear she would kill herself, the attack on the house, the visit last evening from Flores and Barstow, Phil's death, the phone message. "You can hear it later, it's still on the machine. He said Tommy was murdered."

"No shit. Who would have guessed, a knife in the belly? That was probably the Satans. You saw them dealing out of the Mermaid."

The front door opened. "Okay if we come in?" Ginn asked.

"Sure." Bobby shot Matt a hard look as he left the kitchen to kiss Ginn's cheek. "Good to see you, Ginn." He smiled down at the top of Sophie's bent head. "Hi. Come on in. My name's Bobby."

"Sylvie at work?" Ginn asked.

"She's with her sister in San Diego for a couple of weeks."

"Oh, nice."

The young girl kept close to Ginn. As soon as she spotted Barney, she put her hand down to her side and waggled her fingers until the Lab left Matt's side and went to her. Ginn led her to the nearest couch in front of the fire, but the girl went to the other side of the coffee table, and perched on the edge of the sofa facing the door.

"I called my mom from the car," Ginn said. "She's coming straight here after her breakfast meeting. I hope that's all right, Bobby?"

"Sure, I like to keep open house. Come one, come all."

Ginn laughed. She filled a couple of mugs of coffee, sat next to the girl and put an arm around her shoulders.

"She's shaking," she said quietly. "Why don't you guys go and look at the scenery outside while we girls watch the fire?"

Bobby picked up his cell phone and coffee, opened the French door to the patio, followed Matt outside to the old redwood picnic table under the sycamore. The fire had done the same erratic dance here as it had elsewhere in the mountains, the garden edging the canyon was verdant and untouched. Matt sat on the table, his feet on the bench.

"I've got some contacts in the CHP," Bobby said. "Maybe I can find out something about Phil." He tapped out a number, gave his name and rank. "Is Charlie Brandon around there? Yeah, I'll wait." He glanced at Matt, nodded, then said, "Charlie, Bob Eckhart. I just heard a friend of mine was killed on Latigo last night. Yeah, Dr. Philip Halliburton. What happened?"

Bobby got up, paced along the edge of the brick patio, listening, asking questions, his voice all but inaudible. After a few minutes conversation, he disconnected and returned to the table.

"They've got a witness who says she saw Phil's Mercedes and a vehicle that sounds as if could be an SUV racing down the canyon. She didn't actually see Phil's car go off, and there's only one set of skid marks where Phil lost control and crashed through the barrier. But according to the witness, the other vehicle did stop, and a man got out, but as she came around the curve and slowed to look herself, he got back in and took off at high speed. The witness, an older woman, was pretty shaken, it was a wonder she was able to call 911. She didn't know the make or color, just that it was dark. She didn't get plates, so there is no identification. She couldn't describe the guy who got out."

"So Phil was helped into the bottom of that canyon."

Bobby shrugged. "Sure sounds like it."

"What chance does the CHP have of finding out who it was?"

"None to zero. No make of car, no license plate. The Mercedes is a total wreck, they've got nothing to go on. You want to make a guess how often this happens in the city?"

"This is not the city, Bobby, this is Malibu. Have you heard of a rehab house for rich kids maybe up in the hills?"

Bobby shook his head. "No. There's no such thing, we'd know about it. Why?"

"The night he died, Tommy told me someone had been into the Mermaid asking questions about runaways from a rehab." Matt nodded toward the house. "Look at that kid inside. She doesn't speak, she's been physically abused, she's got scars on her body like the girl who died, she's terrified of men. It doesn't take much to guess she's been sexually abused as well. Sure, those kids looked like runaways, but definitely not rich runaways from a rehab. One of them was only ten. Another girl's dead. So who are they? What are they doing out there alone?"

The crease between his eyebrows suddenly deeper, Bobby looked at him. "What are you saying?"

"Phil was involved in something that got him killed. A ring of pedophiles, maybe."

"Man, I can't sit on this." Bobby stared at his house as if he could see the young girl through the thick adobe walls. "I'm sorry, Matt, I'm going to have to report it."

Matt stood up. He ran his hand over the stubble on his chin. "Then they'll come for that girl in there and lock her up. Ginn's an officer of the court, she's harboring an illegal alien, and I've already denied seeing anyone. They are going to come down hard."

"What else can I do? These kids are connected to a dead girl. Even if the case is closed, I can't wait on this any longer, Matt, I'm a cop, remember? The law?"

"That girl in there is the key to what Phil was involved in. I just need some time while we try to find out something about her."

"What do you want me to do? You know I can't let it go."

"But you can hold off. Just hold off, that's all. Why not? The bodies are missing, the case is officially closed, what difference does it make?"

The sound of a car turning into the driveway interrupted the discussion.

"That must be Gabby," Matt said.

Eckhart shook his head in frustration. "Jesus, you are one big pain in the ass."

CHAPTER 21

Gabrielle's arm appeared out of the car window. She waved, then parked her Renault behind Matt's Range Rover, and called a greeting as she got out. A woman emerged from the passenger side, looked warily over the door at Barney, barking as he rushed to greet them and stayed where she was.

"He's okay," Matt called. "Come on, Barns. Into the house." He grabbed the dog's collar, walked him inside, closed the door, and returned to the group standing in the driveway.

Gabby continued with the introductions she had already started, nodding at Matt. "And this is Matt Lowell. My colleague, Mrs. Amira Ghoni, Matt. Mrs. Ghoni comes from Bosnia, she's an expert in Slavic languages and kindly offered to come and speak to our little girl, see if she can find out something about her."

"That's very good of you," Matt said.

They shook hands, and started toward the house. Amira Ghoni was carefully made up, her pale eyebrows plucked into an arc, her well-cut hair loose around her face, but her skin was deeply lined, and weathered as if she had spent too much time exposed to the elements. She could have been any age from forty to sixty, and gave the impression of a great sadness. It didn't help that she was dressed in unrelieved black, trousers, sweater, jacket. Even her scarf was black.

"The girl does not speak, I understand." Amira's English was fluent and precise. "I hope I can help. I give whatever time I can to the refugee agency that helped me when I first came here." She glanced up at Matt. "I was myself displaced, lived in a camp for many months, maybe Gabby told you."

Gabby hadn't but Matt nodded. Televised images leapt to his mind, traumatized refugees peering out of tents surrounded by mud, too numb to protest their exploitation by camera crews. He had the feeling that Amira Ghoni had lost all that mattered to her.

Bobby opened the front door and stood back to allow the two women to enter. Ginn stood as they came in, her hand resting reassuringly on the girl's shoulder.

Gabby smiled at her daughter, then sat on the edge of the coffee table in front of the girl. She picked up Sophie's hand, holding it between both of hers while she spoke slowly and softly in English.

"I've brought someone to talk to you. There is nothing to be afraid of, she wants to help. Her name is Amira Ghoni."

The girl's eyes flickered, and Barney thumped his tail gently as she held the roll of loose skin above his collar.

Gabby moved to allow Amira to take her place.

"Zdravo," Amira said gently. *"Moje ime je Amira. Kako se zoves?"* She leaned forward. "Do you understand me?"

The girl remained motionless, her hand deep in Barney's coat as if he were her lifeline, but her already pale face became ashen, then flooded with color.

At the kitchen counter, Matt said softly, "Do you know what she's saying, Gabby?"

"Amira introduced herself and asked her name, then I think

she asked whether Sophie understood her. If she doesn't, Amira speaks several Slavic languages, she'll keep trying."

"I think she understood this one."

Sophie slid her eyes toward the two men, then stared at Amira Ghoni. Her unspoken message was clear. She would not respond until the two men left. Matt touched Bobby's arm, nodded toward the door to the patio.

It was close to noon when Ginn stepped outside. She stood motionless, as if she needed time to bring herself from another time and space to her present surroundings.

Her eyes locked onto Matt's. "She talked to us. I had no idea, not like this. Not personally, you know?"

"Yes," Matt said. He didn't know what she was talking about but could see she needed a response. "Is she all right?"

Ginn shook her head. "I don't think she'll ever be all right, Matt. Never."

She sat down next to Matt at the picnic table, and across from Bobby. "Her name's Laila. She's fifteen. She comes from a place called Filipovici. It's a small town in Bosnia."

"Bosnia!" Matt was astounded. "So where are her parents? Are they here with her?"

Ginn shook her head. "No. Her father's dead, at least she thinks he is. And her brothers." She looked from Matt to Bobby. "They were taken away. The men in her town were rounded up by Serbs and taken away. None of the men have been heard from since. Her father, two brothers, one fourteen, one fifteen. They were driven like cattle out of the town. Anyone who fell was clubbed to death right there, no bullets. There was blood everywhere, rivers of it, she said. Her brothers kept walking, Serbs drove the women back when they tried to reach their children..." She stopped.

"I'll get you a drink." Bobby started toward the house.

"No, don't go in, Bobby," Ginn said. "Mrs. Ghoni's still talking to her. It's taking some time, you know, to find the right questions to keep her talking. She says her mother and sister Nadja were also taken away, but they came back a week later. A few days after they got home, Nadja hanged herself. She was only thirteen. Laila was seven. She and her mother are all that are left of her family."

A moment passed in frozen silence.

"Where's her mother now?" Matt asked.

"She won't say, or can't say, I don't know. She won't tell how she got the marks on her body, either. When Amira asked her, at first she just shook her head. Amira pressed her and she started to rock and make that sound." Ginn looked at Bobby. "She sounds like I think a dying animal must sound when it's caught in a steel trap. I had to get out of there for a minute, I couldn't..." Ginn got up. "I'd better get back."

Gently, Matt caught her arm and urged her back down onto the picnic bench. "She's got enough people in there, and she's got Barney."

As he spoke, the patio door opened again and Amira Ghoni came out of the house. The sound of the girl's keening reached them.

"Oh, my God," Bobby said. His face was suddenly pale.

Matt glanced at him. In spite of all that he'd seen as a cop for the last fifteen years, Bobby had never become hardened. Other people's trouble still got to him. He'd been the same when they were kids.

Mrs. Ghoni pulled the door closed softly, and crossed the patio. She looked as distressed as Ginn.

"I used your telephone," she said to Bobby. "I hope that is all right?"

"Of course, sure."

"Ginn told you about this little girl? Laila?" She spoke to the two men. "What has happened to her?"

Bobby nodded. "Some of it."

"Well, I think what she says is just the tip of something. When I asked her about how she got here to the United States, it was as if she went away, her spirit went somewhere else, I don't know how else to say it. She started to make that terrible sound. I do not believe it is good to make her go on, not without expert help, a doctor maybe, or someone to help her." Mrs. Ghoni's English was suddenly uncertain, as if she were thinking in one language and her thoughts were outpacing her ability to translate into another before she spoke. She took a breath, said, "I'm sorry. Please, forgive me. I told you I do work for the Coalition for Aid to Balkan Refugees, yes? I called my colleagues there, and told them about her. They are getting in touch with ASTA to find someone who can ascertain if I am right."

"What is that, ASTA?" Matt asked.

"Anti-Slavery and Trafficking Alliance. I think this girl has been trafficked."

CHAPTER 22

An open Jeep swung into Bobby's drive and parked by the cedar. A tall lanky form swung easily to the ground—early forties, long patrician face, narrow, wire-rimmed glasses on a beak of a nose. He was dressed in chinos, lightweight urban hiking boots, suede windbreaker. Everything about him signaled success.

"John Cargill. I'm a lawyer. I do pro bono work for ASTA. They told me you have a girl here you think might have been trafficked. Is that right?"

Matt nodded. He was still struggling with what Mrs. Ghoni had told them about trafficking, the modern day version of slavery. If Matt thought about slavery at all, which was almost never, it was Uncle Tom's Cabin, John Brown and Harper's Ferry, the Civil War, Abraham Lincoln and the Gettysburg Address.

He introduced Mrs. Ghoni, then himself and Bobby Eckhart—Ginn had gone back into the house to be with Laila. At Bobby's insistence, he left out the fact that Bob was with the sheriff's department until they were sure the guy wasn't a newshound likely to call the media and name names for the sake of getting publicity for his cause. Bob considered his career was already in enough jeopardy.

Cargill shook hands while walking toward the house. "So what makes you think she's been trafficked, Mrs. Ghoni?"

"You will see when you talk to her. She knows you are coming, she will speak to you. First I think you should talk to Mr. Lowell. He found her."

"You found her?" Cargill stopped. "You want to tell me how that came about?"

The words were friendly, businesslike, but with a distinctly wary undercurrent. Ginn could come up with the same lawyerly tone.

Matt went over the bare bones of what had happened, ending with Tommy Aguilar's murder, and Phil's death two nights later. Cargill listened without interruption until Matt finished, then asked a few questions, the condition of the other youngsters, the area in which they had been found, had they been seen since Aguilar's death.

"You understand I am not interested in the investigation into the deaths of your friends, or anything else. My interest here is in the trafficking, if indeed that has taken place, but we'll talk more later. Right now I want to see this girl, find out what she can tell us. It would be better if you both stay outside."

Bob looked as if he was about to protest, but there would be no argument from me, Matt thought. Three guys coming at her through the front door would look to that kid like a bunch of storm troopers.

Mrs. Ghoni led Cargill to the house, knocked, called a greeting in the same language she had used earlier.

Bobby waited until the door closed behind them. "I'm a cop and whatever she has to say, I need to hear it first hand. I know we can't crowd her, but you and I can go in through the kitchen."

"No, there are too many people in the house already. I'll stay here."

Matt walked over to the edge of the canyon. A deer path led to the bottom, and he could see the creek was running with water again after the recent rains. The mist still hung in milky patches below the rim, but mostly it had burned off. A couple of miles down canyon, the Pacific Ocean was a wavering patch of blue.

It was a great view, quiet and peaceful above the real world it seemed, the only sounds birdsong and the rustle of leaves. Overhead, a couple of red tail hawks had caught a thermal and were turning in lazy circles, watching, hunting for anything that had survived the burn.

An hour passed, the minutes were dragging when a grim-faced Bobby emerged from the house, Ginn and the lawyer behind him. Matt walked toward them.

"Are you all right, Ginn?" He knew it was a stupid question as he said the words. She was not all right. Her eyes were red and puffy, her skin tight across her lovely cheekbones.

"I'm numb, I think."

Cargill lowered his long frame to the redwood bench.

"Okay, so let's talk." He waited until everyone had taken a seat. "This appears to be a genuine case of trafficking, and if what Laila says is true, my guess is what you've uncovered is the tip of a very nasty iceberg."

"Of course it's true," Ginn said. "How could she make up a story like that?"

"You'd better fill me in first," Matt said.

"Yes, well, her family appears to have been decimated by the war in Bosnia. Her father and two brothers were driven away, her older sister committed suicide—"

Ginn interrupted. "He knows that, I told him earlier."

Cargill nodded. "Okay. So Laila and her mother spent the last winter of the war hiding in the ruins of their home. Her childhood is nothing short of a horror. During the day, soldiers roved the streets shooting anything that moved. The mother ventured out only at night to scavenge for food. Laila stayed alone, hidden in the cellar. Somehow they survived, the war ended, but the town was virtually destroyed. Few men were left. The surviving women, eight years later, are trying to cope. Rape continues to be commonplace.

"Last spring, a woman who said she represented a U.N. organization spoke to Laila's mother about a new summer program in Germany, languages, computers, early job training. The lady was well dressed, had the right documents, official papers for the mother to sign. Obviously the papers were forged, but the mother had no way of knowing that. The poor woman had to scrape together 350 marka, about a couple hundred dollars, to get Laila accepted into the program. It was a fortune, but somehow she did it."

"What did she think she was paying for?" Matt asked, appalled.

"Well, supposedly for papers and visas, and to help with the schooling Laila was going to get in Germany. Any mother would be suspicious of a free ride. So Laila and three other kids she didn't know left together, a boy, two girls. She never saw them again after they reached Berlin. She was taken to a house, raped as soon as she arrived, beaten and subsequently raped daily."

Bobby Eckhart met Matt's eyes. He looked sick. "Sons of bitches."

"Other kids were there, it appears these people specialized in youngsters. They were told their families would be killed if they tried to get away," Cargill said. "Just after she arrived, two girls tried it anyway. They were beaten to death. Their bodies were left on the floor of one of the rooms for a couple of days as an object lesson."

Matt broke the strained horrified silence. "Okay, that was Germany. How did she get to Malibu? How did she even get into the country?"

Bobby snorted. "Our borders? Are you serious? You just walk in."

"There are a number of trafficking routes, but in this case, that's just about right," Cargill said. "She left Germany with six other kids. The official story was that they were students on their way to study in Mexico. The group leaders, a couple she knew as Bernhard and Juliette Pfeiffer, held their passports, also forged of course. The kids were warned to shake their heads and smile if anyone spoke to them, but if immigration insisted, or spoke to them in their own language, they were to confirm they were going to study in Mexico and were changing planes at Los Angeles."

Cargill took a thin cigarillo out of his pocket, stripped the wrapping, lit it with a gold lighter. Sweet smelling blue smoke drifted in the air.

"At LAX, passengers in transit are met by a uniformed security guard who escorts them from terminal to terminal. The guard who met Laila's group simply escorted them out of an exit door. A van was waiting at the curb, they ended up at a house that she thinks was about an hour away from the airport. A couple of guys there made sure all seven kids knew what lay in store for them."

"Laila said they were Albanians here and in Berlin," Ginn said.

"Did she see anything on the way from the airport?" Matt asked.

"No, the van was windowless. All she knows is that there were other youngsters already there at the house, she was raped again, she slept. But for some time after that, a week or so, no one touched her. She was fed. Her burns and bruises healed." Cargill shrugged. "She stopped speaking, but no one cared about that. She's a pretty girl, she was going to a high-class place."

"You mean to a brothel here in Malibu?" Matt shook his head. "No. No way. I've lived here all my life, so's Bobby. We would have heard of it. Remember the Albatross across from the old sheriff's station, the stories about that, Bobby? No way."

"Not a brothel," Cargill said. "It sounds more like some sort of private club." Throughout, his voice had remained devoid of emotion, no outrage, no passion.

"This doesn't surprise you, all this?" Matt asked.

Cargill shook his head. "No, I wish it did. I've heard it all before, and worse. These kids are just merchandise to be used over and over. Usually they're sold on every two or three months until they die from an overdose of drugs, commit suicide, or are killed, sometimes by their owners, sometimes by customers. There's always a fresh supply."

Matt slid a glance to see how Ginn was taking this. Her face was tight, her normally ivory skin had the sallow tinge it got when she was ill.

"Laila is not addicted to drugs," she said flatly.

"No, I'm sure she isn't," Cargill replied. "I'm surmising that wherever this place is, it is the first stop, and whoever runs it wants youngsters who are new to the life, not a bunch of addicts whose habits have to be fed. They have an interest in keeping them healthy. Later, I can assure you, it would be a different story."

Bobby was grim as he looked at Matt. "During the fire it was the boy who saw his chance and grabbed it. The gates opened for cars to leave, everyone was panicked, he slipped out in the smoke and chaos. A couple of the girls grabbed our Jane Doe, someone got hold of the youngest kid, the black girl, Laila followed and they headed downhill to the beach. She says the baby was born dead, they dragged the mother along with them, and finally they holed up in the canyon. When she died, they carried her up onto the road where she'd be found. What I can't figure is why they didn't just keep on going and get as far away as possible."

"Where do you think a bunch of brutalized, scared young kids with no money and no papers, who couldn't speak the language, would go, Bobby?" Ginn asked. "To the police? These are girls who'd had just seen a baby born and a girl die, they've had it beaten into them that no one would listen, that their mothers would be killed if they talked. They are just children, Bobby. Children."

Ginn got up from the table, walked to the edge of the canyon. Silently, the three men avoided each other's eyes, then Matt got to his feet, crossed the patio to stand behind her. He could feel the rage emanating from her rigid body in waves of energy. "Ginn, we'll get the bastards who did this."

"Yes? How?"

"We're going to figure that out."

A moment passed then Ginn reached a hand behind her. Matt took it in both of his. Her hands were small and surprisingly strong. She let out a long breath and turned.

"Okay."

She squeezed his hand, then walked back to the table, slid onto the bench. Arms folded, Matt leaned against the sycamore just behind her.

"Sorry," she said shortly. "So let's talk about the next step."

"What do you think, Bobby?" Matt asked.

Cargill looked up at him.

"Bobby's a deputy sheriff," Ginn said. Matt and Bobby exchanged a glance. Neither of them had explained to her Bob's reticence about revealing his profession.

Cargill's eyebrows rose. "I see. No one mentioned that. It is not a good idea to bring the police in officially at this point. Laila will be treated as an illegal engaged in prostitution, whoever is behind it will get away, and she will pay the price."

"Are you suggesting lousy police work? Or payoffs?" The muscles around Bobby's mouth were tight.

"It's what happens, Bob." Cargill gave a chill smile. "Just check the record. The trade in human beings is a thriving enterprise, the people running it are connected at every level internationally. Plenty of money changes hands to make sure the engine runs smoothly."

"Well, in our little corner of the world, linking it up with a dead girl is the way to throw some sand into that engine," Bobby said.

"Good luck. I'm just telling you that at this level the police will have no choice, they will have to take Laila into custody. She'll be thrown into a detention camp with every sort of underage felon awaiting trial, accused murderers, rapists, violent young criminals. The FBI has to ascertain whether she has indeed been trafficked, and those wheels turn very slowly. She will have no one to protect her and after what she has experienced, suicide is obviously a risk. If she survives—" Cargill swept his glance over the three people listening to make sure they understood what he was saying "—she will likely be deported back to her country of origin. You will have exposed her to all that for nothing."

An appalled silence followed his words.

"Isn't there a safe house, something like that?" Matt asked.

"The best she could hope for would be a homeless shelter, or a battered women's shelter. More likely is the detention camp."

"Then she stays where she is, with us," Ginn said.

Cargill nodded. "It's the best solution for her right now."

"And then what?" Bobby asked.

"The best advice I can give you is to leave this with me for now. I have some good contacts in law enforcement, sympathetic people I've worked with before. I will contact them first thing tomorrow. We'll know better how to proceed. Don't worry, I'll keep you informed. But please, you have to consider your own safety, this is a dangerous business." He glanced at his watch. "Look, I'm sorry, but I have to go. Ginn, if I can be of help in any way, legal or otherwise, feel free to call me." He got to his feet, reached to shake hands with Bobby. "Good to meet you, deputy. Matt, if I could have a minute?"

"Sure." Surprised, Matt led him along the side path to the front of the house.

At his parked Jeep, Cargill turned to look at the mountains rising in seemingly empty layers of silver and gray and purple, the patchwork of black from fire damage as perfectly arranged as in a Japanese painting, with no hint of the San Fernando Valley, and its millions of residents, on the other side.

"This is a lovely spot, mountains, ocean view. Pretty expensive piece of real estate."

For a beat, Matt didn't answer. "You mean for a deputy sheriff? It always puzzles me that people look at Malibu and assume no one lived here before the latest real estate boom."

"Look, what I'm saying is a house of horrors exists somewhere in Malibu, and someone knows about it. The people who deal in human beings are the most remorseless killers I've ever heard about. You want to be very careful whom you trust, that's all. You understand?"

What he understood was that he wasn't going to explain or defend Bobby Eckhart to a stranger. "Thanks for coming."

Cargill looked at him for a moment as if contemplating another comment, but he nodded silently, slid behind the wheel and turned on the ignition. The lingering stink of exhaust fumes hung in the air long after he'd made the turn out of the driveway. Matt waited until the sound of the engine faded, then went over to Ginn's car, looked in the glove compartment for the Glock. He took it out and slammed the door. Footsteps crunched over the gravel behind him.

"That the cannon you took from your invaders?"

He turned at Bobby's question. "Yes. I am not going to apply for a license, so don't suggest it."

"Wasn't going to. Come on, I'll get you another clip for it." Bobby opened the door to the three-car garage, flipped on a light. The garage was immaculate, Bobby's precious Harley covered by a fitted tarp, Sylvie's space left empty. Bobby led the way past his restored '75 Chevy pickup to a sturdy cabinet hung on the rear wall. He fiddled with the combination lock until it clicked open to reveal a bank of drawers, and three handguns mounted on the wall beside them. Bobby pulled open one of the drawers. "What did Cargill have to say that was so private?"

"Just a warning, be careful who we trust."

Bobby handed Matt an extra clip for the Glock, closed the drawer, reset the combination lock. He leaned a hip against the hood of the Chevy. "Don't you mean who you trust? Somehow I got the feeling the guy thinks I might be on the take, or know someone who is." Bobby shook his head in disgust. "The hell with him."

Matt looked out of the window high on the wall. Before the fire it opened into the green depths of the old cedar. Now all he could see was the endless expanse of the sky. Sylvie had had an arborist look at it and he'd said the tree was over a hundred years old.

"I feel as if I've taken a toxic bath just hearing what happened to that kid in there. I can't begin to imagine what she…" Matt stopped, unable to voice the enormity of what had happened to her.

"Yeah," Bobby said shortly. "So what's next? I can't sit on this. I meant it when I said the way into it is through our Jane Doe. I have to report it."

"Not through the chain of command in Malibu, that would be crazy."

"The guys I know are clean, Matt, I'd stake my life on that."

"Yes, but why risk it? What about Barstow and Flores? They're specialists and they're outside the loop. I got the sense they're good cops, I know it pissed them off that the case was closed and two bodies just disappeared. If I go talk to them, will you hold off?"

Bobby rubbed a thumb over a speck on the immaculate paint-work of the cherry red pickup. "I could get canned for sitting on a witness like this."

"Bob, we nail these bastards, they'll make you chief."

CHAPTER 23

The detectives room was quiet and smelled of old coffee and stale cigarette smoke. No Smoking signs were prominent, derisory comments added by a black felt pen, so the cigarette smell had to be clinging to the clothes of the smokers in the room. Only half of the dozen or so desks were occupied. Everyone seemed to be on the phone, busily scratching notes as they spoke. But earlier Matt had been pinned by every eye as he came through the door.

"You got us here on our day off for this?" Detective Flores leaned back in his chair on the other side of the desk. He wore a bright red muscle shirt with Los Hombres de los Angeles emblazoned across the front, battered jeans, heavy white socks and sneakers. His denim jacket hung on the back of his chair.

"Hold on, Ed." Barstow was perched on the edge of Flores' desk, a scuffed cowboy booted foot propped on a chair. Matt was aware that both men had placed themselves to their own advantage, Flores in the place of authority behind the desk, Barstow looking down at Matt seated in a low, uncomfortable visitor's chair.

"Just let's go through this again, Mr. Lowell, so you can see exactly what you've brought us." Barstow counted off on his nicotine-stained fingers. "You've got a young girl you refuse to identify or produce but whom you say is the victim of trafficking, smuggled into the country and forced to work as a prostitute."

Matt interrupted. "No, that's not what I said. That's just the point. The girl is not a prostitute, she is the victim of serial rape and sexual slavery. She wasn't paid, she wasn't willing, and she managed to escape. She's fifteen. She was taken from her home, brought here illegally—"

"Right there you're breaking the law by harboring her," Flores cut in. "Turn her over to INS and we'll go talk to her."

Matt shook his head in frustration.

Barstow held a cautionary hand up to his partner and continued. "You're right, Mr. Lowell, my mistake. She's not a prostitute. Anyway, let's go on. You have no information on where the girl was forced to work, nor who forced her." He counted off another finger. "You say there are several other victims who also escaped from this same unknown place, including our Jane Doe, and they are now wandering around Malibu somewhere, but you don't know where." Finger number three. "Your own house was attacked by mysterious unknown gunmen, but you didn't report it, and neither did anyone else."

"Only last Wednesday, you denied seeing anyone in the canyon where the dead girl was found," Flores said. "You've changed your story, admitted you lied, and now you've decided to come clean you think we can just snap our fingers, somehow produce the manpower to jump-start a search for these mysterious victims, all based on your uncorroborated word?" Shaking his head, he expelled a heavy breath as if he had difficulty believing anyone could be so dumb.

Barstow held up finger number four. "You've got this phone message from a friend who says Aguilar's been murdered. He sounds unnerved. Understandable. Aguilar was shot, then had his guts ripped out with a knife, a nasty way to go." He tapped his thumb. "The guy who left the message then dies in a traffic accident on a narrow winding road at night, unfortunately not an unusual occurrence, people drive too fast on those roads all the time. But we'll pull the report, Mr. Lowell, to be sure nothing was missed." Barstow tapped the small tape recorder Matt had brought containing the tape he had removed from the answering machine. "He says he got in too deep, he doesn't know how, he's sorry. He says he couldn't do it. What couldn't he do? Sleep with your girl? Prescribe controlled substances to the rich and famous to finance a fancy lifestyle? And maybe he supplied also to Aguilar, who was known to consort with the Sons of Satan, as evil bunch of drug dealers as you're ever likely to meet, and who very likely killed him. Or maybe he killed himself. He says he's going to end it. Either way, both men are beyond questioning now. There is nothing concrete here, Mr. Lowell."

Flores rocked back in his chair, his hands clasped behind his head. "You're a bright guy. You didn't figure out that lying in a police investigation was not a wise move? Now that Aguilar, the only other person who saw these mysterious kids, is dead we've only got your word they even exist and your word doesn't inspire much confidence around here. And just suppose they do exist? If they've got any sense, they're long gone."

"No. They've got no papers, no money and they don't speak the language. Why would I concoct a story like this?"

A thin smile curled Flores's lips. "How about deflecting attention? Works for me."

The guy had his mind locked around one idea and couldn't let it go. "I offered to pay for a funeral. That's it. Can't you see beyond that?"

"Two funerals."

Shaking his head slowly, Matt held Flores's cold brown eyes. He sensed Flores was just trying this on to see where it would take him. The worst thing he could do was lose sight of what he was here for and get bogged down defending himself.

Flores was the first to break eye contact. "Ah, the hell with this bullshit." The legs of his chair banged against the floor. He leaned forward, put both hands on the desk in front of him. "If we'd had this when Aguilar was alive and the cases were open, yeah, we could have got the manpower for a search. Now it's too late. You think about that next time you decide to lie to the police."

"What Ed means is that our hands are tied," Barstow said. "As you know, the bodies of the girl and the baby are gone. The cases are closed."

"What would it take to get them reopened?"

Flores slid a glance at his partner. An unspoken message flashed between them. "More than you've got here, *muchacho*. But I tell you what. We're homicide, but you give us something real, some hard evidence about this alleged trafficking, we'll work it on our own time. If we find anything, we'll even turn it over to the feds because it would be their jurisdiction. Right now, you got dick. I'm going home."

Barstow stood. The meeting was over. Matt got up.

"Well, thanks for your time."

"Yeah," Flores said.

Politely, Barstow walked with Matt across the room, then at the doorway, then stood back to allow a man to enter.

The newcomer, slender, thinning fair hair, nodded his thanks. "Jim." He looked over at Flores standing at his desk, and raised a hand in greeting, then addressed Barstow, a note of amusement in his pleasant baritone voice. "Since when have a couple of senior detectives been pulling Sunday duty? Please don't tell me y'all are going to be putting in for overtime?"

Barstow gave a polite laugh. "No, Mr. Lowell here came in with some suggestions for us in one of our closed cases. The Jane Doe in Malibu. This is our boss, Commander Peters."

Peters nodded without offering to shake hands. "Well, good. I'm sure the detectives here appreciate your input. Thanks for coming in." He smiled, and continued walking.

Barstow took out a business card, leaned on an empty desk and wrote a couple of numbers on the back. "My home number, and Ed's. You get anything, give us a call. Have a good day."

Matt looked back before he left. The two homicide detectives were deep in conversation with their boss. Peters was frowning, but he was nodding, listening intently.

They were going to do it, Matt thought. They were actually going to try to get the case reopened.

The narrow gorge of Malibu Canyon opened up at the Presbyterian Church on the crest of the rise, the Pacific came into view, and the temperature dropped its usual fifteen degrees. Moisture glistened on the red clay tile roofs of the Malibu Villas where Annie Lautner had her condo.

Matt swung left into the condominium driveway, parked in one of the visitor's spots, turned off the engine. He sat for a moment planning what he would say. Annie sounded as if she was still in shock when he'd called from the 101—not surprising, she and Phil had been together for years. Best case, she'd know what Phil meant by that phone call. Worst case, she'd think Matt an insensitive clod for asking questions. Anything in between could be useful. He got out, locked the car.

Steam rose from the Olympic-size pool and he could see people working out in the brightly lit gym on the other side, treadmills busy, weight machines in use, beautiful bodies in the maintenance shop. The brick paths were lined with lantana and ferns, and littered with leaves from the sycamores, the air smelled fresh and green. He ran up the stairs to Annie's condo, rang the bell, waited a couple of minutes.

He rang again. "Annie, it's Matt Lowell." Hers was the only door on this level and his voice echoed in the empty passageway. Matt stood back, looked at the stunning view of the Pacific framed in the opening at the end of the passage. Rays of the sun pierced the ocean fog, the dark mass of Point Dume rose in the west, looking like a smaller version of Hawaii's Diamond Head.

He put his mouth close to the beveled glass set into Annie's front door, and rapped on the wood with his knuckles.

"Annie. Are you there?"

The door bounced open, hit the wall, bounced back. "Hey, Matt. Long time. Come on in." Annie wore a pale apricot satin wrapper and had her small white dog Sammy hanging uncomfortably from beneath one arm. Dark hair straggled around her face, her smoke gray eyes were bloodshot. Without waiting, she padded back along the hall on bare feet, trailing sweet smoke in her wake and leaving Matt to close the door and follow.

"How are you doing, Annie?"

"Okay. Want a drink?" She threw the words over her shoulder. "I'm doing martinis."

"No, thanks, Annie. I just wanted to have a few words about Phil—"

"He's dead. That's it. Dead." Annie dropped the dog into the corner of a huge black-silk sectional and flopped down beside it. Her decorating style was startling, black floor, black furniture, white walls, paintings that looked as if they'd been chosen for their brilliance of color rather than artistic merit, although a couple of them had both. The living room gave onto an open kitchen and dining area, a wall of glass doors drew the eye to a landscaped balcony and the view across the bay toward the Palos Verdes Peninsula.

Matt looked at the oversized martini glass on the black granite coffee table in front of her, the joint she held delicately between finger and thumb. "Are you okay, Annie?"

"No, but I'm taking the edge off." She waved the joint. "Here, try some. It's good stuff."

Matt shook his head. If she had been at this as long as it appeared she had, poor Sammy must have a secondary high. "No, thanks, I don't—"

"I've got some blow in the bedroom if you want. Or a drink?"

"No thanks, I just have a few questions and then I'll go, leave you in peace."

"Shoot." She laughed as if she'd just made a joke. "Shoot me."

He said gently, "I'm sorry about Phil, Annie. I know you'd been together a long time."

"Over five years." She started to cry, the sobs soft in her throat.

Helplessly, Matt suppressed the impulse to offer a friendly shoulder. Annie loved to think of herself as a wild child, there was no way of telling where an offer like that would lead.

"Shit!" Like a child, more hurt than wild, she rubbed at her face, the tears mingling with the mucous running from her nose.

Matt got up, went into the guest bathroom. It was like entering an exotic cave, black walls splashed with crimson birds, the focal point a pelicanesque creature about to dive into a cantilevered black toilet bowl. His reflection wavered in the dark smoked mirror and he thought of the last time he'd been there, a crazy Malibu crowd scene on New Year's Eve a couple of years ago. He and Ginn had left early, he remembered, to get to Ned and Julie's. He'd been having fun, but Ginn wanted to see Ned's two boys before they went to bed.

Life had been so good then, he hadn't realized how good. Now he'd stumbled into something so evil it made his skin crawl. People were dying, Ginn made his head reel, insisting she was still out of his life, but making love like they'd never been apart; a smart-ass lawyer he'd only just met had planted a nasty seed about a guy closer to him than a brother and a couple of sheriff's detectives seemed to think he was a killer. Buried in all this was something irritating his memory like a splinter of wood under the skin. He didn't know what the hell it was, but he had the feeling it was important.

"What are you doing in there, Matt? You won't find anything," Annie called. "I hide everything interesting."

"It's okay. I found it." Matt returned to the living room and bent to put a heavy black container of tissues on the coffee table in front of her. Annie reached for it, the box slipped from her grasp, hit the ashtray, scattering shards of glass and the ashy remains of the weed she'd smoked across the carpet.

"Oh, shit!" She raised her voice. "Tuti!"

On the other side of the kitchen, a door opened and a voice said, "Miss Annie?"

"Come clean this mess up."

Matt looked to see who she was talking to, and a moment later, brush and dustpan in hand, a small Asian woman crossed the room. Matt smiled at her, but she avoided his eyes, and dropped to her knees.

He felt a small weight of anxiety drop off. "I didn't realize someone was here with you, Annie. Maybe she could stay tonight, so that you're not alone." He didn't add, "because you're stoned out of your mind."

"Of course she'll stay tonight, where else would she go? She lives here."

"Oh, I didn't know that." In a two-bedroom condo, he wondered where she slept. It certainly wouldn't be in Annie's fancy guest room.

"So what's so urgent you had to see me about?" Annie said. She motioned to the maid to hand her another tissue, dabbed at her eyes, blew her nose and dropped the tissue on the floor.

Tuti picked up the used tissue, put it into her dustpan, and inched along on her knees working on the carpet. Matt had an uncomfortable flash of the picture they made, two large Caucasians lounging in overstuffed furniture while a small-boned Asian woman inched along on her knees, cleaning the floor.

Annie followed the direction of Matt's eyes and obviously misunderstanding his look of concern, shook her head impatiently. "Oh, don't mind her, she won't understand what you're saying. She doesn't speak to anyone, anyway."

Matt looked at her. Annie Lautner might not be most aware woman he'd ever met, but he didn't remember her being this insensitive. It had to be the dope she was smoking and there was nothing he could do about that. "Annie, did Phil discuss his work with you?"

"His work? What, his medical practice? No, of course not.

That's not ethical. Sure, sometimes he'd tell me which gorgeous movie star fancied girls instead of boys, or vice versa, that kind of thing. Nothing important, though. Why?"

"Anything about a rehab clinic up in the hills that catered to troubled kids, rich kids?"

"He wouldn't talk to me about that. I'm not interested in kids." Annie tapped the maid's shoulder, pointing with an arched foot. "You missed a bit. Sammy could cut his feet." She looked back at Matt. "What's this about?"

Her work finished, the maid got up, looked a silent inquiry at Annie, who waved her away. Matt kept his eyes on Tuti's back as she left on silent feet. Even if Annie only behaved like this when she was stoned, Tuti had to really need this job to put with such treatment. He wondered where she slept.

"How long has she worked for you?"

"Who, Tuti? She's always been here. Five years. Phil bought this place when we got together, and she came with it. Why?"

She made Tuti sound like a stray cat. Matt found himself asking a question that, before this morning's conversation with Cargill, would never have occurred to him. "How much do you pay her?"

"I don't know, Phil pays her. He takes care of all the bills." Her breath caught in her chest. "I have to see a lawyer. I don't know what's going to happen now, we weren't married so I didn't sign a pre-nup, and I don't know what plans he made for me. Maybe nothing, he was only forty, he didn't expect to die."

Gently, Matt asked, "How did he seem to you last week?"

"Seem? I don't know. Like always. What do you mean?"

Annie leaned forward to pick up another joint, allowing her satin robe to gape, revealing the perfectly formed breasts she had giggled were the best that money could buy, a gift from Phil on one of his own birthdays. Matt forced himself to look away. Real or not, they were pretty damn magnificent. Annie looked up at him through her lashes, aware of the effect she was having, and took in a deep lungful of smoke. She closed her eyes, held the smoke in her lungs for a long count before allowing a faint whisper of blue smoke to trickle from between her lips.

"He called me the night before he died," Matt said. "He sounded as if something was really troubling him."

"Phil? What could Phil be troubled about? His life had never been better, he had everything he wanted, a lot of money, lovely house. Me. We had a lot of fun together. That's what makes this so awful." She leaned back, propped her feet on the table. "Well, he wasn't much interested in sex for a couple of weeks, and that wasn't like him. Usually we did it about every day."

Every day? Phil Halliburton? "What was he doing on Latigo that night, did he tell you?"

"No, Phil never told me where he was going."

"Did he keep anything here at your place? Any papers?"

"Like what? A will? No. I wish."

"No, not a will." Matt didn't know himself what he was looking for, it was a stab in the dark. "Anything else, any files, work notes, letters, anything like that?"

Annie shook her head and shrugged. She took another hit. "Why are you asking all these questions, all of a sudden?"

"He had some papers of mine, and I need them."

"Well, I don't know where they are. Probably in his office." Her tone changed. "You know the night it happened? Well, I went to the house to pick up some things, you know, private things, stuff I didn't want his mother to see." Tears welled, misting her gray eyes. "He came from some redneck town near Bakersfield, and his mother's one of those, you know, holy roller evangelicals. She doesn't think anyone should even do it unless they're married." She sniffled. "I don't know why I'm so nice to her, she's such a bitch. Maybe I'll go back to the house tomorrow. I could take anything I want, he's got some nice things there. He'd want me to have them, anyway."

"You've got keys?"

"Well, sure, it's like we were married. Oh, God, this is so awful." She laid her head back on the sofa and closed her eyes.

"Annie, these papers of mine Phil had. I really need to go get them."

"God, Matt, what did he have that's so important?"

"It's a business deal we had going together, some property. I've got to have the papers for a meeting tomorrow. If I can borrow your keys, I can look for them."

Annie looked into her glass, saw that it was empty. "I'm going to have another drink. Sure you don't want one?"

Matt shook his head.

"Okay, but I don't have keys to the office, only the house, and I have to have them back first thing in the morning because I'm going there. He'd want me to." She gave a wide gesture with her empty glass. "They're in that drawer in the kitchen."

Matt got to his feet, made his way around the counter separating the living room from the kitchen. He glanced at Annie, saw that she was at the bar splashing gin, measuring drops of vermouth into a narrow glass jug, stirring with a rod. Quietly he cracked the door to the service area. Tuti was sitting cross-legged on a narrow futon spread on the floor in front of the laundry machines, almost hidden by freshly ironed sheets suspended from a line strung across the small space. A shelf held skimpy piles of clothes, black cotton pants, white T-shirts. Up close, Tuti was older than he'd thought, at least in her mid-forties. She scrambled to her feet and Matt put a finger to his lips. He closed the door, found the keys in the drawer, and returned to the living room.

"Annie, one more thing and I'll leave you in peace. Can you call Phil's nurse, ask her to meet me at his office?" The medical building Phil owned was only a few minutes south on the coast highway.

"What, now?"

"Yes. Does she know about the accident?"

"She saw it on the news. At least she called me, and that's more than his awful mother did. She was just some poor old drunk still living in the same beat-up old trailer in the Sunset

Trails Trailer Park or whatever the hell it was called until Phil bought her a big fancy house and got her out of there."

Matt's mind was reeling. Annie was fueling her resentment with every drag on the joint, every sip of booze, and he'd learned more about Phil Halliburton in five minutes than he'd discovered in ten years.

He chose his next words so as not to scare her to death. "Annie, listen, I want you to be careful. Don't open the door, and don't go out tonight. I'll get Phil's keys back to you first thing tomorrow."

"What, you think I'm too stoned to talk to anyone? Well, I'm not. If you find a will anywhere, let me know right away, don't wait until tomorrow, okay?"

"No, I won't, don't worry. Now call Joan Brassart and ask her to meet me." If she was home, he thought she would agree. They'd gone through school together from Webster Elementary to Malibu Park Junior High.

Annie wobbled over to the wall phone in the kitchen, almost stumbling over Sammy circling around her feet. To Matt's relief, Joan picked up. A couple of minutes, a question and answer, and she agreed to open the office for him.

On the way Matt hit the button programmed for Ginn's cell phone. When she answered, he said, "It's me. Is everything all right?"

"We're fine. Gabby has taken Amira back to town, and then she's going home from there. What did Flores and Barstow say?"

"The short version is that we don't have anything concrete, but I think they might make a stab at getting the case officially reopened. I'll fill in the rest later. You are going to stay tonight at Bobby's, aren't you?"

"Yes, after what John said, I won't do anything to risk Laila, don't worry."

Impulsively he said, "I love you, Ginn."

"Hullo, hullo, I can't hear you, Matt, I'm losing you. I'm hanging up."

"No, wait a minute, I'm sorry, I won't say it again. Listen, I've just come from Annie Lautner's—" He put the phone down. He was talking to empty air.

He cut through Cross Creek Road, turned onto the Pacific Coast Highway. For the first five years in Malibu, Phil had rented a small medical suite in a building on Cross Creek Road close to the Country Mart. Then he bought a dingy real estate building on the Pacific Coast Highway and spent a fortune turning it into one of the most elegant spaces in Malibu.

A lone Honda Accord occupied the tree-shrouded lot behind the building. Matt parked and got out, went to ring the bell. As he got closer, he realized the door was ajar, the lock broken.

"Joan? It's Matt Lowell." He pushed the door open, found himself in the working center of the practice. The asphalt tile floor was strewn with patient files, glass-fronted cabinets had been smashed open, computers, printers, medical equipment swept off desks and counter tops.

He called out again and heard a responding voice, then Joan Brassart's substantial figure appeared from the front of the building. Her normally ruddy complexion was pale, her prominent blue eyes wide with shock.

"Annie Lautner called and said to meet you here. Anyone else and I wouldn't have come on a Sunday afternoon. Good thing I did, when I got here, I found this. Somebody's broken in." Her voice quivered in outrage. "Can you believe this, Matt? First Dr. Halliburton is killed, then our office is broken into?" Joan turned back into the office. "I bet some addicts saw on the news that he was dead and came looking for drugs."

"Is anything missing?"

"I haven't had time to check, I just got here, saw the lock broken and called 911."

Then he hadn't much time, Matt thought. He did not want to be here when the patrol car arrived and find himself explaining his presence to one more suspicious deputy sheriff.

Joan was filled with nervous excitement, talking non-stop. "I don't know, Matt, Malibu never used to be like this when we were kids. It's all these new people moving in, changing everything. This used to be a nice ordinary little beach community."

"Joanie, doesn't sound as if you and I grew up in the same town."

Joan pressed her lips together. "Annie Lautner said you had papers here, or something. She wasn't too clear. She sounded stoned."

"I need the papers Phil had on the treatment facility for teenagers he was involved with." Matt spoke as if he knew what he was talking about, and so would Joan.

"Dr. Halliburton kept everything to do with that facility on his laptop. Why do you need them?"

Matt managed to keep the surge of triumph he felt from reaching his face. He'd found a thread, a link, something to go on.

"We were partners in it and we had a meeting with the bank tomorrow. I'll have to explain what's happened, but I'll need everything he had."

"I can't help you. He dealt with it himself."

"What about the billing?"

"No, I told you. He kept everything about it on his laptop. I only know about it because an invoice did come here once from a drug company, and I opened it with the other bills and asked him what account to use in paying it. He just snatched it out of my hand, told me I had no business opening it. He acted as if it was my fault, can you imagine?" Her small well shaped mouth started to tremble. "And I've been with him since he came to Malibu. Ten years."

"Did the invoice show the address of the place?"

A small puzzled frown creased her brows. "I thought you said you were a partner. Don't you know the address?"

Matt thought fast. "I need to know if there has been a breach of confidentiality, Joan, that's all. The clients are the kids of high-profile people and a total blackout is a major part of the package we offer. If there is a breach, not by you but by the drug company, I have to know because from now on, I'll be dealing with them. I need the name they used on the invoice."

"I don't remember, it was a couple of years ago."

"Are you sure? Think for a minute, it's very important."

"I don't remember, Matt," she said impatiently. "Doctor Halliburton wanted me to forget it, so I did. We treated a lot of famous people for a lot of strange ailments so I certainly know how to keep a confidence. We've never had another invoice here so I don't know why you think you have to come down hard on anybody."

"What about the name of the company?"

"What's wrong with you? I don't remember. Do you know how many bills come in here? It wasn't a company I was familiar with. I told you. Everything about that facility was on his laptop."

"Then I'll have to take that."

"No, you can't. I'm sorry."

"Is it here?"

"Well, I haven't searched, if that's what you mean, but he had a real thing about that laptop. He kept it with him all the time, practically chained to his wrist."

"I'll just take a look in his office." Matt walked toward the front of the building where Phil's office faced the highway. A quick glance was enough. If the laptop had been here, it wasn't now.

Joan stood in the doorway. "Look at this, they've been in here, too. My God. Anyway, I can't allow you to take anything out of this office, Matt. The police are coming and they'll need to see."

"No, you're right." He started back down the hall, Joan on his heels. "Thanks for your help. I'm going to leave now before the cops get here. I don't want to be tied up with the sheriff's department and have to answer a load of questions, why I'm here, what I want, that kind of thing. Can you keep my name out of this, not mention I was here?"

Her blue eyes sparkled with interest. "Yeah, I heard they've

Shirley Palmer

been talking to you a lot lately. About the baby you found on the beach and all, and then that girl in the canyon. You know, the mother."

Matt looked at her over his shoulder. "I found the baby, Joan, not the mother."

"Oh, don't worry about it, Matt, I told you, I can keep a confidence, had to in this practice. If they don't ask, I won't volunteer anything. But if they do, I'll have to tell them."

"Fair enough. I'm sorry about Phil, Joan. He was a good guy."

Joan Brassart shrugged. "He was all right." Her voice broke on the last word.

He left by the back door, inched the Range Rover carefully through a space between the stand of eucalyptus trees separating Phil's lot from the fried chicken joint next door. He was turning left out of the Colonel's driveway as a sheriff's black and white slammed to a stop outside the front door of the medical building.

Two minutes later, he was at Phil's home on Carbon Beach.

The house presented a blank front to the Pacific Coast Highway, an expanse of pale walls with a deceptively simple wood door that only the cognoscenti would recognize as rare Hawaiian purpleheart. Matt pressed the doorbell, waited a couple of minutes then selected a key from Annie's key ring. Two keys later, the tumblers clicked into place and Matt slipped inside, pulled the door closed behind him, shutting the traffic noise from the PCH down to a distant hum. Quickly, he followed a black rock path through the trees, opened the door into Phil's four-car garage, and disarmed the alarm as Annie had instructed.

A wooden staircase against the south wall led up to an enclosed loft and a walkway with three doors overlooking the garage. Maybe an office, he thought, probably storage, but worth a look before going into the house.

He poked his head around the first door, expecting to see the gear most people shoved into their garages, stuff too good to give away, not good enough to use. What he found was a small room with clerestory windows, one bunk bed, both tiers perfectly made up, two small whicker chairs, an empty chest of drawers. Apart from that, nothing. A door led to an adjoining bathroom. A quick glance revealed a toilet, small shower, no tub. Empty and clean. A connecting door led into a small bedroom. Slightly more fancy. A regular bed, made up. Another empty chest of drawers. This room had an easy chair with a little a table, a nice rug. Nothing more.

So where had they gone? Phil's help lived in, his housekeeper was Latina, Matt thought from Mexico, and Phil also had a couple of maids, small anonymous figures. Now that he'd met Tuti, Matt thought they could be from the same part of the world, maybe South East Asia.

Behind the remaining door he found the used stuff he'd expected, tables, a sofa and matching overstuffed chairs piled with an assortment of heavy drapes. He closed the door and left the garage.

Before entering the house, he looked around as if seeing the enclosed garden for the first time. It was lush with tropical plants, giant ferns from Hawaii, full-sized trees. A stream of water meandered over black pebbles before splashing into a black swimming pool designed to look like a watering hole in a forest, edged with rocks and ferns and soft green moss. The front wall of the house was frosted glass etched with the same theme, a forest glade with birds and animals. The moisture laden air was warm and sweet with the scent of plumeria so somewhere the heat source was still turned on.

Phil Halliburton had to be a very, very rich man. Why had he never given a thought to that before? Matt wondered. Phil's neighbors were mostly entertainment billionaires and industrialists. Along here, Malibu's Gold Coast, ten million dollars would get you a tear down. Phil had done an extensive remodel instead, kept the same footprint and moved in only four years ago. Even for a successful doctor, this was some establishment.

Behind the etched glass entrance, the house was dark. Matt

selected a key from Annie's ring and it turned at the first try. The air inside felt static and smelled old.

The foyer led into a huge space that took up most of the ground floor. It was luxuriously furnished in a vaguely Indo-Chinese style, rich woods, warm and inviting, professionally decorated—nothing of Annie here. Glass doors opened onto a wide deck above the sand. Catalina Island was a long, dark shape on the horizon, and the sweep of the Santa Monica Bay stretched for twenty miles before rising with the terrain on the Palos Verdes Peninsula to the south. At night, the view would be of the Queen's Necklace, the stream of lights the followed the curve of the bay.

"Anyone home? Lupe?" Matt called again without much hope of an answer. The house felt empty.

He looked around, his neck rippling uncomfortably. There was a sense of disturbance. Pictures were crooked as if they'd been taken off the wall, and carelessly rehung. A smooth flush dark wood panel that was actually a door to the enclosed entertainment center had been left open. A long cabinet Matt remembered as being centered on one wall was no longer centered. Nothing much, but after Phil's office, each displacement resonated like a warning bell. He took the Glock out of his pocket, kept it in his hand as he walked, his footsteps too loud in the silent house.

The kitchen had all the latest and greatest bells and whistles, a couple of double fronted refrigerators and stoves large enough to cook for an army. A small room behind the kitchen was temperature controlled, racked from floor to ceiling with bottles of wine, furnished with a tasting bar and upholstered chairs.

In the kitchen, pantries were stacked with cans and paper goods, fine china and silverware and linens. He returned to the foyer and the sweeping double staircase.

A bedroom suite overlooking the ocean occupied the second floor. A larger than kingsize custom bed on a platform faced the ocean. A quick search of a bedside table turned up nothing of interest to Matt, no laptops or papers. A built-in white terry cloth couch stretched the length of one wall of the pale marble bathroom, a double vanity occupied another. A sunken tub the size of a swimming pool was close to the window so that the bather could watch the surf. Clear glass enclosed an onyx-lined shower larger than Matt's spare bedroom. In the cedar-lined dressing room, individually bagged suits were piled neatly on the floor, dress shirts on top. Drawers had been emptied of underwear and socks. Nothing remained on the racks. In an adjoining room, Annie's things, dresses, slacks, tops, filmy lingerie were in a similar pile.

So far, the only thing he'd learned was that Dr. Phillip Halliburton certainly knew how to live well.

The floor above was divided into smaller spaces: a workout room with mirrored walls, treadmill looking out to Catalina, weight machines, a dance barre; next door was a small movie theater complete with banked theater seats. The corner room was furnished as a small retreat, book-lined, easy chairs and sofas, a small bar.

Matt picked up a silver framed photograph from a table. It showed a tired-looking woman and a small, skinny boy about ten years old standing in front of the open door of what looked like an aluminum sided house trailer sitting on bare earth. The boy was grimacing, and had one hand shading his eyes from the sun. The woman's hair was held back by an Alice band, her loose housedress came to mid calf, bare white feet were pushed into sandals. He bent to retrieve a matching frame from where it had fallen, half hidden under a chair. The same woman, alone this time. Her now blonde hair was stylishly short. She wore a green two-piece summer suit with elbow length sleeves, white pumps. Behind her was a house in what Matt thought of as the Italianate public library style of architecture, a vast pale peach stucco monster similar to those that littered the landscape of southern California. In Los Angeles, where land was like gold dust, they were usually built out to the lot line in every direction. Phil's mother's home, though, sat in the middle of heavily landscaped acreage. Even in Bakersfield, it could not have been cheap.

Matt placed both frames on a bookshelf. Someone had had instructions to strip the place clean. If a laptop had been here, it was gone now. In the entire house, he had found not a single scrap of personal paper. Not a bill, or a check book, or an address book. Even the phones had been stripped of any message and the tapes removed.

The sun was dropping toward Point Dume, only an hour or so of daylight remained. Matt took out his cell and called Bobby Eckhart.

"I'm at Phil Halliburton's," he said when Bob answered. "The place has been searched. There's nothing here, not even a check book, or a bill."

Bobby blew out a heavy breath. "How did you get in?"

"Annie Lautner gave me the key."

"So maybe she took everything away to sort through at her leisure."

"Maybe, but she told me this morning that she'd come by for some personal things on Friday after she heard Phil had been killed. She would have mentioned it if she'd taken everything else. I was at Phil's office on the Coast Highway. It's been broken into as well."

"So what do you think they were looking for? Come to that, what are you looking for?"

He realized he hadn't spoken to Bobby since he'd left to meet the homicide detectives. "Joan Brassart said that Phil had an interest in a drug rehab for teenagers here in Malibu, but that's all she knew. He kept everything about it on a laptop and I thought I might find it here. I didn't but just to cover all bases, can you find out if a laptop was recovered from Phil's car?"

"I can give my guy in CHP a call, sure. What about Barstow and Flores? Ginn says they might step up to the plate."

"Yes, maybe. I'll tell you about it when I see you."

As soon as Bob disconnected, Matt called Annie. On the tenth ring, she answered.

"Annie, does Phil have a safe at his house?"

"Well, sure, there's a little one in the dressing room. You press the third panel on the wall just inside the door. It pops open."

"Is it big enough for a laptop?"

"No, it's for jewelry, and cash, that kind of stuff. Phil kept his important things in a safety deposit box." She stopped. "Maybe that's where he kept his will. But I don't know what bank."

Matt took a breath. In as gentle a tone as he could muster, he said, "Annie, do you know the name of Phil's lawyer?"

"Yes, it's Duggan & something, I don't know, Duggan & Thumper, something like that. They're downtown."

"Look in the Yellow Pages under attorneys, go down the names and see if you recognize it. If you do, get the number and call them tomorrow. They'll have a copy of the will. Do you have the combination of the safe?"

He jotted it down, then returned to the dressing room. Annie was right. The safe revealed a diamond collar, a couple of gold watches, some other bits of expensive stuff. Nothing of interest to him. He was walking back through the house when his cell phone rang. Bobby Eckhart's voice said, "Matt, the car was totaled, nothing was recovered. No laptop, nothing."

"Did they search?"

"Well, it was a routine traffic accident, so they ascertained that no other bodies were thrown out, but they probably didn't make a detailed search of the canyon. They had no reason to. Where are you now?"

"I'm still at Phil's house. You remember those maids he had?"

"No, you're talking to a lowly deputy sheriff. I didn't socialize with Halliburton except at your place on the Fourth of July. What about the maids?"

"Well, Phil said one of them was legal. But the other two are Asian. I don't where from, I never spoke to them." He had a sudden flush of guilt, remembering how he had not really seen them. They'd been like pieces of furniture, there to be useful, replenishing glasses, refilling plates, handing out fresh napkins. "I've searched this house from top to bottom. They all slept over the garage, but they're not there now and there's no trace of them. No trace, Bobby. It's as if they never existed. Annie Lautner's maid's also Asian and she sleeps on a futon on the floor of the service area. Annie treats her dog better than she treats that girl."

"You're losing me, Matt. Phil's dead so the help went home, and Annie Lautner, gorgeous, but not the brightest berry on the bush from what I remember, doesn't treat her maid well. What are you talking about?"

"Trafficking. Cargill mentioned trafficking domestics as well as the sexual slavery. It looks to me like Phil Halliburton was involved in all of this up to his eyebrows. His misfortune was rediscovering his conscience. It got him killed."

Bobby was silent for a moment. "Yeah, okay. Sounds like you're on a roll."

"What time you leaving for work?"

"I'm on the eight to four shift tonight, so I'm out of here in a few hours."

"I'm going to have a look at that crash scene before it gets dark, see if the laptop is there."

"Matt, you want to be careful with this."

"I'll be back before you leave."

CHAPTER 24

The accident scene was unmistakable. Fifty-foot skid marks wobbled across the tarmac where Halliburton had fought to keep control before smashing like a battering ram through the low stone wall marking the edge of the canyon.

Matt headed for the viewpoint twenty yards beyond the gap in the stonework, made a three-point turn in the narrow road while it was still daylight, parked the Range Rover, and walked back.

From the trail of destruction, smashed rock, the sheered stumps of trees and brush, it looked as if the Mercedes had bounced down the steep hillside before hitting the bottom. It wasn't clear whether the car had burst into flames upon impact. The canyon was black with earlier damage from the wildfire that had taken a hell of toll here. The houses he could see on the ridgeline were mostly burned-out shells.

He listened to the silence, examined the skid marks close-up, looked at the deserted ravine, thought of Tommy Aguilar dead with a knife in his belly, Halliburton crushed in a car. He had hiked and ridden through these hills and canyons all his life, and never once had he had to wonder whether it was safe. Until now. It made him very angry, as if something precious had been violated.

He went back to the Range Rover, picked up the flashlight he kept for emergencies. In an hour, the shadows would be dense.

It took him less time than he'd thought to get to the bottom. The fire-parched earth had soaked up the recent rains, leaving the creek as dry as if it were midsummer. Matt eyed the terrain, mentally dividing it into a grid for a search. It was a stark landscape of blackened earth and gray boulders. Downed trees littered the ground, bits of metal from the Mercedes had lodged in the charred branches, the stink of gasoline still lingered in the air.

He started at what looked to be the point of final impact, walked west for one minute toward the ocean, probing every dark patch with the beam from the flashlight, then turned south on his mental grid, continued for half a dozen paces before turning east for another minute.

He heard the sound of a car approach on the road above, but it continued, climbing up into the hills; a moment later there was the sound of another car traveling downhill toward the highway. After that, there was only the thud of his boots striking rock. The running conversation in his head was not encouraging. He was looking for an article that was black or silver gray, about twenty by thirty inches, that might or might not have been thrown from a car that was totaled, that may or may not tell them anything they wanted to know, and if by some stroke of unbelievable luck he actually found it, it would undoubtedly be in as bad a shape as the car. But he was here, he told himself, he still had some daylight.

He probed a shadow in the charred brush with the flashlight and picked up a shape that looked promising. He made his way to it, sat on his heels and turned over a blackened twisted rectangle, not surprised that it turned out to be the door of a discarded oven. Something caught his ear, and he looked over his shoulder.

The scrap of oven jumped as if alive, the whine of bullets following in a nanosecond.

Matt hurled himself behind a boulder, adrenaline pumping, his heart banging against his ribs. Mouth dry, he hunkered down, pulled his legs up tight against his body.

This was rapid-fire, not single-action. With the noise reverberating off the walls of the canyon, it sounded like a war zone.

The firing stopped. He eased the Glock out of his belt, and listened, but with the bouncing echo, there was no way of pinpointing the location of the gunman, he could be anywhere. Moving cautiously, Matt picked up a large stone, threw it to the side as far as he could without exposing any part of his body. It struck the ground, gunfire swept the area.

Okay, he thought. Okay, the guy was west of him, on the same level, not firing down from a somewhere up on the hillside.

He studied the area. It was getting darker, the shadows deepening. He threw another rock, larger this time, toward the wall of the canyon, and at the same time jumped in the other direction, rolling behind an outcropping, and praying he did not disturb a torpid rattlesnake curled up beneath the rocks.

The gunman took the bait, a fusillade sprayed the canyon wall. Under the cover of the noise, Matt jumped to his feet, raced toward a downed sycamore, skidded beneath a tangle of branches.

He rubbed his damp face, found it sticky with blood. He hadn't felt a thing, but he must have been hit by a bit shard of rock. Gingerly he fingered his scalp, located the wound above his hairline, and winced. Blood was flowing down his face and he mopped his sleeve across his forehead to keep it from dripping into his eyes.

He looked around, thought of trying the decoy stone routine again, dismissed it as being too risky. But when the light started to go in the canyons it went fast. He could already see it the late afternoon sun retreating up the canyon wall, darkness advancing along the creek bed. He studied the area, decided on the next refuge—an uprooted oak thirty feet closer to the hillside up to the road. He steeled himself for the move, forced himself to count to three, rolled out of the sheltering embrace of the sycamore onto his feet, and launched himself at the ground behind a battlement of roots and earth.

Gunfire raked the sycamore, shattered the top edge of the massively tangled and gnarled roots of the oak, the noise deafening as it bounced through the gorge. Finally, it stopped. Through the ringing in his ears, he heard a shout from the road above—unintelligible, but he could swear it wasn't English. Matt inched his way on his belly from the protection of the roots but if the shadows favored him, they also covered whoever it was firing at him—all he could see were dark shapes of boulders, the twisted limbs of burned-out scrub.

Then he heard the thud of running feet. Going west, he thought. Away from him. A surge of adrenaline drove him to his feet. He tightened his finger around the trigger of the Glock, fired at the sound, the shock of the recoil slamming into his shoulder. The murderous bastards were going to get away. He braced for returning fire, but the sound of boots on rock had receded into silence.

He shoved the gun back in his belt, grabbed the trunk of a scorched toyon, dug his feet into the earth, hauled himself up the steep slope. He kept his mind on the next bush he could grab, the next embedded rock that would give his boots purchase. He got to the stone wall edging the road just yards from the Range Rover. No other car was in sight. Matt remembered the engines he'd heard earlier. It could have been a single vehicle that turned around and parked farther down the road, out of sight and out of earshot.

He put the Glock on passenger seat, jammed the key in the ignition, and peeled out. Halfway down the hill, skidding around a curve, he picked up taillights. Matt pressed on the gas. The gunmen would be forced to stop at the intersection at the bottom of the hill, give him a chance to see the license plate.

He was wrong. They shot past the stop sign, took the left turn onto the highway, crossed four lanes of traffic without pausing.

Matt followed, bursting through the same stop sign, weaving through the skidding tangle of cars, ignoring the blast of horns, his eyes on the taillights. But it was already too dark, the red lights melted into the flow of Sunday beach traffic streaming south to Santa Monica, and the freeway. He'd lost them.

He eased up on the gas, took in a couple of deep breaths. He was shaking, his heart still pounding from the adrenaline rush. A dark-colored SUV had forced Phil Halliburton to his death. A dark SUV had raced away the night of the attack on his house. The attackers that night had called to each other in a foreign language. The voice on the ridge just now had used the same language to call off the gunman below. They'd then driven away in a dark SUV. None of that would stand up in a court of law, but it was enough to convince him these were not coincidences.

The phone in his pocket buzzed, he reached for it. A voice said, "A friendly warning, Mr. Lowell. We could have killed you, but we chose merely to show you what we can do. Now, do your part. Stop the questions. You've got a good life. Don't waste it. There is nothing here to concern you."

"Fuck you." The words were out of his mouth before he could stop them. "I'm coming after you, you sick bastard!" But whoever it was had disconnected.

He knew that voice. Unlike the gunmen, this guy was an American. How the hell had he got his number?

CHAPTER 25

"Bobby, I don't know where they picked me up." Holding the phone to his ear, Matt walked over to the hotel window, twitched the drape, and studied the cars below. Even armed with the Glock, his own house had suddenly seemed too vulnerable so he'd taken a room overlooking the parking lot at the Malibu Inn. Above the lights in the parking lot the sky was black and moonless. "I didn't see them but they must have followed me from Phil's place." He swept his eyes over the lot, saw that it had the same number of vehicles as it had when he checked in fifteen minutes ago, each of them in the same place. Two were sports utilities, one a silver Lexus, the other a dark gold Mercedes and had been there when he arrived. Both license plates were from out of state.

"So I take it you didn't find Phil's missing laptop?"

"No, but I didn't get a chance to make any kind of real search."

"Did you get a shot off at least?" Bobby asked.

"Yes, but it was hopeless, I'm no marksman, I couldn't see anything, and it sounded like World War III out there. But the voice on the phone? I knew it, Bobby, and I've heard it recently, I just can't grab where. Anyway, after this, I won't risk coming up to your place. Can you call in sick tonight?"

"I'm supposed to be leaving in half an hour... Oh, hell, what am I saying? Sure, I can get a touch of belly flu for tonight. I haven't taken a sick day in I don't know when. Years, anyway. Are you okay, Matt?"

"Yes, fine."

"Ginn's right here, do you want to talk to her?"

Ginn's voice said, "Matt, are you hurt? What happened?"

The concern in her voice sent a rush of warmth straight to his heart. "Yes, sure, I'm okay. Same guys, I think." He told her what had happened. "Bobby's going to skip his shift tonight, but let's play it safe, Ginn. Don't go to work tomorrow, stay at Bobby's with Laila."

"Gabby will be here. If I just disappear off the screen, that sends a message, too. If anyone is looking at me, which we know they are not."

"No, we don't know that, we can't be sure of anything except that these men and the people behind them are vicious. You need only think about they've done to Laila. They operate on a level completely foreign to us. There are no rules."

He heard her start to protest, and a wave of exhaustion hit him as the adrenaline drained out of his body. He crossed the room to sit on the hard, queensize bed. "Babe, I'm running out of juice. I'll call you first thing and we can discuss it then. I'll be more up for it."

"Okay. Sleep well, Matt."

His head felt as if it was inhabited by a team of Japanese kodo drummers, the bed seemed three times the size of his own and without Ginn to share it, was about as cozy as an airplane hanger. He glanced at his watch. 5:00 a.m. Too early to call her. He swung his legs to the floor, made his way to the bathroom, rifled without much hope through the little baskets of soap and body lotions for aspirin.

He used the john, washed his hands, and caught his image in the mirror above the sink. He leaned closer. He looked like hell. Last night, the young woman at the desk had refrained from comment about his dirt stained clothes, his hair sticky with blood—he'd cleaned himself up as best he could before checking in and he'd paid in advance. After a sleepless night, he looked worse than he had then.

He was thirty-six, he thought, only four years younger than Phil Halliburton had been when he died. His thoughts turned to Ginn. Maybe she was right when she said he was skimming the surface of a pool of grief. Maybe he was too scared to look down in case he was drawn into the depths. He'd built a wall around his mother's death when he was ten. She was gone. Life went on. Closure. He hated that word.

But if he didn't at least try to find out why he couldn't seem to give Ginn what she had a right to expect from him, he'd certainly lose her, and for the first time since she'd left, he felt she wasn't really gone, that he had a chance to get her back. They were talking, arguing, even laughing together. Two weeks ago, there had been only silence.

He showered, put his filthy clothes back on, shoved the Glock in his belt, and left the room. Except for a sleepy desk clerk, the lobby was deserted. Matt nodded a good morning, pushed through the door into a cold morning. The lot had the same number of cars, the same configuration he'd memorized when he'd last checked at 2:00 a.m. Even so, after he pulled away from the hotel lot, he made a loop on his way home, turning inland at Cross Creek Road, past the public library, City Hall, and then the giant cross erected by Pepperdine University at the top of the hill, winding north for a few miles, circling back to the coast highway, and heading south to Malibu Road. If they wanted him, they knew where to find his house, so it was unlikely he would be followed there, but after yesterday, he was taking no chances.

His small clapboard house looked sadly empty, almost derelict behind the charred stumps, the open, battered garage. He drove past, parked fifty yards farther on, and went down a neighbor's stairs to the beach. The Glock in his hand close against his leg, he walked back to his own house across the soft sand. In ten minutes, he was shaved, dressed and out of the door, a Band-Aid covering the gash on his forehead. The air was cold and moist, the ocean mist was stained with pink from the sunrise, and after a couple of Advil, the throbbing in his head started to ease.

At PC Greens, he picked up coffee, got back in the Range Rover, juggled the cardboard container and the cell phone and managed to hit Bobby's number. He was going to try to persuade Ginn to stay home from her office today, but early morning was not the best part of Ginn's day.

"Ginn had her coffee yet?" he asked when Bobby answered.

"She's not here, Matt. She went to John Cargill's with Laila. She hasn't called you?"

"What? No, she hasn't. When did this happen?"

"Last night. Just after you hung up, Cargill called to see if everything was okay. Ginn and I had been talking, trying to think this thing through. I called in sick last night, and glad to do it, there's no question, but you know I can't keep it up, Matt. I have to report for work, they can't stay up here alone. Besides that, Sylvie's coming home in a couple of days. I'm already into this up to my rear end, but I don't want Sylvie's career compromised as well. It seemed to us both that Cargill's house was a good solution to our problem."

Matt tried to remember whether Cargill had mentioned a wife, but they'd all been so wrapped up in Laila's story, everything else was just a blur. "So where does he live?"

"West L.A. Off Beverly Glen."

At least she was not that far away. "I wish you'd checked with me first."

"Why? You'd had a hell of a day, and you'd crashed. Ginn said she'd call you this morning, first thing."

Which for Ginn did not mean 6:00 a.m. "Does he have my dog, too?"

"Ah," Bobby said. "You mean as well as your girl? Yes, Laila won't go to the john without Barney."

"Do you have his number?"

"A couple of them. You got a pen?"

"I'm on the highway, I'll have to call you when I get to the office. At least, I'm going to get my dog back."

He could hear Eckhart laughing when he hung up.

It was just seven when he got to Brentwood, but the construction business started early and already the phone was ringing through the empty office as he opened the door. He got to his desk, grabbed the phone before it stopped.

"Matt Lowell."

"And how are you this bright Monday morning?" Mike Greffen's voice said. "Open for business?"

With an expensive new wife, a huge mortgage, and a lot of alimony he liked to complain about, particularly after a couple of drinks, Mike Greffen started his working day as early as construction people did. "Good morning, Mike. What's up?"

"I've got a nice little building that's just come onto the market. Eight stories, ground floor used to be a bank, so there's some good stuff inside, mahogany paneling, lovely mouldings. Very well preserved. Downtown, so I thought I'd call you first. It's a great opportunity."

"Another opportunity like the dump on San Julian Street?"

Greffen had the grace to laugh. "No, but that's gone already. Full price, all cash deal. You didn't move fast enough."

"Who took it off your hands?"

"The same people that bought the building across the street, Aurora Borealis Company. They've picked up a lot of stuff in the garment district. My guess is they're Canadian, you know, the northern lights you can see up there in the Yukon all winter. All summer, too, I'll bet. Canadians are coming on strong right now in Los Angeles. You might want to look into them, check your competition. What about this bank? Interested?"

"Yes, sure. Send over the paperwork and we'll run some numbers."

"Don't hang around if you want it. You got some big sharks starting to swim in your waters. I hear the Donald's in town."

"Mike, do you really think I'm going to worry that we're head to head with Trump for a derelict eight-story bank building?"

Greffen laughed. "You'll have the paperwork on your desk this morning. Get back to me if you want to see it, and we'll set something up."

Matt disconnected, then called Ginn's cell, listened impatiently to her recorded voice, left a message to call him immediately. Next he phoned Bobby, jotted down Cargill's home and office numbers. He called Cargill's home first. No luck, so he left a message there and another at his Century City law firm, then called Ginn's office in case she'd decided to go to work in spite of his warning and left word again for her to phone him.

He'd covered all the bases he could think of. He sat back in his chair and stared down into the plaza at the poinsettias and fake snow, the stores with Christmas displays in place. Thanksgiving was still a week away and for a second he mourned the loss of his favorite holiday, trampled in the rush for the Christmas trade.

He swung back to his computer, booted up. Trump was no competition, Lowell Brothers were definitely nowhere close to playing on that field. The Canadians, however, were a different matter. He tapped a few keys but Aurora Borealis Company did not have a Web site. It was a long shot anyway.

On a hunch, he brought up the general plan for the city of Malibu and studied the screen. He'd always felt a real kinship with May Rindge, the last owner of the vast Spanish land grant known as Rancho Malibu Sequit. She went down fighting to keep the ranch intact, spent her fortune in court battles that spanned a quarter of a century. As late as 1920, old May still had mounted gunmen patrolling the fences to keep the Pacific Railroad from crossing her land. Of course, the railroad won, he and Bobby had found traces of the old rail line, long gone now. The highway pushed through in 1929, the twentieth century moved in, the ranch was broken up. All that remained of the Rancho Malibu Sequit that once stretched from Santa Monica to Point Mugu were land parcels and beach lots.

Matt typed in Phil's address, got a parcel number and a map of Carbon Beach. He zoomed in on the lot, a hundred feet along one of the most exclusive stretches of coast in California.

He looked at his watch, saw that it was past eight and reached for the phone. Anything he wanted to know about a piece of property he could get from the title company Lowell Brothers used. They had the software to search for ownership, encumbrances, liens, and could establish from the tax stamps attached to the deed how much was paid every time it changed hands.

"United Title Company," a female voice said.

"This is Matt Lowell, Lowell Brothers. Bill Winer, please."

Almost immediately, a voice said, "Good morning to you, Matt. What can I do for you?"

"Bill, good morning. I need a quick title search. A lot on Carbon Beach in Malibu."

"How quick?"

"Right now." Matt knew Winer would make the search without demur. Their relationship had been cordial and mutually rewarding for the fourteen years Lowell Brothers had been in business.

"Okay, give me the details, I'll get back to you."

While Matt waited, he called Annie Lautner and wasn't surprised when he got a recorded message. If he had to guess, he'd say Annie was not an early riser at the best of times, and this surely was not that for Annie. He didn't leave a message.

His other line rang and he picked it up. Bill Winer's voice said,

"Matt, that parcel on Carbon Beach." Winer started in on a history of the property.

Matt cut through the legalese. "Just the last five years, Bill."

"Okay. The property changed hands five years ago. Present owner of record, Aurora Borealis Company. Purchase price, fifteen-twenty-five."

Matt's heart beat a sudden tattoo. He was on to something, but he wasn't quite sure what. Not yet. But the same company that was buying big downtown owned Phil Halliburton's house, paying over fifteen million dollars, which did not include the cost of the remodel and that had to have been plenty. Halliburton had lived in what could be a twenty million dollar property and that was a lot of celebrity patients. "Dr. Phillip Halliburton's name appear anywhere?"

"Just a minute."

Matt waited impatiently, then Winer said, "No, just Aurora Borealis Holding Company."

"Who's the field agent?" A holding company was impenetrable, but tax bills and official documents had to go somewhere to be handled. The field agent was usually a law firm.

"Duggan and Thurman." Winer gave an address on Figueroa Street in Los Angeles.

Duggan and something, Annie had said. Duggan & Thurman. Phil Halliburton's lawyers were the field agent for Aurora Borealis Holding Company. They owned his house, they were buying up derelict buildings in the garment district. Or maybe Halliburton was into real estate. A lot of real estate. In all the years Matt had known him, Halliburton had never mentioned real estate holdings, and in Los Angeles real estate was the number one topic of conversation. But there was a hell of a lot Halliburton had never mentioned.

"Matt, are you still there?" Winer asked.

"Yes. Bill, I need to know if Aurora Borealis Company owns anything else in Malibu." He thought a moment. Halliburton had been killed on Latigo Canyon Road. "And I'd like a list of the owners of record of every parcel of land in a two mile radius around Latigo Canyon in Malibu. And contiguous plot maps blown up to a twenty-four-inch square."

"How soon?"

"How soon can you get it together?"

"Noon okay?"

"Thanks. As soon as they're ready, messenger them over."

He called Annie Lautner's number and let it ring a dozen times before hanging up. Annie probably had a head full of kodo drummers, too, after the amount of dope and booze he'd seen her put away. God knows how much more she'd had after he left.

Ned ambled in at 9:30. Matt brought him up to speed on the conversation with Mike Greffen and they spent fifteen minutes discussing progress on a couple of their projects. Matt called Annie again. This time he left word on her answering machine that he was on his way out to drop off the keys she had lent him.

Matt drove into the driveway of the Malibu Villas and parked the Range Rover in the same visitor's spot he'd used the day before. A serious swimmer was using the pool for laps, and through the windows of the gym, he could see one lone twentysomething in a bright pink leotard working her already shapely glutes on the step machine.

Matt ran up the stairs to Annie's unit and rang the bell. No one answered, so he banged on the door. Annie's fancy front door was the only door on this level, but the hallway led to an opening that framed the view of Point Dume. Matt waited a moment, then went down the hall to lean over the wrought iron railing. He could see Annie's balcony, landscaped with large terra cotta urns planted with a variety of palms, brilliantly red geraniums and white impatiens. A filmy drape had caught in the sliding glass door, and moved in the slight breeze.

He returned to the front door, rang again, hammered a fist against the wood.

"Annie. It's Matt Lowell. Are you okay?"

No answer, and he couldn't wait around. As he bent to push

the keys beneath the front mat, his attention was caught by a flash of white. He heard a small whimper.

"Hey, what are you doing out here?" Matt held out his hand to Annie's tiny dog who was cowering behind one of the tubs of dwarf palms flanking the door. The little Maltese terrier wagged his tail and practically jumped into Matt's arms. All eight pounds of him were trembling. Matt ran a soothing hand over his coat, and looked at the heart-shaped tag attached to a jeweled collar. Sammy Lautner, he read, followed by Annie's phone number.

"Well, Sammy Lautner, how did you manage to get out? Where's your mom?" A ripple of disquiet touched the hair on the back of his neck. Even as stoned as she was when he left her, Annie would never allow Sam out of the house alone. Neither, surely, would the maid, Tuti.

Matt chose a key from the set Annie had given him and slipped it into the lock. It turned first try and he opened the door. The air was stuffy, and sour with the smell of stale marijuana and the camellia-scented candles she had been burning the day before.

"Annie," he called again. "It's Matt. I've got your keys."

He stepped inside and closed the door behind him. He lowered Sam to the floor and walked through the foyer into the living room.

It was empty. The sliding door was slightly open, he crossed the room, closed it, then went through the kitchen. Nothing in the sink, and though the dishwasher was filled, the dishes were shining and clean.

"Tuti?" He knocked, then pushed open the door to the service area. It too was empty, the floor powdery with laundry detergent that had been spilled and then swept up. But there was no futon, no small stacks of black trousers or white T-shirts. No sheets suspended over a line. In fact, there was no line.

It was as if Tuti had simply vanished.

Déjà vu, he thought.

Quickly, he went from room to room. There was no sign of

Annie, but as at Phil's there was a sense of disturbance, as if someone had searched, and put things back but not quite in order. The bed was made, the black silk spread pristine, but the towels in the bathroom had not been used, and there were no damp towels in the laundry basket.

In the kitchen, Sam was nosing a dry water bowl on the floor. Matt filled the bowl with water, left Sammy drinking while he searched for dog food. He fed Sammy, picked him as soon as he had finished eating, then left the condominium as he had found it, locked the door, dropped the keys into his pocket. Sammy tucked under his arm, Matt ran downstairs, checked Annie's carport in back. Her space was empty, her seafoam green Jaguar missing.

"She would not have left you outside, so what happened, Sam?" Matt murmured. "Any ideas?"

He knew Sam was her constant companion. Annie rarely went out without him, carrying the little terrier in a shoulder bag with only his small fluffy white head visible.

Briefly, Matt considered calling the sheriff's department, but what did he know for sure? Very little. He could hear himself explaining: "Well, her dog was outside, her maid's gone, her car's gone, the house is stuffy, and I have the feeling something's wrong because her dead boyfriend's maids have also left."

Carrying Sam, he walked over to the gym. The girl with the perfect body was still working the step machine to the rhythm of techno rap, her back to the door.

Matt lifted the dog, stared into the brown button eyes.

"If this doesn't work out, Sam, I'll come get you. You've got my word." He opened the door to the gym, put Sam on the floor just inside, closed the door again to prevent him from following.

The girl with the model's body probably knew Annie and that Sam belonged to her. But if she didn't, Sam was wearing his tags, he was irresistible and alone. If Annie did come back, she'd get her dog. If she didn't, eventually the girl would get in touch with the authorities and tell them Annie was missing.

At least, that's what he hoped.

CHAPTER 26

Matt stood in front of floor to ceiling windows in John Cargill's reception area on the seventeenth floor of the Two Thousand Building on Century Park East. The view was spectacular, from Century City across Beverly Hills to the high-rise towers downtown and beyond to the San Gabriel Mountains, shrouded by haze and smog much of the year, but often startlingly clear in late fall and winter as they were today, topped by snow from last week's storm.

On the way in from Malibu, he'd called Ginn again. He didn't know whether to start to panic or whether Ginn was out of range, or out of batteries.

He turned as John Cargill emerged from his office. "Sorry I haven't had a chance to return your calls. It's been a hell of a morning. You know how Mondays are. Come on in."

Matt did know something about Mondays and since Cargill was the only one who might be able to give him answers to some questions, he'd come in person instead of waiting for his call to be returned at the end of a crammed day.

Cargill indicated a visitor's chair, went around his desk in front of windows that showcased the view behind him, flipped a switch on his intercom. "Nikki, coffee, please." He lowered his long frame into his own leather chair. "I know you must be anxious, but I'm waiting for my law enforcement contacts to return my call. It might be a couple of days before I can tell you anything."

"That's not why I'm here, John. I understand you picked up Laila and Ginn and my dog Barney."

"Oh, I see. They're okay, Matt, quite safe. When I called last night to find out how things were, it was clear that a problem was going to arise for deputy Eckhart. So I offered my place. Just temporarily. Nice dog by the way."

The door opened, a young woman placed a tray with cups and saucers, a coffeepot, a plate of sugar cookies on Cargill's desk.

"I would trust Bobby Eckhart with my life," Matt said when she'd left. "I'm sure you didn't come out and say this to Ginn, but I'm guessing that's another reason you encouraged her to leave, because you don't."

Cargill did not agree or deny. Instead, he said, "I'm sorry, maybe we should have kept you in the picture, but Ginn told me about the attack on you and the phone call warning you off. She mentioned you'd had a hell of a whack on the head, so we decided it was best to let you rest last night."

"That was thoughtful. She hasn't called me yet today."

"The young girl takes up a lot of energy. Look, they really are all right, I can assure you of that. I'll give you my address, go on over there." Cargill slid a discreet glance at his watch.

Okay, Matt thought. He had given time enough to being pissed off. Time to move on. He needed some answers, and Cargill was the expert. "You said something yesterday about people being trafficked into the domestic trade and sweatshops."

"Yes, it's a big problem, and it's growing yearly."

"I went to Phil Halliburton's house yesterday. He was the doctor who came to see Laila initially. I mentioned that he was killed on Friday night. He had three live-in maids, two Asian, one Latina. They are all missing. His house had been searched."

Cargill started to speak, and Matt held up a hand to stop him. "Wait a minute, there's more. Annie Lautner, Halliburton's girlfriend has a maid, also a small Asian woman, who appears to live in the laundry area off the kitchen. I went to see Annie again this morning, to see if she was all right. No one was there. She and the maid both seem to be missing."

John leaned back, steepled his fingers. "Matt, listen. When you first get involved in this kind of thing, trafficking, I mean, you start to see it everywhere, even where it doesn't exist. Maids work for agencies. They can get new jobs overnight."

"Yes, that's possible. But I ran a title search on Phil's house on Carbon Beach. It's got to be at least a twenty million dollar establishment. He also bought a spread for his mother in Bakersfield. Although I can't prove anything yet, I'm beginning to think he was the major player in all this."

Cargill nodded. "All right, I can pass that word along. It's a lead. But if you want my advice, drop this now. It really is more dangerous than you know."

"Something else," Matt said. "Do you know anything about a firm called Duggan and Thurman? They're downtown on Figueroa."

"I know of them. Why do you ask?" He sat up, his attention engaged.

"They're Phil Halliburton's lawyers. They're also the field agents for Aurora Borealis Holding Company. Aurora is buying old factory buildings in the garment district and throwing up some impregnable fences around them. I'm wondering if they could be sweatshops."

"What I know off hand is that I can make some calls if you like, get a private investigator to look into Duggan and Thurman, see what we can dig up about this Aurora Borealis Company."

"Thanks. I knew Phil for years. It's hard to believe that he was involved in anything as terrible as sexual trafficking. I thought I might find something on his computer notebook, names, maybe even a location, but the computer's gone and his house has been stripped bare of every scrap of paper. It's a dead end."

Cargill frowned, perplexed. "Paper? That's strange."

"Not if you think about it. Someone searched, couldn't read English, and took everything."

"That could be, I suppose."

A soft, discreet knock at the door was followed by Nikki. "Your 11:30 appointment is here, Mr. Cargill."

Matt rose to his feet. "I won't keep you any longer. Thanks for seeing me."

Cargill scribbled a few lines on a pad, tore off the page and handed it across the desk. "This is my address. It's a couple of miles up Beverly Glen. Easy to find."

Cargill's rambling Spanish hacienda occupied the entire end of a secluded enclave of half a dozen houses in a quiet box canyon not far from the UCLA campus. Gabby was in the doorway when Matt arrived. An ecstatic Barney threw himself against Matt's legs.

"Where's Ginn?" Matt asked. He dropped a kiss on Gabby's cheek, rubbed Barney's ears.

"She went to see Phil's housekeeper, Lupe Vasquez."

The raucous cry of blue jays seemed louder in the sudden silence as Matt stared, speechless, at Ginn's mother. "Lupe?"

"That's what she said, cheri."

Matt took his cell phone from his pocket, jabbed a finger at Ginn's number and got her voice mail. "She's still not answering. I've been leaving messages all morning. Gabby, this is crazy, why did she do that?"

"Well, Bobby told her that Lupe was not in the house, and she thought it would be a good idea to make sure Lupe and her daughter were all right."

"And you let her go?"

Gabby raised her finely shaped eyebrows. "You think I should have stopped her?"

"Of course you should have stopped her. What's she going to do, knock on doors until she finds her?"

"No, what are you talking about? She's going to the place Lupe goes every month on her weekend off." Gabby took in the surprise on Matt's face. "I forgot, you don't know, it was after you and Ginn separated. Lupe called her out of the blue one day. Her daughter got into some sort of trouble, and Lupe was afraid Dr. Halliburton would find out. She knew Ginn was a lawyer. Ginn got the girl back in school and then arranged for the child to get some counseling."

Only Ginn, Matt thought. He hadn't even known Lupe had a daughter. There was no reason why he should, there was no reason why Ginn should either. But that was Ginn.

"Where is this place?"

"I don't know, she didn't say."

Matt's cell rang, he held up a finger, asked Gabby to excuse him. "Ginn?"

"No, it's Ned. Matt, we've got some trouble at the Contessa. Can you get down there right away?"

"Now? What kind of trouble?"

"A bunch of homeless guys have taken over some completed apartments. They're demanding a meeting and it has to be with you."

"With me?"

"That's what they say. Matt Lowell."

"Can't Manny Gonzales deal with it?"

"He's tried, but they insist on you."

"I can't get there. Have Manny call the cops."

"No, they claim to be veterans, Matt. Manny says no, but we can't risk having cops dragging homeless veterans, if that's what they are, out of a Lowell Brothers project. How do you think that would play if it got on the news tonight? Just go down there, find out what they want, and fix it."

"Ned, I can't get away, I'm tied—"

Ned cut in. "Hey. I would be glad to go myself but I've got the brass from the mayor's office here in ten minutes, and Chet Barnes is already on his second cup of coffee in our conference room. Now we've got a business to run here, Matt, and whatever you're doing I can tell you right now it is not a priority."

"Listen, you don't know what's going on—"

"No, you listen. People are expecting to move into those apartments this weekend. Whatever you've got on, shelve it. Matt, I've gotta go. Call me from the job." He hung up.

Matt snapped the phone closed. "Goddamn it."

Gabby looked at him. "What?"

"Ned thinks there's a crisis on one of our jobs but that's Ned. He thinks everything's a crisis." Although to be fair, community relations, whatever that community happened to be, was his responsibility, not Ned's.

"You have to go?"

Matt shook his head. "No. I have to talk to Laila."

"How can you do that without a translator? You go, take care of your business matter and I'll call and ask Amira to come. By the time you get back, Ginn will probably be here, too."

Matt thought about it and reluctantly agreed. He had a responsibility to Ned he couldn't ignore. "Okay, I'll be back as soon as I can, but if you talk to Ginn before I do, please have her call me."

Matt strode into the Contessa's reception lobby to be greeted by one of the leasing agents almost hidden by a huge flower arrangement on the granite countertop. Face creased with distress, she said, "Those people didn't come through here, Mr. Lowell. We would have stopped them. They must have snuck in when no one was looking."

"It's okay, Molly, no one's blaming you."

The lobby smelled of fresh paint and scent from the flowers, Italian tapestries and mosaics hung in place on the walls, leafy ficus trees filled the internal garden now bright with the early afternoon sun. On the other side of the lobby, Manny Gonzales, the construction boss, was frowning over a roll of plans spread across one of the small leasing desks. At his side, Susan Dean tapped at the sheet with a ballpoint. She had her gold safety helmet pushed to the back of her head, loose strands of red hair curling around her neck.

His heart sank. He hadn't called her as he'd promised, hadn't even thought of her.

"Hi, Susan, didn't expect to see you here today. I haven't been here for a week and the place has really come together. Looks terrific."

She looked up. "Thanks, it's turned out well, I think, and on time. I'm on my way to another job and dropped by to see everything's on track. You've got some trouble, I hear. Manny just told me." She gave him a cool professional smile, then switched her attention to Manny. "I'll be in the Florence." One of the three buildings that comprised the Contessa, each named for an Italian city and separated by lawns and gardens with paths winding beneath a variety of newly planted trees. "When you get through, come find me, and we'll finish going over these interior details. It shouldn't take us long."

Susan picked up a clipboard, flipping though pages as she walked through the front door, into the shade of the jacarandas lining the street.

Matt stared at her departing back, then took a deep breath. He'd hurt her, the last thing in the world he'd want to do. He started toward the community room, the superintendent at his side. "Okay, Manny, fill me in."

Manny was an ex-marine and looked it, grizzled hair razored in a Marine Corps cut, a spine like an iron bar, Semper Fi tattooed on one forearm, a bald eagle with a sheaf of arrows gripped in its talons on the other.

"I did what you said on the phone. Worked like a charm. I bought out the roach wagon, offered lunch and that got them out of the apartments. I put them in the community room." The building they were in, the Roma, was flanked by the other two, and housed the community rooms and library, the full-sized gym as well as two floors of apartments. "They're still in there, eating lunch."

"So what do they want?"

"To talk to you. I was in 'Nam, and the first Gulf War. One or two may be vets, but I don't think so. Ask me, they're a bunch of nutcases holding us up to ransom, and I'd haul their sorry asses out of here but Ned won't go for it."

Matt opened the door, and tried not to take in the combined odor of unwashed bodies, burritos, sour breath and roach wagon coffee. Manny had covered the central conference table with a plastic sheet and it was littered with grease-stained paper plates and crumpled napkins, cans of soft drinks and plastic cups.

Matt cast his gaze around the ten or twelve seated men, a racial mix, black and white. They were dressed in a variety of dirt stained T-shirts and ill-fitting pants, cheap sweaters, a few jackets made of shiny synthetic material. Maybe some of the garments had once had color, long lost.

Immediately Matt's gut told him something here was not right. There was constant movement round the table, fingers tapping, bodies shifting, knees jerking. This was clearly not a cohesive group.

"I'm Matt Lowell," he said pleasantly. They had asked to see him, yet not one of them looked up. "I'm told you want to see me."

Silence greeted him. "Maybe one of you had better do the talking." Matt spoke to the man closest to him. "How about you?"

The skinny black man looked up, his eyes wide with anxiety. He shook his head without speaking. The man next to him, his white skin pitted with the acne scars of a crystal meth addict, said, "We want a nice apartment in this fancy building."

"What's your name?"

"Spike."

"Okay, Spike, good enough. Now, what can I really do for you?"

"A nice apartment in your nice fancy building."

"Didn't Manny here explain we had nothing available?"

A black guy on the other side of the table, his hair dreadlocked by grime, said, "A nice apartment and jobs so's we can pay you a righteous rent."

"You wouldn't know what to do with a job if you had one," Manny said. "Didn't I offer you a broom a few months ago?"

Matt looked again at the men around the table. They belonged in a hospital, most of them, on medication. There was no point in going on with this discussion.

"Give me a minute." He got up and walked to the window and stared at the gardens Benny Pressman, the landscape architect, had created on the other side of the road. Something about this situation smelled, and it wasn't just the defeated men doing their best to keep to a script somebody had given them. He looked at his watch. Almost one and Ginn still hadn't called. On the way downtown, he'd phoned her office, tried to persuade her assistant to give him Lupe's address. She'd refused but promised to get back to him as soon as she got permission. He turned and resumed his seat.

"I'm sorry, our apartments are already rented. If you like, Manny here will give you the names and addresses of a couple of other places. As for jobs, Manny might be able to find some cleanup work for minimum wage."

Spike looked around nervously. "So we gonna call, you know, the ACLU, and the TV news, and the *L.A. Times*."

"What are you talking about? Who put you up to this?"

Another of the men on the far side of the table said suddenly, "A nice apartment in this nice fancy building."

The construction superintendent looked disgusted. "I asked, and not one of these jokers can give me their unit, their name, rank or serial number. If they're veterans of any war I know about, I'm the leader of the free world. I say haul their asses out of here, and let me get back to work."

"Hey, you wait a minute, a nice apartment in this nice fancy—"

He did not want to pursue this, but suddenly out of patience, Matt cut in. "Who's behind this stunt? You tell me who put you up to it and you get two nights at the Adlon over on the Nickel." The Adlon Hotel was a good flop, as these places went, on East Fifth.

"Fuck that, no way," Spike said. "No fuckin' Adlon, they got a shitload of rules there." He grinned, exposing a mouthful of brown rotted teeth. "Take cash, though."

"No cash," Matt said.

"Couple nights at the Adlon sound ace to me," a voice said. "Get me a shower. Sound good, man."

"Okay." Matt walked over to the speaker. He pushed aside a paper plate, perched on the table and folded his arms. "So what's this about, dude?"

The man shot a defiant look at Spike and said, "Got ten bucks each guy, get Matt Lowell down here, keep talking—"

His voice was suddenly lost in a blast that roared through the room. A babble of terror rose and Matt found himself in the middle of a rush of men pushing through the door into the lobby. He struggled free, ran to where he'd last seen the young leasing agent, found her crouched under the counter.

"Are you okay?"

She looked up shakily. "I guess so. Is it an earthquake?"

"No, an explosion. One of the other buildings. Call 911, but stay here." As he raced outside, he yelled over his shoulder, "911! Right now!"

The men he'd been talking to had scattered, but Manny and his crew of workmen were converging on a rising cloud of dust. He sprinted after them—the ex-marine carried twenty more years than he did—and they reached the scene of the explosion.

"Christ on a crutch," Gonzales said.

From the middle of the street, a crowd of dust-covered workmen and women stared in shock at the rubble. Thirty feet in the middle of the front wall had collapsed, newly planted trees were uprooted, cars had their windows blown out, their bleating alarms adding to the turmoil. He turned, searched the crowd for a gold hardhat.

"Where's Susan?"

"Oh, God Almighty," Manny said. "She said she'd be here. She was doing a random check before the final move in."

Matt started toward the building at a run, Manny on his heels. "Anyone else inside?"

"No," Gonzales panted, "it's closed up, move-in ready." He turned and shouted, "Jaime, take a head count. Stay back, take a head count."

Matt scrambled over a beam, stumbled into a cracked sink blown from an apartment. The dust was settling and he could hear sirens and power horns in the distance. He made his way into the small elevator lobby. It looked like a war zone, shattered marble, a gaping hole instead of a polished walnut cab, elevator cables ripped and dangling.

"Susan! Can you hear me?"

"I'll bring up equipment, move some rubble." Gonzales was still with him.

"Yeah, okay, but keep everyone out. And shut everything down, gas, electricity."

"Got it." Gonzales turned back through the tangle of construction debris and was gone.

"Susan!" The groan of trembling masonry greeted his shout. He felt nauseous with panic. "Susan!" His fear for her was taking over and he knew he had to get it under control. He took in a couple of deep breaths and choked on the dust-filled air. "Susan, can you hear me?"

"Matt? Matt, I'm here." The sound of her voice was faint but unmistakable.

She was alive. The sound was coming from the ground floor, thank God, not the elevator shaft. His panic subsided. He turned toward the direction of her voice.

"Are you okay? Where are you?"

"Apartment four."

"Are you all right?" He started down the hall.

"Yes, I think so. I can't get out, though."

"Okay, Susie, take it easy. I'm on my way."

The hall was an obstacle course of downed light fixtures, mouldings and plaster hanging in sheets from the ceiling, the carpet already deep in water. Electrical wires fizzed and sputtered and Matt tried not to think of the gas escaping from cracked pipes. Apartment four was two apartments down on the right, facing the street, the door hanging drunkenly off the hinges. He shoved the door out of the way, crunched over smashed floor tiles.

"Susan!"

"Master bedroom." Her voice had weakened.

She was lying across the threshold between the master bath and bedroom, the front of her thick red hair was caked with white plaster that was ominously streaked with scarlet, her face smeared with blood. The bathroom countertop was across her legs.

"Matt, I can't move."

"You're going to be okay, Susie." He heaved the countertop aside, glad it wasn't granite as they'd originally planned, then discarded because of cost. Her pants were ripped, but her legs seemed okay, not broken, as far as he could tell. He thought quickly. Best choice was not to move her but Manny hadn't had time to shut down the gas and power, so Matt couldn't wait for the medics—the place could explode again at any time. "I'm going to get you out of here. Can you put your arms around my neck?"

"Yes, I think so."

Matt dropped to one knee onto the shards of the bathroom mirror. "Okay, here we go." He slipped an arm around her waist, the other under her knees. Somehow he got to his feet—he couldn't smell the gas, but he knew it was there, he was beginning to feel the effects, and Susan had to be feeling worse. She groaned and he said, "Hold on, Susie, we'll be out of here in a second." He made his way through the living room, over the collapsed wall into the patio, out into the increasing chaos of arriving emergency vehicles—fire trucks, police cars, ambulances, lights whirring, sirens adding to the chop of news helicopters overhead. A shout went up as Matt stumbled into the street, a couple of medics unloaded a gurney and raced toward them. Matt lowered Susan onto it, and stepped back to allow them to attend to her.

He turned away, wracked by a spasm of coughing. His lungs and throat felt much as they had during the Malibu fire. One of the medics glanced at him from across the gurney.

"You okay, buddy?"

Matt nodded. "Yeah, I'm all right, thanks."

He took a few breaths then turned back to smile as reassuringly as he could at Susan. She had a neck brace already in place, and she was being strapped to a board. She grasped his hand as he walked beside her to the waiting LAFD ambulance.

"What happened? Matt, it just exploded," she said. "What happened?"

"I don't know yet. Don't worry, Susie, they'll take care of you. I'll call later."

She put a hand to her face, then looked at the blood on her fingers. "I must look a mess," she said.

He heard the fear in her voice. "It's a scalp wound, Susie, they bleed a lot, but your face is fine. You look beautiful."

The medics lifted her into the ambulance. Matt stood back, smiled and waved. "I'll call you later."

"Can I take that to the bank?"

"Lloyds of London, Susie."

The doors closed and the ambulance pulled away, lights and siren blaring. Another team insisted on checking him out. Matt took a hit of oxygen, told them the day of the week, the name of the president, followed a moving pen from left to right, refused transportation to the hospital, promised he'd come in if he felt sick or sleepy.

A female reporter he recognized from a local news channel shoved a mike into his face. "What's your name, sir? Who was that you just rescued? Is she your girlfriend?"

"Excuse me," Matt said. He pushed past her, scanning the crowd until he spotted Manny on the other side of a fire truck. He was in the center of a group of men in suits talking to him earnestly, and even from this distance, Matt could see the look of relief on his face as Manny caught his eye and waved him over. Matt started through the crowd of firefighters and emergency response people, stepping over hoses, avoiding equipment and running men.

It was unreal to hear the insistent buzz of his cell phone. He answered with his name and the elusively familiar voice said, "You did not take me seriously. This can get worse. Back off, keep your mouth shut, walk away."

Matt's heart pumped. Keep calm, he told himself, keep him talking, and listen. Listen hard.

"You did this?"

"Well, a gas leak blew. That's what investigators will find, an accident. Easy to rig, you know that. We can do more damage than you want to know, Matt."

Frowning, Matt listened, his eyes roving, moving on and then returning to the group of men around Manny. "Okay, I'll back off. How do I know you'll leave us alone?"

"Well, Ned's kids will stay healthy. Play it smart, Matt. Stop asking questions, keep your mouth shut, live the good life. Think about your girl, Ginn. You want to keep her safe, don't you?"

Susan's blood was damp on his shirt, and suddenly Matt lost it. "You son of a bitch," he shouted. "She's nothing to do with this."

He felt eyes on him, saw the swivel of heads in his direction, reporters practically salivating as they leapt into action, pushing through the milling crowd of workmen being held back by the police.

A cop, he thought. Yes.

CHAPTER 27

Ginn cruised slowly, leaning across the passenger seat to check the numbers against the address her assistant had given her earlier over the phone, but the cars jamming both sides of the street made it impossible to see anything painted on the curb, and only the letter carrier familiar with them could find numbers on these buildings.

The neighborhood was a mixture of small houses with miniscule front yards protected by chicken wire fences, shabby three- and four-story apartment buildings, some old Spanish-style fourplexes surviving from a more prosperous time. A couple of car lengths ahead, a battered Toyota pulled away from the curb, and Ginn slipped the BMW into the vacated spot in front of a stained yellow stucco apartment house. She got out, walked up the chipped flagstone path to the building's bank of mailboxes, and discovered she was standing in front of No. 603. She clicked the key lock for her car, and started back down the block.

The street was busy for a Monday, people coming and going.

A couple of collarless pit bulls nosed the gutter, rap blasted from a boom box hung on a fence, and a group of well muscled young men, their white tank tops showing off a variety of tattoos, were half buried under the hood of a glossy low-rider. They looked up as she passed, making loud comments in Spanish. These were the guys keeping order on this street, Ginn thought. She flashed a smile, and kept walking and checking house numbers.

The address she had occupied the lower left of a bougainvillea-draped Spanish fourplex with black iron grilles over the windows. Cars lined the crumbling driveways on either side of a patch of struggling grass.

She pressed the bell and out of the corner of her eye saw a front curtain twitch, and turned so that her face could be seen. She heard a hurried exchange of voices from the other side of the door then a dead bolt slide back, a chain rattle as it was being removed. The door opened a few inches and an old woman peered out at her. Her face had aged into an ancient wrinkled beauty, hooded dark eyes, her thin white hair was pulled back tightly from her face.

Ginn smiled at her and said, "*Buenos dias, senora.* I'm looking for Lupe Vasquez. Is she here?"

A fragile, arthritic old hand reached out and pulled her into a small foyer. The old woman stared at her, and Ginn realized she was scared to death.

She spoke gently. "Is Lupe here, *senora?*"

The old woman shook her head. Ginn ran her eyes over the sparsely furnished living room, a sofa and a couple of mismatched chairs, a TV set on a stand, a card table covered by a green and white checked oilcloth and bearing a vase of plastic flowers. On the walls were pictures of the Virgin Mary and Jesus, and both slain Kennedys. The room was cold. A couple of suitcases stood by the side of an open door through which Ginn glimpsed a narrow bed, a bedside table and tiny lamp.

Lupe Vasquez came through the door and pulled it closed behind her. Lupe looked as the old woman may have looked in her mid-thirties—soft mocha colored skin, large dark eyes, a mass of black hair twisted into a loose knot at the nape of her neck.

Avoiding Ginn's eyes, she crossed the room and put an arm around the old woman and spoke softly in Spanish. The woman asked a couple of questions in a tremulous voice, shooting anxious glances at Ginn as Lupe helped her to shuffle back to her chair in front of the TV. The sounds of a Spanish-language soap filled the room.

"She's very scared," Lupe said. "She is Maria Ortiz, I told you about her."

But she hadn't said Maria Ortiz was in her eighties. "I'm sorry," Ginn replied. "I didn't mean to frighten her."

Lupe shrugged and gestured at the room. "This is what she has. She rent out her room for a little extra and she think the landlord find out, he make her leave. She don't read, she don't write, all her life she is a cleaning lady. Like me. Why did you come?"

Ginn looked at her more closely and was shocked at the change in her. Lupe was a beautiful woman, but today her face looked as if the muscles that held it together had been pulled apart. New creases from her nose to her mouth marred her skin, her large black eyes were sunk deep into their sockets, the skin around them smudged from lack of sleep.

"I came to see if you and Angeline were all right. May I sit down?"

"Please, yes. Sit down." Lupe crossed to the card table and dragged out a metal folding chair for Ginn, seated herself in another.

Ginn took the chair offered. "How is Angeline?"

A familiar immigrant story, Ginn had thought when Lupe had come to see her. Lupe had to work to support them, so she boarded her daughter with a friend, Maria Ortiz. All she wanted, Lupe had told her, was to give her fourteen-year-old daughter a better start in life than she'd had. But Angeline had her own ideas, started to run with bad kids, got into trouble, until finally she was suspended from school. Ginn got her off a charge of vandalism, reinstated, and into counseling. For her services, she had sent Lupe a bill for thirty dollars.

"She's gone away," Lupe said.

"But she's all right?"

Lupe nodded. "She's with my brother in the desert."

"You're leaving, too, I see." Ginn looked at the suitcases.

The sound from the TV increased suddenly. Lupe got up, adjusted the volume, then returned to her chair. She pressed her lips together and swallowed. "I don't know why you are here, Miss Ginn. I don't know anything."

"You don't know what I'm going to ask. And maybe you know more than you think you do." Ginn leaned forward. "I'm glad you and Angie are okay, but I want to know about the other two women who worked with you? Betty and Eva, aren't those their names?"

"Dr. Phil called them that."

"Did they get other jobs?"

Lupe shrugged.

"Lupe, you remember my…Mr. Lowell? He went to Dr. Halliburton's house yesterday and couldn't find any trace of any of you. Did they leave when you did?"

Lupe turned her head to stare at the images on the TV screen.

"Lupe, please," Ginn said. "I think you know where they are."

"Dr. Halliburton is dead." She shrugged. "They went away."

"Did they leave an address?"

Lupe shook her head.

"Then how could they get their final paycheck? They must have money coming to them."

"I don't know."

"What about you, Lupe? Did you get a final paycheck?"

"Dr. Phil pay me cash. I don't pay no taxes."

"Did he pay Betty and Eva the same way, under the table?"

Lupe shrugged, and reached to straighten the plastic flowers in the vase. Her hand was shaking.

Ginn covered Lupe's hand with her own. "Lupe, what are you afraid of?"

The frightened woman turned her hand to grasp Ginn's.

"My Angeline, she's a good girl and she's okay now. You very good to us, Ginn." Lupe took a shaky breath. "Men came and took Betty and Eva. Maybe they are dead. I don't know, I was very scared and I run outside onto the sand, they don't see me."

"My God! Lupe! When did this happen?"

"Friday night after Miss Annie came. She cry, tell us Dr. Phil killed in accident. Then Betty and Eva went to bed. I stay in the house, I sit in the living room, you know, pretend like it was mine. I hear people come in, then see lights in the garden. I went out to see. Men go up garage stairs to our rooms. I heard Betty and Eva scream and I run. I wait a long time, then go back inside. Everything very neat, very tidy but Betty and Eva gone. I pack my things and Saturday, I get first bus and come here." Her mouth shook. "I send Angeline to my brother, but I stay to help Maria. Now I go, too."

"Why didn't you call 911?"

Lupe flashed her a look that said how stupid she thought that suggestion was.

"But you have a green card now, Lupe, you have nothing to fear from the police."

Lupe shook her head mutely.

"What if I go with you?" Ginn asked. "We'll go today, now, and we'll tell them what happened. Men can't take people away like that, not in this country."

As if needing to get away from the sound of Ginn's urging, Lupe got up, went into the tiny kitchen.

Ginn followed her, watching while Lupe filled a kettle at the sink, then struck a match to light the gas and put the kettle on to boil.

"There's something you are not telling me," Ginn said.

Silently, Lupe opened a cupboard, took down a can of a store brand of coffee.

"Start by telling me where they come from."

Lupe turned to face her. "Okay. Indonesia," she said, defiantly. "That's what they say. Village in Indonesia."

"Do they have friends here in Los Angeles?"

"No. No friends." A muscle by her right eye twitched and Lupe put her fingers against it.

Ginn felt a chill of apprehension. "Lupe, please," she said again. "What is it you are not telling me?"

Lupe rested a hip against the counter, leaning as if the small flash of defiance had drained the last of her resistance. She took a deep breath that caught in her chest. Fighting tears she said, "They work, Betty and Eva. All the time, all the time, all the time. They don't go out, don't get money, not speak much." She reached into a drawer, took out a tissue and scrubbed at her eyes. "They cry and cry for their children, all the time cry. They want to go back to their village, but they don't got passport, no papers, no money. Nada. They think their families get hurt if they run away, and they got no place to go here anyway. Dr. Phil say to me everything okay, they eat good, get clothes, is okay, go home one day with lot of money." The words tumbled over each other, as if now that she had started speaking, she couldn't stop. "Dr. Phil say to me I run his house good, speak English good, be the boss of everyone. Dr. Phil is good to me, Ginn, like you. He help with the amnesty, green card for me and Angeline. I need my job, for my daughter, maybe soon bring my son from Salvador. I go to police, they say I help illegal people, I lose my green card. I see Father Galvan in confession, he say I must go to police, but I think better I go far away." Her face twisted and a strangled sob escaped from her throat. "They hurt Betty and Eva. Maybe even kill. Maybe they come for me, maybe police take me if I tell them."

Speechless, Ginn crossed the kitchen and put an arm around her. Lupe's terror was palpable. And no wonder. Phil Halliburton. She'd always sensed something wrong about him, an empty place where his heart should be. It was clear in the way he treated Annie Lautner. He robbed her of her humanity, never spoke to her, never asked her opinion, or listened when she spoke to him. She was a doll to dress, to hang with jewelry, to show off as his possession.

"Lupe. This is an awful thing to have happened. Look, I have a friend, a lawyer who knows about things like this, about people who are forced to work without pay. I'll go with you and he will tell us what to do. It will be all right, nothing will happen to you."

Lupe shook off Ginn's arms. "How do you know that?" she asked angrily. "Men came into Dr. Phil's house, Ginn, into his house. They hurt Betty and Eva. I saw them. I think of my Angeline and I say to you what I say to Father Galvan. No." The kettle whistled and Lupe went to the stove and turned it off. "I am going to my daughter, and my brother in the desert. We'll be safe."

CHAPTER 28

Matt ignored Manny's beckoning wave and managed to get away before the reporters could reach him, walking rapidly to the reception building. Molly had emerged from beneath the counter, and hovered anxiously just inside the glass doors. They were still intact, Matt noted, not even a crack.

"Oh, Mr. Lowell, what happened? No one has told me anything."

"A gas leak. Susan Dean was hurt, but she's on the way to the hospital."

"Is she going to be all right?"

"Yes, I think so. Molly, I want you to call Ned, let him know what's happened here."

"I did that already, as soon as I'd called 911. He's on his way, he should be here any time now."

"Good, thanks. When he gets here, tell him I'll call him later."

"You're leaving?"

"Yes."

He closed the door on the anxious young woman, and made

his way to where he'd left the Range Rover, on the street far enough away for it to be undamaged.

Five minutes later, he was on the Santa Monica freeway, driving west to the 405. He'd left downtown at the height of commuter traffic so it was an hour before he hit the Wilshire Boulevard off ramp, and already dark when he walked into the office in Brentwood. He found a staff eager for news. Half a dozen of their people had been with him and Ned virtually since the beginning, and no one had gone home. He fielded a barrage of questions, reassured everyone that he was all right, that no one had been killed, that Susan Dean's injuries were not life threatening, finally escaping into the quiet of his own office.

Matt went into the bathroom, washed his hands and face. He needed a shower, but failing that, he used the towel to remove as much of the white plaster as he could from his hair. The wound from yesterday's encounter in the canyon was oozing again, and he dabbed at the blood with a clean facecloth, then made a pass at the crud on his clothes with the damp towel. He gulped some Tylenol to quiet the banging in his skull.

A small cardboard tube was lying on his desk with a note from Marni saying she'd gone down to the Contessa with Ned, would probably see him there, and here was the material United Title sent over earlier today. Matt shook the maps out of the tube, scanned them briefly, then rerolled and put them back to study later—he couldn't concentrate on anything until he knew where Ginn was. He tried her number again, got the same dead air. He picked up the map tube, turned off his light, called a general good-night toward the voices he could still hear in the drafting room, and left.

Her silver BMW was parked in Cargill's drive, by the side of a white Taurus, and behind Gabby's Renault. He sat in the dark for a moment staring at it. It had been a hellish day, but then so had yesterday, and the day before that. He'd been living in a nightmare world for the past two weeks. He felt obliterated with exhaustion, groggy from the toxic fumes of today's explosion, and from anxiety about Ginn. He took the first easy breath of the last twelve hours, got out of the car and started toward the house.

Ginn was standing in the open front door before he had time to ring the bell. She stepped outside onto a porch darkened by a curtain of trailing bougainvillea.

"Ginn, don't you pick up your messages? I've been calling you all day." He put his arms around her and pulled her close. Briefly, she returned his embrace, then stepped back as if suddenly remembering she did not do that anymore. He dropped his arms. "Why did you do that, race off like that without letting me know you were leaving Bobby's?"

"I'm sorry. You were so tapped out Sunday night, I thought the kindest thing to do was to let you rest. I had to take care of a few things in the office this morning, so I called you from the car. All I got was static." Ginn pulled the door closed behind her. "Lupe Vazquez told me that the night Phil died, men came to Phil's house and took his two maids away. By force. Lupe hid under the house, but it scared her to death. She sent her daughter to stay with her brother in Barstow, and I took her to the bus this afternoon so she could join them."

Before he could respond, Gabby's voice floated from inside the house. "Ginn, is that Matt?"

"Let's talk later." Ginn squeezed Matt's arm. "Don't say anything, I don't want them frightened."

He followed Ginn into the house, across the entry, down a couple of steps into a large, softly lit living room. Drapes were drawn against the night, white couches faced each other on either side of a stone hearth. The walls were hung with an eclectic mix, a few impressionists, a Bracque, a Klimt. If they were originals, they'd be worth a fortune.

Gabby came toward them. "I told you Ginn would be here when you got back." Her eyebrows arched as she took a closer look at Matt's face. "Where have you been, *cheri?* You look as if you've come from a war zone."

Ginn registered his battered appearance for the first time. She took in a sharp breath.

"There was an accident at the Contessa. Probably a gas leak. It's a mess, but nothing that can't be fixed." He'd tell Ginn the truth later when they were alone. "Is John here? I didn't see his Jeep."

A look of amusement flitted across Ginn's face. "He drives a Bentley to work. The Jeep is for weekends. Doesn't fit the Century City image, I guess."

Matt looked around. "Does Laila know I want to talk to her?"

Ginn nodded. "She's waiting. She'll be okay."

Dressed in green pants and matching sweater set, the girl was sitting with Barney in a cozy book-lined den off the living room, Amira by her side on a sofa in front of a fire. The room smelled sweetly autumnal, a mingled perfume of chrysanthemums, burning logs, the ancient leather-bound books on the shelves.

Matt bent to greet Barney and said gently, "Hello, Laila, you are looking a lot better." He'd almost said very pretty, but realized in time that was probably not what this particular young girl wanted to hear. But she looked more than pretty. It was possible to see a real beauty beginning to emerge. Her hair was a shining black curtain just touching her shoulders, the dark smudges were gone from beneath her eyes, the wide cheekbones were brushed with natural color. Most of all, it seemed as if at least one layer of sadness had lifted.

Laila raised her head and for the first time her black looked directly into his. Matt was unprepared for the tumult of emotion that suddenly rocked him, a sense of responsibility for her, a desire to protect her, even a strange sort of gratitude. He had been unable to save the child on the beach, but this young girl would have a chance to live. And he would do everything, he vowed silently, whatever it took, to find out who had brought her here.

He smiled, and saw her lips curve in response. The smile was faint, but it penetrated his heart like a beam of light. He touched a gentle finger briefly to the back of her hand, and she did not flinch.

Matt spoke to Amira. "Thank you for staying." Careful to keep his voice low and even, he went on, "Mrs. Ghoni, I want to know more about the house where Laila was held. I believe it's in Malibu, but I need to know what else she can tell me." Then he looked at Laila and spoke directly to her. "Laila, could you see the ocean from the house?"

Her eyes were fixed on his, as if she were struggling to understand his words.

Mrs. Ghoni translated, and Laila answered. Her voice was soft, delicate. "From the top windows."

Top windows. That meant more than one floor. "How many stories did the house have?"

"Two, ground, and an upstairs."

"How many rooms?" Were they talking one of the small old two-story houses, or a mansion? Like the rest of Los Angeles, almost every new house in built in Malibu since the early nineties was gargantuan.

Laila shook her head. "I don't know. Many."

Not a small house, then. For half an hour, Matt asked questions through Mrs. Ghoni. The girl was painfully earnest in giving her answers. Matt noticed that she kept one fine-boned hand on Barney's head, while the other hand rested in her lap. The aura of hysteria that had seemed a part of her had vanished.

"Did you have your own room?"

"Yes."

"Laila, what did you see from your window?"

"Trees. And hillsides."

"What about the rest of the house?"

"From a different window, I could see a fountain and some statues."

"Good. What kind of statues?"

"White."

"Statues of people?"

The girl nodded.

He continued with that line of questions. The statues were in front of the house with a large fountain in the middle of a graveled forecourt where cars could drive around. She had seen other buildings on the other side of the forecourt.

"Was the house on a mountaintop?"

The girl shook her head. "No. There were hills all around."

"So you were in a canyon?"

"Yes, but I could see the ocean."

The house could be anywhere in Malibu. "Okay, what about the gates. What did they look like? Were they made of iron?"

"I don't know."

"Yes, Laila, you went through the front gates when you escaped. Can you tell me what they looked like?"

Mrs. Ghoni spoke softly to Laila, listened intently, then asked a couple more questions before repeating the girl's words. "They were big gates that closed in the middle. They had big stone pillars on each side."

Matt nodded. Now a much harder question. "Would you recognize any of the men who—" he hesitated, trying to find the right words "—who visited the house?"

The girl shook her head, and murmured a reply. "I saw no one. Just big cars. I came there the day before the fire started."

That explained why Kanita knew nothing about her, not even her name.

"How close was the fire to the house when you and the others got out?"

Laila shook her head, then wrapped her arms around her body and started to rock. A small whimper came from her throat. Matt tried to put an arm around her, but she resisted, her body shaking. Ginn left her chair in the corner of the room and Matt stood back to allow her to gather the girl close.

Something he had just said had frightened her. But what?

Matt saw Mrs. Ghoni to her car, then returned to stand in front of the fireplace in the living room. The house was silent except for the crackle of logs, the softly-lit room inviting. A picture perfect scene on a chill November night if you didn't know that a teenager from Bosnia who'd been brought here to used as a sex slave was sequestered in an upstairs bedroom. He stared into the flames and went over in his mind what he had learned. It wasn't much.

Ginn entered the room. "She's quiet now. Gabby's going to stay with her."

"Did she say anything more?"

"No." She sat in the corner of a sofa.

"I asked how close the fire came. I wonder why that frightened her?"

"Oh, Matt, who knows? That kid's been through so much, she could be having all kinds of flashbacks." She looked up at him. "What really happened downtown today? You've got blood on your shirt."

He told her about real nature of the explosion and the anonymous call he'd received. "I know I've heard that voice, Ginn. If I continue with this, they're going to come after you, and they are going to go after Ned and his family."

"Then you've got to tell him."

"Not yet. He'd go right to the cops. I know I would in his position."

An almost imperceptible frisson of pain passed over Ginn's face. She turned her head and looked into the fire and Matt realized immediately what he had said. In Ned's position, he would be a husband and father. If he loved her, as he said he did, he would be her husband, the father of their children.

They'd been getting closer, but suddenly it seemed as if the abyss yawned again at their feet.

"Does your law firm still use that private investigator, you know the guy I mean?" Matt heard himself say.

"Yes, the ex-cop. Wendell Graff."

She sounded okay. "You trust him?"

"We wouldn't use him otherwise. Why?"

"Would he baby-sit Julie and the boys?"

"Graff will do anything you ask him to do, within reason. And if he's tied up, he's got a number of ex-cops working for him."

"Good. Can you call me with his number?" Matt got up, picked up his jacket from the back of the sofa where he'd left it earlier. "First thing tomorrow, I start looking in the hills for a big two-story house with large wooden gates neither of which may have survived the fire."

Ginn walked with him to the front door. "Are you sure you ought to be doing that?"

"You heard Laila. I've got a personal stake in finding these bastards, Ginn. I can't wait around for John Cargill's contacts to get back to him. I know Malibu. I might be able to track something for them to work with."

"What are you going to tell Ned?"

"Enough so that he'll keep the boys at home from school, not enough so that he'll go to the police before we're ready."

"Where are you staying tonight?"

She looked reluctant to have him leave. Or was he imagining it? "I'm going home."

"Don't do that, Matt. Go to a hotel, or go to Bobby's. Don't go home."

"Hey, don't worry."

"I do worry. I mean it, Matt. Go stay with Bobby, please."

He looked at her earnest face, bent down and brushed her lips with his before she could protest. "Okay. Call me with that number."

He followed the unlit, winding road up Las Flores Canyon Road, turned in at the charred stump that was all that remained of Bobby and Sylvie's hundred-year-old cedar. He switched off the engine and sat for a moment studying the house. The windows were dark except for a crack of light around an edge where the drape didn't quite meet. Surprising. Bobby was on nights this week, and as far as he knew, Sylvie was in San Diego. He felt the heft of the Glock in his pocket and quietly got out, walked over to the house, peered through the space at edge of the drape.

Bobby was in his favorite position, stretched out on the sofa watching an old black-and-white movie on television. Matt went to the door, knocked, called out as he entered, "Thought you were on nights."

"The duty roster changed." Bobby clicked off the set. "What happened to you?"

"It's a long story. For a beer and a sandwich I'll give you the details."

"Sit down. I'll broil a steak." Barefoot, Bobby padded into the kitchen. "You look as if you've had yourself a day." Bobby excelled at understatement. He reached into the refrigerator, emerged with a couple of cans of Rolling Rock, shoved one across the counter to Matt.

"You could certainly say that." Matt popped the top and took a long drag.

While Bobby busied with the steak, emptying a bag of spring greens into a salad bowl, mixing olive oil and red vinegar, Matt told him the highlights, answered questions, discussed what Laila had told him.

Bobby slid the steak onto a plate, passed a basket of warm rolls. The minute the food hit his tastebuds Matt realized he was ravenous.

"So what has big wooden gates flanked by stone pillars?" he asked between bites.

"Just about everything in Malibu these days. And statues and fountains." Bobby leaned his back against the sink. "No one has called in about a missing woman so either Annie's back or no one else has noticed that she's gone. But the RV park up by Solstice Canyon did report a break-in. A guy said he thought it was done by a pack of kids he'd seen hanging around the park for the last week. They took some of his wife's clothes, some food, and left a portable TV and other electronic stuff untouched.

Woman at the park office said she saw a bunch of girls couple of days ago but thought nothing of it. She hasn't seen them since, but she hasn't been really on the lookout either. She did say one of them was a little black kid, maybe about ten. The others were older, blonde, teenagers."

"She didn't see the boy?"

"No, but from what she says, I'm guessing these are the missing kids. I left my number and asked her to call if she sees them again."

"I'll go down there and talk to her."

"No, I'll keep on it, Matt. I also went down and had a look at Halliburton's accident scene." Bobby went into the living room, picked something up from a shallow bowl on the table, and returned to the kitchen. "No laptop, but I did find these." He held out his hand. Resting on his palm were half a dozen bullet casings. "I left a bunch more down there."

"I've got three that I picked up at my house."

"Good. If we can match them to the same weapon, we've got a link."

"Tomorrow, I'm going on a hunt for this place. My first bet's on Latigo Canyon, so I'm starting there. I've got plot maps and a list of owners for every parcel in a three-mile radius. Only a few hundred properties are tucked into those hills. If the house is there, I'll find it." Matt sounded surer than he felt. "If I get real lucky, maybe someone will take another shot, and I'll get a chance to take him out."

Bobby grinned. "Now that's what I call intrepid, Matthew."

Matt could barely muster a return grin. He got to his feet. "I'm bushed. All right if I stay the night?"

"Sure."

"Okay, I'm going to hit the shower." Matt tossed the empty can into the blue bin under the sink, casually thumped Bobby's shoulder with his fist. "Good night."

CHAPTER 29

After a merciful night of dead sleep Matt awoke at first light. Even so, his body felt like a stone. Bobby was already up and drinking coffee when Matt emerged from the spare bedroom. Words between them were few and they left the house into a dull, overcast November day with the moisture hanging low over the tops of the hills. The air was cold, pungent with the mixture of damp ash, and resurgent rosemary, the smell of salt drifting up from the sea. Bobby took his Harley and followed Matt down Los Flores to the café at the bottom of the hill. They ate quickly, Bob left for his shift and Matt went out to his parked Range Rover to call the ex-cop Wendell Graff on the number Ginn had left for him earlier while he was in the shower.

"Yes, Ms. Chang called and said you'd be getting in touch. What can I do for you, Mr. Lowell?" Seven a.m. and Graff had picked up at the first ring. A good sign.

Graff listened while Matt explained what he wanted, a couple of days, a man in front of Ned's house in Santa Monica, a man in the alley behind. Both armed. To begin immediately.

"We're licensed to carry firearms," Graff responded. "But if you have a problem that's likely to require that kind of force, my advice is to go to the police." His voice was deep, assured, professional.

"That is what I am planning to do, Mr. Graff. I'm getting a case together." He didn't say about what, and Graff didn't ask. "But I need a couple of days to do that."

After a moment's silence, Graff said, "Okay. Ms. Chang vouches for you, that's good enough. I'll take the front of the house, and I'll have a man in the alley. I'll need some details. What are we looking for?"

"I have to make a call and get back to you on that. Be within the hour."

Matt disconnected. The café parking lot was filling up, people stopping at the newsstand to pick up the morning paper, going about their normal lives as he used to. Now he was hiring guns to protect his brother's family, and he, too, was armed. It was as if he were leading some kind of parallel life, not really his own. But for now, it was his life. He speed-dialed Ned at home. After a general back and forth about Susan Dean, the mess they had to clean up at the Contessa, the insurance status and the official investigation already underway, Matt got to the crux of his call. "Ned, are the kids and Julie there?"

There was a moment of silence on the other end. "Of course they're here. Where else would they be? It's seven o'clock in the morning. The boys are eating their cereal in the kitchen, and Julie's with them."

"Listen, some things have happened. I'm going to tell you everything later, but right now, I need you to do as I ask. Keep the boys home from school today, and have Julie stay with them. You, too, Ned. Stay home today. I'm sending a man called Wendell Graff to the house. He'll have another guy with him. They are both ex-cops, good men." He was stumbling over his words.

"What? What are you talking about? Have you completely lost it? You're beginning to scare the shit out of me, Matt. Did you get hit on the head by something yesterday, an I-beam fall on you?"

"No. Listen to me, Ned. This all has to do with the baby I found on the beach, and the teenaged girl found dead on the road."

"You'd better tell me what's going on."

Matt could hear the cold knife of alarm in his brother's voice. "I can't, not right now, there's no time. There's a lot to tell. You will have to trust me. Give me a day."

"Is my family in danger?"

"I'm not sure, Ned. That's why I'm sending protection. Wendell Graff and his men will be watching the house, front and back. They'll be armed. Keep Julie and the boys inside. And don't mention anything of this to anyone, not the police, not even Julie if you can help it." Matt knew Ned's wife would hit panic level if she thought her kids were in danger. "I promise you'll know as much as I do by the end of the day."

"Have you done something I should know about, Matt?"

"You mean did I have anything to do with those deaths? Did I kill anyone? No, of course not. I don't really know exactly what's going on myself yet, that's what I need the day for, to find out. But I do know there's some bad muscle involved. That explosion was no accident, Ned."

"Not an accident?" Ned's voice thundered through the phone.

"No," Matt said shortly. Now was not the time to give Ned more information. Silence stretched between them. He could almost hear Ned thinking.

"Okay, Matt," Ned said finally. "I'll give you your day. I'll work at home and I'll keep Julie and the kids inside today. But I want to hear from you tonight. No later, no matter what, you call me or come by. Understand?"

"Yes. I'll call. Take care." Matt clicked off, blew out a heavy breath, and called Graff to give him Ned's Santa Monica address north of Montana Avenue, an exclusive neighborhood of tree-lined streets and multimillion-dollar houses. "Don't let anyone in, that simple, front or back," he instructed. "My brother knows you're coming."

A day, Matt thought. He'd better make it count. His watch read eight. Still early. First thing to do was check on Annie Lautner. He had to pass her condo on his way to Latigo.

The gym was deserted, no sign of the girl with the fabulous glutes, nor any sign of Annie's green Jag. Taped to the front door was a handwritten note. "Hi, Annie. Sam got out, but he's safe with me. Call when you get home and come have a drink. No hurry to pick him up, though, he's a sweetie. Kate."

From Annie's, he drove north, turned right off PCH onto Latigo Canyon Road, a turnoff marked only by a small street sign, an old bus bench, and a scruff of brown grass. His foot heavy on the gas, Matt snaked up the first half of the eight-mile climb without stopping. The broken wall where Phil Halliburton's car had plunged off the road flashed by, then the black marks where Phil had laid down rubber before being hurled to his death. Matt forced himself to slow down. Latigo was a series of switchbacks and curves, and even without a tail forcing the pace, could be treacherous.

Phil had been traveling downhill that night. If he had come from the house Laila described, as Matt suspected he had, then the house had to be situated somewhere beyond this point higher in the canyon.

For the next three hours he scoured the hills, an eerie patchwork of black and bright green, the charred remains of fire juxtaposed with the new growth brought into being by the recent rain. It should be a terrific spring next year, he thought. Wildflowers in these hills were always spectacular after a wildfire. Burned-out properties bordered those untouched by flames and he studied them all. He turned in at stands of mailboxes that were the only indication of a dozen or so houses tucked down an unpaved road; ignored "No Trespassing" and "Private Road" signs and explored the remote labyrinth of fire breaks, and unmarked roads, checking the site maps frequently to be sure he did not miss a property that could be tucked behind another.

By late morning he was in a rugged side canyon looking at the small community of Monte Verde. According to the local newspaper accounts of the fire, Monte Verde had been among the first places evacuated. With a shift in the wind, for a time it looked as if it might be spared, but the firestorm eventually swept through. The devastation was complete. Matt wound his way through melted appliances, torched cars, the remains of brick chimneys and concrete foundations, the coal-black skeletons of trees and chaparral.

The road T-junctioned at the burned hulk of a water tower. As he debated which way to turn, something flickered in Matt's memory. Twenty years ago he and Bobby come up here on a dare from a bunch of surfing buddies to see Guru Bannerjee, a skinny Indian kid about their own age who used to ride around Malibu in a gold Rolls Royce with a surf rack and boards on top. The guru had built a palatial ocean-view estate up here, and he and Bobby just drove up, knocked on the gate and offered to give the guru surfing lessons. Guys in turbans politely refused to allow them in, but they'd managed to get a glimpse inside the gates. Not that they could see much through the trees, just an asphalt drive and a bit of a large two-story white building with a lot of windows. Then overnight, it seemed, Guru Bannerjee and his followers left and the place was sold.

Matt turned right onto the narrow one-lane road that led out to the canyon's edge. Twenty years ago, the road had been a tunnel of sycamores and native oaks, colorful with oleander and wild yellow tobacco. Now it was barren, exposed to the open sky. He followed the twisting lane for a quarter mile until it suddenly dead-ended at the entrance to the old estate.

The pillars were as he remembered, tall square structures of river rock that had survived the fire pretty well, but a brand-new eight-foot chain-link gate had replaced the richly carved-wood original. He hadn't thought about this place in years, and he'd only been here that one time, but still, he should have remembered those gates. White plastic strips was woven into the new chain-link, continuing into the fence that ran along both sides of entrance, effectively cutting off all view of anything that remained on the other side.

What, he wondered, could be that important, it had to be hidden, and so quickly after the fire passed through here?

Matt backed up, turned the Range Rover just in case he had to make a quick exit, and parked well away from the entrance. He picked up the Glock, checked the cartridge, shoved it into his pocket and started back to the gates on foot. The silence was profound, no birdsong, no rustle of wildlife, or hint of a breeze in the still moist air, but as he got closer, he heard the sound of male voices on the other side of the fence. A heavy diesel engine coughed into life.

Pulse racing, Matt reached for a handhold on the top of the closest pillar, scrabbled to jam his boots against a fissure in the rock, and hauled himself up until he could see into the compound.

About fifty feet inside the gates, a silver Airstream trailer was parked straight across an uneven, fire damaged used brick driveway that before the fire had been clearly tree-lined. Beside the Airstream was a black Bronco and twenty-five yards beyond was a pile of rubble, all that remained of what had once been a very large house. Part of a marble staircase had survived, leading now to a phantom second floor. More debris littered a great circular forecourt; chunks of alabaster statuary, the cracked and crumbled remains of a marble fountain and its pedestal, none of which had been there in Bannerjee's time. Well away from the main house were the burned-out shells of other structures, guest quarters maybe, offices, garage. A few walls remained standing.

He spotted a backhoe, still stationary. The engine noise came from a bulldozer working to push rubble off the foundation slab of the house onto an area beyond. His eyes returned to the

Airstream and the Bronco. On the other side of them he could see the curved grille and hood of another vehicle. Seafoam green with a distinctive hood ornament, a leaping Jaguar. Annie's car.

Matt quickly dropped back to the ground. He checked the Glock again, and followed the high chain-link fence to where it ended abruptly, as he'd hoped it would, at the cliff's edge, a straight drop at this point down to the canyon bottom. Matt grabbed the metal fence post, felt for a foothold until he struck an embedded rock. He wedged his boot against it, and then swung his body around the post, onto firm ground inside the fence.

The noise of the bulldozer masked any sound of his footsteps, but the fire had destroyed the landscaping and almost every semblance of cover. Crouched low, he ran to an outbuilding and dropped to his haunches behind a half-ruined wall.

He scanned the scene. From the sharply defined marks left by the teeth of a backhoe along the edges, it looked as if the earth beneath some of the debris had been freshly turned, the rubble then piled back on. A faint, foul stink hung in the still air.

Matt broke from behind the wall and made for the Bronco, skidding behind it in the instant the door of the Airstream opened. A harsh voice shouted to the driver of the bulldozer. The engine kept chugging, and the owner of the voice muttered a short single word. He lit a cigarette, left the trailer and strolled over to stand in front of the bulldozer where the driver could see him, and slashed his hand across his throat. The engine sputtered to a stop, the two men exchanged a couple of sentences before the driver of the 'dozer grabbed the edge of cab and jumped to the ground.

Matt held his breath. He was close enough to see the scabbed-over wounds left by Barney's teeth on the smaller of the two men, the driver of the bulldozer. He wasn't sure about the taller guy. Could be the same man who'd raided his house, but he hadn't had a clear view of him in the rain that night. Not that it mattered. If this was the place, these men were in it up to their necks.

For the first time in his life, Matt wanted to kill.

The two men started back to the Airstream, passing within feet of the Bronco. Slowly, carefully, Matt eased the Glock out of his pocket. Then the cold clear voice of reason spoke in his brain. These were the bottom feeders. If he took them out, the men at the top would run, free to start over somewhere else. Silently, he watched them mount the steps on booted feet, and disappear inside. Their time was coming, he thought. It just was not now.

The sound of a voice floated from an open window—fractured English, the words not clear, the meaning garbled, and Matt realized he was listening to half of a phone conversation that one of the men had just made. It was not incoming, he was close enough to have heard the ring or buzz of a telephone. He memorized the number plate of the Bronco, ventured a look through the closed window of the Jaguar. White leather interior, it had to be Annie's, but he memorized that number, too, just to be sure the car belonged to her. Moving quickly, he retraced his steps, feeling the tingle in his exposed back where a bullet could shatter his spine. He reached the metal post and surefooted now, swung himself swiftly to the other side of the fence. On the periphery of his vision, he caught the movement of a figure traversing a steep, bare deer path toward the bottom of the canyon. He knew immediately. Hasan. What the hell was he doing up here? He dismissed the urge to call out, his voice would echo and reverberate in all directions in this empty landscape. It was too big a chance to take for both of them.

Matt followed the perimeter of the fence back to the safety of the lane and the Range Rover, parked just as he'd left it. Driving as fast as he dared on the main canyon road, he pulled into the first wide turnout, jumped out and scanned the hillsides but there was no sign of the boy. He called his name, listened without much hope for a response, then got back into the Range Rover.

Keeping to the speed limit now, he continued down the steep grade, catching intermittent glimpses of the heavy marine layer hugging the coast below, mulling over the newspaper account of the fire. The order to evacuate had come as the fire threatened to sweep over the mountain and funnel into the canyon. There had been a panicked couple of hours of clogged roads before the wind changed and eased the threat. Using wildlife paths and gullies worn into the sandstone by winter storms those kids, already survivors of unimaginable horrors, could have made it down to the beach. Not easily, but with the driving force of a fire behind them, guts and a chance to escape their nightmare world, certainly possible.

At the bottom of Latigo, he called Bobby. "I think I've found it. You remember the guru, Bannerjee?"

A beat of silence, then, "Yeah, sure, I remember. Secluded, on the edge of that little canyon off Monte Verde."

"I saw Annie Lautner's car on the property and I've got the license plate numbers of a black Bronco. I took the number of the Jag to be sure. Can you run them?"

"Sure. Good job, dude."

Matt gave Bobby the numbers. After some discussion, they arranged to meet at Bobby's house where they could talk. He disconnected, picked up the site maps from the front passenger seat. He checked the parcel number of the property, then flipped through the list showing the owner of record.

His eyes fixed on the name. He sat back, oddly unmoved. It was as if all feeling had abandoned him leaving his brain and his body ice-cold. Strangely, though, he found he could barely pull the next breath into his lungs.

CHAPTER 30

"I want to nail this bastard," Bobby said again. "We have to get more proof, Matt, or he's going to slip away."

Between hot, muttered outbursts from Bobby, they had been tossing around ideas for how to do just that for almost an hour. Matt felt numb, but beneath the ice he knew he was in a killing rage.

Outside, the sound of a car horn announced that Ginn had arrived—he'd called her on his way up Las Flores. Bobby took another mug off the shelf and reached for the coffeepot while Matt went to the door. Ginn was already out of the car. She looked pale, but her jet-black eyes were gleaming.

"You found it." She put both arms around him, held him in a fierce embrace.

He returned the pressure, holding her hard against him, his hand tangled in her long black hair. "Looks like it. I saw Hasan, too, so the kids are still hanging around."

"Oh, that's good news. Don't worry, Matt, we'll find them, and we'll get them the help they need." Ginn released him, walked into the house. She unwound her cashmere shawl, threw it over the back of a chair, then went to examine the map spread out across the kitchen counter.

"So where is this place?"

Matt leaned over her, traced his journey up Latigo Canyon Road, then stabbed a finger on the outline of a large solitary parcel located past the network of roads that was Monte Verde.

"How do you know this is it? Did you see the house?"

"The remains of it. The fire destroyed it, but it's the place, Ginn. I saw at least one of the men who attacked us, he's got Barney's teeth marks all over his arm. And there's a black SUV, a Bronco on the property." He didn't mention Annie's car, he wanted to break that to her more gently. He told her about the view of the ocean, the broken statuary and fountain, the account of the evacuation order in the local newspaper. "They got out, and down to the canyon by the deer paths, then they must have followed the creek to the beach. It couldn't have been easy, but that's how they did it. Laila will be able to fill us in on that."

"Who owns it?" she asked grimly.

"Quickdraw Enterprises." Matt took a deep breath. "That's Jake Broagan, Ginn."

Speechless, she turned to look up at him. "Jake Broagan?" She repeated the name as if she could not believe she'd heard correctly. "What do you mean? What makes you think it's Jake?"

"Quickdraw was the nickname he picked up when we were kids on the beach," Bobby said. "He used to put the make on all the girls. He thought it was pretty cool when we started to call him that. He was a deviant little bastard even then."

Ginn groped for the stool behind her. "That's not much to go on, just a name."

"It's not enough for a search warrant, but it's enough for me," Bobby said.

"You don't think it could be one of those crazy coincidences?"

"Quickdraw?" Matt shook his head. "Not likely. Besides, we

have the beginnings of a solid link. Phil didn't own the house he lived in. A holding company owns it. Bobby called in the license plate number on the Bronco. It's registered to the same holding company, Aurora Borealis. It's not much of a leap from Phil to Jake Broagan. Jake took him up as soon as he arrived here. Introduced him around, and there he was, overnight, one of Jake's courtiers."

"Living like a billionaire in a mansion on the beach, even if he didn't own it," Bobby said. "All he had to do was keep his mouth shut, turn a blind eye, make sure the merchandise was healthy, collect his dough, keep the turnover in human flesh a going concern. We find those kids, they'll tell us what he did."

"There's something else." Matt took Ginn's hand. "I saw a green Jaguar on the property. Bobby ran the plates. It's definitely Annie's."

"Did you see Annie? Of course not." She answered her own question. Tears welled in Ginn's eyes.

The kitchen wall phone rang and Bobby picked it up, moving a few feet away in order to listen.

Ginn pushed a finger at the map as if it were toxic. "Even if Jake owns this place, it doesn't prove he's involved, Matt. It could be he doesn't know what it was used for. I mean, why would he do it? What would have been his motive? It can't be money, he's got all the money in the world."

"Not money. Power. Jake lived in the shadow of a legend he knew he couldn't possibly measure up to. So he's doing what he could to destroy it. He's always been the same. He uses defenseless human beings, abuses them, throws them aside. Obviously it's escalated over the years. This is the worst possible thing Jake could do to his father. Think of the old man's background, who he was, what happened to the people he came from, what he saw when he was young."

"Oh, that's more than sick, that's evil. This is someone we know. We know his wife, and his children. He always seemed to love those children."

Matt said nothing. Ginn had to have time to process the shock, but he could see in her eyes the dawning acceptance. She knew he was capable of this, she knew of the whiff of corruption that clung to Jake Broagan.

Bobby put the phone down. "That was the woman down at the RV park in Solstice." He told Ginn about the burglary complaint. "She says she saw a couple of girls flitting about the place this morning, but she doesn't know if they're the same ones from yesterday. She called out to them, and they ran. She didn't see where they went."

Matt's heart pumped. "Just a couple of the girls?"

"That's what she said." Bobby picked up his keys. "I'll go down now and see what I can find."

"No, wait a minute, they see a police car and a man in a uniform, they'll run. As long as Hasan is still here, my guess is that they're not going anywhere. I think we have to get Jake on that property and see what he has to say."

"And if you're wrong?" Ginn asked.

Matt shrugged. "I'll tell him I'm sorry."

"How do you propose to get him there?" Bobby asked. "Drive downtown, strong-arm him out of his fancy office without anyone noticing something's up?"

"I'll call and ask him to meet me."

"He could turn you down, Matt. He's a busy guy, got a lot on his mind."

Ginn reached for the phone. "I can help with that."

Matt stood just inside the door of the Ivy at the Shore, on Ocean Avenue in Santa Monica. At this hour, 3:30 on an overcast afternoon, the restaurant was quiet, the wall of French doors onto the patio closed and only a handful of people seated at the wicker tables in the bar area. Soon, it would be standing room only, a hip young crowd from Santa Monica's new movie studios and advertising firms winding down after a long day's work, or winding up for the evening ahead.

He spotted Jake, a glass in front of him on a small table tucked away discreetly in a far corner of the bar. Matt stepped behind a large palm and studied him. Well-tailored, meticulously groomed, an indefinable aura that said good schools and exclusive country clubs.

Impassive, Jake looked at his watch, then the door and turned back to his drink. Quietly, Matt exited the restaurant and walked through the landscaped patio around the side to the French door located behind Jake's table.

At the click of the opening door, Jake turned. As his eyes locked on Matt, a fleeting shadow crossed his face, instantly veiled by a broad smile. He got to his feet.

"This can't be Matt Lowell, not in a bar in the middle of a working day."

"How are you doing, Jake?"

"I called your office as soon as I heard about the Contessa," Jake said easily. "Ned said you had a major problem down there. Anything I can do to help, just pick up the phone." He looked over Matt's shoulder. "I'd ask you to sit and have a drink but I'm meeting someone."

"Ginn sends her regrets."

Jake's lips thinned and the arrogant olive green eyes seemed suddenly flat. Matt flashed back twenty years. A party on the beach at the Broagan's summer home in the Malibu Colony, a couple of guys up from the public beach, a girl Jake was romancing all over one of them, shaking her hair, flirting, laughing over the guy's shoulder at Jake. Jake had watched all evening with this same reptilian stare. Two days later, the girl's ten-year-old sister was raped. The rapist was never found.

Jake laughed and the moment passed. "Okay, don't get a hard-on. Ginn called me, I didn't call her." He resumed his seat and beckoned a waiter. "Sit down and tell me about the gas leak. How's Susan Dean?"

Matt waved off the waiter. "Finish your drink, Jake. I've got something I want to show you."

"What is this?" Jake gave a short half laugh. "First Ginn calls out of the blue to set up a little rendezvous, then you arrive to announce she's changed her mind and now you want me to take a drive. What am I missing here?"

"It won't take long."

Jake made a show of looking at his watch. "Well, I'm afraid we'll have to make it some other time, Matt. I can carve an hour or two out of my schedule for a pretty lady, but otherwise, you know how it is." He drained his glass and got leisurely to his feet. The smile was gone from his face. He dropped a twenty on the table, walked through the restaurant to the front door. If he knew Matt was hard on his heels, he gave no sign.

Commuter traffic was picking up on Ocean Avenue, the wide sidewalks busy with pedestrians. On the Santa Monica Pier across the street, the brightly colored lights of the Ferris wheel were hazy in the afternoon fog over the ocean, snatches of calliope music from the merry-go-round drifted through the drone of the passing cars.

Jake retrieved his parking ticket from his pocket, and waved it at the valet. Matt reached for it. "We'll take my car."

"What do you think you're doing?" Jake protested. "I'm not going anywhere except back to my office."

Matt took his arm. "The Range Rover, see it there?" He'd parked on the street in the red in anticipation of this moment.

Jake tried to jerk his arm free. "If this is about Ginn Chang, I told you, she called me. Leave me out of your lovers' quarrel, if that's what this is."

"It's not about Ginn." The sound of her name on Jake's lips made him sick, but Matt kept his voice pleasant. The parking attendant was watching them curiously. He tightened his grip on Broagan's arm.

Jake's voice hardened. "Get your hands off me, Matt. You're beginning to piss me off."

The parking attendant was now conferring with a colleague, both men eyeing them suspiciously. Matt dismissed the urge to jam the Glock against Jake's kidneys. He knew he wouldn't shoot Jake down on a crowded sidewalk. All it would do was encourage him to yell for the cops and run for cover. Matt dug his fingers deep into Jake's bicep. "This won't take long."

"You're way out of line here, Matt. What's wrong with you? What about my car?"

"Don't worry, I'll bring you back." Matt shoved Broagan into the passenger seat, raced to slide behind the wheel. Jake had reopened his door, and Matt grabbed a handful of fine Brioni tailoring, jerked him back inside the vehicle, reached across and slammed the door closed.

His face suffused with blood, Jake threw a punch at Matt's shoulder, connecting hard. "What the hell do you think you're doing?"

Matt pulled away from the curb into the flow of the traffic. "Calm down before you break a blood vessel."

"Fuck you, calm down. If this isn't about Ginn, what the hell is it about?"

"A piece of property."

Jake's voice rose. "What? And for that you decide to kidnap me? What happened to calling and making an appointment?"

Matt blew through the changing light at the California Incline, took it down to Pacific Coast Highway, bombed north in the fast lane.

Jake expelled a heavy breath. "All right, so where is this goddamn property I have to see so urgently?"

A house of horrors, Cargill had called it. Matt gripped the wheel with both hands, struggling with a surge of anger. He took a breath then turned on the radio full volume. Billie Holiday's incomparable voice reverberated through the small space, heartbreak in every note as she sang of strange fruit. Jake threw up his hands in disgust, but at least he was silenced.

Just past the intersection at Civic Center Way in Malibu, Bobby Eckhart's Harley paced the Range Rover for a few seconds then dropped back and tucked in behind. Before leaving

Las Flores, they had talked, deciding that Ginn would go down to the RV park, find out if any of the motor homes had been there for a while with the owners coming out from town only on weekends. If so, she would walk through the park, keep her eyes open, check them out. Bobby had to finish his shift, but then he'd watch for Matt on PCH.

Jake turned and looked out of the rear window at the dark helmeted figure. Abruptly, he reached over and turned off the radio. "Okay, I guess you're making some point here. Just tell me what it is, or so help me, I'm calling someone higher up the food chain than our pal Eckhart back there." He pulled a cell phone from his pocket.

"You do that. Tell him to meet us at the house off Monte Verde."

Jake dropped his hands into his lap. His body was suddenly still, the air inside the vehicle buzzing with tension. "What house?"

Matt slowed for the turn onto Latigo Canyon Road. He glanced into the mirror to see that Bobby was behind him, and took in Broagan's white-knuckled hand gripping the cell phone. Matt could smell the fear in the car, the sour sweat that beaded Jake's face.

"What house?" Broagan's voice was unsteady as he looked out of the window. "What the hell are we doing up here?"

Matt kept silent—he'd already said too much, given Broagan time to dredge up some story. The mist was drifting in nebulous clouds, creeping along the bottom of the canyon. With the overcast, it was getting dark sooner than he anticipated, they probably had only another half an hour before the light faded altogether. He increased speed, slowing only slightly for the tight turn off the main road. In the lane leading to the house, he cut the engine and coasted to a stop fifty feet from the gate. Bobby had done the same, and in the silence, the heavy throb of a diesel engine came from the other side of the fence. With that much noise, no one could have heard them approach. They'd have surprise on their side.

Bobby removed his helmet, put it on the seat of his bike and walked over to the Range Rover. He was wearing his heavy boots, but he had changed from his uniform. Matt knew that beneath the leather bomber jacket he was armed with a Beretta 9mm in a shoulder holster.

"Out of the car, Quickdraw," Matt said.

The muscles in Broagan's face shook. His Adam's apple bobbed nervously above his impeccable tie. Matt pulled the Glock from his belt and took pleasure in jamming it into Broagan's side. "Get out, Jake."

Broagan stared down at the weapon. A line of sweat trickled slowly from temple to chin. He looked as if he was about to throw up.

Bobby opened the passenger door. Unceremoniously, he dragged Broagan out, slammed him against the side of the Range Rover. "Hey, Quickdraw. You've got yourself into some pretty deep shit here. No Hoffmann ready with the bribes and blood money today, my man."

Broagan's eyes skittered from Bobby to Matt on the other side of the vehicle, and back to Bobby. "No, wait a minute. I'm in the dark here. I do own this property, I mean Quickdraw, sure, I can't deny I own it, but I lease it out to a company who uses it for conferences, you know the kind of thing, motivational weekends, a bit of howling at the moon maybe. But look at it. It burned down in the fire. There's nothing here now."

Bobby reached under his jacket and took out the Beretta. "I can't see a goddamn thing through that fence, so why don't we just go take a look."

"I tell you I lease this place out. I can't just barge in there without notice. Anyway, it's locked and chained. I don't have a key."

Matt couldn't bring himself to speak to this piece of garbage in a three-thousand-dollar suit and handmade shoes. Silently, he shoved the Glock back into his belt. He opened the Range Rover's rear door, picked up the bolt cutters he'd taken from Bobby's garage and strode toward the gate.

Urged by the Beretta against his spine, Broagan stumbled after him. "I don't know why you're doing this. I don't know what they used this place for. Honest to God, I don't."

"Then you've got nothing to worry about, Quickdraw," Bobby said. "But we've got half a dozen kids who were held here and they can tell quite a story."

Broagan staggered as if his legs had lost strength. He slumped against the fence, his face ashen.

"I see you know what that means," Bobby said. "Juries are pretty harsh when it comes to crimes against children."

Matt snapped through the chain threaded around the metal posts, flipped up the latch, swung the gates open, stood back to allow Eckhart to shove Broagan through the gate and down the brick driveway ahead of them. Annie's car was where Matt had seen it earlier, but a black Lexus was now parked behind the Bronco. The noise came from the backhoe.

Matt kept the Glock against his leg as he walked toward the Airstream. "There are a lot of people here. Better keep old Quickdraw out in front where they can see him."

The teeth of the backhoe continued to bite into the earth, digging a wide, deep trench, then the blur of a face turning toward them said the driver realized he was being watched. The engine cut out, the stink of diesel fuel hung visibly in heavy blue clouds. The man jumped down. Muscular, mid-fifties, moving easily.

"This is private property, and y'all are trespassing," he called. "You men just turn around now, and leave."

Matt felt suddenly as if all other sound dropped away and he could hear only that voice. *The slight drawl, the southern accent. The voice on the telephone. The voice of the man at the Broagan dinner with the expensive young wife wearing red satin and loaded with rubies; the voice of the man in the doorway at headquarters on Sunday who went on to talk to Barstow and Flores. The splinter in his memory. He should have known.*

The tall figure was dressed in dark suit pants, white shirt

sleeves, loosened tie. He strode purposefully toward them, polished loafers covered in black ash.

"That's Rafe Peters," Bobby murmured to Matt. "Commander Rafael Peters. Top brass."

Peters came closer, his eyes locked on Broagan, a dawning recognition crossing his face. "Mr. Broagan, you shouldn't be here. Mr. Hoffmann already called. I'll deal with it." Peters took in Matt and Eckhart behind Broagan. The blood left his face. In the half light his skin looked like that of a dead man. He recovered quickly, went on as if he had never seen Matt before. "I'm a law enforcement officer and this is a crime scene. I must ask you to leave. Now, please." Clearly he did not recognize Bobby, out of uniform and one of hundreds of deputies under his command.

He was going to tough it out, Matt thought. "Where's Annie Lautner?" he asked.

Peters blinked, his mouth tightened. "I've warned you once, but I'll repeat it. You are interfering with a criminal investigation. I'll give you men one minute to turn around and leave, then I'm calling in backup."

"We just get to walk out of here, no harm, no foul?" Bobby asked pleasantly. "You including Quickdraw here in that offer?"

Matt had the uncomfortable feeling they were under scrutiny. He could feel the pressure of eyes. "Watch it, Bobby," he said softly. "Two other men are here somewhere."

He nodded toward the Airstream to let Bobby know what he intended, then gun in hand, he ran up the steps, and looked inside. He stood back, gulping, trying not to gag. One swift glance, and the picture was imprinted on his retina—two men sprawled on the filth-encrusted floor of the trailer, their torsos ripped open from stab wounds. Both shot in the head, one with the face obliterated, the other with the back of his head missing. The smell was sickening, fresh blood and loosened sphincters, garlic and fried onions and stale cigarette smoke. The two men had been surprised while eating—paper plates of half-eaten food still lay on the small pullout table—shot at almost point-blank range. The killer had then dragged them off the benches and used the knife.

Matt had never witnessed a murder scene before, but even he could see the rage and hatred that had driven this attack. Shaken, he retreated down the steps.

"They're both dead," he said to Bobby. "Shot in the head and stabbed."

"The Satans have been here?" Bobby asked, incredulous. "That's how they killed Tommy."

"No," Matt said. "Not the Satans."

"Yes, it was a drug deal," Peters said quickly. "The men in there were dead when I arrived."

"Then you see the backhoe and figure you might as well to do a bit of landscaping while you're here?" Bobby kept his eyes, and the Beretta, trained on both Broagan and Peters. "We've got to call this in, Matt."

"I've already done it," Peters said. He hesitated for a breath before saying, "I'm Commander Peters, Sheriff's Department. Now just put that thing down, and let me do my job." He started toward the Lexus.

"He's going for his twelve-gauge," Bobby shouted.

Matt jumped forward, grabbed Peters. The man, fit and solid, wrenched free, broke into a run, had the door of his car open as Bobby fired, shattering the window. Peters reached inside beneath the dash, whirled, pumping the action of a shotgun.

Before he could fire, a single shot cracked. Jake Broagan dropped to his knees, both hands at his neck, a fountain of arterial blood arcing through his fingers. Another shot struck his chest and he swayed, pitched forward. He was dead before his body hit the black, soot layered ground.

Without hesitation, Peters fired at the threat behind the crumbling garage wall, then swung the shotgun on Eckhart. Matt pulled the trigger of the Glock at the same moment that Bobby fired. Peters fell back into the open door of the Lexus, the shotgun spinning out of his hands.

Matt didn't wait to check whether Peters was dead, Bobby was there ahead of him anyway. He raced over to the collapsed garage wall, scrambled over the rubble. The slim, still form was where he knew it would be. The gun was still clutched in his right hand. Jimmy McPhee's gun. Tommy had known the Satans were brutalizing the girls, and he had done nothing to prevent it. Hasan had shot him, and his rage had done the rest.

Matt dropped to his knees. Hasan's body, clad in the old gray sweats Matt left under the trees in the canyon ten days ago, had been shredded by the blast from the shotgun.

The boy's lips moved. Matt bent to listen.

The whisper was as faint as the rustle of a breeze in the grass. "Dead?"

"He's dead. You killed Jake Broagan, Hasan."

The boy sighed. The light faded from his bright blue eyes.

Matt gathered the boy into his arms, held him against his chest and rocked him. "You paid the debt. You're a good man."

Annie Lautner's body was lifted from the ground at midnight. The charred remains of other bodies had already been uncovered from a common grave in the same trenched area. A grid had now been established by crime scene investigators, and K-9 cadaver units were to be brought up at first light.

A generator hummed a low note beneath intermittent bursts of sound from police radios and the voices of the people working the scene. Light bars flashing red, blue, amber from the tops of the dozen or so vehicles parked along the driveway and out into the lane merely deepened the surrounding darkness.

Detectives Eduardo Flores and Jim Barstow detached themselves from a group clustered around the open trunk of the Lexus and walked to where Matt stood with John Cargill watching the work progressing under the harsh white glare of the lights. While Bobby had used Peters's radio to call in what was at minimum a quadruple homicide, Matt had first called the two homicide detectives. Then he thought about John Cargill, working pro bono for years in the snakepit of human trafficking, and knew John should be there.

Looking grim, Flores lit a cigarette, carefully pocketing the spent match. "Thought you'd want to know we found a laptop computer locked in the trunk of Peters's car. It's pretty banged up, but we've got good tech people. If there's anything to find, they'll find it."

"Peters is already filling in some of the blanks. The son of a bitch is seriously interested in saving his own tail," Barstow added. He looked bleak. "Never would have believed it. Rafe Peters. Medals for bravery. Great career. Would have trusted him with my life. Jesus."

Peters had been removed by ambulance with a gunshot wound in his right arm. Eckhart had applied a tourniquet, but only after wondering aloud whether he shouldn't just let him bleed to death. Bobby was immediately pressed into service at the scene, answering questions, taking orders, but before the first responding sheriff's car had arrived, Matt had prevailed upon him to have a short-term memory loss regarding one small piece of the whole story—the call from the woman at the RV park. A homeless shelter or an INS detention camp was not going to happen to those kids, not after what they had survived. All that was needed was a little time to figure out what to do.

Barstow went on to fill in Matt and Cargill on the highlights of what they'd learned so far from Peters.

"This property was owned by Jake Broagan. He ran this operation. He's one of the billionaire Broagans here in Los Angeles." He squinted at his notes.

"The dead men in the trailer are Albanian nationals. Names Gazmir and Fakaj. They were the security, made the pickups at the airport, made sure the victims toed the line."

"You're lucky you survived, Matt," Cargill interjected. "The Russian mafia is behind most global trafficking, but they like to use Albanian muscle. Killing is their first choice."

Barstow shook his head. "Luck wasn't involved. Peters claims he advised against killing Mr. Lowell. He could disappear a couple of little Jane Does—the baby you found on the beach, Matt, and the body found on Encinal. But if Mr. Lowell was killed, Peters wouldn't have been able to prevent a full-on investigation, which could have led to Broagan and to Peters himself. So the muscle was told to intimidate only, to seriously threaten Matt and the people around him."

Flores dragged on his cigarette, blew a stream of blue smoke. "The Albanians recovered that laptop from the bottom of Latigo Canyon, and an Erik Hoffmann sent Peters up here personally to get it."

"Oh, God," Matt said softly.

"You know this man, Hoffmann?" Flores asked.

"Yes, he's an eighty-year-old friend of Jake Broagan's family." Anything else, Matt decided, they would find out for themselves. He thought of Jake's father as he had seen him a couple of weeks ago, already frail.

"To finish up with Peters then," Barstow said. "When he got here on his errand, he found two men dead. He had no idea who killed them, he searched the property, made sure the killer was not around, and was cleaning up the mess, getting ready to bury the bodies when you and Eckhart, Matt, turned up with Broagan."

"A fortunate arrival, I'd say," Flores added. "Peters doesn't know anything about the boy he killed. For the moment we'll proceed on the assumption he is one of the trafficked victims, taking his revenge." He looked at Matt. "You want to add to that, Matt?"

Matt realized that Flores was making up for the attitude he'd displayed on every previous meeting. "He's one of the kids I told you about."

"Have you any idea where they are now?" Flores asked.

Matt caught Cargill's eye and looked away, fastening his gaze on Flores. "No. I wish I did."

"Well," Flores mused. "They're the only ones who can tell us why the others didn't get out of the house when they did. Why they burned to death." He looked at Matt. "Be good questions to ask them if we could."

Non-committal, Matt nodded. Those kids were still far from safe. Traffickers did not allow victims to escape and live to testify.

"What about the bodies that have been found?" Cargill asked softly. "Do you have a count yet?"

Shaking his head, Flores let out a heavy breath. "At least ten. That's very preliminary, bodies are still being recovered. Early indications are they were mostly young. The bodies are badly burned, so it will be some time before we have answers."

"They must have had maids here, too, gardeners, people keeping the place running smoothly," Barstow said.

The men were silent for a moment.

"Does Peters know who they are?" Cargill asked.

Barstow shook his head. "Claims he never came here as a club member is how he put it. That wasn't his deal. He's got a young and expensive new wife. He needed the big bucks. Says he was only one link and he only provided protection from the law. Only." Pain lurked in the deepening creases of Barstow's exhausted eyes. "We are hoping that the laptop is going give us names. Names of the club members, the victims, where they came from, where they went."

The men moved back to allow an unmarked sedan to pass. The driver found a spot to park among the phalanx of vehicles, and four dark-suited men climbed out into the floodlights, flashing color of the police lights playing across their faces.

"Well, the Bureau has arrived," Barstow said dryly.

Cargill studied the four men. "That's Special Agent Pierce and his crew. Ian Pierce. I've worked with him on a couple of cases. He's a good man. Excuse me."

They watched Cargill shake hands with the federal agents, then walk with them toward the group scouring Peters's car.

"We gotta go." Flores peered at Matt's face. "You doing okay?"

Matt shrugged. His head throbbed, his body ached with a bottomless exhaustion. He felt as if he had been hollowed out and drained of all feeling.

"Yeah." Flores sighed. "Know what you mean. Any consolation, a lot of bad guys are going down because of what you did here." He patted Matt's shoulder. "Yeah. We gotta go."

And no hard feelings, Matt thought. He took out his cell phone, called Ned as promised. Ned was awake, waiting for him to call. The conversation was long but could have been longer. He fielded a few questions, didn't promise to be in the office first thing, and hung up.

He took a moment to look around. It was surreal.

He called Ginn.

CHAPTER 31

The soft night air on the deck smelled keenly of salt and fresh seaweed. A bright first-quarter moon threw a silver path across the dark water. It was one of those crisp and diamond-clear evenings that often grace the coastline in early December.

Matt closed his eyes and breathed in deeply. He never grew tired of the smells of the ocean, or its sounds.

"The seals are out on the reef," Ginn whispered. "Hear them?"

Ginn was curled up with Matt under a favorite plaid wool blanket they used to use for sitting out in the fresh air of the deck on cool nights just like this one. Matt touched the warm nape of her neck. His arm felt the natural curvature of her body. We fit, he thought.

"Yes, I hear them." A chorus of barks rose over the low bass tones of the waves on the beach below. Matt gazed out over the water, his eyes following the lights of a night-fishing boat sweeping north toward Point Dume. He could hear Barney gently snoring at his feet.

In the last three weeks, Matt and Ginn had had few quiet nights like this one. A media storm had broken over them, reporters and cameras camped on Malibu Road in front of Matt's for the first seventy-eight hours. Every day it seemed another name was added to the list of prominent men under investigation. The *Los Angeles Times* had a crack team of reporters assigned to the story, no doubt headed for a Pulitzer. But Matt was getting most of his information from his two new insider pals, Barstow and Flores, on permanent assignment to the case. It was from them he'd first learned that Erik Hoffmann had been arrested, and that a superior court judge had committed suicide.

Within days of uncovering the unthinkable in the hills above Malibu, the case had blown wide open and into the largest discovery of human trafficking in the history of Los Angeles. In the nineties, there'd been the notorious sweatshop bust in El Monte, but nothing this big or far-reaching or odious. The sex-slavery operation on Jake Broagan's property occupied just one vile tentacle of a multi-headed monster, an underground criminal network that also consists of trafficked domestic workers in every area of the city and trafficked garment workers in factories downtown. The Aurora Borealis shell had been surprisingly clumsy in putting its name on the deed to Halliburton's house. This had led Matt, and ultimately the FBI, straight to the barbed-wire sweatshops on San Julian Street, and others nearby. Otherwise, this might have remained a single case of violent, forced prostitution.

John Cargill and the FBI had given Matt a quick course on sexual trafficking that he wished he'd never had to take.

Exclusive private sex clubs like the one in Malibu specialize in the cream, which means the young ones and the beauties, and sometimes even virgins, who are increasingly in demand and fetch some of the highest prices in the international sex trade. Halliburton's computer notes had included financials for Jake's place, no surprise given Phil's obsession with money. Annual membership was a cool hundred thousand, plus joining fees.

Matt had learned that such exclusive high-priced clubs are rare. For a newly trafficked girl or boy or young woman, who's been purchased by such a place, it's only a first stop. After being used up, if he or she survives, the trafficked person is shuffled into a chain of down-and-dirtier brothels. Clearly, that's the fate that would have awaited Laila and the others if they hadn't escaped during the fire.

"I spoke to John Cargill today," Matt said after a long silence. "Nate Broagan called him today. Poor old man's devastated. But he wants to do anything that would help. John decided to take him up on his offer. Broagan Enterprises has a lot of powerful friends in Washington."

"Right now the urgent need is a place for the girls. They can't really stay where they are much longer. Wendell Graff's got his men there round-the-clock, but it's really not safe enough and John needs his space."

Ginn had found the girls hungry and tired and frightened in an empty trailer in the Solstice RV park. The only safe place she could think to take them was to join Laila at John Cargill's.

"I talked about that with John today," Matt said. "I offered to get them a place of their own. But John told me he'd already arranged with Mr. Broagan for the five girls to go to Hannah's House. Mr. Broagan is going to provide all the protection they need."

With everything else they knew, the surviving girls were also direct witnesses to murder. Except for Hasan and the five girls when the fire came close the thugs had locked up everyone, maids, gardeners, four other girls. When they ran, they could hear them screaming.

"That will be so good for Mr. Broagan and for the girls. They'll be safe, have the doctors they need, they can restart their education, and they'll be together. If we find their mothers, there'll be room for them, too."

Cargill was working on getting the girls T-visas, the special documents issued by the State Department to trafficked victims willing to testify. Every one of them—Kanita, Iris, Nives, Laila, even the little Sudanese child Mura—had said they would appear in court although it take a while to build a case. The FBI believed the magnitude of the case pointed to a single international crime syndicate.

"I've missed this," Ginn said softly. "The sound of the ocean and the seals on the reef."

This is the moment, Matt thought. He found himself nervous, searching his mind for the right words. Suppose she turned him down? After the emotional turmoil he'd put her through in the last two years, he wouldn't blame her if she did.

"Let's tear this place down, and build a real house. What do you think?"

"Is that a proposal of some kind?"

"Yes. It is."

She smiled. "You will have to give me time to think about it."

"All the time you need, *Mei Hua*." Matt took her hand. They sat together for a while longer on the deck's weathered rattan sofa.

Ginn stretched. "I'm going in to take my bath." This was a nightly ritual with Ginn. She never missed.

"I'll be in," Matt said.

With Barney at his heels, he took the narrow wooden stairs down to the beach, crossed the soft sand to the water's edge. His mind roved. He thought about Bobby, wondered how he could get him to accept a couple of tickets to some islands somewhere. He'd forgotten his father's birthday. He'd call him tomorrow, and then get over to see the horses. He remembered Hasan, the first and the last time he'd seen him. And Ginn. He thought about what he was asking her to do, daring to love him once more.

He picked up some driftwood and threw it for Barney. So many people had died. The first of them had been the baby who had changed his life. Ginn had told him that the little girl had been born in the Chinese Year of the Horse and the element of the Horse is fire. Horse children invariably leave home young and Horse years are notorious turning points.

He did not don't know what was going to happen next but he knew he was ready.

AFTERWORD

The United Nations reports that four million women and girls, some as young as five, are traded against their will every year into domestic, sweatshop and sexual slavery.

Eastern and Central Europe have emerged as major points of origin for this trade. A primary trade route runs from the Balkans through Germany, sometimes directly into the United States, sometimes through Mexico or Central America.

The United States is a major destination country into which individuals from more than 50 countries are routinely trafficked. Los Angeles is a major destination city.

The Victims of Trafficking and Violence Protection Act of 2000 was landmark legislation passed by the Congress of the United States. Under the provisions of this new federal law, if a victim dies in the course of a trafficking crime, the traffickers can now be put away for life.

$$2\ 2\ 6\ R$$

$$15\overline{)\ 0\ \ \ 5}$$

$$B$$

$$8\ \ 0\ \ \ C$$

$$6\ \ 6\ \ \ C$$

$$3\ \ 6$$

$$4\ \ 5\ \ 8$$

$$5\ 0\ B$$

$$6\ 0\ 8$$